"Recommended. Shetterly captures the rhythm, feel and language of rural Florida, its legends, and the clash of cultures."   —*Library Journal*

"In this poignant coming-of-age tale, pearls of childhood memory are strung on a fine strand of fantasy. The tale's true wellspring of magic is the enchanted childhood Chris conjures from reminiscences of his family and the popular culture of the day."   —*Publishers Weekly*

"Shetterly's latest novel is a pure delight."   —*Rapport*

"A lovely, dark, gentle book. The story runs from the simple pleasures of the narrator's childhood to the mysteries of adult interactions, seen through the memory of a child."   —*San Diego Union Tribune*

"An ingenious novel. The prose is deceptively simple, hiding a depth of interpretation and implied events."
                                          —*Detroit Free Press*

Don't get left behind!

STARSCAPE

Let the journey begin . . .

From the Two Rivers
The Eye of the World: Part One
by Robert Jordan

To the Blight
The Eye of the World: Part Two
by Robert Jordan

Ender's Game
by Orson Scott Card

Jumper
by Steven Gould

Briar Rose
by Jane Yolen

The Cockatrice Boys
by Joan Aiken

Mairelon the Magician
by Patricia C. Wrede

And look for . . .

Ender's Shadow (5/02)
by Orson Scott Card

Wildside (9/02)
by Steven Gould

The Whispering Mountain (5/02)
by Joan Aiken

The One-Armed Queen (9/02)
by Jane Yolen

Orvis (6/02)
by H. M. Hoover

Jumping Off the Planet (10/02)
by David Gerrold

The Garden Behind the Moon (6/02)
by Howard Pyle

The College of Magics (10/02)
by Caroline Stevermer

The Dark Side of Nowhere (7/02)
by Neal Shusterman

Deep Secret (11/02)
by Diana Wynne Jones

Sister Light, Sister Dark (7/02)
by Jane Yolen

City of Darkness (11/02)
by Ben Bova

Prince Ombra (8/02)
by Roderick MacLeish

The Magician's Ward (12/02)
by Patricia C. Wrede

White Jenna (8/02)
by Jane Yolen

Another Heaven, Another Earth (12/02)
by H. M. Hoover

It was a dream, then a place, then a memory. My father built it near the Suwannee River. I like to think it was in the heart of Florida, because it was, and is, in my heart. Its name was Dogland.

Some people say you can know others if you know the central incidents that shaped their lives. But an incident is an island in time, and to know the effect of the island on those who land there, you must know something about the river they have traveled.

Dogland

Will Shetterly

A TOM DOHERTY ASSOCIATES BOOK
NEW YORK

This is a work of fiction. All the characters and events portrayed in this book are either products of the author's imagination or are used fictitiously.

DOGLAND

A Starscape Book
Published by Tom Doherty Associates, LLC
175 Fifth Avenue
New York, NY 10010

www.starscapebooks.com

ISBN: 0-765-34233-2

Originally published in hardcover by Tor Books, 1997

First Starscape edition: April 2002

Printed in the United States of America

0 9 8 7 6 5 4 3 2 1

This novel is dedicated with love
to Mom, Dad, Mike, and Liz

Contents

1

The Way to the Feast of Flowers

It was a dream, then a place, then a memory. My father built it near the Suwannee River. I like to think it was in the heart of Florida, because it was, and is, in my heart. Its name was Dogland.

Some people say you can know others if you know the central incidents that shaped their lives. But an incident is an island in time, and to know the effect of the island on those who land there, you must know something about the river they have traveled.

And I must warn you before we begin, I don't know that river well. I visit that time and place like a ghost with poor vision and little memory. I look up the river and see fog rolling in. I look down the river, and the brightness of the approaching day blinds me. I see shapes moving behind me and beyond me, but who they are and what they do, I cannot say. I will tell what I know is true, and I will invent what I believe is true, and that, I think, is all you can ask any storyteller to do.

I learned the Nix family history from the stories Pa

told. Even at the age of four, I suspected that Pa's stories might not be perfectly true. When Pa said we Nixes came to North America as indentured servants working our way out of debtor's prison, Grandma Bette would make a face and say he couldn't know that. When he said we Nixes had Lakota and Ojibwe blood in our veins, Grandma Bette would say she wasn't prejudiced, but it simply wasn't so: she and Pa and his brothers and sisters were dark because her people were Black Dutch, from a part of Holland where everyone had black hair and black eyes. And then Grandma Bette wouldn't say a word for half an hour or more, a very long time for Grandma Bette to be quiet.

Pa usually told the family stories when driving to the store with Little Bit and me, while Ma stayed home with Digger. Little Bit would sit on the front seat of the station wagon with Pa, and I would stand in back, straddling the transmission hump with my arms wrapped over the front seat. After a while Little Bit or I would ask for the Little Big Horn story, or the Light-Horse Harry Lee story, or another of the Nix family histories, like:

"Tell us 'bout that bad man."

"What bad man is that?"

"Our great-great-great-great-great-great-grampa!"

"That's a lot of greats."

" 'Bout the bad man!"

"You mean the horse thief?"

"No." The horse thief story was hardly a story at all. A Nix was caught for stealing horses and hung, that was all. Pa only told that story when Grandma Bette was visiting.

" 'Bout the bad man."

"In jail."

"An' the train."

"An' the man ran off with his wife."

"That story! Tell us *that* story."

"Tell us that story. Please?"

"Pretty please. Pretty please tell us that story."

"Well, there's not much to tell."

"Please, Pa! Please, please, please!"

"Well, okay. There was this man—"

"A Nix."

"—a Nix." Probably a farmer. Most forgotten Nixes were probably farmers. "And some fellow ran away with his wife." The farmer was old, forty-five or fifty, with stubbly, hollowed cheeks and staring eyes. He wore overalls. His wife was young, barely twenty, pretty and plump and blond. The other man, a lanky salesman with clean-scrubbed skin, was from the city. He wore a nice suit and had a shy smile, and he parted his hair in the middle. "They were on a train. They thought they'd gotten away."

"But they hadn't, had they, Pa!"

"No, they hadn't." The couple sat side by side in the train. The wife-stealer sat by the aisle with his hat in his lap. He wore a green plaid suit, and he kept twisting the hat, a derby, with his smooth, clean fingers. He grinned his shy smile while staring happily into the eyes of the woman. She'd glance at him, glance away, then glance back, then glance away again. She was nervous, not afraid that her husband would find her but merely embarrassed to be so obviously the object of the young man's love. She feared he expected too much of her and would be disappointed once they'd lived together. She loved him as much as he loved her, and she could not believe two people could be so perfectly created for each other.

"He caught up with them, didn't he, Pa?"

"Right in the train, right?"

"That's right." The passenger car's interior was like the train in *The Man Who Shot Liberty Valance*, only in color: seats of plush green velvet, heavy drapes by the windows, walls paneled in red oak. Happy people in Sunday clothes waited to depart. Men had moustaches that waggled in easy grins above their cigars. Women carried parasols and wore long dresses. The conductor looked like Captain Kangaroo with his plump belly and his white walrus moustache. He talked to a tiny old woman with sugar-white hair coiled on her head who wore square wire-rimmed glasses with lenses no bigger than cough drops, and no less thick.

"He managed to follow them. Left his farm as if he didn't plan to come back. Came after them with a Bible and a shotgun."

"Oooh."

"He caught up with them on the train." The conductor felt someone brush by him, saw someone dressed wrong for traveling by train. He turned away from the old woman, called, *Hey, you!* The man, the Nix, my ancestor, stopped to look back. The conductor stared at him. The old Nix wore a stiff black jacket over faded overalls. He carried a shotgun at his side. The conductor said, *You can't bring that gun in here.* The old man looked at the conductor, looked at the shotgun, looked back at the conductor, said, *It's for hunting.* He walked on.

The young couple did not see or hear the old Nix. The other people in the car did not notice the old Nix. He was an eccentric farmer, nothing more. The old man walked up behind the couple and called the young man's name.

The young man in the plaid suit turned; he had never seen his beloved's husband. He said, *Yes?* Beside him, the young woman turned, too. She raised her hand to her mouth, but in that moment, no words could come from her lips. The old man never looked at her.

"He said, 'You *sure* you're so-and-so?' asking the fellow's name again to be safe."

The young man smiled as he nodded. The young woman spoke a word then, perhaps the young man's name, perhaps my ancestor's. As the young man looked toward her, the old man raised the gun—

"—blew the man's brains out, right there in the train."

The shotgun's explosion was loud, but the young woman's scream may have been louder. The old woman covered her wrinkled mouth with a white lace glove. The conductor's eyelids opened wide as if he could not get enough light to his pupils to see what had really happened.

"Then what? Huh, Pa? Then what?"

"Nothing, really. They locked him up. He didn't try to get away or anything. He'd done what he had to do."

"An' then?"

"He hung himself in the jail cell." The old man dangled from his belt (I never wondered why my ancestor wore both overalls and a belt), which had become long enough to tie to a convenient wooden beam. The walls of the cell had been built with blocks of gray stone. The old man spun slowly. His boots had holes in them. Sunlight shone obliquely between the bars of the single window. The shadows stretched across the floor, across the old man's faded, battered boots.

"Oooooh."

I learned my personal history from Ma. She told me about my birth in 1955 on an army base in South Carolina, and about the Mexico trip when everyone smiled at the happy gringo baby with curly red hair, and how proud Pa was. She told me that after they brought Little Bit home to the farm in Minnesota, they'd hear her cry and rush into the room to find me already there, patting her head and saying, "Don't cry, baby, don't cry." It took them several weeks to realize that I would pinch her when we were alone, then comfort her as the adults arrived. That story always made me laugh.

I liked the old stories because they changed a little with each telling. Sometimes an old story inspired a new one that I had never heard, a story that told me about something I hadn't suspected I hadn't known. That was how I learned about the drunken man at the hospital when I was born.

Ma told me that story one night when I was four or five, soon after we moved to Florida. I asked, "Ma? D'you 'member the hairy man an' the tree lady at Mardi Gras?"

She shook her head and set aside the copy of *Reader's*

Digest that she'd been looking through. "There were an awful lot of people dressed up that day, and I wasn't really paying much attention to any of them." She smiled.

"The tree lady that helped you."

"The nice Negro woman?" Ma smiled and glanced toward our TV set. We always had secondhand televisions that never delivered clear pictures or sound; one was usually playing in the background of any family conversation. "Oh, yes. But I don't remember anything about her and a tree." I thought Ma wouldn't continue, but then she said, "It's funny how you were all born under such odd circumstances."

"We were?" No one else was in the living room. Digger and Little Bit had to go to bed half an hour before I did, and Pa was out in the yard working on the station wagon again.

"Well, not very funny," Ma said. "But having Digger in the middle of the Mardi Gras parade is pretty funny." She smiled and blushed at the same time, and so did I.

"Yeah." I laughed. "Pretty funny."

"And on the day Little Bit was born, an entire flock of quail landed outside my room. You hardly ever see quail in northern Minnesota. Several of them settled on my windowsill and started whistling away. Dr. Jim said you could've hunted your dinner with a shopping bag. One of the nurses went to shoo them away, and they just flew around her, a-singing and a-singing. But as soon as Dr. Jim walked toward them, they flew off."

I knew the punch line to that one: "Figure he forgot his shopping bag?"

Ma set her hand on my head and ran her fingers over the bristles of my crew cut. "I suppose so."

"And what about me, Ma?"

"What about you?" Ma winced the tiniest bit, then smiled. "Oh, that. It's nothing, really."

"It's funny?"

"Well, there was a drunk man in the waiting room, say-

ing you were his boy. I was afraid Luke would hit him, but
the orderlies took the man outside."

I could see a drunken cowboy staggering into a hospital room wearing chaps and six-guns. "What kind of
man?"

"Just some man. There are some very strange people
in this world, Chris. You have to be careful."

"Yes'm."

I couldn't remember the farm in Minnesota or the trip
down to New Orleans, but Digger's birth was one of my
earliest memories and one of the first stories that I could
tell, though it didn't seem like a real story to anyone except me. It wasn't like the things that no one else remembered because they probably weren't important to them,
like my earliest memory, of a day in the living room in
Louisiana when the TV screen suddenly went dark in the
middle of a show. A white dot lingered at its center as if
the whole picture had fallen in on itself, and then the dot
faded to black. Pa walked across the living room and did
something to the back of the set, but that's where that
memory ends.

Everyone in the family remembered the day of Digger's
birth, even Little Bit and maybe even Digger himself, but
everyone remembered it a little differently. He was born
in 1958, soon after my family came to New Orleans. Pa
had been away selling encyclopedias, and Grandma Letitia hadn't come down to be with Ma yet because the baby
wasn't due for three more weeks. Ma had called us in from
the yard and said that Little Bit and I would have to come
with her in a taxi, and we'd have to be very good and take
care of her like she usually took care of us.

I fetched the pink suitcase that Ma had packed a month
before, and Little Bit carried Ma's purse. No one said
much. A neighbor came out and offered to drive Ma, but
just then the taxi arrived. The driver, a red-nosed man
who looked like Santa Claus with a flattop, kept saying,
"Don't you worry none; we'll get you to the hospital fine.

Wish it weren't Mardi Gras. Traffic's gonna be hellacious. But don't you fret now, ma'm. We'll get you there jus' fine, you'll see."

The taxi could not reach its destination, but a parade of costumed drunks were not enough to stop my brother from reaching his. Ma said, "The baby's coming," and the driver yelled into the crowded street, "He'p me! He'p me! A woman's havin' a child! Somebody he'p me!" Little Bit and I sat very quietly beside Ma, watching her breathe, watching the costumed crowd, watching for a white-haired doctor in a long white coat with a gleaming stethoscope around his neck and a black leather bag at his side.

"I know 'bout birthin' babies," said a fat black woman with oak leaves sticking to her hair and her long green dress.

"Oh, thank Jesus," said the taxi driver.

"I do, too," said a scrawny, bare-chested white man with goat horns at his temples and shaggy trousers covering his legs. "I know to get everyone out of the way."

"Yes, sir. That's right. That's a fine idea." The driver and the goat man began hustling people away from the cab. I listened to Ma's breathing, and I felt myself getting more and more scared. Ma smiled and kept saying it was okay, but she was sweating and red and gasping.

"You chil'en wait outside the cab," said the woman with oak leaves. "Your mama won't have no trouble at all, now."

"Ma?" said Little Bit.

Ma smiled more easily, and her breathing grew deeper, slower, and more even. "Go on, you two. I did all right with you, didn't I? Stay"—she gasped, then smiled again—"by the car, okay?"

The tree woman glared at the people clustered around us. "Y'all turn your backs and give this poor woman some privacy, hear!"

The watchers, white and black, young and old, rich and poor, all nodded and obeyed. In the middle of a street packed tight with bodies, under a bright midday sun, Ma had more privacy than she would in any delivery room.

The taxi driver lifted Little Bit onto the hood of the car. They played patty-cake while the Mardi Gras crowds surged around Ma's shielding ring of people. Everyone ignored me, which comforted me; it meant there was nothing I was supposed to worry about. I couldn't see Ma, and I could only see the back of the tree woman, which wasn't that interesting, so I studied the hairy man.

Every kid knows about Halloween suits made of crinkly cloth in colors unknown to nature. The hair on the man's legs was dark brown and matted with beer or sweat. His hooves were muddy, and one was chipped. His horns stuck out from the curly hair on his head, which was the color of the hair covering his legs. The horns were small and dull black and didn't quite match. He smelled like a dog that'd been in the rain.

The hairy man put his fists on his flanks and said, "What you lookin' at, son?"

"You," I said, because Pa had taught me to answer adults, and then, "sir," because Pa had taught me to be polite.

The hairy man nodded, then belched. I smelled something like Grandma Bette's breath after she drank port—soda pop for grown-ups, only stronger. Then the man laughed. "Think you see good, son?"

I had never thought about how well I saw. Ma and Pa both wore glasses, and Little Bit and I didn't, so I nodded.

The hairy man laughed again. "You ain't seen a thing till you've seen it straight on *an'* out the corner of your eye, both. Near any fool can do one or the other."

As an approaching band broke into "When the Saints Go Marching In," the tree woman said, loud enough that I could hear over the noise of the parade and the crowd, "You got a son, ma'am. A beautiful son, and he's doing just fine. You rest easy now, hear?"

A white policeman—a real policeman with a real pistol on his hip, not someone in a costume—had joined the ring of people standing around the cab. Someone began to cheer, and others joined in, even people far away in the parade who couldn't have known what was going on. The cries—"She had a son!" and "A boy's been born!" and "Hallelujah!"—rippled up and down Bourbon Street.

"She wants her chil'en," the tree woman said. A few leaves fell from her hair as she brushed against the roof of the cab. One dropped into my hand. It seemed fresh and green, as if the woman had plucked the finishing touches for her costume only minutes before.

"Where's her children?" the policeman asked.

"Ma!" I yelled, suddenly frightened. "Ma, I'm here!" I lunged between the adults' legs, between hairy legs in Bermuda shorts, smooth legs in dresses, blue trousers that belonged to the policeman, blue jeans that belonged to farmers, black cotton trousers that belonged to jazz musicians, baggy red-and-white-striped breeches belonging to pirates, rough leather chaps belonging to cowboys, fringed brown trousers belonging to Indians, tight white pedal pushers belonging to motion picture starlets. "I'm here, Ma! I'm here!"

The tree woman grinned at me as she stepped away from the open taxi door. Her gold tooth reflected sunlight, and I was blinded by the sight of her and my mother and the baby. When my sight returned, I saw Ma lying in the back of the taxi. Her blue print dress was all rumpled and stained, and the taxi seat was, too, but that was okay. Ma was smiling. In her arms, she held a wet little red thing that looked like an ugly puppet or a shaved monkey. "Chris," Ma said. "Say hello to your little brother."

"Ma?" I whispered. "You okay, Ma?"

"I'm fine, Chris. Let Little Bit see, too."

"Yes, Ma." As my sister squeezed past me, I backed away, back through the sea of legs, and started to turn to run as fast and as far as I could. A hand gripped my shoulder, and I looked up into the hairy man's face.

"Ugly li'l bastard, ain't he?"

I nodded hesitantly, not sure whether I should let anyone talk that way about my new brother.

"But he's beautiful, too. It's tough to understand, but there it is. Chew on it awhile, son."

"Yes, sir."

The policeman, by the cab door, grinned like the drunkest of the festivalers. "Sure is a handsome li'l fellow. Got a name for 'im, ma'm?"

"We're not sure," Ma said gently, which meant that Pa hadn't said if there was a name he wanted Digger to have.

"George'd be good," said the hairy man. "Means he works with the earth."

"George?" Ma spoke as if she were tasting the name on her tongue.

"George is right nice," said the fat woman with oak leaves, and she smiled at the hairy man. A breeze touched the taxi and the crowd, erasing the damp Louisiana heat for a moment.

Ma smiled. "George." She stated it in the quiet voice that she almost never used, the voice that meant she had decided something and nothing anyone, even Pa, could do or say would ever change her mind.

"George!" someone in the crowd shouted. People called, "Good name, ma'm!" and "Let's hear it for George!" and "Who the hell's George?" I couldn't make out much else in the joyous babble. Someone put a dark bottle in my hands and I drank deeply, thinking this was soda pop. When I began to cough, someone grabbed my shoulder. I thought I was about to be spanked for drinking wine, but the hand belonged to the policeman, who pushed me toward the taxi. "Get on in, boy, your mama still ought to get to the hospital."

I looked around. The hairy man and the woman in oak leaves had gone. I nodded, mumbled, "Yessir," and got in next to Little Bit.

The police car ran its siren all the way to the hospital. Little Bit sat next to me in the taxi and kept sliding onto my side of the seat to look out the window, but I didn't mind. Ma sat with the baby and smiled and whispered to him, and the taxi flew so fast that the wind whipped through the window, so fast that the Louisiana heat couldn't catch us, and Little Bit laughed, and everything was as wonderful as it could be, even if I did have a shaved monkey doll for a brother.

Pa came home five days later. Grandma Letitia, who'd arrived the night of Digger's birth to take care of Ma and us kids, went right back to Minnesota. I tried to tell Pa about the tree woman and the hairy man, but Pa said that's Mardi Gras for you, people'll do any damn thing for fun, and why'd the hospital expect us to pay the full bill when Ma never even got a peek inside the delivery room?

I was sorry that Ma didn't remember the hairy man. I'd wanted to ask if he had looked like the drunken man at the hospital in South Carolina when I was born.

I have few memories about the pink house in New Orleans that Ma loved, and the few that I have are suspicious, as if they come from things I was told rather than things I lived. I believe I remember running around in a small yard of lush green grass with a Coke bottle in my hand, but that may come from Ma telling me how all the neighbor kids drank soda pop, and we Nixes would want some, so she would give us orange juice in a Coca-Cola bottle, and for a while that satisfied us.

I think the end of our street curved, rather than came to an intersection. I remember running with other kids around a winding sidewalk. Where it took us, I have no idea.

I do remember moving from the pink house. Some people took away our swing set—in the back of a pickup truck, I think. Little Bit and I, and maybe Digger, too, ran behind it, watching it go away. I think we cried. (Ma said once that I watched our possessions being sold, and she explained that we would be getting a new house, new furniture, new friends, and new swings. I considered this for hours, then asked, "Mommy, will we be getting a new daddy, too?")

Ma must have cried, too, as she said good-bye to her neighbors, her pink house with its pink General Electric appliances, and a life of some security, no matter how small. In South Carolina Pa had brought home a check from the Army, and at the farm in Minnesota he had worked part-time as a butcher, and in New Orleans he had been paid by the owners of the horses he had trained, and later by the bank for which he had sold insurance. But now he was going to work for his dream, and dreams can't be counted on when it's time to pay your bills.

Pa sold everything that would not fit into or on top of our station wagon. When the pink house was bare, we drove away. Remembering later trips, I can guess some of the details of that one: Pa sang "Little Joe the Wrangler" and "The Streets of Laredo," and Ma sang "Baa, Baa, Black Sheep" and "Roll Over, Roll Over." I sang the Daniel Boone theme song, and Little Bit sang any words that passed through her mind. We ate at hamburger stands and truck stops and Mom and Pop roadside restaurants where Pop tended the grill and Mom made a special of the day in the back kitchen. We stayed in little motels run by elderly couples in partial retirement. We drove all day, departing in darkness and arriving in darkness. If we drove past something that interested any of us, we did not turn back. If we missed a road we had intended to take, Pa told Ma to find the next one that would intersect the one we wanted. In the afternoon we stopped by city parks or country streams, and Pa napped while we kids ran around, chasing each other and yelling and doing our best to get a full day's playing into half an hour. Ma sat in the shade with a magazine, sometimes reading, sometimes fanning herself, always glancing at us through large sunglasses to be sure no one was eating dirt or chasing large dogs.

That must have been the trip when Digger got his name. George Abner Nix had a metal construction crane with black rubber wheels and a movable front scoop. He played with it constantly. He rarely talked, but one of the words he knew and used was "digger," the name of his toy. Pa started calling him that, and everyone, including Digger, thought it was funny.

Little Bit got her name because she had trouble pronouncing Letitia Bette Nix. She was a tiny girl with short brown hair and big brown eyes; "Little Bit" seemed appropriate to Pa and to everyone.

I never had a nickname other than Chris. I knew I had been named for Mark Christopher Nix, my father's brother, the brother who'd taken care of him when he was little, then gone off to the Second World War, that great war that followed the Great War to End All Wars, and died a hero. I didn't know then that he'd been shot down over Italy by American forces after returning from a successful mission; I didn't know then that the good guys kill the wrong people, too. I had seen a picture of Uncle Mark looking like John Wayne in his pilot's uniform. Ma was keeping his little pin-on silver wings for me until I was old enough to take care of them. Being named for him was better than any nickname could be.

As we drove toward Florida, land of flowers, where Spanish moss and oranges grew on every tree, Pa told me Grandpa Wade and Uncle Mark stories late at night, when I had the navigator's job of keeping the driver awake while watching for the next road that we wanted, and Mom and Digger and Little Bit slept in the backseat.

Wade Nix, so far as I knew, sprang like Adam from the American Midwest at the beginning of the twentieth century. He married Bette Kalff, a girl much younger than him, and they settled on a farm in northern Minnesota among the descendants of Norwegian and Swedish pioneers. In photos, they are a small, dark, handsome couple, but they may only seem small and dark next to their tall, fair-skinned neighbors. A picture exists in which a lean, weathered farmer smiles with a laughing baby on his knee; Wade Nix died soon after meeting me, before I had a chance to remember meeting him.

The Grandpa Wade story I heard most often was from late in his life. He and Bette had taken a trailer house down to Florida for the winter. Every morning he would go out and look at the sky, then shake his head. After sev-

eral weeks of this, he said, "Another goddamn beautiful
day," hitched up the trailer, and started back to Minnesota.
Pa always laughed when he told that one.

Wade and Bette Nix had six children: a daughter, a
son, a daughter, then three sons. From the names Bette
Nix gave them, you would think she was a devout Christian. The boys were Matthew, Mark, Luke, and John; the
girls were Hope and Faith. Whether Charity died young,
in the womb, or was never conceived, I do not know. What
a fifth son might have been named, I cannot guess. I know
that Grandma Bette believed in the Lutheran church for
human company, but she found her spiritual comfort
among the beans and tomatoes of her gardens, and the
tribulations of the shadowy actors on her afternoon soap
operas.

What the young Bette Nix might have believed or
sought, I cannot say. Pa would say Grandma Bette believed in having her children do her work and sought to
keep them working. The only story he told about Bette was
about how he would run down to the creek beside their
farm whenever she chased him to beat him. If he made it
to the creek, he was safe. She was too fat to scramble
down the steep bank after him.

The only story Grandma Bette told that I remember
was about crossing a river in a covered wagon when she
was a girl. The water came up through the floorboards,
but they crossed safely.

When her second son was born, Bette said his name
would be Mark. My Grandpa Wade, who Pa said never
spoke unless he had something to say, looked at her and
at the red-faced baby and said, "Mark Christopher." Bette
stared at him, but he offered no explanation and left their
bedroom.

The first names of her children seemed to satisfy
Bette's wish to shape a pattern for her neighbors to admire. The children's middle names were those of dead rel-
atives and presidents. Pa's middle name was Homer, but
he always signed himself "Luke H. Nix." When he was in

the Merchant Marine, he had his middle name legally changed to "H." so he could continue to say, as he always had, that the "H." stood for nothing.

After Uncle Mark was born, several years passed before the birth of my father, and then the birth of his younger brother. The Nix girls had school and chores around the farmhouse to keep them busy, and the oldest boy, Matt, had school and field work with Grandpa Wade, so Uncle Mark served as Pa's baby-sitter at least as often as either of his sisters.

Soon after Pa entered school, Matt Nix left it. Uncle Mark became the oldest male Nix at a tiny public school filled with Hansons, Olsens, Petersons, and Lundgrens. When the Nixes got into fights with blond town boys, Uncle Mark was the family champion. Pa began to start fights with older boys, knowing that Uncle Mark would come to his aid, until the day Uncle Mark saw what was happening and let Pa get beat thoroughly. Pa had a bloody nose and a broken tooth from that one. He laughed whenever he told about it, and so did I.

The Nix boys had a reputation for an easy way with girls, according to Pa. When Uncle Mark was a teenager, he had the easiest way of all. He was tall and good-looking, he played the guitar, he drove a shiny Studebaker convertible, and he was the captain of the football team. It's true that almost every boy in that community was tall, and Mark only knew a few songs and probably didn't play them well, and the Studebaker was secondhand, and there were so few high school boys in that small town school that anyone who wanted to could be on the football team. But it's also true that boys and girls both liked Uncle Mark's smile, and not everyone was brave enough or driven enough to sing in front of others, and the Studebaker's paint gleamed and its engine hummed, and even if anyone could be on the team, only one could be captain, and that one was Uncle Mark.

And it's also true that my pa got in a lot of fights when

he was young, and the person who'd sit him down and hear his story and tell him he'd fought well whether he'd won or lost was Uncle Mark.

The story about Uncle Mark and Grandpa Wade goes like this:

"Mark and your Grandpa Wade and I went into town one Saturday morning for supplies, and this fellow I didn't know came out of the store and stopped in front of us. We didn't think anything of it; we just began to move around him, when he says, 'Mark. You, Mark Nix. You afraid to face me?'

"Now, this fellow was big, a Swede farmer with shoulders that you get from working fourteen hours a day when work needs to be done. Being afraid of him seemed like a perfectly natural thing to me, and probably to your Grandpa Wade, too. I don't know if Mark was afraid, or if he just felt funny having this happen in front of his pa and his little brother. There wasn't much Mark could do but shake his head and say, 'No, Carl, I'm not afraid of you.'

"The Swede grins and says, 'All right, then. You and me, right here, right now.' And he begins to roll up his sleeves.

"Mark says, 'She said she wasn't your girl anymore.'

"The Swede kind of loses his grin and looks real mean. He says, 'You chickening out, Nix?'

"Mark looks at Pa and looks at me and says to the Swede, 'If you want, I'll meet you tonight at the Nitehawk.'

"The Swede says, 'Why should I wait up all night when you're right here?'

"Now, by this time, there's a few people inside the store listening, and there's a couple more on the sidewalk, and we're blocking the doorway, even though everyone around is more interested in whether there'll be a fight than in getting past us. Mark's kind of blushing, 'cause he knows everyone's going to be talking about this, no matter what he does.

" 'Hell,' the Swede says, real disgusted. 'You're yellow,

Nix. Little yellow pretty-boy. Come on, I'll give you the first blow. Hit me, if you're man enough.' He sticks out his chin. 'I dare you. Hit me.'

"Mark looks at your grandpa, and your grandpa just says, 'Well, son, *hit* the man.' "

Pa would laugh and repeat that: " 'Well, son, *hit* the man.' " And then the story would end the way it had to: "So Mark cold-cocks him, right there. One punch to the chin and the Swede's on the ground, wondering what train went over him. One punch. Your grandpa says, 'Come on, son,' and we went about our business. They were helping that poor Swede out of the store as we left." Pa would shake his head and grin then. "One punch."

Uncle Mark joined the Army Air Corps when the U.S. went to war. Pa, too young to join the Army, became a radio operator in the Merchant Marine. One day at sea he learned that Uncle Mark had been shot down over Italy. A week later he overheard a radio report that a ship carrying thousands of American bodies back from Europe had been sunk. The news never reached the public.

The U.S. government buried a coffin and set up a tombstone with my name on it at the military graveyard on the outskirts of Minneapolis. None of the Nix family traveled to the funeral. A few weeks after the funeral, Bette and Wade Nix received an American flag in exchange for their son.

If Pa was bitter about the end of Uncle Mark's story, I never heard that. I heard pride when he said that Uncle Mark and his copilot stayed in the plane until everyone else had parachuted safely, and then it was too late for them to bail out, too. What followed after that was just the way the story ended, no different from Custer at the Little Big Horn or the charge of the Light Brigade.

Ma told stories of our past, too, when she drove and Pa rested. Hers tended to be quiet afternoon tales. Mystery and violence were usually replaced with humor, but sometimes the grim things lurked in the corners of Ma's stories, outside the telling and making themselves known by their shadows, where none of us saw them unless we looked.

What should have been the best story of all was, in Ma's telling, a simple statement of fact: we were related to General George Armstrong Custer through Grandma Letitia, who had been born a Kuster with a "K," a cousin or a second cousin of his, or perhaps they'd come from the same German village centuries before. The details didn't matter. One of America's most famous heroes was one of ours, even if Ma had nothing to say about his life or death. Pa did his part to enrich this simple detail for Digger, Little Bit, and me by pointing out that our Indian blood meant we had ancestors on both sides of the Battle of the Little Big Horn, among its losers and its winners.

I don't remember any of Ma's stories about Grandpa Abner. Ma loved him, and so did we, because he was a happy man who was always finding ways to make us laugh. Maybe because of that, we didn't need any stories about him. He was the druggist in Rosecroix, Minnesota, a small town about a hundred miles from the farm where Pa grew up.

Ma's favorite story about Grandma Letitia was of a Sunday afternoon when they had gone driving. Grandma Letitia had seen a sign advertising a new soft drink, 7-Up, and she had said, "What's Zup?" Grandpa Abner had smiled and said, "I don't know, dear. What's up?" "No," said Grandma Letitia, pointing adamantly at the billboard. "What's Zup? What's Zup?"

Ma was an only child, so she had no stories to tell about brave or foolish siblings. She had been a happy and an obedient child, and as the daughter of one of the three richest families in town (the druggist comes after the two other wealthy "D"s of every small town, the doctor and the dentist), Ma had been protected

But Ma knew one story whose mystery I had never appreciated. Grandma Letitia was one of four Kuster girls. The oldest, Rose, had been a journalist for a good newspaper. Rose Kuster was a tall, independent woman, the quintessence of the 1920s free women. She wore short, fringed dresses; she bobbed her hair; she smoked cigarettes and raced roadsters; she kept her father's Colt .45 in her luggage. She never married. Grandma Letitia thought her oldest sister was a scandal and a delight.

Sometime between the two world wars, Rose Kuster took an ocean liner to Europe and never arrived. No one knew what happened to her, whether she fell overboard, was thrown, or threw herself. Her trunk came back to the U.S. without any hint of the fate of its owner.

Maybe I never appreciated the story because Ma would suggest that Rose had lost her memory and married a count, or had run away with a man who had not won Rose's father's approval. Those conclusions could not compare with struggling to land a shot-up B-17 in the dark hills of Italy. Only when I was older did I think of a moonless night on the ocean, and a ship cruising away while a dance band played a fox trot, and a woman in an evening gown swimming gamely after it, knowing her cries and the waving of her hand would never be noticed.

Only one set of family stories remains to be told before my story begins. These are the stories I learned as a child about Susan Genevieve Uvdal and Luke H. Nix.

When Ma graduated from high school, she went hundreds of miles away to the city, to Minneapolis. At the university, she danced late into the night at fraternity parties and hotel ballrooms, and eventually, homesick, she returned to her parents' house. She became a Wave during the Second World War. In photos of her in uniform, she looks like Judy Garland, another Minnesotan. After the war, with three others whom she called girls but who must have been young women, she spent a summer driving through Mexico. Handsome men were always available to help them whenever they had trouble with their car. When Ma returned to Minnesota, she was engaged several times, but she always found the men too stolid to marry.

Pa stayed in the Merchant Marine for some time after the war. In Germany he was jumped by two men, perhaps for his money. Pa knocked one down, straddled his chest, and tightened his fingers around the man's throat. The second man kicked Pa in the chin, so Pa banged the first man's head against the cobblestones. They repeated this like figures in a cuckoo clock striking an hour that would not end. At last, the first German quit kicking Pa and carried away his friend, or maybe the military police arrived. That night left Pa with a patch of mottled skin on his jaw where his beard would never grow.

When he left the Merchant Marine, he came back to northern Minnesota, but not to the family farm. He rented a cabin on Lake of the Woods, and he bought a used red MG convertible, the only sports car in several counties. One summer, he and his brothers and sisters put on the first waterskiing show on Lake of the Woods. His cabin became the county's weekend party house. He lived the life Uncle Mark might have led.

Pa was tending bar at the Nitehawk on the evening he met Ma. She came in with another man, and when Pa asked her what she'd like, she said, "In Minneapolis they knew how to make highballs, but no one knows how to make them up here."

Pa said, "Sister, if you can drink 'em, I can build 'em."

That was probably the true moment of my conception.

2

In the Foundations
of Dream

At the Florida welcome station, three pretty women with their hair piled high on their heads gave us smiles and small paper cups of orange juice. When I held out mine for more, Ma said, "Chris! What do you say?"

I said, "Please," and the pretty woman refilled my cup. I kept saying please until I could drink no more.

Ma gathered brochures of tourist attractions and showed us pictures of pirates in Tampa, mermaids in Silver Springs, and cowboys in Ocala. Pa said soon there'd be a brochure for Dogland here. He asked one of the pretty women with high hair if they had any literature about Latchahee County. The pretty woman frowned, said "Excuse me," and went to speak with a prettier woman with higher hair.

Little Bit whispered, " 'Piders."

I said, "What?"

Little Bit said, "In her hair. 'Pider nest."

I shivered and stared.

The youngest of the three spider women returned. "I'm

sorry. We're all out of brochures on Latchahee County. There isn't much there—"

"Now," Pa said.

"Beg pardon?"

Pa smiled. He always smiled at pretty women, and they always smiled at him. "Isn't much there now. But there will be."

"Oh, yes, sir," the woman said. "Florida's the fastest growing state in the nation. And as you visit here—"

"Settle here," Pa said. "Doing our bit to keep you growing so fast."

"Well!" said the woman. "Welcome to Florida! You, too, ma'm."

Ma said, "Thank you. We're looking forward to living here."

The woman looked at us. "And you, li'l chil'en? Are you looking forward to living here, too?"

I looked at my cowboy boots and nodded. Little Bit hid behind me. Digger just stared at the woman.

Ma said, "They're tired. It's been a long trip."

"Yes," said the young woman, smiling even more. "I'm sure it's been." At the end of the counter, the other two women watched us. Laughing, they waggled their fingers toward us like spiders walking.

Ma said, "Say good-bye, Chris, Letitia Bette."

I whispered, "G'bye."

The spider women laughed and called, "Be seeing you."

In Florida, nature has not been taught its place. Plants and animals do not know the forms they're permitted up north, so you find thick gray swatches of Spanish moss in the trees, and snapping turtles with heads shaped like those of eagles, and deep carpets of saw grass growing along the bottoms of the rivers, and walls of green palmetto spears making dens in the countryside for rattlesnakes and wild pigs.

As we drove to Latchahee County, Ma said, "See, Letitia Bette? The moss is waving hello."

Little Bit smiled and waved. "H'lo, moss." Digger giggled. I thought of Halloween witches with thick gray hair.

I pointed with an empty cowboy cap pistol. "Turtle."

Ma said, "Seven animals for Chris. One to catch up to Digger, six to catch up to Letitia Bette."

I always hated car games.

Pa said, "They call that a gopher down here. Turtles live in the water, gophers live on the ground. Their heads look different. Down here, they don't have hairy gophers like up north. Down here, lots of things are different."

Little Bit pointed. "Fire."

In the light of the sunset, a cross burned before an old wooden house. Several people stood around it wearing sheets.

I said, "Is it Hall'ween?"

Pa laughed, loud enough to surprise me. "No, son. You've got a couple of months to go."

Digger, pressing his hands and nose against the window of the station wagon, stared at the distant flame. Ma patted the back of his head.

Little Bit said, "Can we make a fire?"

Pa said, "Next time we go camping, we'll make a fire."

"Can we have mushmellows?"

Pa nodded. "We can have mushmellows."

"Can I have my own bag of mushmellows?"

"No."

"But—"

"No."

Ma tucked a strand of hair behind Little Bit's ear. The burning cross soon disappeared behind us.

Little Bit pointed. "Deer."

A fawn stood under the pines, long enough to be counted, then slipped into the shadows of the woods.

Ma said, "Fourteen for Letitia Bette."

I said, "I quit. I give my points to Digger, so he wins."

Ma and Pa always gave their points to Digger. Often

we'd catch him looking at an animal that none of us had
seen, and we'd give him those points, too. The only animals he would call were dogs and cats, and then he would
only whisper, "Robberlee" or "Nax." Robert E. Lee had
been the neighbors' dog in New Orleans, and Max had
been their cat.

Little Bit said, "That's not fair. Chris can't give his
points to Digger, too."

Ma said, "He can give his points to anyone he wants,
Letitia Bette."

Pa said, "Life's not fair."

Little Bit said, "But we're s'posed to try to be fair anyway."

Pa nodded. "That's about the size of it."

"But that's not fair," Little Bit said.

Pa reached over and ruffled her hair. "Who's my girl?"

"Me!" said Little Bit.

"Is that fair?"

Little Bit nodded vigorously.

Pa laughed. "No, it's not. I'm just luckier'n I deserve."

I pointed my pistol at her and whispered, "Bang."

"Chris's pointing his pistol at me!"

Ma said, "Did he hurt you?"

"No."

"Then that's okay."

I stuck my tongue out at her.

"Chris's sticking his tongue out at me!"

Ma said, "Chris, do you want a little bird to land on
your tongue and go to the bathroom?"

I pulled my tongue in fast.

"Ha-ha!" Little Bit said, pointing at me. "Ha-ha!"

We drove on in silence, finally broken when Pa said,
"Down here, you'll hear white people call Negroes 'niggers.' If any of you use that word, you'll get the whipping
of your life. Understand me?"

I said quietly, "Yes, sir." Little Bit bounced on the seat
and said, "An' don't say 'ain't.' "

Pa said, "You know why?"

Little Bit said, " 'Cause 'ain't' ain't right!"

They laughed, and Ma smiled, and Digger clapped his hands together. I pointed a cap gun into the night and whispered, "Bang."

Besides watching for animals, we watched for interesting billboards. U.S. 19 had been decorated with signs promising wondrous things if only we would travel a little farther: Reptile World, Seminole World, The Old Plantation, Six-Gun Territory, Busch Gardens, Beautiful Miami, Scenic Tallahassee, Historic St. Augustine, all kinds of motels with "beach" in their names that usually added a line saying they were "right on the beach!" Ma thought that was funny and said we'd better not stay at any beach motels that weren't on the beach. Pa pointed at two signs, for the Fountain of Youth Motor Inn and Suwannee Riverboat Rides, and said they were just down the road from where we were going.

Almost all of the billboards had pictures of pretty white women in one-piece bathing suits, but they also had snake heads and seashells and panthers and automobiles and clowns and old black men singing and fat black women laughing. None of us kids could read yet, but I knew most of the alphabet, and Little Bit and I had both learned to recognize a few words, especially when they were near pictures of our favorite meal: "Hamburgers! Hamburgers!"

Ma said, "Two nights in a row?"

Little Bit and I said, "Yeah!"

Pa shrugged. "It's a vacation."

So we stopped for dinner at a hamburger stand and had burgers, french fries, and chocolate milk shakes on tables set between two rows of parked cars. Behind the stand were older cars and a table where a Negro family ate. The air smelled of burnt meat and burnt gasoline, the smells of travel.

The men's room was locked, and Pa thought I was getting too old to be taken into the ladies', but they had a third door next to the first two. The word on the door didn't start with "W" or "L," so it wasn't for girls. It didn't start with an "M" or a "G" either; it started with a "C," which looked like a broken "G." When I tried the door, it opened, and there was a toilet inside, so I used it. When I came out, a Negro woman at the door looked at me and smiled slightly, and I felt bad. I hadn't known anyone had two women's rooms.

A white boy coming out of the men's room saw me ducking past the woman. He laughed and said, "That's the lightest nigger I ever saw!"

At the table I asked Ma, "What's see oh el oh ar ee dee?"

She said, "Oh, that's the bathroom for the colored people. Why?"

I shook my head. Ma took Little Bit and Digger to the ladies' room. When she brought them back, Little Bit, holding Ma's hand and twisting to look over her shoulder, said, "There's colored men and women using the same bafroom!"

I looked, and it was true. A whole family, a man, an old woman, two boys, and a girl, had formed a line at the bathroom I had used.

Ma said, "Shh."

Pa took his pipe out of his mouth, looked at it, and said, "They only get one in most places in the South. Wasn't any different in New Orleans. You never noticed?"

I shook my head.

"You think they should be using the bushes?"

Little Bit's eyes opened wide, and she shook her head.

Pa said, "All right, then," and put his pipe back in his mouth.

After dinner, as we drove into the gathering darkness, Ma said, "Should we get a motel room?"

Pa shook his head. "We're almost there."

"Everyone'll be asleep."

"I'll call the realtor."

"You don't even know if we have beds."

Pa frowned. "There's the mattress on the roof. You've got sheets."

Ma nodded.

"I'll call the realtor." Pa was at the pay phone for a minute or two. When he came back, he said, "Don't look like that, Susan. You'll be sleeping in your own house tonight."

Ma nodded. "Who wants to ride in front?"

Little Bit and I said, "Me, me!" Pa looked at Ma and didn't say anything.

Ma said, "You rode up front this afternoon, Little Bit. It's Chris's turn."

I grinned in triumph and jumped in. The front seat was best because you could see everything, including the car's control panel. Since we almost never had more than the driver and a passenger in the front, you had an entire half of the seat to yourself.

Ma, Little Bit, and Digger fell asleep quickly. Pa found a radio station that played Johnny Cash and other good country music, but when the signal turned into static, I couldn't find anything else on the dial.

I woke up sometime after that, when Pa said, "That's the Suwannee River up ahead." I saw the silhouette of a steel girder bridge against the dark sky, and a black ribbon of river to either side of us as we rattled over it. I knew the song, the first lines, anyway, and I would have sung them if I had been asked. Pa only said, "Watch close, son. The turn off to Dickison's easy to miss."

I sat up and squinted hard. The next light in the darkness was an electric sign for the Fountain of Youth Motor Inn, a small pink motel with a swimming pool in its courtyard. At the far end of the pool, water gushed from a giant bowl molded in concrete.

As we passed it, Pa said, "There's a springs back behind

the hotel. The owner said you kids can swim there any-time you want."

We drove for a mile. Pa said, "Damn," pulled into the gravel parking lot of Gideon's 19-cent Hamburgers, and turned around. For the first time on that trip, we drove the same stretch of road twice. I sat there, unable to say any-thing, but Pa pointed into a dark field and said, "Dogland."

I saw the shape of a building and the outlines of some trees, and nothing more. Pa said, "Needs just a *little* bit of work," and laughed, so I nodded.

When we got back to the Fountain of Youth Motor Inn, Pa said, "Damn it to hell," and we turned around again. I looked in the backseat. Ma and Digger still slept. Little Bit lay against Ma's shoulder, but her eyes were open wide.

Pa said, "Now, how'n hell'd I miss that turn?" Little Bit closed her eyes then, and I looked up front. In our station wagon's headlights, a narrow blacktop cut off from the highway. Beside it, a sign said, WELCOME TO LATCHAHEE COUNTY.

Pa turned onto the new road. A second sign said, FLORIDA 13, and a third said, DICKISON, 12 MI. Pa said, "Al-most there."

Florida 13 wound through forests and farmland. Just when I was about to fall asleep again, we left the darkness to pass a wooden roadhouse called Red's where electric lights burned and several speakers under the eaves played Jerry Lee Lewis very loudly for a parking lot filled with pickups, semitruck cabs, and convertibles with their tops down.

Under the lights, Red's was a movie set. A vignette played just for me while we approached: a black-haired boy and a blond girl leaned against a crimson Cadillac as they kissed. His hair was long and slicked back; hers was caught in a ponytail. He wore a white T-shirt; she wore a black blouse. He wore tight blue jeans; she wore tight white pedal pushers. I couldn't see her face. He looked up as our station wagon passed, and he smiled at us. Then, as he put his lips to her neck and she arched her back in pleasure, the movie set was gone in the darkness.

We came to a motel and a gas station where Pa began to slow down. A sign said, DICKISON, POP. 1,137. Pa said, "They'll have to pop five more now that we're here," but I didn't get it and Ma was still asleep.

Main Street consisted of several blocks of buildings, mostly one-story, flat-roofed, single-windowed structures that fronted on sidewalks shaded by water oaks, live oaks, and chinaberry trees. We parked in front of a small storefront with white lettering on its window: CENTRAL INSURANCE AGENCY AND REAL ESTATE, A. DRAKE, PROP. The office was dark. A note had been tucked in the screen door.

Pa and I got out. He looked the note over and headed back for the car. I ran to get into the passenger seat, and we drove several blocks to Mr. Drake's house. Over half of the houses in Dickison were old, high-roofed, square wooden boxes with a couple of windows and a porch in front and a shed in back. The rest were new, flat-roofed, rectangular cement-block boxes with a large living-room window, either no porch or a tiny porch large enough for one person to huddle out of the rain, and a carport attached to the living-room side of the house. Mr. Drake lived near the Christ the Redeemer Baptist Church in one of the new houses. A yellow light burned next to his front door, and a statue of a Negro jockey waited to hold horses next to the asphalt driveway.

Ma had woken by then, but she didn't say anything; she just watched. Pa parked behind the Drakes' shiny blue Buick, and he and I went up to their door. Pa pressed the buzzer. An eye and a mass of brown hair appeared in one of the three glass panes set in the front door, and then that door opened. A teenaged girl in a poodle skirt stood behind the screen. She smiled and said, "Hi. You folks lookin' for my daddy?"

Pa nodded. "If he's Mr. Drake."

"Just a minute." The girl ran back into the house, then

returned with a tanned man in a white, short-sleeved shirt and brown trousers.

The man stepped out, thrusting his hand toward Pa. Lots of people were taller than Pa, but Mr. Drake was almost a full head taller. "Mr. Nix? Wasn't sure you folks'd make it tonight."

The men grinned as they shook hands. Pa said, "Sorry to bother you so late, Mr. Drake. I have your check. We'll take the key and get out of your hair."

Mr. Drake had very little hair to get out of; his brown crew cut looked like a Marine's version of Friar Tuck's tonsure. He shook his head. "No, it isn't any trouble. I'll get you folks out there and show you where everything is." He lifted a hand to forestall any protest. "Got to let a man earn his living. Call me Artie." He motioned toward the girl. "That's Gwenny, my pride and joy."

Pa nodded. "I'm Luke. This is my boy, Chris. The rest of the family's sleeping in the car."

"You put in a couple of long days."

I said, "Yes, sir. All day long, sir."

Mr. Drake laughed. "I bet." He turned and called, "Gwenny, pick me up at the old Hawkins Motel. In about half an hour."

"Sure thing, Daddy."

"And don't call that Tepes boy and tell him you're home alone." He pronounced the name "teeps." I didn't learn the spelling until I saw Johnny Tepes's name in the *Dickison Star* several years later.

Gwenny may've exaggerated her indignation for us. "Daddy!"

He laughed. " 'Cause I will be expecting you in half an hour."

She may've exaggerated her resignation, too. "Yes, Daddy."

Mr. Drake asked Pa, "Mind if I drive you out? It's a sight easier'n following me or my directions."

Pa squinted. "We passed the property on the way in."

Mr. Drake laughed again. I could smell a little beer on

his breath. "Oh, I doubt you'd get lost on the highway. But I thought I'd show you a shortcut. And it's a mite tricky."

"Shortcut" was always a phrase of seduction to Pa. Suggesting that the route was difficult was the setting of the hook. Pa shrugged. "Fine."

"Good." Mr. Drake reached inside the door to pick up a long silver flashlight. "You want to carry this, Chris?"

I smiled. "Yes, sir!" The flashlight was heavy and twice as big as any of Ma's little house flashlights. I loved anything that was bigger than it was supposed to be, so long as it wasn't scary.

Mr. Drake said, "Don't turn it on until we need it."

I nodded. "All right."

Gwenny Drake smiled at me. "Nice meeting you, Chris, Mr. Nix." She gave her father a kiss on the cheek. "See you soon, Daddy."

"And don't drive over fifty. And take the highway!"

She laughed. "Yes, Daddy."

At the car, Digger didn't wake up for introductions, but Little Bit did. Mr. Drake said, "What a little charmer," and Little Bit grinned. He added, "It's apparent where she gets it, Mrs. Nix."

Ma smiled, tired and pleased. "I see I'll have to warn her about Southern flattery."

"Oh, some folks just have to state the obvious, and I fear I'm one, ma'm."

Pa said, "Get in, Chris." I hadn't been dawdling, but I slid into the middle of the seat fast and grinned. Mr. Drake got behind the wheel, Pa got in beside me, and we backed out onto Church Street. As he drove, Mr. Drake said, "Dickison's named for Captain J. J. Dickison of the Confederate Army. In February of 1865, he turned back two regiments of Yankees who tried to march inland from Cedar Keys. He was nearly the last Floridian to succeed in turning back Northerners." Mr. Drake's smile was in his voice, and Pa laughed, so Little Bit and I did, too.

I sat in the dim glow of the headlights and the dashboard and saw Confederate cavalry chasing Union troops

while cannons exploded in the sky. My family came from
the North, but I was Southern-born. Besides, the Confederates had better uniforms than the Yankees.

Mr. Drake shrugged. "The last time was a month later,
some of our troops and a bunch of schoolboys repelled a
Yankee invasion of Tallahassee. That was up north a ways
at a place called Natural Bridge. Did you know Tallahassee's the only Confederate capital east of the Mississippi
that wasn't captured by the Union?"

"No," Ma said. "I didn't."

"I figure that either means the Yankees never completely whupped us, or we've always been able to work
deals with the North, whether we liked it or not."

Pa said, "There been any hard feelings about us buying the Hawkins land?"

Mr. Drake glanced at him, then laughed and glanced
back at the road. "Oh, no, sir, not at all. Not enough Yankees settling in Latchahee County to bother anyone. Down
south and along the coast, some folks call it the North's
second invasion, but no one really minds. This time it's an
invasion of money, not soldiers, and no one's come trying
to tell us how we ought to live."

Pa said, "Good to hear that. Susan and I'll always be
Yankees, I suppose, but the kids'll be talking like little
rebels in a month, I bet."

Mr. Drake laughed. "Kids're like that." He turned onto
a rutted gravel road, marked only by a sign saying COUNTY
666, and pointed a finger out into the night. "Captain Dickison turned back the Yankees near Otter Creek, but the
townsfolk there were happy enough with their name.
Around here, we didn't much like our old name of Creek
Town, so we took on Dickison in 1866. Our old name
wasn't on account of any creek running through town. In
territorial days, a Creek Indian village was here.

"We'll pass by Old Dickison, the site of Creek Town, in
about half a mile. Isn't anything there to see in the dark."
Which was certainly true. Away from Dickison, there was
only the night. The whole of the world lay inside our car

and in the strip of gravel that rolled through our head-lights and beneath our wheels.

"The Creeks and the whites lived in peace in Creek Town, same as in Chiefland over in Levy County. And, same as in Chiefland, they were forced south as more and more whites moved in. Some of 'em prob'ly ended up in the Everglades. Most of 'em were prob'ly sent to Oklahoma after the Seminole Wars. Anyways, the only Creeks you'll see around Dickison are the Dickison Warriors on home-coming weekend. We always put on a nice parade. Gwenny'll be a drum majorette this year."

He pointed toward a dark strip on the black horizon. "Old Dickison. Not a heap more to see in daylight. Folks keep talking about turning it into a county park. Maybe that'll happen when they finish this road." He laughed. "That's kind of a local joke. Seems like they've been work-ing on this road forever."

We passed a big yellow grading machine and a little caterpillar with a shovel on the front. On the side was sten-ciled, TOPHET CONSTRUCTION CO. Drake laughed again. "See what I mean? S'posed to connect Dickison with a little beach on the Gulf of Mexico, open up the county for tourism. I wouldn't hold my breath."

Ma said, "History is your hobby, Mr. Drake?"

"Yes, ma'm. That and religion. If you don't know those things about folks, you don't know dirt about 'em. And it's natural enough to me, being in insurance and real estate. Gods and the past, yes, indeed, ma'm."

He gestured again at the night. "Folks think this is a new land, call it the new world, but it's old. People been coming to Florida for near as long as there's been people. When the Spaniards came in the 1500s, two tribes held most of this part of the peninsula. The Timucua and the Apalachee. The Suwannee River divided their territory."

Apalachee sounded like Apache. I began to see John Wayne in the desert, and warriors circling the wagon train.

"There was an Indian village around the property

you're buying, which probably would've been Timucuan.
They called the river the Guasaca Esqui, the River of
Reeds. De Soto called it the River of the Deer. But its last
Spanish name was the San Juanee, the little St. John.
Folks say the coloreds corrupted the name to Suwannee,
but I reckon we all did, since that's what we all call it." He
nudged me. "Might find arrowheads on your property.
Would you like that?"

"Yes, sir!" I said.

"You find anything special, you let me know. I'm an
armchair archaeologist, too. But I know some real ones
at the University of Florida. You know what an archaeologist does?"

"No, sir."

"An archaeologist is an active historian. Gets right in
there with the clues folks have left us and figures out how
they lived."

"Oh." Archaeology sounded more like something for
Digger than for me.

"The tourist board likes to say Florida's belonged to five
nations, Spain, France, Britain, the Union, and the Confederacy. That's prob'ly 'cause they only want to use one
hand to count with. When the Spanish came, there were
four nations already here, the Calusa, the Tegesta, the
Timucua, and the Apalachee. We don't know the names of
the folks who came before 'em, but we know of some that
came after. The Creeks came down with the British
colonists, before the American Revolution, helping 'em
fight the Spanish and enslave the local Indians. Some of
the Creeks stayed here and got the name of Seminoles.
That means Runaways. You know about the Seminoles,
Chris?"

"No, sir."

"Great warriors, and good people. Before the U.S.
owned this land, slaves would run south to be free. Some
of them set up their own community, took over an old
Spanish fort. Others of 'em married into the Seminoles. A
woman named Morning Dew who had some Negro blood

married a warrior named Osceola, or As-se-he-ho-lar, which means Black Drink. That was a ceremonial brew, sort of like beer."

I nodded.

"Morning Dew gave Osceola four children, and then some settlers carried her off as a slave on account of her Negro blood. In those days, they had terms for how much Negro you had in you. An octoroon was an eighth Negro, and I don't know if Morning Dew was even that much Negro. Anyway, Osceola never forgave the Americans for stealing his wife. A war lasted seven years. Might've ended earlier, but Osceola came in to talk under a flag of truce, and the American leader—I hope a Yankee—captured him. Another Seminole, Wild Cat, kept the war going. Cost the U.S. fifteen hundred soldiers' lives and over forty million dollars in expenses and property damage."

Pa said, "Sounds like Florida's got a history of losing battles."

Mr. Drake laughed. "Don't say that to anyone but me. Folks know I'll say any fool thing 'cause I went off to school." He laughed again. "You're right, though. A history of losing wars and losing lands. But keep in mind that every one of those losses was hard-fought."

Ma said, "What happened to Morning Dew?"

Mr. Drake gave her the same look he'd given Pa. "You know, I've bored countless people with that story, and you're the first to ask. I'll find out."

Ma said, "Thank you."

A car slowly approached and passed us; our headlights flashed across a pale, elderly couple sitting close together in the front seat. Mr. Drake said, "Tourists, most like. Surprising number of people travel this road, maybe just to see where it goes. Which is a few miles past Dickison into absolutely nothing at all." A new set of headlights approached from the north, then crossed the road far ahead of us, continuing south and letting us know we were almost to the highway.

Mr. Drake said, "There, the shortcut prob'ly saved you

a whole minute and a half." We came onto Route 19 next
to Gideon's Hamburgers. Mr. Drake jerked his head toward the tiny restaurant. "Gideon Shale's one of your
neighbors. Nice old coot. Makes a fine hamburger. As long
as you don't mind hearing a little Jesus every ten or twenty
minutes, you'll get on fine with him."

"What is he?" Ma asked.

"What church?" Mr. Drake shook his head. "Baptist, to
be sure. Near everyone down here's Baptist. What kind of
Baptist, I can't say. He's a happy one though. He thinks
Latchahee County is the site of the Garden of Eden."

Pa sounded as if his nose had clogged up.

Mr. Drake said, "Lots of people in Florida get their notions. For the most part, folks figure you can believe any
fool thing so long as you let them believe their own non-
sense." He let his foot off the gas and flipped the turn signal. "This is all sacred ground around here."

Ma said, "Oh?"

"Sorry, I'm getting so wrapped up in ancient history
that I'm forgetting near history." He eased the car onto a
gravel driveway. "Mrs. DeLyon's willing to knock five thousand dollars off the buying price."

Pa made a grunt of interest.

"The old house burned down a couple nights back."

Ma gasped. Pa made a grunt that only said he'd heard
what Mr. Drake had said. I said, "Ooh," and wished I'd
been here to watch.

"Wasn't anything in it. You must've seen it was in sorry
shape when Mrs. DeLyon showed it to you."

Pa grunted again. Ma said, "But where'll we live?"

Mr. Drake said, "The manager's quarters have been
kept up nice."

"Luke said they were small."

"Yes, ma'm." Mr. Drake parked our station wagon beside a pale green square building with large windows on
three sides and a CLOSED sign in one of them. The window
lettering said, HAWKINS'S HOME-STYLE CAFE. The headlights
shone on a dirt trail through an overgrown yard to a low

cinder-block building with two doors. "If you don't think you'll be comfortable, we'll head back into town and put you up at our place. Won't be any trouble."

"Well." Ma looked at Pa. Pa stared out at the charcoal night beyond the car's twin beams of light. Ma said, "We've come this far."

Little Bit said, "We're here?"

I said, "Of course we're *here*. Where d'you think we are, *there?*"

Ma said, "Chris, everyone's tired."

"But she couldn't even tell—"

Pa said, "Chris."

I said, "Yes, sir," and shut up.

Mr. Drake said, "I 'spect I'll need that flashlight now."

I handed it to him and felt useless. Pa was already getting out of the car, so I scrambled after him, and felt a little better as soon as my cowboy boots crunched onto the gravel.

Pa said, "That's two fires here."

Mr. Drake said, "Nothing suspicious about that. The row of motel rooms burned last year 'cause of a fellow smoking in bed. Did you know that cigarette companies add things to their tobacco so the cigarettes won't go out fast when you're not puffing on 'em?"

Pa glanced at him.

Mr. Drake laughed. "Sorry. My daughter says I always take shortcuts when I drive and the scenic route when I talk."

Pa nodded.

Mr. Drake turned the flashlight on and cut the night with its beam, revealing the charred ruins of a house. "Rooster Donati—that's the sheriff—says a party got out of control. Someone built a campfire behind the house, away from the highway, and didn't pay any mind to it till it was too late. Prob'ly kids broke into the house to, ah, fool around and forgot about their campfire. Or might've been tramps. Anyways, the only damage was property damage."

Pa nodded. "Anything else I should know?"

"There is one more thing, but I'd prefer to show you around first. Reassure you that everything else is just the way you saw it."

Pa said, "My check won't clear for a couple of days. I've got plenty of time to assure myself."

Mr. Drake nodded. "Let me give your family the quick tour and finish up the ancient history, first. If you don't mind."

Pa shrugged.

Mr. Drake smiled and handed me the flashlight. "Shine that over there, Chris."

I aimed the light where he pointed. Alone in the night, far from any other tree, stood a huge live oak draped in Spanish moss. Jack the Giant-Killer could climb that tree and find riches. The Swiss Family Robinson could build a city in its limbs.

Mr. Drake said, "They call that the Heart Tree. No one's sure why. S'posed to've sprouted when Columbus landed. No one's counted rings, but the botanists who've looked at it agree it could be that old." He smiled at me and Little Bit. "That tree's nearly five hundred years old."

"Ooh," I said.

He nodded at Ma. "Remember when I said this was sacred land? Before the Spanish came, the natives marked the trees in a ring five miles out around this place. Apalachees and Timucuans who'd been wounded in battle would come here to heal, and no one would fight on this ground. Some say it was the Heart Tree that was sacred. Some say it was Hawkins Springs, back behind the Fountain of Youth Motel. In either case, it doesn't matter. Sacred ground."

I nodded and looked at my family. Everyone was listening to Mr. Drake, except for Digger, who sat on the dirt and grinned as he picked up sacred ground and dropped it on his clean dungarees.

Pa nodded. "Plenty of firewood there." Mr. Drake gaped, and Pa laughed. "Don't worry. We'll put a sign in

front of that tree for the tourists. Maybe we could hire you
to write its history."

Mr. Drake's nod was almost a bow. "I'd be honored."

Ma said, "Where were the motel rooms?"

Mr. Drake tapped my shoulder and pointed. I turned
the beam of the heavy flashlight and revealed a long scar
in the earth that tall grass and small bushes were beginning to reclaim. Mr. Drake pointed toward the woods. "I
think they dozed the rubble back into there, by the
Hawkins's garbage dump. Nothing salvageable in either
fire."

He took from his pants pocket a ring of keys with a
round white tag, led us to the restaurant door, opened it,
and snapped on a light mounted to the outside of the
building, then a light inside. In the electric glare, the Heart
Tree was just a big tree, the Hawkins's Cafe was an old
roadside restaurant, and the land where the motel had
burned was ugly instead of mysterious.

As Pa went to turn off the station wagon's lights, Mr.
Drake waved at the restaurant and said, "You can tell it
needs a good cleaning."

Ma's lips tightened, and she nodded. The windows and
walls were thick with grime. Digger stood beside Ma, resting his head on her leg. She picked him up in both arms
and whispered, "It'll be fine." He put his head on her
shoulder and immediately went to sleep.

Mr. Drake said, "Maynard Hawkins wasn't much of a
handyman, and when the title went to Mrs. DeLyon, she
saw no need to fix up a business that'd just compete with
the Fountain of Youth. So there's plenty to keep you busy
here. But everything's sound. It'll be worth the work."

Pa said, "Hmm."

Mr. Drake held the screen door open for us. The restaurant was a dusty version of the places we usually ate in
when we traveled: large windows, a few bare lightbulbs in
the ceiling. The cinder-block walls had once been white or
light gray. Eight or ten square, Formica-covered tables
were stacked in twos on one side of the room; the upper,

upside-down tables thrust their iron pedestals into the
air, where their feet made "X"s. Next to the tables was a
cluster of steel-tube chairs with pink padded plastic-
covered backs and seats. Just inside the door, a counter
ran along the wall, with twelve high stools bolted to the
floor in front of it. The stools had dark bases, like the tables, but they ended in round seats with shiny aluminum
sides and padded red vinyl tops. Behind the counter was
a pass-through into the kitchen, next to scarred swinging
doors.

Mr. Drake said, "A few hours with soap and paint, and
it'll be beautiful."

Little Bit and I jumped onto two high stools and began
to spin ourselves around. When we laughed, Digger woke
up, looked at us without any expression, and went back
to sleep.

Pa said, "This'll be the souvenir shop until we're ready
to expand."

Ma looked at him and Mr. Drake and didn't say anything.

Mr. Drake said, "Everything works. The grill, the hot
water, the refrigerator, which was bought new three years
ago, the freezer, everything. If you decide you don't want
to run a restaurant, you could sell the furnishings for a
good price."

Ma looked at Little Bit and me. "You'll get dizzy." We
were already dizzy, but her warning was a fine excuse to
stop spinning, so we jumped down from the stools. Ma
looked at Mr. Drake. "The manager's quarters don't have
a kitchen."

"No, ma'm, they don't. But you've got everything you
could want for cooking right in here." He pushed open the
swinging doors to the restaurant's kitchen. I ran in with
Little Bit right behind me, and Mr. Drake laughed.

The kitchen seemed darker than the front room because its walls were hung with cabinets and its ceiling had
been stained with smoke. A heavy table dominated the
center of the room, big enough to butcher a pig or a per-

son. Little Bit and I peered under the table, then raced around it.

Pa looked at Ma, his face still, waiting as if he could wait forever. Ma opened the oven, turned a gas burner on and off, then smiled the tiniest bit and nodded. Pa turned to Mr. Drake. "Looks fine."

"Good. On to the manager's building?"

Ma said, "What're you children looking at?"

Little Bit and I stood in front of a closet door. I closed it quickly. "Nothing."

Ma looked in the closet. On an old calendar, a naked blond lady was stretching out on red cloth like she couldn't get comfortable enough to sleep.

Mr. Drake said, "I'm sorry. You may not be able to tell it, but some tidying up was done after Maynard left."

Ma told us, "I think you've looked at that long enough."

Pa smiled. I felt a little embarrassed about looking at a grown-up without any clothes on, even if it was a picture of a grown-up. As Ma closed the closet door, Little Bit pointed at the calendar and said, "She's going to take a bath."

Ma said, "You'll have to wait until tomorrow to take yours." She asked Mr. Drake, "Any surprises in the manager's house?"

He smiled. "I surely hope not, ma'm." He made a gesture like tossing a ball underhand, indicating we should all leave, then turned off the lights and locked the restaurant. He said to me, "You like pirates?"

I nodded very affirmatively.

"Pirates sailed up the Suwannee, way back when. So did smugglers, and during the War Between the States, so did blockade runners. There were bootleggers running liquor on the Suwannee during Prohibition, so you might as well add gangsters to the list."

Ma said, "Pirates, Mr. Drake?"

"Yes, ma'm. Blackbeard, Black Caesar, Gasparilla, Jean Lafite, John Davis—you can just about take your pick." Mr. Drake looked at me. "A pirate couldn't think much of

himself if he didn't visit Florida at least once." He pointed
back at the restaurant. "Might be this place is named for
a pirate."

Pa said quietly, "Oh?" then added, "Keep that light on
the path, Chris."

"Yes, sir," I said. We followed the dirt trail through
long grass. Sand spurs stuck to my pants. When Little Bit,
bare-legged in a dress, said, "Ow!" and brushed at her
calves, Pa picked her up and set her on his shoulders.

Mr. Drake said, "Captain John Hawkins was an English
pirate and slave trader. His ship was the *Jesus of Lubeck*,
the first English ship to visit Florida waters. That would've
been in 1564."

I aimed the light at the building we were approaching.
Like the restaurant, it was flat-topped, built of cinder
block, and painted pale green. Two doors divided its front
into thirds. Beside each door was a long louvered window
with narrow horizontal panes of milky glass.

"Hawkins preyed mostly on the Spanish, I believe. No
one knows if he really sailed up the Suwannee, but his log
does mention a 'beautefull sprynge where all do live in
peace.' Properly, the local spring's named for Colonel
Josiah Hawkins. He showed up in the early 1800s and
built a plantation on these grounds. He said he was one
of Captain John's descendants, and he filed a claim for all
these lands, but one of Mrs. DeLyon's ancestors went to
court arguing that the springs and the land around it were
theirs. The law came up with a perfect compromise—it
made everyone unhappy. The DeLyons kept the springs.
The Hawkinses got most of the land. The Hawkinses and
the DeLyons were at odds for nigh on a hundred years, but
that's all history now."

Mr. Drake fumbled with his keys, then opened the
right-hand door and asked for the flashlight. I gave it to
him; he aimed it inside, reached in, and turned on a light.
"You folks mind waiting on the porch?"

Ma and Pa both studied him. Pa said, "Kids can stand
the sight of another calendar."

Ma didn't laugh. Mr. Drake said, "I won't be a second."

Pa drawled in the way that meant he was giving you one chance, and no more. "All right."

I peeked in as Mr. Drake entered. The room looked like a motel room: blue block walls, a chipped dresser, a double bed with a beige chenille spread that had a couple of moth holes, a night stand that had a few cigarette burns, and a mottled black-brown-and-white linoleum floor. Mr. Drake disappeared through a door next to the closet, then came outside thirty seconds later through the farther door.

Pa said, "Well?"

Mr. Drake laughed. "Didn't want to alarm you, but Ethorne—he's a local Negro who does odd jobs for Mrs. DeLyon—said he'd chased out a rattler when he brought the furniture. Mrs. DeLyon said if you have no need for these things, let her know and she'll have Ethorne haul 'em off to a needy family."

Ma looked at Pa. He put his hand on her arm and said, "Now, Susan. You knew there'd be rattlesnakes."

"Not in the house, I didn't."

"Well, there aren't any." Pa looked at Mr. Drake. "Are there?"

Mr. Drake told Ma, "No, ma'm. That one probably slipped in while Ethorne left the door open to fetch something. He said he looked all around to make sure there weren't holes in the floor or the walls, or any likely nests under the foundation. I trust Ethorne. He's a better man than most whites you'll meet."

Pa glanced at us as if he was going to say something, but didn't.

Mr. Drake said, "Snakes don't like folks any more than folks like snakes. You'll see one now and then, but once there's activity around here, they'll keep their distance."

Ma said, "If you say so," and went inside. The rest of us followed her. While Ma put Digger down on the bed, I pushed open the sliding door of the closet and saw a room just long enough for me to sleep in.

Ma said, "That was thoughtful." Someone had picked a handful of small blue flowers and put them in water in a Coca-Cola bottle.

Mr. Drake smiled. "Ethorne, I bet."

"It was kind of Mrs. DeLyon to see we had beds our first night."

"I mentioned your husband had said you'd be buying furniture when you got here. She's a fine lady, is Mrs. De-Lyon."

I ran to catch up to Pa and Little Bit, who were following the route Mr. Drake had taken on his search for snakes. The right-hand bedroom's inner door led to a small yellow bathroom consisting of a white porcelain sink and toilet, and a sheet-metal shower. A door opposite the first opened on the left-hand bedroom, which was a fun house mirror image of the right-hand one. The furniture in the second bedroom had seen even more use than the furniture in the first, the walls were green, the blue flowers were in an Orange Crush bottle.

Ma said, "There's not a lot of space for a family."

Pa said, "Got a big yard."

Ma smiled slightly, then shook her head. "All three children in one room?"

"It's big enough for 'em while they're small. I never had a room of my own when I was a boy. We can build on, someday, or build a new house once Dogland's a going concern."

"Well—"

I went into the closet, closed the door, and called, "This is my room!"

Ma said, "That's the closet, Chris."

Little Bit said, "Do I get my own bed?"

Pa said, "Not tonight, little darling."

Little Bit said, "I want my own bed."

Ma looked at Pa. He said, "We can bring in the mattress. If we're staying."

Ma said, "Well—"

Mr. Drake spoke from the bathroom doorway. "I don't want to pressure you. I'm serious about being happy to put you up at our place."

Pa laughed. "A little hard sell, a little soft?"

Mr. Drake shrugged. "I won't deny that I want you folks to stay. Time's passing by Latchahee County, and it doesn't have to be that way. The kids, white and black both, leave for the cities, where pay's higher and there's excitement every night. Seems the only folks who stay are losers and dreamers." He touched his chest and grinned. "Myself, not excluded. But you folks seem to be dreamers *and* doers. I like that. Latchahee County needs people like you."

Pa looked at Ma. "Write the check?"

Ma said, "Well—"

Mr. Drake said, "You can write it now if you want, but I won't deposit it till you call and say to. 'Cause there's one thing I haven't told you yet."

Pa said, "I hadn't forgotten." His smile had gone.

"They'll be building the interstate a good hour east of here. U.S. Nineteen's going to lose some traffic in the next few years."

Ma gasped. I didn't know what that meant, but I knew it must be worse than rattlesnakes in your bedroom. I went to stand beside her. Little Bit took her hand.

Pa said, "We knew that was a possibility when we picked this place."

Ma looked at him.

Mr. Drake said, "Planning for the worst doesn't mean you expect it. We know that."

Pa said, "Just means there won't be as many tourists visiting accidentally. We'll have to get them to visit on purpose."

Ma said, "Can we?"

Pa said, "If that's the choice. I assume they won't be shutting down Nineteen."

Mr. Drake laughed. "No."

Pa nodded. "Then all we'll really lose are folks in a hurry to get to south Florida. The ones who're traveling for scenery will still come this way. They're our real customers."

Ma said, "If you say so."

Pa said, "So. Write the check?"

We kids saw he wanted Ma to say yes. She looked at Mr. Drake. "It's really all right to sleep here tonight and decide tomorrow?"

An automobile horn sounded up by the restaurant. Mr. Drake smiled. "That's my girl." Then he said, "That'd be fine with Mrs. DeLyon. The longer you stay, the more you'll like it here." He handed Pa the ring of keys. "Only thing you didn't see was the pump house, and it ain't much."

Pa said, "The water's running. It's probably fine."

"Give you a hand with the mattress?"

Pa looked at Little Bit. "Thanks."

The horn sounded again. Pa said, "C'mon, Chris."

Ma looked in on Digger, who slept, as always, quite soundly, then she followed us up to the restaurant where Mr. Drake's new Buick blinded us with its headlights. Gwenny identified herself as the shadow in the driver's seat by calling, "You ready, Daddy?"

"Just about. Was the Tepes boy at Red's?"

"No, Daddy," she said, very patiently, and she brushed her sand-brown hair forward over her shoulder. The collar of her yellow shirt with red polka dots had been turned up.

Mr. Drake smiled. "That's too bad. Gwenny, this is Mrs. Nix and Little Bit."

"Hey," said Gwenny.

"Hi," said Ma.

Little Bit said, just loud enough that I could hear, "Her neck."

I squinted and stepped closer to the car. Gwenny smiled at me and said, "Hi, handsome." I blushed and stood still.

Ma said, "Do you baby-sit?"

Gwenny shrugged. "Now and then."

Mr. Drake smiled. "She's the finest baby-sitter in Latchahee County."

Gwenny looked at me, then tugged a thick strand of her hair forward again, hiding a reddened area at her throat. "Daddy tell you about the pirates?"

I nodded.

"He's still working on getting Billy the Kid down here."

Mr. Drake said, "You don't remember old man Goode, Gwenny. Died when you were a baby. Some said he was the Kid, and Pat Garrett lied about killing him."

Gwenny laughed. "Oh, Daddy." Little Bit and I laughed, too.

Mr. Drake put his hand on my head and ruffled my crew cut. "I didn't tell a single stretcher tonight, Chris. Might've set you up for a few later, though. 'Cept for that business about old man Goode, which was Gwenny's fault. He wasn't really Billy the Kid."

I nodded. "I knew that, sir."

Mr. Drake said, "He was John Dillinger." He held his hands out as if he were holding a machine gun and went, "Ratta-tatta-tatta!"

"Daddy!"

Mr. Drake winked at me. I blinked both eyes at him, which was the best I could do. Ma smiled at him and said, "We shouldn't be keeping you."

"You kidding? Gwenny just got her driver's permit. This is a great night for her, cruising alone and driving the boys wild." Gwenny wrinkled her nose at him. Mr. Drake stepped over to the station wagon, where Pa had finished untying the mattress. "Here, I got this end, Luke."

Pa grunted, then said, "Bring the blue suitcase, Chris."

"Yes, sir!" I used both hands to drag the heavy case from the rear of the car.

Little Bit told Gwenny, "You're pretty."

Gwenny laughed and said, "Wish the boys thought so. But you, you're cuter than a bug."

I said, "I think you're pretty." Then I looked at my cowboy boots.

Gwenny nodded. "Then you're my boyfriend. Want some help with that suitcase?"

I shook my head and began to haul it toward the house, clutching the handle in both hands and bumping my knees with every step. "Uh-uh."

Little Bit said, "Chris has got a girlfriend, Chris has got a girlfriend."

"Do not."

Gwenny said, "You're *not* my boyfriend?"

She sounded hurt. I said quietly, "I'm your boyfriend, but I don't got a girlfriend. Okay?"

I hadn't realized Ma had heard. She laughed and said, "Isn't that just like a man?"

The night ended soon after that. Pa and Mr. Drake put the mattress for Little Bit in one corner of the green bedroom and pushed the double bed against the wall for Digger and me. Gwenny helped Ma put on sheets from a box out of the back of the station wagon. Pa wrote a check for the property after Ma said, "Well, all right." Ma and Pa both shook hands with Mr. Drake, everyone smiled, Gwenny and Mr. Drake drove away, and I had to go to sleep with Digger.

A plastic night-light plugged into an outlet in the cinder-block wall kept our bedroom from becoming part of the kingdom of night. Its dim red light held the room in the borderland, in the land of shadows. The night lay under our bed and crouched in the closet and peeked through the louvers of the window over our heads. On the wall above our bed, a chameleon was perfectly still. Whether it was watching, sleeping, or dead, I could not tell.

Digger rolled against me. I pushed him onto his side of the bed. He didn't wake. I hoped he'd pee on his side of the bed if he had to pee in bed; he could sleep in a damp bed, but I hated moist sheets and always had to get Ma to change the linen no matter which of us had wet them.

I lay curled in a ball and thought about pirates and cowboys and Confederate troops, and all the dogs that would be coming to Dogland, and Indians in the woods watching the settlers who'd come to build a tourist trap close to the banks of the Suwannee. I thought about Mr. Drake, who seemed like he'd be a nice father. I thought about Gwenny Drake, and wondered if I would marry her when I grew up. I don't think I thought about my family; they were too much a part of me. I might have wondered whether Pa would be happy here, and whether Ma would like this place as much as she liked the pink house in New Orleans. At some point, my thoughts became dreams, and I slept through the warm Florida night.

3

Things Seen in Black and White

I woke at dawn when Digger climbed over me to get out of bed, and I woke again an hour later when Pa called, "Everyone up who wants breakfast!" Across the room, Little Bit was dressing in a T-shirt and jeans that had been mine a year before. Ma had put a stack of clean clothes at the foot of the bed for me. I dressed without caring what I put on. The only important items were my cowboy boots and my Roy Rogers belt with two holsters for cap guns, even though I only had one cap gun left, and its trigger was broken.

When I used the toilet, I sat on the front edge of the seat, watching the water beneath me, and scooted off as soon as I was done. I had seen a cartoon in a book at Grandpa Abner's that showed a fish leaping out of a toilet bowl and a woman staring at it with big eyes. I thought that was funny and I knew it was impossible, but I didn't think there was any reason to take chances.

Ma called, "Little Bit has to use the bathroom."

I yelled, "I'm almost done."

Ma called, "Are you off the toilet?"

I yelled, "Yes!" Ma opened the door and brought Little Bit in. Squeezing toothpaste onto my toothbrush, I said, "I wasn't done yet."

Ma said, "Your father's making breakfast in the restaurant." That meant we should hurry, so I slid the brush over my teeth while Little Bit sat next to the sink, and then I ran out of the house.

Stepping into the sunlight was stepping into Florida. I didn't smell oranges—Ma had explained that oranges grew farther south—but I smelled a humid pinelands that was not like the New Orleans suburb I had known. I drew my pistol and watched for Injuns and rustlers in the weeds or behind the bushes. I knew where they were: the clearing for the former motel and restaurant was enclosed on three sides by straight walls of the old forest. But no bad guys showed themselves as I followed the path to the restaurant, so I entered through the back door.

Pa grinned and said, "Morning, Christopher."

I said, "G'mornin'," and sat next to Digger at the big table. In one skillet, Pa tended pancakes (bubbles were just beginning to appear on their tops as the first side fried) and in another, bacon, which sizzled and shriveled and, in its way, bubbled, too.

Digger had a bowl of Rice Krispies and a box decorated with the three elves, Snap, Crackle, and Pop. He was happily loading his mouth with milk and sugar-drenched cereal, using a spoon that he held tightly in his fist. Whitish drool oozed from the corners of his mouth.

"Digger's dribblin'," I announced. Pa had piled plastic bowls and spoons in the middle of the table and set out a carton of milk. I grabbed the biggest bowl and heaped it full of Rice Krispies.

"He dribblin' on you?"

"No, sir." Several open mason jars were in the center of the table with spoons in them; some of the spice containers had gotten wet when we had packed in New Orleans, so Ma or Pa had transferred the contents. I grabbed a jar with white powder and put three spoonfuls on my Rice Krispies.

Pa flipped bacon and pancakes. "Then don't worry about it."

"No, sir." I filled my bowl with milk until the cereal became a floating island, and listened to the snap-crackle-pop, which was never as good as it was on television. Then I put a spoonful in my mouth and said, "Bleh!"

Digger looked at me and grinned. Pa looked at me and said, "What is it?"

"Tastes bad," I declared.

Pa flipped pancakes and bacon onto two plates and set them in front of us, then looked at my cereal bowl. He frowned and said, "You put salt on it."

"Oh." I reached for the syrup bottle to drench my pancakes.

"Finish your cereal."

"Tastes bad," I repeated.

"Waste not, want not," Pa said, which had no meaning that I could understand. When I hesitated, he said, "That was your doing. Now you live with it."

Ma and Little Bit came in then. Ma said, "Smells wonderful." Pa grunted. Ma went straight to Digger and wiped his face, but when I looked at Pa, he didn't seem to have noticed that I'd been right.

Pa gave plates of pancakes and bacon to Ma and Little Bit. Beside me, Digger used his fork to break apart the center of his pancake, then lifted mush into his face. I sat there, looking at my huge bowl of salted cereal.

Ma said, "What's wrong, Chris?"

I shook my head.

Pa said, "He dumped salt on his cereal. Now he won't eat it."

Ma said, "Why'd you do that, Chris?"

Little Bit quit eating to watch. Digger kept merrily breaking apart his pancake.

I said, "I thought it was sugar."

Ma nodded and told Pa, "He thought it was sugar, Luke."

Pa said, "I heard." He sat down with his own plate of pancakes. "Everyone eat, now."

I stared at the bowl.

Ma said, "Luke, if he didn't know—"

Pa said, "He's got to learn to eat what he takes."

Ma said, "But if he didn't know—"

Pa said, "He could've looked. He could've asked. The salt was right next to the pepper, and the sugar was way the hell off to the side."

Ma said, "It was a natural mistake."

Pa said, "Life doesn't forgive you for natural mistakes. Everyone eat now."

Little Bit looked at me with sympathy and began to eat. Digger seemed to have finished eating; he kept making mounds on his plate with pancake mush.

Ma looked at Pa, who was concentrating on his breakfast, then said, "Go on, Chris. It may taste bad, but it won't hurt you."

I shook my head.

Ma said, "If you don't eat it, you won't get to eat your pancakes. They're good." She took a bite to show me.

I shook my head again.

Pa said, "You took it, son. Now you eat it."

I shook my head a third time.

Pa said, "What do you say?"

I whispered, "No, sir."

Pa said, "On the farm, we ate when we had food. When we didn't have food, we didn't eat. Have you ever been short of food, Chris?"

I shook my head.

"Eat, then."

"I'm not hungry. Sir."

Ma said, "If he misses his breakfast, surely that's punishment enough."

Pa said, "I'm not trying to punish him. He's old enough to be accountable for his actions, that's all."

Little Bit said, "I'll eat some. I like Rice Krispies."

Pa said, "Chris took 'em, now Chris'll eat 'em. I don't want to talk about this anymore."

I said, "They taste bad, sir."

"Jesus! You think you're going to go through life eating things that taste wonderful? Eat that cereal."

I shook my head.

"You asking for a spanking?"

I shook my head again.

Ma said, "Luke? Surely he doesn't deserve a spanking for—"

Pa said, "I gave him an order. He heard it." He looked at me. "I'm going to count to three, Chris. If you haven't started eating by then, you'll get a spanking. And you'll still have to eat the cereal."

In my mind I said, "That's not fair." I didn't dare say it out loud.

"You understand?"

I nodded.

"One."

I lifted a single kernel of cereal in my spoon.

"Real bites," Pa said.

I scooped a spoonful of salted cereal and held it in front of my face.

"Two."

"Go on," Ma whispered.

I grimaced.

Pa said, "I'm not fooling, Chris."

"I can't!" I threw the spoon into my bowl, splashing the table with milk and cereal, and jumped from my chair to run. Pa caught my arm.

"Luke!" Ma cried. "Don't!"

Pa bent me over his thigh and began spanking me, hard, with the flat of his hand. "I told you, damn it. I gave you fair warning."

I didn't make a sound. Pa's spankings followed set rules. He spanked you until you cried. Little Bit understood that; she would cry after the first swat. Digger didn't

need to understand that; he would cry before the first
swat. I understood that, but I also understood that men
didn't cry. What was worse was that I knew that men didn't
get spanked. The fact of being spanked was worse than the
act.

Ma winced with each blow of Pa's hand, and so did I.
Little Bit and Digger stared in horror, fascination, and,
since the spanking hadn't been provoked by something I
had done to them, pity. I always tried to keep my face from
showing anything, but I doubt I was successful. I usually
began to cry around the eighth or ninth blow, maybe to
make Pa stop, maybe because I had to, and that satisfied
everyone. This time was no different.

Pa gripped my shoulders to straighten me up from his
knee. "It's done. You can stop crying and eat."

I wiped my nose with my hand and nodded.

"And clean up the table where you spilled."

I nodded again.

Ma went to the sink for a rag. Pa said, "Chris made the
mess." Ma handed me the rag. I wiped up the spatter of
milk around my bowl and wished I'd spilled it all. Pa said,
"If you don't stop crying, I'll give you a reason to keep crying."

I nodded and sat with my face ten inches from the
bowl.

"Well?" Pa said.

I began to eat like a robot. Pa was right. It didn't taste
horrible. It didn't taste like anything at all. When I finished
the cereal, I ate my pancakes. They didn't taste like anything, either.

By the time I finished, Digger and Little Bit had gone
out to play. Pa said, "Learn anything?" I nodded, got up,
and walked toward the door. Ma said my name and
reached for my arm, but I twisted away from her and
went outside.

A green cement sidewalk circled the restaurant. I sat
on it, around the corner from the back door where no one
could see me, and stared at the ground. I said, "Ee-yuch!"

several times, but I couldn't make myself throw up. Ants
had built a hill between the sidewalk and the gravel parking lot. I considered eating some to show everyone how
sick I was. The idea made me ill, so I didn't.

I was watching a line of ants carrying bits of a dead
caterpillar into their home when a shadow fell over me. I
didn't look up, 'cause I thought it was Pa, and then I knew
it wasn't. The person smelled wrong—smoky, but not like
Pa's cigars, and flowery, but not like Pa's shaving lotion,
and warm, but not like Pa's sweat. I looked up.

I must have talked to black people in New Orleans,
though I don't remember any. I'm sure I gaped at the
small, very dark man standing before me. He said
solemnly, "How do."

Ma and Pa had taught me to answer the greetings of
adults. I said, "Fine, sir. How're you?"

The man's eyebrows drew together, and then he smiled,
and then he laughed while shaking his head, "Oh, I's very
fine, yes, sir-ree. But why's a well-spoken gentleman like
yourself off a-cryin' by hisself?"

I wiped my nose, which must've betrayed me, then
wiped my hand on my shorts and shook my head. The
man smiled again. "Mind if I sets?"

I shook my head.

"Thankee, sir." He sat. We studied each other. He had
a narrow moustache and iron-gray hair, which was not
clipped close to his scalp like that of most black men I had
seen. His hair was long, glistening with lotion and parted
high on one side of his head. He wore faded Levi cover-
alls, a blue work shirt that had been laundered almost to
whiteness, and heavy brown work boots, all of which
seemed a little large for him. He looked like a singer Ma
liked, Sammy Davis, Jr., but he dressed like a comic strip
character I liked, L'il Abner, except for the Panama hat in
his hands with an eagle feather in its cloth band. He said,
"Go on and cry if you want. Don't mind me."

I said, "Wasn't crying."

He nodded. "My mistake. Not that it matters. Some-

times a man gets so frustrated he just gots to cry, and
that's all there is to it. Cleans you out, like. Shoot, I s'pose
a man ought to cry every now and then whether he's got
a reason to or no."

I squinted at him.

"They calls me Ethorne."

"Mark Christopher Nix." I wiped my hand on my
shorts, then held it out.

Ethorne smiled, and we shook. His skin felt strange.
His palms were hard and rough like tree bark. I decided
that all Negroes must have skin like his. "Pleased to meet
you, Master Nix. I seen you watchin' the ants."

I nodded.

"Ants is somethin' else. They busy all the time, bustlin'
all about. I 'xpect they think they seen it all and know it
all. Got them a purpose, which is to work. They know
who their friends is, which is ants from their hill. They
know who their enemies is, which is ants from anywheres
else. Think it'd be good to be a ant?"

I stared at him and shrugged.

He nodded. "Can't really say I know, neither."

Behind the restaurant, Pa called, "Chris?" Before I
could answer, Pa walked around the corner. He looked at
us, and I had time to wonder if I was talking to strangers,
which I wasn't supposed to do. Pa looked from me to
Ethorne and said in a firm voice with a hint of a question,
"Hello."

Ethorne stood, stiffly and gracefully at the same time,
and nodded. "How do, sir." He didn't offer his hand. "I's
Ethorne Hawkins. I do a li'l work for Mis' DeLyon, up at
the Fountain o' Youth."

Pa studied him for an instant, then held out his hand.
"Luke Nix."

Ethorne took the hand. "Mist' Nix. This your boy?"

Pa nodded.

"He's a fine boy."

Pa glanced at me. "Sometimes." I looked away, then
back as they continued to talk.

Ethorne studied the yard. His gaze lingered on the burned ruins of the old house. "I 'xpect you got a mess o' work needs doin'."

Pa nodded. "I expect so."

"I work hard when I got a mind to. You ask Mis' De-Lyon."

"And when you don't have a mind to?"

Ethorne laughed. "Then I don't work none at all, Mist' Nix. That's the best part o' bein' free."

Pa smiled. "We can probably keep you busy, if you've a mind to work just now."

"That's what I hoped to hear."

"Hawkins, you say?"

"Yes, sir. My people was slaves of Co'nel Josiah. When we was freed, all we kept was his name."

Pa said, "Malcolm X didn't."

Ethorne smiled a little differently than he had before. It was almost like Grandpa Abner taking off his Santa Claus suit at Christmas. He was still the same man, but the smiles were smaller, and they meant more. "Folks 'round here's knowed me as Hawkins nigh on forever. Shoot, I knowed me as Hawkins nigh on forever, too. An' I kind o' like knowin' the only folks still named after Co'nel Josiah is li'l black babies."

Pa said, "I can see that."

We all stood there, not really looking at each other. Several hundred feet away, cars passed steadily on the highway, mostly new cars of tourists and old cars of local people. Birds made bird sounds (I never paid attention to the kinds of birds that lived around us when I was a boy) and in the woods, something rustled the bushes, probably squirrels.

Pa said, "Dollar and a quarter an hour be fair?"

Ethorne grinned. "Dollar and a quarter an hour be very fair."

"C'mon." Pa turned. Ethorne looked at me, and we both followed Pa around the back of the restaurant. Ma came out with a broom in her hand, maybe to see what

Digger and Little Bit were doing. Pa said, "Susan, this is Ethorne Hawkins. He'll be helping us get the place fixed up."

Ma brushed a lock of hair back from her forehead with the back of her hand, smiled her usual wide, delighted greeting, rubbed her hand against her skirt, and thrust it out. "Mr. Hawkins. Glad to meet you."

Ethorne looked at the ground. I was the only one low enough to see his face; he looked shy or embarrassed or pleased. When he glanced up, he smiled easily and shook Ma's hand. "Mis' Nix, I'm most delighted to make your acquaintance. Please, call me Ethorne."

Ma laughed. "Then you call me Susan."

Ethorne shook his head and grinned. "Oh, no, ma'm. But you call me Ethorne. Mr. Hawkins was one bad, bad man. All I got is his name, and I wouldn't be so content with it if I had to hear it all the time."

Ma frowned and looked at Pa.

Pa said, "His people were slaves here."

Ma took a quick intake of breath.

Ethorne smiled. "Long, long time ago, ma'm. Not forgotten, but gone." He pointed past the woods, toward the Fountain of Youth Motor Inn and Hawkins Springs. "Wasn't 'xactly here, neither. The old house was up thataways, and so was the fields an' the nigger shacks. Old house done burned. Fields're overgrowed now. Don't hurt me none to see it like this."

Ma said, "The Colonel was a bad man?"

"I say that? Oh, I misspoke myself, ma'm. Gettin' old. He was a hard man. He did good as he saw it, to whoever he figured needed it. That's 'bout all I can say."

Pa said, "People have long memories around here."

Ethorne laughed. "You been talkin' to Mist' Drake. Him and me, we live more in the past than the present, I 'xpect. Most folks 'round here are just folks, same as anywheres."

Pa said, "You must've heard the joke."

"Oh?"

"My pa used to tell it. A house is for sale. A fellow

comes to buy it, asks the old-timer living next door how the local people are. The old-timer asks how they were in this fellow's last home. Fellow says they were mean ess oh bees. The old-timer nods and says, a-yup, the locals are pretty much like that. The fellow decides not to buy the house."

Pa glanced at me, and I looked away, as if I wasn't listening. Pa said, " 'Nother fellow comes to buy it, asks the old-timer how the locals are. The old-timer asks how they were in this second fellow's last home. Fellow says they were the friendliest bunch of people you were ever like to meet. The old-timer nods and says, a-yup, the locals are pretty much like that."

I threw a rock into a palmetto clump. It rustled the leaves as it fell.

Ethorne said, "No one's payin' a black man more'n a dollar an hour in Latchahee County."

Pa said, "Can't be true. I am." He added, "I don't expect you to do less work than a white man, so I figure I better not pay you less money."

"Thank you, sir." Ethorne put his straw hat onto his head, and the eagle feather bobbed. "Where you want me to start?"

"Got a lot of ground to clear. There was a scythe in the pump house when I was here before."

Ethorne nodded. "I's a fine hand with a scythe, Mist' Nix."

Pa said, "Luke."

Ethorne said, "Mist' Luke."

Pa shrugged. "All right. We'll call you what you want, and you call us what suits you. I warn you, I might not answer to son of a bitch."

Ma said, "Luke!" and looked at me.

Pa said, "Well, I wouldn't. Chris doesn't know that, it's time he learned." He grinned at me, and I smiled for the first time at him. Pa jerked his head. "C'mon." He headed toward the pump house, a wooden, flat-roofed shack with peeling lime-green paint.

Digger and Little Bit were playing in the gravel parking area, which was dotted with high, lone weeds trying to reclaim the land for the woods. Pa shouted at Little Bit, "Don't play near the bushes. Might be anything in there!"

We walked up to the pump house, Pa leading, followed by Ethorne, then me. I kicked the dirt as I walked. I wanted to go away and play, but I also wanted to see the inside of the pump house, and Pa had not dismissed me.

He unlocked the padlock and opened the door, a plywood rectangle reinforced with two-by-fours and hanging from two rusty hinges. Some light filtered through two dusty windows. My first impression was of dirt, tools, and machinery. As the door opened wide, there was a sound like hissing or pebbles tumbling against themselves.

Pa stepped back fast. "Jesus Christ!"

Something like a fire hose moved in the gloom beyond the water pump and tank. Its eyes were bright beads. Two curved needles shone within its smile.

Ethorne said, "Move easy. Rattler don't want no more trouble'n we do."

Pa breathed quickly. I stared, unable to move until Pa said, "Back off, Chris. Slow."

I stepped backward, watching the snake undulate on the pump house's wooden floor.

Pa said, "Guess we'll have to buy a gun."

Ethorne said, "You mean to kill it?"

"If we scared that thing off, would it come back?"

"Hard to say. If it thinks that's home, most like it would." Ethorne sounded sad.

Pa said, "Then we kill it."

Ethorne said, "They's a scythe in there, you say?"

Pa snorted a harsh laugh. "I didn't look too close."

Ethorne nodded and stepped toward the door.

Pa said, "I hope you know what you're doing."

Ethorne said, "Me, too, Mist' Luke." He pushed against the half-open door. It swung against the far wall. The sound startled us all, except the snake. Sunlight didn't seem to bother it. Its skin was like a chain-mail shirt made of precious metals. Its eyes were jewels. Its flickering tongue was a taunt.

Ethorne moved slowly, like a man in one of the silent films that Grandpa Abner showed in his basement with the projector turned to half speed. He approached the door as though his shadow, preceding him, had more substance than his body. He seemed to be trying to keep his shadow from falling on the snake, as if that much disturbance would make the rattler attack.

At the door, Ethorne peeked in, then reached his arm inside to feel along the wall.

Pa whispered, "You know how high a snake can strike?"

Ethorne shook his head. "Don't aim to find out." He withdrew his hand, showing us a shovel. "Scythe's too far back." He glanced at us. "Back off some, now, hear?"

Pa brushed his hand in the air at his side, trusting me to obey. I did.

Ethorne raised the shovel overhead like a spear, then thrust it down into the pump house. Something thrashed violently as the shovel struck the floor. Then Ethorne swept the shovel across the wooden planks, flinging something like a man's fist out onto the grass. The thrashing continued within the pump house.

Ethorne whirled toward us, calling, "Stay 'way from it!"

The snake's severed head snapped its jaws open and closed, over and over again, bouncing it around in the long grass. Ethorne said, "Snake needs time to study out it's dead."

Little Bit and Digger had seen that something interesting was happening. Pa spotted them as they approached us. He yelled, "You kids, stay back!" Little Bit grabbed Digger's hand. They stood, staring as the snake's head continued to seek escape or a victim.

Ethorne turned with the shovel and plunged it back into the pump house. Pa and I turned to watch him sweep out the snake's writhing body.

Little Bit screamed. I looked at her. Little Bit was still twenty feet away from the snake's head, but Digger, laughing, ran toward it on pudgy, unsteady legs.

Pa shouted, "Digger! No!" Digger, usually the most obedient of us all, did not seem to hear. He stretched a small hand out for the shiny thing that danced in our yard.

Pa and Ethorne both ran forward. Pa held his arms out to grab Digger. Ethorne lifted the shovel as if he hoped to bat the snake head away. Digger stopped still in mid-squat, his hand six inches from the snake's head, and looked at the two men running toward him. His smile faded. He squinted as if he was trying to decide whether he had done something for which he should cry.

The snake's jaws thrashed once more. The head sprang into the air, its jaws open to their widest. They closed around Digger's hand, enclosing it within its bite. Its fangs buried themselves into Digger's wrist. Its eyes glistened.

Digger stared at his arm, terminating in the head of a snake that smiled as it watched the boy puzzle out what had happened. Then Digger screamed, waved his arms, and tried to run back toward the restaurant where Ma was working.

Pa caught up to him as he tripped and fell. Pa seized the snake's jaws in both hands and ripped the head apart. Blood dripped from Digger's wrist and Pa's fingers. Digger continued to scream as if he would squeeze every bit of breath from his lungs before he could inhale and begin again. Pa snatched him up, patted his back, saying, "Easy, son. Easy," and began carrying Digger toward our station wagon.

Ma ran from the restaurant with a broom in her hands. She cried, "Luke! What's—" Then she saw Digger and dropped the broom. "George! Oh, my God, Georgie!"

Digger screamed louder when he saw Ma and reached for her with blood-smeared hands.

Pa said, "Susan, don't get excited. We've got to stay calm."

Ethorne said, "Let me help, ma'm. I know what to do."

Digger struggled in Pa's arms, reaching for Ma. She grabbed him from Pa, saying, "Oh, Georgie, Georgie," and then, to Pa, "What happened?"

Pa said, "Snake bite."

Ma gasped.

Ethorne pulled out a red bandanna, twirled it between his fingers into a rope, and telling Digger, "This be all right, now," tied the bandanna around Digger's arm, above the bite, then tested it with his finger to see that it was snug enough to slow the flow of blood, yet not so tight as to stop it. A little blood continued to ooze from the two holes.

Digger tried to wrap his arms around Ma's neck. Ethorne caught Digger's wrists and brought them down gently, telling Ma, "Keep his bitten arm low, closer to the earth than his heart. Poison slows some when it has to work uphill."

Ma closed her arm around Digger's shoulders to trap his arms at his side. "We've got to call—Who has the nearest phone? Oh, my God."

Pa asked Ethorne, "Is Dickison the nearest hospital?"

"Ain't no time, Mist' Luke." Ethorne's hand came out of his jeans pocket with a pearl-handled folding razor and a box of Red Devil matches. "Got to get some o' the poison out of 'im now."

Ma said, "But—"

"I knows what I'm doin', ma'm. I'd do this for my own chil'en."

Digger continued to scream. Ma pressed her cheek against his, while Pa stood beside the station wagon, ready to open the back door. Pa nodded. "All right."

Ma looked at him, then nodded, too. She continued to say, "Easy, Georgie, easy." She didn't seem to see that Digger knew something bad was happening because she used his real name. When Little Bit touched his leg and said, "It's okay, Digger," he quit screaming and only cried.

Ethorne lit a match in one hand, snapping the head with his thumbnail, and flicked open the straight razor in his other hand. Passing the flame under the blade, he said, "Now, don't be scared, Mist' Digger. I got to cut you, but I won't go so deep as ol' Mist' Snake."

Digger continued to cry, wrapping his arms around Ma's side. Her dress and her face were flecked with his blood. Ethorne glanced at Pa. "We got to."

Pa had been pressing his own cut fingers against a handkerchief. He pocketed it, took Digger's bit hand, and held the arm straight out. "Easy, son," he said, surprisingly helpless. "Easy."

Ethorne rested his hand on Pa's, pressing downward. Pa lowered Digger's arm.

Ethorne said, "Goin' be fine, Mist' Digger." He cut four shallow slits, each less than half an inch long, down the length of Digger's arm. As he made the incisions, he said for the rest of us, or maybe for himself, "Two cuts at the bite marks. Two a little lower, where Mist' Snake spurted his poison. No need to cut deep. Just the surface, so the blood'll let the poison out. We be mos' careful o' the muscles and the nerves, um-hmm."

Digger screamed louder as dark blood sprang from the cuts. Ma pressed her head hard against the side of his, saying, " 'S all right, baby. 'S all right." Pa continued to hold Digger's wrist in one hand. He rested his other lightly on Digger's upper arm.

Ethorne picked something out of one of the wounds and tossed it aside. He leaned over, fastening his lips around Digger's cuts, then spat blood out with a grimace. He did this several times, then paused to say, "We need to get over to the Fountain o' Youth now. Mis' DeLyon's good with these troubles, an' she has a telephone to call the doctor."

Pa said, "All right. Susan—"

"I'm going." Ma used the hard voice we rarely heard.

Pa nodded. "We're all going. You kids, hop in front, fast."

Ethorne, Mom, and Digger slid into the back. I had been squatting nearby, running my fingers through the gravel; I scrambled into the front seat with Little Bit, where I dropped the fang that Ethorne had thrown aside into my shirt pocket. As doors slammed, Pa drove away more quickly than I had ever known. Gravel slid beneath our wheels as he backed up, and when he turned onto the highway, the rear end of the station wagon slewed sideways to line up with the front wheels, and we hurtled up Route 19.

Ethorne kept applying suction to Digger's arm and spitting the result out the car window, spattering the rear glass. Digger had stopped crying, which was scarier than his crying and screaming had been. He lay against Ma like he was going to nap. Tears ran from Ma's eyes, but her voice was calm as she said, "It's all right, Digger. Everything's fine, now."

At the Fountain of Youth Motor Inn, Pa screeched the brakes as we halted under the carport by the office. Ethorne was the first one out. He yelled, "Mis' DeLyon! A child needs you!"

A dark woman stepped from one of the guest rooms, pulling the door firmly shut behind her. In a place where most people's race was obvious, hers was impossible to guess. Her skin was a brown that might have been its natural hue or might have come from years in the sun. Her hair, drawn back in a tail, was thick and black. Her eyes were as dark as her hair; the skin around them was lined from weather and laughter. She was small without being slender; she looked as if she could carry her own weight on her shoulders and walk all day without rest. She wore no makeup or jewelry. Her clothes consisted of a short-sleeved white shirt, blue jeans, and white tennis shoes.

That may have been the first time I knew my mother was pretty. I'd always known that Ma was beautiful, but this was the first time that I saw another woman and compared Ma to her. Ma was a little taller and bustier than Mis' DeLyon. Ma's eyes were green, and her hair was short and curly and reddish-brown. She wore red lipstick and a necklace of white beads with her light blue dress and

white sandals. Her face, as I looked, was etched with an-
guish for Digger. Mis' DeLyon's face was calm, concerned
but confident, and I realized that Ma's face always showed
her feelings, joy or fear, but rarely confidence.

Mis' DeLyon saw Digger's wounded wrist, then looked
from it to Pa's fingers. Ethorne explained, "Snake bite,
Mis' DeLyon. Mist' Luke tore its mouth off o' Mast' Digger
here."

Mis' DeLyon looked at Pa. "There's a phone in the office with a list of numbers beside it. Call Dr. Lamont and
tell him you'll be bringing your boy."

Pa nodded as he headed into the office. Ma started to
follow, but Mis' DeLyon touched her shoulder. Ma turned
back, frowning. Mis' DeLyon took Digger's wrist in her
hand. He opened his eyes when she did that, then closed
them again.

Ethorne said, "I been suckin' the poison out o' him. But
he's mighty small."

Mis' DeLyon said, "Come." She strode across the blacktop to the swimming pool. We followed as obediently as
we would follow the Pied Piper of Hamlin.

The pool was a typical small Southern motel's outdoor
pool, a rectangle with a diving board at the deep end and
a shallow end for nonswimmers. But next to the shallow
end was the motel's trademark, the green cement fountain
shaped like a sports trophy. Water bubbled from its top,
spilling into a metal-lined basin, then into the pool. Next
to the fountain was a plastic dispenser for paper Dixie
cups.

Mis' DeLyon yanked free a cup and dipped it into the
basin. "This," she told Ma, "is piped from the springs behind the motel. There's no water purer, I assure you." She
poured it on Digger's wrist and washed the slits with her
fingers, then sprinkled some drops onto his forehead.
When he opened his eyes, she smiled. "Hello, Master Digger. Drink this."

Digger's head rolled from side to side.

Mis' DeLyon said, "For your mother's sake." She put the cup to his lips.

"Uh," Digger said, perhaps in protest. As his lips parted, Mis' DeLyon poured water into his mouth. He sputtered, and water dripped over his chin, onto his shirt and onto Ma's dress.

"Drink," Mis' DeLyon repeated, tipping more water into his mouth.

His eyes opened wider and he began to drink deeply. Ma laughed, and Mis' DeLyon smiled again. Digger bobbed his head once and announced, "Good." As Mis' DeLyon filled a second cup for him, Ma laughed louder, and hugged him harder.

Mis' DeLyon looked at Ethorne. "I suppose you haven't rinsed out your mouth."

"Ain't been time, Mis' DeLyon."

Shaking her head without losing her smile, she set her hand on his upper arm. "Oh, Ethorne." She took a clean handkerchief from her jeans pocket and tied it over Digger's cuts while Ethorne snagged a paper cup, filled it, rinsed his mouth, spat, then filled his mouth and drank.

Pa came out of the motel office. "They're expecting us."

Mis' DeLyon said, "Let me see your hands."

Pa stood at the driver's door. "They're expecting us."

Mis' DeLyon said, "If this makes a difference, it will be for the good. Come."

Pa's eyes narrowed, then he strode toward Ma and Mis' DeLyon. I may have seen him, too, for the first time that day as someone other than my father. I had always seen a wild force in Pa: he never needed to rest when something needed doing. That force drove him toward us now. But there was something else I had never seen, a helplessness before the threat to Digger that scared me. I knew how easily Pa's helplessness could turn to anger.

I also saw that Pa, unlike Ma or us kids, looked like Mis' DeLyon. His hair and his eyes were black. His skin tanned quickly and darkly and almost never burned beneath the sun. Though his face showed emotions as easily as Ma's, a fierce confidence always lurked beneath his expressions.

He stopped in front of Mis' DeLyon. "Well?"

She reached for his hands and turned the palms upward. "From its teeth?"

He nodded. "I feel fine."

Ethorne said, "One o' the fangs tore off in Digger."

Pa said, "The other didn't get me."

Mis' DeLyon poured water from the fountain onto Pa's hands. "You can't rely on strength alone."

He gave the humorless laugh. "You rely on what you've got."

She patted the cuts clean. "Exactly." Before he could respond, she said, "You were luckier than your son. Have Dr. Lamont look at these, just to be sure."

"Hell, I don't need—"

"And if you feel weak on the way, have someone else drive. Understand?"

He looked at her and, to my amazement, nodded.

Mis' DeLyon said, "Ethorne, will you guide them?"

"Sure thing, ma'm."

Ma said, "Mis' DeLyon—"

Mis' DeLyon shook her head. "Neighbors must help each other."

Ma smiled. "Thank you."

"Go. Dr. Lamont will worry." Mis' DeLyon refilled Digger's cup and handed it to Ma. "Keep him warm, and give him all the water he wants. He'll be fine."

Pa said, "C'mon." We all got into the station wagon in the same places where we had sat before. Pa nodded to Mis' DeLyon, and we drove away. Mis' DeLyon stood at the edge of the highway and watched us go.

Little Bit waved back at her and whispered, "She's a nice lady."

As we turned toward Dickison, Pa told Ethorne, "Had trouble finding this road last night in the dark."

Ethorne smiled. "Oh, it be easy, now you belong here."

* * *

At Dr. Lamont's house, Ma and Digger went into the office with him and his nurse. Pa, Little Bit, and I went back outside, where Ethorne waited by the car. He smiled at us, then walked around the doctor's yard with Little Bit, telling her the names of the plants. Pa and I sat in the sun on the hood of the station wagon. The metal was warm and hard under my butt, but I liked sitting there with my cowboy boots resting on the bumper. I watched Little Bit and Ethorne, and wondered about whether Digger would get better, or if he would die, and if he died, would he get a Viking burial on a burning boat pushed out to sea. Pa was quiet beside me, and he didn't seem angry, so I didn't think about him at all.

Without warning, Pa said, quietly enough that only I could hear, "When I was a boy and I'd done something wrong, my pa beat me with a razor strap. You know what that is?"

I shook my head.

"It's a strap of leather that you use to sharpen a razor. You strop the razor back and forth on it." Pa closed his hand as though he were holding a straight razor and turned his wrist from side to side.

I nodded.

"Worst part was he'd send me to bring the strap from where it hung on a nail in the barn. I hated fetching it more than I hated the beating. I never knew whether it was better to walk slow, to put it off as long as possible, or to run, to get the whole thing over fast."

I nodded again, but Pa didn't see that. He had been looking at his scuffed engineer boots. Now he looked up, not at me but at the doctor's big white wooden house. "And when my pa was a boy, his pa would take a whip to him when he acted up. You imagine what that's like?"

I grimaced. "Bad?"

Pa gave a harsh bark of a laugh. "Oh, yeah. Bad's a start on what that's like." He shook his head, then looked at me.

"Spanking only hurts a little while, doesn't it?"

I said, "Yes, Pa."

He nodded. "So maybe things're getting better for the Nixes. That's what I tell myself. That's all you can hope for, isn't it?"

The question wasn't directed to me. He spoke it to his open hands. I was glad, since I didn't have an answer.

Dr. Lamont, a thin, brown-haired man a little older than Pa, came onto his porch. "Your boy'll be fine. We're done for now, if you want to come in."

Pa looked at Ethorne. "You want to come in?"

Ethorne laughed easily. "Oh, I like it outdoors on a pretty day like this."

Pa nodded. "I like it outdoors, too."

Dr. Lamont looked at Pa, then shrugged. "Your boy's resting easy. No reason he can't go home with you. Doesn't look like any poison got into him, but you'll want to watch him careful. Skin tends to get ugly 'round a rattler bite. It'll usually slough off, leaving an ulcer there, danger of gangrene, all kinds of potential problems. Could be expensive, too, if it called for reconstructive surgery. But it looks like your boy was sure lucky. Considering, of course."

Dr. Lamont tapped out a Camel cigarette, held the pack out to Pa, then lit one for himself when Pa shook his head. "Some docs'd cut out the bit area, just to be safe. But his color's good, the skin around the bite seems healthy, his breathing's easy. I'm of a mind to leave it be, for now, leastways. Your rattler must've sprayed near all its poison 'fore it latched on to the boy's wrist. Then since you treated him fast, you got out most of what poison was left on the fangs."

Dr. Lamont dragged deep on his cigarette. "Or it might just be a miracle. I'll take payment, but I can't take credit."

Pa smiled and nodded. "Thanks, Doctor."

Dr. Lamont said, "Your wife said you'd been cut by its teeth."

Pa shrugged.

Dr. Lamont said, "I don't charge to look, not when you're already here."

Pa said, "Well." He held out his palms. "Mis' DeLyon cleaned 'em up." The cuts had closed, leaving a thin scab line.

Dr. Lamont looked closely. "Your snake must've been shooting blanks. Keep your hands clean and bandaged till that's healed. If there's any inflammation, or if you just get to feeling poorly, tell me immediately, hear?"

Pa nodded. Ma and Digger showed up on the porch then. Ma's dress was damp from where she'd tried to sponge away Digger's blood, but the cloth was drying quickly. Ma carried Digger, and he seemed to be asleep, but when the sunlight fell on his face, he looked at us and, smiling, waved his bandaged wrist.

"Hey, Digger," Little Bit said.

Pa grinned. "You're a tough kid, Digger."

Ma said, "He was very brave."

Digger smiled, then slumped back against Ma's shoulder. I wished the snake had bitten me instead of him.

Dr. Lamont said, "Give him plenty of liquids and plenty of rest. Kids bounce back in no time."

Ma said, "We haven't opened a local checking account yet—"

Dr. Lamont said, "I understand. We'll send the bill." He and Pa shook hands, and we all got into the car.

Driving toward downtown, Ethorne said, "Dr. Lamont, he takes good care o' the white folks. Coloreds has their own doctor up in Waycross."

Ma looked at Pa. He grunted to say he'd heard Ethorne, and Ma relaxed. Pa said, "Since we're in town, we might as well get some business done." He glanced at Ma. "You haven't changed your mind about staying?"

Ma stroked Digger's head.

Pa said, "We'll get the land cleared back, fast. Activity'll keep the wildlife away. You'll see."

Ma shrugged.

Pa said, "Can't keep kids perfectly safe anywhere,

Susan. All you can do is watch 'em, and do what you can when things go wrong. Seems to me today proved there's good people here."

Ma said, "I know that."

Pa said, "Then I'll tell Drake what we decided."

Ma said, "Yes." It was resignation, not agreement. We all knew that. No one said anything.

Dickison in daylight looked like any of the small Southern towns we'd driven through on our way to Dogland. I spotted a Five and Dime, which I pointed out to Ma, in case she needed to buy someone a new cap gun or a bag of plastic army men. She smiled and said something about needing to buy some thread, which made Pa say, "If there's time."

We stopped at the Dickison State Bank. A happy man gave us kids lollipops while Ma and Pa got account books, including savings accounts for each of us with the five-dollar bills that Grandpa Abner had sent. Which would've bought me a Fort Apache toy set of blue U.S. Cavalry and Indians in red and yellow, but Ma said the account was so we could learn how to save. Little Bit said, "I'm going to have *lots* of money," and everyone laughed, including the banker.

When we drove to Artie Drake's office, he was at his desk, reading a thick, leather-bound book. He heard the door, looked up, then closed the book on an envelope to mark his place. "Hi, y'all. Come on in. How was the night?"

Pa said, "Night was fine. Morning was a little rough."

Mr. Drake's eyes widened as he saw the bandage on Digger, asleep in Ma's arms.

Ma said, "A snake bit him."

Mr. Drake said quietly, "I'm sorry."

Pa said, "I don't know what got into Digger. He ran up to it before we could stop him."

"Kids," said Mr. Drake.

Pa nodded.

"He'll be fine?"

Ma said, "Dr. Lamont thinks so."

"Good."

Pa said, "We just wanted to tell you to deposit our check. We're staying."

Mr. Drake said, "Sure you're not rushing the decision?"

Pa laughed. "You're one hell of a salesman, you know that?"

Mr. Drake shrugged. "There's enough business in the world dealing with folks who're content. No need to make money off folks who aren't."

Ma smiled at him. "I agree one hundred percent."

Pa said, "You give people a fair deal. If they're not happy with it, that's their problem."

Mr. Drake said, "So, no refunds at Dogland if you don't like what you see?"

"You give folks what you said you would, and no one'll want refunds."

Mr. Drake smiled. "You have a lot of faith in human nature, Luke."

"Not a bit. Just being practical. Never give anyone grounds to use against you, and you'll get by."

Mr. Drake looked at Ma, then back at Pa. "Ah. I expect you could make that argument."

Pa said, "Have to make it some other time. Work's waiting. If you're out our way, drop in. I can argue all night."

Ma laughed. "That's no exaggeration. Do drop by. And say hi to Gwenny for us. Right, Chris?"

I looked at my boots. "Okay."

Pa said, "Mind if I use your bathroom?"

Mr. Drake said, "Not at all." He pointed toward the rear of the office. "Through that door."

"Thanks." Pa left.

Mr. Drake looked at Ma and said gently, "I'll hold off another day on depositing that check, if you'd like. What happened to your boy—" He shook his head. "That'd drive a lot of people away."

Ma said, "The best way to get Luke to stay somewhere is to try to drive him away."

The toilet flushed. Pa came out, and we went outside.
Mr. Drake followed us to the car. Seeing Ethorne in the
backseat, Mr. Drake said, "Hey, Ethorne. How's things?"

Ethorne said, "Like silk, Mist' Artie. Had a li'l bump
over a seam, but we back on the silk now."

"And Mis' DeLyon?"

"Oh, same as always."

We waved to Mr. Drake as we drove away. Little Bit
whispered, "He likes her."

"Mr. Drake?"

Little Bit nodded.

"Likes Mis' DeLyon?"

Little Bit shook her head. "Ma."

I nodded. Everyone liked Ma.

At the Winn-Dixie Grocery Store, Ethorne said, "I'll
watch over Digger while you shop."

Again Pa looked at him, but didn't say anything. Ma
said, "That's good of you. We won't be long."

We bought groceries: hamburger, milk, eggs, white
bread, Sugar Frosted Flakes, and cans of Campbell's soup,
corned beef hash, cream corn, and string beans. I lingered
by a wire spinner jammed full of comic books. I knew the
names of many of the characters, though I couldn't read
them: Batman, Superman, Dennis the Menace, Jerry
Lewis. Ma tugged me onward, so I followed.

In the car, driving home, Little Bit and I ate Baby Ruth
bars and drank from big bottles of grape Ne-hi, my favorite. Digger slept in the back on a blanket, next to the
groceries, and Ethorne sat beside us. Ma, in the front,
said, "Mr. Drake seems like a nice man."

Ethorne nodded. "Oh, Mist' Artie's a fine fellow."

"We met his daughter, but not his wife."

"Oh, he don' got no wife. Not since his troubles."

"Troubles?"

"Well, it's not a secret, 'xactly. It was a long time ago."

"Oh?"

Pa said, "Susan, don't make the man tell anything he
doesn't want to."

Ma said, "I couldn't make anyone tell anything they didn't want to! How could I possibly—"

Pa laughed. "You can make anyone agree to anything, when you put your mind to it."

"But I don't try—"

Pa reached an arm along the top of the bench seat and gave her a hug. "Which is the only thing that saves us all."

"Well." Ma smiled enough to say she had forgiven him, though she did not think he deserved it.

Ethorne said, "Ain't no big deal, I s'pect. You might as well hear 'bout it from someone who likes Mist' Artie. He had him a hard time in the war."

"Korea?" Pa said.

"World War Two," Ethorne said. "He come back to his wife and his job, but he acted kind of strange. He went off to the V.A. hospital for a year or so. When he come back, his wife left him."

Ma said, "Poor man." Then she said, "What about Gwenny?"

Ethorne shook his head. "Her ma drowned a year or two later. Girl was sent back to her pa. He's been a good father to her. Has one o' my girls for a housekeeper. Sarah cares for Gwenny like she was another of her own babies."

Ma, delighted, said, "You don't have grandchildren, Ethorne!" She added with less certainty, "Do you?"

Ethorne laughed. "Oh, yes'm, I do. A passel."

Pa said, "Start young enough—" He grinned at Ethorne. "I don't have any that I know about."

Ma said, "Luke, honestly." Ethorne chuckled, maybe at both of them.

Pa lifted his chin, pointing up the road. "Who wants hamburgers?"

Little Bit and I both shouted, "I do, I do!"

Ma said, "You don't have to scream."

Pa said, "All right," and turned onto the gravel parking lot in front of Gideon's 19-cent Hamburgers.

As we rattled to a stop, Little Bit said, "Ma likes Mr. Drake, too."

I squinted at her. "Ma likes everyone." Then I yanked on the door handle, and we ran toward the source of God's most perfect food.

Gideon's was a drive-in carryout hamburger stand with a porch on one side covering several wooden picnic tables. A door in the center of the building opened on a small room divided by a long counter. On one side of the counter was space enough for six or eight people to stand while placing their orders. On the other side was a griddle, a refrigerator, a wooden cutting table, and the few other basics that a fry chef requires.

Little Bit and I came to a stop as soon as the screen door closed behind us. On the back wall, between two draped American flags, were pictures of Jesus. There were Jesuses on place mats, postcards, and cardboard fans. There were little paintings of Jesus in wooden and plastic frames. There were newspaper cutouts of black-and-white pictures of paintings of Jesus, and photos of people dressed to look like Jesus, and photos of things that looked like Jesus if you squinted, like a cow with markings on its side that resembled a bearded man's face.

Behind the counter and in front of the collage was a short, skinny, tanned man with white hair in a crew cut. Despite the heat, he wore a long-sleeved white shirt buttoned to his neck. He saw us and said, "God bless you, children! Welcome, welcome!"

Little Bit smiled, saying, "Hi. We're going to have hamburgers."

"Well, the Lord surely directed you to the right place," said the small man.

Little Bit walked up to the counter, but I stayed back, studying the Jesuses. Some cried, and some laughed, but most looked as if they had not had enough sleep. A blackboard hung over part of the collage. It was covered with writing that did not look to me like a menu, because there were no rows of items with corresponding rows of prices.

The screen door opened again. I had to jump forward to make room for Pa and Ma. Pa looked around the room,

and Ma glanced from the collage to Pa. The small man
said, "Welcome. Your girl says you've come for hamburgers, and I'm mighty glad to hear it. That's all we serve that
you can sink your teeth into, though the good word's available if you'd like some meat for your soul, too."

Pa nodded at the collage of Jesuses. "Friend of yours?"

"Oh, yes, sir," said the small man. "A friend of yours,
too, though you may not know it. And a friend of the
Hamite in your car, as well."

"Hamite?" said Pa.

The small man nodded. "The unfortunate race with
God's mark on their skin. But if they serve dutifully in this
world, they'll be rewarded in the next. The Negro is to be
pitied, not despised."

Ma looked at Pa again.

"So," said the small man, "what can I fix you?"

Pa began, "I don't know—"

Little Bit cut him off with, "A hamburger, please, an' a
starberry milk shake!"

"We're your new neighbors," Ma said. "We bought the
Hawkins land."

"You did? I'm delighted!" The small man wiped his
hand on a dishcloth and offered his palm to Pa. "I'm
Gideon Shale, sir. If there's anything, anything at all, I
might help you with, you let me know. I've done a few
things in my time."

Pa glanced at Ma as he took the man's hand. "Luke Nix.
This is Susan."

Ma held out her hand, and Mr. Shale said, "A pleasure,"
as he took it.

Pa said, "That's Chris and Little Bit."

"Well, you look like fine helpers for your parents!" Mr.
Shale shook hands with us, too. His fingers felt like talons,
strong and fleshless, but his hand shook slightly in my
grip.

I shrugged at his statement. Little Bit said, "I'm going
to have any dog I want."

"You are?" said Mr. Shale.

Little Bit nodded.

"Have you decided what kind you want?"

Little Bit nodded. "Every kind!"

Mr. Shale laughed. Pa said, "We're building a tourist attraction. When we're done, we'll have over a hundred and twenty breeds of dog on display. American Kennel Association recognizes a hundred and thirteen currently, but in the world, there's more'n four hundred breeds. We'll have plenty of room to expand."

Mr. Shale nodded. "Mastiff, greyhound, mongrel grim, hound or spaniel, brach or lym; or bobtail tike, or trundle-tail—" He stopped abruptly and shrugged.

Pa said, "I don't recognize that."

"Shakespeare. The other good book. Though neither book has much good to say about dogs, I fear." Mr. Shale shrugged. "You came for food for the body, I believe."

Pa nodded. "Six hamburgers."

"Mine plain," I said.

"I can't make you a milk shake," Mr. Shale told Little Bit. "Freezer broke down, and the Lord hasn't provided a new one, yet. I suspect He's waiting for me to pull the motor. We have milk, soda pop, and coffee."

"Four milks." Pa stepped outside and called, "Ethorne! Milk or pop?"

"Anything be fine, Mist' Luke," Ethorne called back.

"What'd be finest?"

Ethorne laughed. "Co'Cola be finest, sir."

Pa stepped back inside. "And one Coke."

"Coming right up." Mr. Shale opened the refrigerator and took out a metal tray full of ground red meat.

Pa looked at the blackboard and read aloud, "It is easier for a camel to go through the eye of a needle, than for a rich man to enter into the kingdom of God. Matthew Nineteen: twenty-four." Ma glanced at Pa again as he said, "Interesting thing for a businessman to have on his wall."

"Oh, I change the teaching every week," said Mr. Shale, shaping hamburger patties in his hands. "That one's to remind me that we make money to live, not the other way around."

"Sounds un-American." Pa nodded toward the two American flags flanking the Jesuses.

Mr. Shale laughed, pointed at cutout letters among the pictures of Jesus, and read, "One nation, under GOD." The word "GOD" was surrounded with gold foil stars. Mr. Shale dropped six patties onto the grill, each adding its sizzle to the noise as it landed. "Nothing wrong with making money, so long as you spend some on Jesus."

"Hadn't heard he was hurting for cash," Pa said.

Ma said, "Luke."

Mr. Shale said, "Oh, I don't mind some funning, Mrs. Nix. There are many ways to spend money on the Lord, if you seek them out. There's always someone doing His work who could use a little help."

"I've read the Bible," Pa said. "I don't remember Jesus asking for handouts."

Mr. Shale frowned at Pa, then flipped each of the burgers, producing new explosions of sound and increasing the smell of cooking meat. As he placed hamburger buns on the grill to toast, he said, "We're all frail. We do what we can for those we can."

Ma looked at Pa and said, "That's what we all do."

Pa told Mr. Shale, "You may be a little hard on yourself. I heard there was a gate in Jerusalem called the Eye of the Needle. And it wasn't impossible to get a camel through the gate. It was just hard."

Mr. Shale shook his head and placed six paper napkins on the counter. "I've heard that, too. I doubt the Lord was unaware of the implications of what He said when He said it." Mr. Shale removed the buns, placed them on the napkins, squirted five with ketchup, then assembled the burgers and folded the napkins around them. "Want these to go?"

Pa said, "We'll eat them here."

"I could eat a horse," I said.

"Oh, that's too bad," said Mr. Shale. "These are all cow." He stacked the burgers onto a cardboard tray and set that on the counter. As he opened the refrigerator to remove four cartons of milk and a Coca-Cola bottle, he said, "If talking about Jesus disturbs you, let me know. I'll be happy to quit my prattling. Jesus comes when you're ready for Him. I can ask you to receive Him, but only you can open your heart."

Pa said, "Tell you what. You don't try to convince me you're right, and I won't try to convince you you're wrong. Is that a deal?"

Mr. Shale laughed. "No, Lucifer, that's never a deal. But my wife, bless her soul, always said I never knew when to let folks be. You have a good meal, hear?"

"Will do." Pa placed a five-dollar bill on the counter.

Mr. Shale started to hand Pa his money back. "We're neighbors."

Pa shook his head. "That's right. This way, on slow days, we'll each know we got at least one customer nearby."

Mr. Shale smiled and counted out Pa's change. "God bless you."

"Bye," Pa said.

"God bless you," Ma repeated.

"God bless *you*," Little Bit stated firmly.

"G' b—" I began, and finished, "bye."

As we walked out into the sun, Pa said, "Why'd you introduce us right off? Old coot'll be over to convert us within twenty-four hours."

"He's our neighbor, Luke."

"You want to be nice to him, you be nice to him. I'll have work to do."

Ethorne brought Digger out of the car. Ma carried Digger to a picnic table; he ate half of his hamburger before he fell asleep again. Pa ate the other half. Afterward, he said, "Well, I suppose I can always listen to ol' Gideon for the sake of a good hamburger."

After we returned to our land, Pa and Ethorne looked

in the grass for the dead snake. The head and body were both gone. Ethorne said, "Critter got it," but he sounded doubtful.

I patted my shirt pocket. I still had a fang to prove the snake had been here. I didn't show it to anyone.

4

Building in Blood

In 1959, these things happened in my parents' world: Ninety miles away from the United States, Fidel Castro's Communist forces defeated Cuba's corrupt dictator and expropriated U.S.-owned sugar mills. The Soviet Union sent the first rocket to the moon. Alaska and Hawaii became the forty-ninth and fiftieth U.S. states. Raymond Chandler, Frank Lloyd Wright, Cecil B. De Mille, Errol Flynn, Buddy Holly, and Billie Holiday died. China crushed a Tibetan revolt, and Tibet's spiritual leader, the Dalai Lama, fled to India. *Ben Hur* won the Academy Award. "Tom Dooley" and "Mack the Knife" dominated the radio waves. For the first time, the number of Americans who had died in automobile accidents (more than 1.25 million) was greater than the number who had died in all previous American wars. The U.S. Postmaster General banned *Lady Chatterley's Lover* from the mail. President Eisenhower sent troops to crush strikes by U.S. steelworkers and longshoremen. Los Angeles won baseball's World Series. Jack Nicklaus won the U.S. Golf Association amateur championship. The star contestant on *21*, America's most popular television game show, admitted that the show's producers had given him answers to their questions.

My world's events happened near the cinder-block motel unit that was home. Ethorne and a crew of young men cleared the ashes of the house that had burned before we arrived, and then they began cutting back the jungle around us. Ma and several hired black women cleaned the restaurant, then Ethorne and his crew painted it pink. A swing set appeared beside our new home, a replacement for the one we had lost in New Orleans, and Little Bit, Digger, and I learned how playing was different in Florida:

When sand spurs are green, you can crush them between the tips of your fingers, if you're careful. When they're brown, the spines will pierce your skin, hurting when they enter, hurting while they're in you, hurting again when you pluck them.

Some ants are busy specks that scurry away when you kick apart their hills. Some ants are fire ants whose bites burn like a lit match.

Some snakes are harmless, but every poisonous snake in North America lives in northern Florida. Rattlers, water moccasins, and copperheads are easy to know by their fangs. The difference between the poisonous coral snake and the harmless scarlet king snake is subtle; it lies in the pattern of red, black, and yellow rings around their bodies. Ma taught us, "Red on yellow, kill the fellow. Red on black, poison lack."

I went to tell an adult whenever I saw a snake, no matter what I thought it might be. Little Bit loved to hunt for grass snakes. When she found one, she called, "Come, Chris a for! Come, Digger! Nice snakey! See?" Digger always waddled to her as quickly as he could to see what made her laugh. His fears were reserved for large, fanged monsters with heads larger than Pa's fist. I always stood back and pretended I was bored by mere grass snakes.

Dogs began arriving before construction had begun on the kennels. The first was a rough-coated collie. Little

Bit saw her and raced toward her, yelling, "Lassie! It's Lassie!"

The second was a white and brown pointer that liked to jump up and bark when he saw people he didn't know. I heard the barking and stepped behind Ma. Pa saw me and said, "Christopher, come here."

Ma said, "He needs time to get used to the dog."

Pa nodded. "That's what I'm going to arrange."

The entire family was watching. Digger and Little Bit had stepped back when the pointer barked, but Pa had not noticed them. I took a few steps forward as if I had merely been walking around Ma to get a better look at the dog.

"Come on," Pa said with less patience. "He won't hurt you."

"Chris doesn't know that," Ma said.

Pa glanced at her. "He will." Ma looked away as Pa said, "Hold out your hand. Toward the dog."

I moved my hand about six inches forward. The snake had enclosed Digger's fist. A big dog could swallow my arm.

Pa patted the pointer. "His name's Beauregard. He's not going to hurt you, Chris. You do what I say, and you'll know how to tell if any dog might bite."

I nodded, but I didn't move my arm any closer.

"Turn your hand over so he can see you don't have anything in it. Dogs usually bite when they're scared. If they can't see what's in your hand, they don't know if you're going to hit them or something."

I showed my palm. Beauregard licked it, and I jumped back. Little Bit and Digger laughed, then so did I. Beauregard began licking my face, and I had to use both arms to hold him back.

Pa said, "Well, Beauregard's too fast to be a good example. But anytime you're dealing with a dog you don't know, let it smell you so it'll know you don't plan to hurt it. If a dog growls at you, just draw your hand back slowly. Never show you're scared, or it'll try to chase you away."

I nodded and let Beauregard lick my hands. It had never occurred to me that something large might be afraid of me.

Pa kept the collie and the pointer chained to the porch in front of the house so they wouldn't run off or get on the highway. That seemed a reasonable solution until a blond, short-haired Chihuahua arrived.

Ma said, "You can't leave that little thing out all night."

Pa said, "On the farm, we never had dogs in the house."

Ma said, "Daddy and Mother have always had house dogs."

"Gretel," said Little Bit, naming Grandma and Grandpa's elderly dachshund.

Pa said, "I don't want a dog in my damn house."

Ma said, "What if something happens to him? Mickey's a champion. If we had to pay the breeder what he's worth—"

"Champion Chihuahua," Pa said. "Champion yappy little lapdog."

"Yappy lappy dog," said Little Bit, petting Mickey.

That night, when we went into Ma and Pa's room to watch *Gunsmoke* on the secondhand TV that Pa had bought at a church sale, Mickey was in a cardboard box that Ma had cut down and lined with rags. Pa looked at Mickey and said, "All right. I don't want a dog in my damn bed."

Ma said, "Fine." All during *Gunsmoke*, while Marshal Dillon and Miss Kitty maintained civilization in Dodge City, Mickey kept jumping onto the chenille bedspread. At first, we kids laughed at the way Ma would catch Mickey and set him down with a shake of her finger and a fiercely whispered, "Stay! Good dog! Stay!"

And then it quit being funny. Mickey would stand on the tiles, then circle the bed and bound back up. Finally, Pa said, "Jesus, Susan, will you just hold that damn dog so it'll quit jumping around?" Ma clutched Mickey like a baby through the rest of the show. He licked Ma's and Lit-

tle Bit's faces, and after a few minutes, they laughed. Pa,
Digger, and I watched *Gunsmoke* as if the Chihuahua did
not exist.

The fourth dog to arrive was Captain, the best Norwegian elkhound that ever lived. I don't know who decided
Captain was my dog, if I did or Captain did, or if Ma or
Pa decided that each of us kids should have a dog that we
could consider our own—though most of the dogs were
on loan to Dogland, it was understood that they would
stay with us as long as they lived. Captain was gray and
shaggy and happy and brave, the kind of dog who pulled
Sergeant Preston of the Yukon through the snow to save
lost people and capture bad men. Captain loved to lick my
face when I petted him, and he always thought it was
wonderful to see me, and I always knew it was wonderful
to see him.

Shortly after my fourth birthday, I was playing in the
gravel parking lot near the restaurant, building a moat
around the Fort Apache set that Grandpa Abner had sent
me, when something large rolled across the rubble behind
me. I turned, gasped, and scrambled backward, caving in
part of the trench I had dug and burying a blue cavalryman who had been about to saber a bright yellow
tomahawk-wielding redskin.

An ancient green pickup truck had coasted in behind
me. The door opened quickly and quietly, slicing the air
within inches of my head. The driver stepped out as the
door swung wide. I saw engineer boots and shapeless
work trousers, and I thought this was Pa until I heard the
man's voice: "Hey, boy. Careful where you play. Might get
hurt."

He walked away so quickly that I barely had time to
note the ways in which he was not Pa. He had a north
Florida accent. He was short and round like Santa Claus.
His skin was reddish-brown, and he wore a work shirt that

matched his trousers. He carried himself with a military erectness that I envied.

He stopped under the shade of the Heart Tree. A few hundred yards away Pa and Ethorne were clearing land with several young men that Ethorne called his boys. The stranger said, "That your Pa with the niggers?"

That was my pa, but I had been told that Ethorne, James, and Seth were not supposed to be called niggers. I had also been told not to correct adults. I stared at the workers as if I had never seen them.

"You too scared to talk," said the man, "you just nod, hear?"

I nodded and whispered, "That's my pa."

The man laughed. Ma came out of the restaurant with a wet sponge in one hand; she and Mayella, one of Ethorne's girls, had been scrubbing walls. Little Bit was helping them. She followed Ma with a small silver, blue, and green metal beach bucket full of sudsy water. Ma smiled and said, "We're not open yet."

The man touched the bill of his cap. "I know, ma'm. That your daughter?"

Ma nodded.

The man said, "I figured she was. She's near as pretty as you. My name's Tom Greenleaf, but they call me Handyman. I hear your husband's got work needs doin'." He smiled. "Ain't much I can't handle right."

Ma frowned. "You'll have to speak with Luke."

Handyman touched his cap again. "Will do, ma'm." He looked at the woods, then said, "Say, you folks ain't seen no sign o' boar, have you?"

Ma said, "Excuse me?"

"Boar, ma'm. Been some good hunts through this land. Got one hog not long ago what weighed near two hun'ed an' fifty pounds."

Ma's eyes widened, and she looked at me.

Handyman smiled. "One I'd like to get is s'posed to be more'n three hun'ed. Big fellow the niggers call Blanche."

"Blanche?"

"Yes'm. A French-talkin' nigger come out of the woods a few years back, all tore up and screamin' something wild. Your neighbor, ol' man Shale, an' Preacher Jones, the minister up at All Souls—that's the nigger church in Dickison—found him. Jones says there was a big ol' boar in the bushes, an' that boar just watched him and Shale put the French nigger in the back of his truck. French nigger said somethin' about Blanche an' the horror an' like that, all in French, which is Greek to ol' man Shale and Preacher Jones. That was all anyone ever got out of him. That nigger's off at the crazy farm now. No one ever figured out where he was from or what he was doin' here."

"Good Lord," Ma said. "The poor man."

Handyman shrugged. "Preacher Jones an' ol' man Shale both been known to take a drink now an' then. Might be you can only find that boar halfway through a jug o' shine. But if you see any sign of a big ol' boar, le' me know, hear? I got a pack of hounds that'll track and hold anything that runs on this earth."

Ma said, "I haven't noticed anything like a boar around here."

"With all this activity you got now, you're not like to, neither. Don't you fret on it none, ma'm."

Ma nodded. Handyman touched his cap again and walked toward Pa and the workers. Little Bit said, "What's a boar?"

Ma said, "It's a wild pig with big tusks. Teeth that stick out from its mouth. If you see any wild animals, you go inside the nearest house immediately, understand?"

Little Bit and I nodded. Ma went back into the restaurant, but Little Bit stood on the green cement sidewalk, squinting in the sunlight. Thinking about wolves and the three little pigs, I trailed Handyman from about thirty feet back.

A few days' toil with a tractor and bulldozer had carved wide, muddy swatches into the woods. Pa and the Negro men were working at the edge of an island of jungle. Pa had his shirt off. His shoulders were red from the sun, but I knew from our trips to the beach that what burned Ma or me would only tan Pa.

Pa and the hired men were hauling a felled tree out of the brush. They were sweating, and their breaths came in gasps, but they all smiled. Ethorne grunted to Pa, "This goin' make—a mighty nice—resting bench, Mist' Luke. Folks come—from miles 'round—just to set on—this here log."

Pa's laugh was interrupted by Handyman saying, "Got them boys working pretty good."

The Negroes quit smiling. Pa looked at Handyman. "They're hardworking men." He and the others didn't slow down.

Handyman grunted agreement. "Long as you keep after 'em." He grabbed a dirt-encrusted root to help carry the tree toward several others that lay in a pile, waiting for Pa to decide how they might be useful. Handyman said, "How you, Ethorne?"

Ethorne said, "Can't complain, Mist' Greenleaf."

Pa said, "Good enough," and everyone dropped the tree. Pa pulled a handkerchief out of his back pocket, swabbed his forehead, then looked at Handyman again. "Help you with something?"

"No, sir," said Handyman. "Might be I can he'p you. I hear you might be needin' a 'lectrician. I'm Tom Greenleaf. Folks call me Handyman, 'cause that's what I try to be."

Pa held out his hand. "Luke Nix." As the men shook, Pa said, "We're hardly ready for an electrician. Got to finish laying this out, maybe get a little more landscaping done first."

"You putting in dog runs," said Handyman, "you'll need plumbing work. I do that, too. You plannin' on some serious landscaping"—he gestured toward the Heart Tree by extending two fingers, making a pistol of his hand—"I work with dynamite."

Pa smiled. "Wife's set on keeping that old tree."

"Give you more room to park cars."

"If we start turning customers away 'cause we're out of parking places, you'll get the first call."

Handyman laughed. "Glad to hear that."

"Check back Monday, if you want. We may be ready to string a few yard lights by then."

"Will do." Handyman nodded at Ethorne, Seth, and James. "See you boys."

Ethorne smiled. "Sure 'nough."

Handyman looked at me. "I got a boy 'bout your age. Might be you two could play together sometime. How'd you like that?" I shrugged and looked at my boots. All of the men chuckled. Handyman said, "Well," and started to walk away.

Pa called, "Tell you what. I'll let you know what we're planning. If you can get up an estimate—"

"Easy," said Handyman.

Pa looked at Ethorne, then at the woods where they'd been working. "Anything in there you think is pretty, let it stand. But all the weeds and most of those bushes have to go. I want to be able to get a riding mower in there, maybe plant some flowers. We'll make Busch Gardens look like some old lady's backyard."

Ethorne said, "You got it."

Pa and Handyman headed toward Handyman's truck. Seth, the youngest of the Negro men, watched Handyman and whispered, "Damn cracker." Though Seth and James were both handsome and wiry like Ethorne, James was tall and dark like a telephone pole, and Seth was short and copper-skinned.

Ethorne looked at me, then shrugged and told Seth, "Boy, pray you never meet a worse white than the Handyman."

Seth said, "Isn't a matter of better or worse." He wiped his dark-framed glasses on the tail of his shirt.

"Oh?" James gave a low laugh. "Say what it be, college boy."

Ethorne, frowning, shook his head, but Seth was looking at me. He squatted on his heels and said, "Hey, cowboy. What's the only good Indian?"

I grinned and drew my broken cap pistol. "Only good Injun is a dead Injun! Pow-pow-pow-*pow!*"

Seth and James laughed. Seth, standing, said, "Some days I wish this world had nothing but good whites."

Ethorne asked me, "You like Mis' DeLyon, Chris?"

I nodded. On hot afternoons, Ma or Pa or both of them would take us kids to the Fountain of Youth, and Mis' DeLyon would let us play in her wading pool.

Ethorne said, "Mis' DeLyon's an Indian."

I squinted at him, then announced, "Pa's part Indian, so I'm part Indian." I patted my hand over my mouth. "Woo-woo-woo-woo-woo-woo-woo!"

James smiled. "You goin' shoot yourself?"

I grinned and fired several times toward the woods with my cap pistol. "Pow-pow-pow!" Then I holstered my pistol, squatted, and shot an imaginary bow. "Whoo! Whoo!" Then I grunted, clutched my chest, and fell full length onto the ground.

Seth clapped. "Marlon Brando's eating his heart out."

Ethorne said, "Paul Robeson be feelin' a mite jealous, too."

James said, "John Wayne got nothing on that boy."

I opened my eyes and grinned at James. John Wayne made the cowboy movies that Pa and I loved. John Wayne was a real actor.

Ethorne said, "We best be gettin' to work."

Seth nodded slowly. "Got to show the white man we ain't no lazy niggers. Ain't that right?" He stared at Ethorne and Ethorne stared back, like gunfighters facing off in a dusty street.

James poked Seth's shoulder. "You ain't 'bout to show nobody nothin' about workin', college boy."

Seth slid his gaze to James. "You're just—" Then he laughed. "About to be proven wrong, farm boy." He snatched up a machete that was lying beside a sickle and a scythe, and he headed toward the woods.

James grabbed the scythe and followed Seth. Stooping for the sickle, Ethorne said, "Your mama be happiest if you play up near the restaurant, Kit Carson."

I saluted, bringing my left hand up above my eyebrow and touching my coonskin cap. Even if he didn't have a TV show, Kit Carson was as good as Daniel Boone and Davy Crockett; Pa had said so. Even better, his first name was my first name. "Ethorne, sir?"

He began to sharpen the sickle with a stone from the pocket of his overalls. "Yes, Mast' Nix?"

"Kit's a good name."

"That is a fact."

"Would people call me that?"

"You'd like that?"

I nodded.

"If you asked 'em nice, they might."

I nodded and ran toward my Fort Apache play set. A little later Mayella called me in for lunch. I ran into the men's washroom, scrubbed my hands, then ran into the restaurant kitchen by the back door.

"Whoa!" said Mayella. "Hurr'cane just blew in."

I grinned at her. Mayella reminded me of Aunt Jemima on the pancake box and the syrup bottle, except she was younger, darker, and not quite as stout.

Ma said, "Be careful when you come inside, Chris. You might've hit someone with the door."

I nodded.

Pa said, "Your mother's talking to you, Chris."

I said, "Yessir," then, "yes, ma'm," and ran to the table.

Ma said, "Did you wash?"

I said, "Yes, ma'm."

Mayella laughed. "Didn't bathe."

I looked at her.

She said, "Got dirt on the back of yo' head. What was you doin', anyway?"

I said, "Injuns shot me."

Pa looked up from a copy of *Newsweek* and smiled.

Little Bit said, "Really?" and Digger stared. When Ma said, "No, Chris is just fooling," Little Bit seemed disappointed.

Mayella grabbed my shoulders and swung me onto a chair. "Now, you stay right there—" She turned away to reach for a washrag, and when she did, I saw down the collar of her white shirt. The skin of her back was striped with black, shiny tissue.

I poked my finger onto the top edge of the uppermost mark. It felt hard and cool beneath my finger. "What's that, Mayella?"

Mayella stepped forward quickly, saying nothing. She bumped against the counter, and everyone looked.

Pa said, "What'd you do, Chris?"

I looked at my boots.

Mayella gave a small laugh. "Oh, Chris just saw where my back got cut up." She lifted the tail of my cap and scrubbed the back of my head with her washrag, hard enough that it hurt a little. I didn't mind, 'cause I knew she was upset by what I'd done, though I didn't know why.

Little Bit said, "What happened, Mayella?"

Ma said, "Don't pester Mayella, you two."

Mayella said, "That's all right, ma'm. I was somewheres at the wrong time. That's how it usually is when you get yourself hurt."

Ma nodded. "Hear that, Chris? Letitia? You always want to be careful, wherever you are."

Pa said, "Being careful isn't always enough."

Mayella glanced at him, then shrugged and began removing golden-brown grilled cheese sandwiches from the griddle.

Pa looked at Little Bit and me. "But there are enough mistakes being made in the world. You don't need to add to them."

For her birthday, Pa had bought Ma a ditto machine so she could send newsletters to friends, family, and Dogland's shareholders. In her first, she wrote, "I smashed my pointer finger, right hand, in car door a week ago and am sill having a kickens of a time using it, so please forgive rrrors." I remember Ma's yell of pain, and my dismay: kids are supposed to suffer; parents are supposed to soothe them. I stood back as Little Bit and Digger ran up beside her.

Pa, on the other side of the car, said, "What in hell—" and ran around to our side. When he saw Ma's hand, he stared, too.

Ma whispered, "It's all right." Her finger was bleeding and ugly. Red drops fell onto the driveway, staining the gravel.

Pa said, "What'd you do that for, Susan?"

Ma shook her head. Tears formed at the corners of her eyes.

Pa said, "Jesus. You need to bandage that up," and he led her into the house.

Following them, Little Bit said, "Does that hurt?"

Ma said, "It'll be fine."

Digger looked at Little Bit. She told him, "Don't worry, Dig-dig. Mommy'll be fine."

When Ma and Pa came out of the bathroom, Ma's finger was covered with a bulbous white gauze bandage. Ma said, "Pretty funny-looking, huh? I've got a clown on my finger." She waggled it once. Digger yowled, beginning to cry fiercely. Ma scooped him up in a hug and said that everything was really fine, really.

Later, when Little Bit and Digger had gone to play on the porch and Pa had gone outside to work, I said, "Does it still hurt, Ma?"

Ma said, "Not enough for you to worry about," and she kissed the top of my head.

That afternoon, we all went swimming at the Fountain of Youth. Afterward, Ma said her finger hardly bothered her at all.

The changing of Ma's bandage became a daily ritual for us kids. When Pa was present, he stayed on the far side of the room, reading or watching TV. Once he said, "Bunch of ghouls." Ma said, "They're curious." Pa said nothing more about it. Over the next days, we watched the finger swell, the bruise darken, the nail fall off, the skin turn pink again, and the new nail grow in clean and straight. It was better than television.

Ma and Pa told us we weren't supposed to play in the front seat of the station wagon when no adults were in the car, but we could play in the back. Sometimes the back-seat was my stagecoach, sometimes it was Little Bit's house, and often it was merely a place where we could sit or lie out of the summer sun. Little Bit liked to crawl in and out through the car window. Sometimes she would perch there, watching traffic on the highway or birds over the woods, or maybe dreaming of wild rides with laughing people, or maybe just basking in sunshine and a rich sense of accomplishment. No one knows why, after weeks of playing safely, she fell backward out of the car window.

Mayella spotted Little Bit lying still on the gravel, and she screamed once. Pa, Ethorne, Seth, James, and all the other workers came running, and so did Ma. Mayella, crouching over Little Bit, said, "Sweet Lord Jesus," and Ma, hurrying near, said, "Oh, Letitia!" and Pa, running from the construction site, said, "What in hell happened?"

I didn't know. Digger and I had been by the Heart Tree, building dirt roads so our plastic cars could run around the tree's thick roots. I was the oldest person present when Little Bit fell, so I knew it was my fault. Pa had addressed his query to everyone, not to me specifically, which was proof of my failure: if I had really been responsible, I would have been expected to answer, even if only to admit my guilt.

Ma reached for Little Bit. Mayella said, "Don't move her, ma'm."

As Ma answered, "I know," Little Bit's eyes opened. She whispered, "Di' I faw?"

Pa laughed. "Yes, little darling, you did." When Little Bit didn't respond, Pa said, "Little Bit?"

"Hmm?" Little Bit looked toward the highway where cars sped past us.

Ma said, "Letitia? Are you all right?" Little Bit looked toward Ma. Her eyes did not focus. Ma said, "Oh, God."

Pa said, "Easy, Susan. Little Bit? Can you understand me?"

Little Bit said, "Umm. Hmm."

Mayella said, "She took a bad fall, Mist' Luke. You got to give her time."

Ma said, "I'm taking her to see Dr. Lamont."

Pa said, "Maybe we should watch her for a while."

Ma said, "Luke."

Pa said, "We've got one doctor bill to pay already."

Ma repeated, "I'm taking her to see Dr. Lamont."

Pa nodded. "I'll drive."

Little Bit sat between Ma and Pa. Digger and I had the back to ourselves, so we rolled our toy cars back and forth across the vinyl seat and tried to be quiet. Dr. Lamont said Little Bit didn't have a fracture, but we should watch her, in case she acted strangely. Pa said, "Well, sure, but what if she acts differently?" Dr. Lamont laughed, though Ma didn't. Driving back, we passed Artie Drake on the street, and he waved at Ma. Ma smiled and nodded at him.

We stopped at Gideon's 19-cent Hamburgers on the way home. As we walked in, Mr. Shale said, "My hounds are bred out of the Spartan kind, so flewed, so sanded; and their heads are hung with ears that sweep away the morning dew; crook-kneed, and dew-lapped like the Thessalian bulls; slow in pursuit, but matched in mouth like bells."

Pa said, "Excuse me?"

Mr. Shale said, "*A Midsummer Night's Dream.* How are you, Miss Letitia?"

Ma said, "We were at the doctor's. She fell."

"Would a starberry milk shake help?"

Little Bit smiled and nodded. Ma and Pa both grinned.

"Good to hear," said Mr. Shale, reaching for an ice

cream scoop. "Jesus told me to get that freezer fixed, and your smile's all the reward I could want."

"Choc'late," I said.

Mr. Shale nodded. "That's a nice reward, too."

A week later, Little Bit began stuttering whenever she spoke, calling us K-k-k-Chris, D-d-d-Digger, P-p-p-papa, and Mmmm-mama. She stuttered for a week, then quit as abruptly as she had begun.

Dogs came to Dogland more quickly than kennels could be built for them. We always had several living in and around our house while their homes were being prepared. Before we could become familiar with one, it would be in its kennel and a new dog would take its place on our porch, in our house, and in our hearts.

Each kennel was designed for five dogs. Ethorne's crew made the houses, long wooden structures with five separate rooms, each with its own porch. The houses came in three sizes. The small rooms were just big enough to hold Little Bit and a Lhasa apso; the big rooms could have been club houses for all three Nix kids.

Handyman and Pa supervised the pouring of the concrete runways, which sloped into a common gutter. Ethorne's crew put up chain-link fences to separate the dogs. Ma made hand-lettered wooden signs that hung on hooks on the dogs' front gates, identifying each by breed, name, and owner. Pa built twenty-four kennels, and though they were never all full, we had more than a hundred pure-bred dogs on our grounds within our first year of operation.

The kennels were arranged in a circle at the back of Dogland. You reached it by going through the Doggy Salon, a pavilion built to house the tiniest dogs and to provide a place to groom and nurse all the dogs. Mickey the Chihuahua ruled the Doggy Salon, barking at all who entered. At Dogland's peak, Mickey shared the Salon with a Mexican hairless that shivered no matter how hot the day might be, and a toy Manchester terrier that loved to lick fingers, and several others.

The only pure-bred dog that often had free run of Dogland was Ranger, a huge, shaggy, white kuvasz whose mouth always hung slightly open in a lazy, wolflike grin. Kuvaszes had guarded Hungarian kings in the fifteenth century; Pa decided Ranger was good enough to guard our family, too. During the day, Ranger stayed in his cage next to the other large working dogs, the Great Dane, the St. . Bernard, the mastiff, and the Newfoundland. During the night, Pa let Ranger out to patrol Dogland.

I remember Ranger as taller than me, but I don't remember being afraid of him. Pa bought a steel cart with bicycle wheels and a wooden bench wide enough that we three kids could sit side by side on it. Ranger pulled us easily whenever newspaper people wanted to shoot publicity photos. (Pa intended to offer dog cart rides to tourists' children, but if the experiment was ever tried, I don't remember it.)

One night when Pa was away and we kids were asleep, Ma heard Ranger barking. She took a flashlight to investigate, and found a drunken man cringing against the Heart Tree with Ranger before him. The man said, "O great white spirit, don' eat me, please!" Ma laughed and held Ranger's collar while the drunken man ran away. When Ma told the story, we laughed, too. Who could be afraid of Ranger? He was our friend.

Dogs arrived at Dogland in many ways. Some were brought by their owners, who wished to assure themselves that the dogs would be properly fed, housed, and exercised. Some were shipped to the Gainesville train station or the Dickison bus stop. Our Doberman pinscher, a lean, seventy-pound black-and-rust beast named Percival, arrived late one day in a cage. Percival barked when anyone came near. He was hungry, thirsty, tired, confused, frustrated, and furious. He had been traveling for at least three days.

James said, "That dog don't like niggers."

Pa said, "That dog doesn't like anyone. He's a liberal."

Seth said, "I'm mighty fond of my fingers."

Ethorne said, "Got to give him time to quiet down. And got to show him we don't mean to keep him in that cage. We might let him out in the ex'cise pen." He looked at Pa.

Pa nodded. The men had recently finished fencing a large, sandy area near the kennels where dogs could run and dig and play. Pa said, "Everyone take a corner."

The four men lifted the cage by its handles. Ethorne told Percival, "Easy, boy. You be gettin' somethin' closer to freedom real soon now." The Doberman circled in the wire cage, barking at its transporters' hands.

Seth said, "Keep something deprived long enough, it's bound to snap out at anything."

"Shoot," said James. "That's just one mean-spirited dog, is all."

"Some things always lookin' for an excuse to bite," said Ethorne.

"Doesn't mean you should give 'em one," said Pa. "Damn Dobermans tend to be a bit in-bred. Once this one gets to know us, he'll be all right."

When we approached the exercise pen, Pa said, "Chris, open the gate."

I said, "Yes, sir!" and ran ahead through the long grass to fumble with the latch. It lifted just as the men arrived, and I sighed and grinned simultaneously. Ethorne grinned back. Pa didn't say or do anything, which meant I'd done fine.

"Ain't goin' to fit," said James, looking from the cage to the gate.

"You sure?" said Seth.

"I got eyes, don't I?" said James.

"Let's try," said Seth. "Never know if you don't try."

Pa nodded. "Might squeeze through, if we're lucky."

Ethorne grinned. "I say that, too, now'n then."

They were not lucky. After one attempt to carry the cage into the exercise area, Seth said, "Why'd they put a dog in such a big box, anyway?"

James said, " 'Cause that's all they had, most like."

Ethorne said, " 'Cause someone had a feelin' for this dog. When you got to cage something you like, you give it the biggest cage you got."

Pa said, "All right. We'll put the cage up to the door of the pen. When the dog goes in the pen, Seth, you close that gate. Fast."

Seth nodded.

Pa said, "Ethorne, you and James pull the cage back out of the way as soon as that dog's out of it."

Ethorne and James both said, "Yes, sir." They placed the cage against the open door. Pa looked at the others, then at Little Bit and me where we stood watching from twenty feet away. Then he reached over the top of Percival's cage, unlatched the front grille, and lifted it high.

It might have all gone as planned, if Ma had known the Doberman had arrived. But Ma had gone out to the kennels to check on the dogs, and since the day was ending, she had let Ranger out. We heard her call "Ranger!" from the far side of the circle of dog pens, and we all looked up. Ranger raced through the island of palmettos and live oaks, approaching like a great ghostly god of wolves.

"Damn!" Pa slammed the grille down a moment too late. It clipped Percival's shoulder as he bounded out of his cage. "Close that—" Pa began, but Percival wheeled in the gateway. As Seth shoved the gate forward, and Ethorne and James yanked the cage backward, Percival leaped, bounding over his cage and charging toward Little Bit and me.

"Get back!" Pa yelled at us as he followed the Doberman. I stared at dark eyes and glistening teeth, then twisted aside, bumped into Little Bit, caught her arm, and began to run, dragging her behind me.

"Don't!" Little Bit shook her arm free and pointed. "Nice dog! See?"

The Doberman ignored us, raced along the exercise pen, heading toward the highway. Ranger intercepted him before he reached the end of the fence. The kuvasz must

have been twenty pounds heavier than the Doberman, yet
Percival did not hesitate. He lunged for Ranger's throat.
Ranger met the attack, twisting aside and snapping his
teeth close to Percival's snout.

Ethorne yelled, "Ranger! Down, boy!" as Pa stepped between the dogs. Ranger backed away, and when Pa
grabbed for the Doberman's collar, Percival sank his teeth
deep into Pa's right forearm.

Pa hit the Doberman once in the nose with his left fist.
Percival did not let go. Ethorne, James, and Seth reached
to pull Percival away, and Ranger circled around them. Pa
grunted, "Hold, Ranger!" and slammed the Doberman
onto his back on the ground. His bleeding arm slipped free
of the dog's bite. His right hand covered Percival's throat
and jaw, extending the Doberman's head back so it was
parallel with the ground. His left hand held the dog's stomach, pinning Percival's torso. The dog's limbs thrashed as
he tried to claw or flee, and he whimpered desperately.
With his head only inches away from Percival's, Pa yelled,
"Who's boss, damn it! Who's boss?" With each yell, Pa
pressed Percival against the ground, then released him
slightly in order to press him down again.

Percival lay still. His whimpering slowed and quieted
to a desperately hopeful plea.

Pa said with disgust and disappointment, "All right,
then." He looked at Ethorne. "Put him in the pen."

Ethorne said quietly, "Yes, sir, Mist' Luke." He clipped
a leash to Percival's collar and said, "C'mon, boy." Percival began to growl. Ethorne, keeping the leash taut, held
out his free hand, palm forward for the dog to sniff.
"Di'n't you learn nothin', boy?" Percival let Ethorne lead
him into the exercise pen. Ethorne seemed to be watching Pa more than the Doberman.

James smiled. "Reckon he knows who's boss now."

Seth, holding Ranger's collar, looked at Pa's arm and
said, "Mist' Nix, I'm sorry, I tried to close him in, honest,
I did." His accent was as thick as James's. It was easy to
believe he was Ethorne's son.

Pa clenched his bleeding arm with his left hand and shook his head. Every kennel had a faucet and a hose on its side for washing the dogs and their runs. Pa went to the nearest and rinsed his arm, but the flow of blood did not slow. The Doberman's bite had opened his flesh in a long, deep tear.

"That's bad," said Little Bit.

"Umm," said Pa.

Ethorne nodded. "Best have Mis' DeLyon look at that, Mist' Luke. Might be the doc should see it, too."

"Don't need a doctor." Pa never needed doctors. He began to walk toward our house. "Susan'll tie it up."

"I'll come along," Ethorne said.

Pa shook his head. "Chris or Little Bit can tell you where my body is, if I fall on the way. C'mon, kids."

Ethorne frowned. "If you say so."

We had hardly gone twenty yards when Ma and Digger came around the path along the kennels. Ma said, "Have you seen Ranger? I let—Oh, my God." She stared at Pa's arm.

Digger stared, too, then began to cry. Little Bit took his hand and said, "Don't cry now, Digger," and he stopped.

Pa said, "Now, Susan, don't get excited. Just run ahead to the house to get some bandages. It's a dog bite, that's all."

"That's all?" Ma said. "You—"

"You prefer I bleed to death here?" As Ma shook her head, Pa said, "Little Bit, you and Digger follow your ma. I'll keep Chris to lean on, if I need to."

"Oh, my God," Ma repeated. "C'mon, kids." She ran toward the house.

Pa and I picked our way over open ground where plumbing had been recently buried and where walking paths had yet to be finished. Pa's skin was damp and pale, and his blood marked our trail from the kennels to the house. In one kind of fairy tale, wolves would follow the smell of the blood, and in another, we would make our way to the princess whose kiss could heal, and in a third,

Pa's blood would turn into red birds whose song would bring joy to the world.

"What'll you do to the bad dog, Pa?" I asked.

"Nothing."

"Nothing?"

"It was my fault."

I blinked at him.

"Should've made sure Ranger was penned before letting the Doberman out. Should've hosed 'em both down instead of grabbing at 'em. That's what you get when you don't think."

"You didn't think, Pa?"

Pa laughed weakly. "No need to rub it in."

I stared at his arm.

"Your pa makes mistakes, you know."

I stared up at him. Things were often my fault, or Ma's, or sometimes even Little Bit's. If Pa was saying he could be wrong, that must be so, because Pa was always right. Had I been two or three years older, that would have been a paradox. At four, it was simply a new truth. To be sure I understood, I said, "You do?"

Pa nodded as we entered the house. He leaned against the door frame, then lurched inside. Blood spattered onto the dark floor tiles.

Ma hurried out of the bathroom with the blue metal first-aid box. Opening it, she said, "What happened?"

Pa shook his head. "Ranger and the Doberman wanted to fight. I got in the way."

Ma whispered, "Oh. I didn't—" As she wiped his arm clean, Pa grimaced. Ma said, "You have to see the doctor, Luke."

Pa shook his head.

Ma said, "You do."

Pa said, "I don't have to see any damn doctor. Especially not that bigot."

Ma said, "If the dog's rabid?"

Pa said, "More likely, I'm rabid. You better worry about that poor Doberman." He laughed, but his shirt was drenched in sweat, and his chest rose and fell as he gasped for breath.

By the time Ma finished taping gauze around Pa's forearm, the bandage was already soaked with blood. Ma said, "You need stitches."

Pa said, "The hell I do," and fainted.

Ma caught him as he collapsed. She screamed at me, "Get Ethorne!"

I ran outside, yelling, "Ethorne! Ethorne!" Ethorne loped across the field toward me, and I yelled, "Ma wants you! Ma wants you!"

When Pa came to a minute later, Ma and Ethorne were carrying him to the station wagon. "I can walk," he said, wrenching himself free of their grip, and he staggered to the car. He hesitated, resting bloody hands on the hood, then went to the passenger door, telling Ma, "You drive."

In the car I began to wonder whether Pa could die.

After Dr. Lamont and Pa came out of the doctor's office, Dr. Lamont said, "You folks're going to pay for the fishing boat I been looking at, if you keep this up."

Pa said, "Yeah, funny."

Dr. Lamont said, "I'll test that dog that bit you. If it's got rabies, you'll be going through a pretty painful process, Luke."

Pa said, "Mmm."

"You going to put that dog down?"

Pa looked at him. "Why?"

Dr. Lamont said, "It's got a taste for human blood."

Pa laughed. "You know how much that dog's worth?"

Ma said, "It's not worth taking the chance that anyone'll be hurt." She looked at Little Bit and me, so I smiled at her.

Pa scowled. "It was my own damn fault. I'm getting tired of having to say that."

Dr. Lamont said, "That land's taking a lot from y'all."

Pa said, "What's that supposed to mean?"

Dr. Lamont smiled. "Means I'll be getting my fishing boat if this keeps up."

"Don't put money on it," Pa said, and walked out of the
waiting room.

Ma smiled at Dr. Lamont. "Well, thanks, Dr. Lamont.
Luke's—"

Dr. Lamont nodded. "It's hard to keep your spirits up
when your arm's hurting. 'Specially if you're the sort who
doesn't like the sight of blood."

Little Bit said, "You *like* seeing blood, Dr. Lamont?"

He said, "Beg pardon?"

Ma said, "Letitia!"

Dr. Lamont said, "Don't you never mind. I couldn't
quite make out what she said."

In the front yard the station wagon started with a roar.
Ma glanced over her shoulder and said, "We have to run."

Dr. Lamont nodded. "Hope the next time I see you is
under better circumstances."

Ma nodded and hurried us out. Pa drove us back, and
no one spoke. Not one of us kids asked to watch when he
changed the bandages. After a week or two, Pa cut the
stitches and pulled them himself.

In the motel unit that was our home, there was a sink in
each of the two bedrooms. Ma kept a chair next to each
sink for us kids to stand or kneel on when we needed to
wash. One morning in our parents' room while Ma was
helping Little Bit and me with our shoes, Digger fell from
the chair. Mickey's food bowl was on the floor beneath the
sink. Digger hit the bowl with his forehead, strewing
blood, broken porcelain, and moist dog food all around
him. When we looked, he lay motionless on the floor.
Mickey yapped desperately and bounded around Digger's
arms. Digger pushed himself up. The skin of his forehead
had been opened from his hairline to his eye. When he saw
Ma running toward him, he began to wail.

Again we made the drive to Dickison. While Dr. Lamont put eight stitches in Digger's forehead, I pondered
the pictures in the comic books in the waiting room, Lit-

tle Bit rolled wooden blocks across the carpet, and Pa leafed through copies of *Life* and *Look*. When Dr. Lamont and Ma came back with Digger, Dr. Lamont said, "I can't promise there won't be some deformity. I'm sorry."

Ma squeezed Digger tighter. Pa said, "He can see all right?"

"Doesn't seem to have affected his vision. Time will tell."

Pa nodded.

Little Bit said, "Can Digger go swimmin'?"

Ma said, "*May* Digger go swimming?" Then she told Dr. Lamont, "We have a little wading pool. And Mrs. DeLyon lets the children play in her swimming pool, too."

Dr. Lamont narrowed his eyes, then nodded. "So long as the boy's in clean water, he should be fine."

Driving home in the station wagon, Ma looked out the window. I didn't see anything except trees and billboards there. She said quietly, "I wasn't watching. I was dressing Letitia, and I turned away. He's never had any trouble washing himself. Never. And I didn't think—"

Pa shrugged, keeping his gaze on the road. "Can't watch kids all the time, Susan. They're going to get hurt. That's just how it is."

Digger, in the front seat between them, began to whimper. Ma hugged him. I said, "Here," and handed Ma Digger's toy crane. He laughed when he saw it.

Ma said, "That was very thoughtful, Chris."

I looked at my boots and blushed. The toy had been lying by my feet. Anyone would have passed it to her.

The next morning Digger, giggling, ran naked from the bathroom into our parents' room. Pa winced and said, "Jesus, Susan, cover up his forehead. Kid looks like Frankenstein's Baby."

Digger stopped in the middle of the room and squinted at Pa, then at Ma. Ma frowned, scooped Digger up, took him to the chair he had fallen from, and began wrapping a gauze bandage around his forehead. I said, "It's not fair."

Ma said, "What's not?"

"Why's Digger get to look like a pirate? I want to be a pirate, too."

Ma said, "Okay. I'll do you next."

Little Bit said, "Me, too! Me, too!"

Pa went to the door and, as he left, said, "You can dress the walking wounded. Ethorne and I need to run into town for more dog food."

While Ma bandaged Little Bit, I ran outside to slice the air with an imaginary cutlass. Seth, James, and Mayella were sitting on the sidewalk around the kitchen, waiting for the workday to begin. Seth pointed at me. "Look-a-there. It's the mummy of King Tot."

Mayella laughed. James said, "King what?"

Seth shrugged. "Forget it."

James said, "No, what?"

Seth said, "It was a joke."

James looked at Mayella. "Must'a' been a funny one."

Mayella looked at Seth. "Took me by surprise, is all."

Seth said, "You know about Egyptian mummies, don't you?"

James said, "Sure," as I said, "No, sir."

The three of them looked at me, then they all grinned. Mayella said, "Sir! Who he talkin' to, I wonder?"

Seth said, "That's one smart kid, that is."

"Yeah?" said James. "He don' know 'bout the 'Gyptians."

"Then you better teach him," said Seth.

"Me?" James touched his chest.

"Since you know all about them," said Seth.

"Yeah," said Mayella. "We listenin'."

"Well," said James, looking around, then settling his gaze on me. "The 'Gyptians was the world's first civilization. And you know where Egypt is?"

I shook my head.

"Africa. The Egyptians was Africans. Most o' their queens looked a sight more like Mayella than 'Lizabeth Taylor." He looked at Mayella and flashed his teeth.

Mayella smiled as she looked away. "No."

Seth frowned and said, "Cleopatra was descended from the Macedonians who conquered Egypt, so she prob'ly did look a bit like Liz Taylor."

James said, "Did I or did I not say 'most' o' their queens?"

Seth nodded reluctantly.

James laughed. "There you is, college boy." He looked back at me. "The 'Gyptians, they was fixed on eternal life. That was why they wrapped up their kings an' queens an' made 'em mummies. They thought there was a tie 'tween the survival of their bodies an' the salvation of their souls. They thought their souls would travel a long ways, crossin' a lot o' bodies o' water to reach the land o' the dead. An' you know who escorted their souls to the land o' the dead?"

I shook my head.

"Anubis," said James. "He was a 'Gyptian god. An' you know what his head looked like?"

I shook my head again.

"A jackal. That's a wild dog. You know that pharaoh hound what come in the other day?"

I nodded. Pa had been very proud of getting the pharaoh hound. It was a sleek tan Egyptian racing dog that might be the oldest breed of domesticated dog.

James smiled. "Ol' Anubis had a body of a man an' a head of a dog. He was the god o' cemeteries and embalming. 'Gyptians didn't know a thing about Jesus."

Seth said, "Who you been talkin' to?"

James grinned. "Ethorne."

Seth laughed. "He told you he was in ancient Egypt, I expect."

James shook his head. "Said he read a lot of books."

Seth nodded.

"Said he met someone who was there, though."

Seth and Mayella both laughed. Mayella said, "That's Ethorne. He tells some tall ones."

James frowned. "He ever lie to you?"

Mayella shook her head. Seth said, "Not about anything important."

James said, "Like what?"

Seth said, "Like his story that he was a slave here.
Come on."

James said, "You think he wasn't?"

"I know he wasn't."

"You can prove it?"

Seth stared at him. "What kind of nappy-headed nigger do you take me for? Nobody needs to prove something
that's impossible is impossible."

"Ethorne knows how the pyramids were built."

Seth laughed. "So do I. Like the ol' South was built.
With slaves."

James shook his head. "Hired folks, mostly, says
Ethorne. Workin' durin' the winter when the crops was in.
An' that's not the question. How'd they lift those big stone
blocks to build the pyramids?"

Seth said, "Wooden cranes, maybe. Swing 'em up
there? I dunno."

James nodded in victory. "They made ramps of sand
and hauled those blocks up on rollers."

Seth shrugged. "Sounds reasonable."

"There you are," said James.

"Ethorne must've read that. Or maybe he made it up.
Doesn't prove a thing about his stories, you know."

James nodded. "Not to you."

Seth jerked his thumb at James and addressed
Mayella. "Can you b'lieve— "

When he stopped speaking, we all looked to see why.
A young white woman had come around the corner. She
appeared to be about as old as Artie Drake's daughter,
which meant she was younger than Mayella, James, or
Seth. She had thin blond hair cut like a football helmet,
and she wore a cotton dress that looked thinner and more
faded than Mayella's. I looked to see if she had come with
her parents and saw she was alone.

She studied us, and we studied her. Then Mayella stood, saying, "Help you, miss?" James followed Mayella's example. He nudged Seth with his foot, and Seth scrambled to his feet.

The white girl said, "This here's the dog place?"

I could hear dogs barking in the distance, but I said nothing. Mayella said, "Yes'm. Ain't open for business yet."

"I'm lookin' for the owner."

"That's my pa," I said.

She looked at me without smiling. "Where can I find him?"

"He went to town with Ethorne," I said. "My ma's here."

The girl nodded. "What's wrong with your head?"

"I'm a pirate."

"Oh." She looked at Mayella and smiled. "That'd 'xplain it."

"Ma's at the house." I pointed at the motel unit. "She's going to make bre'fast. Pa makes scrambled eggs, but Ma makes French toast."

The girl nodded, looked at the four of us, then nodded again and started toward the house.

Seth whispered, "Kind o' cute, for a cracker."

Mayella elbowed him in the arm. "You gone color-blind, stupid, or both?"

James whispered, "Nigger, Emmett Till *died* for whistling at a white woman."

Seth said, "In Mississippi."

Mayella said, "They hang fools in Florida, too." She looked at me.

Seth followed her glance. "Say, Christopher, d'you think that's a pretty young lady?"

I nodded and scuffed gravel with the toe of my boot.

Seth grinned. "Well, I agree with you."

James whispered, "Shee-it."

The screen door opened as the white girl approached

our house, and Ma led Digger and Little Bit out. The blond girl stopped still.

James said, "That's a mess of pirates."

Ma looked at the girl's face, then smiled, indicating Digger with a dip of her chin. "George cut his forehead. The other two are pretending it's Halloween."

"Oh," said the girl. "Ma'm, I'm Francine Carter, an' I'm lookin' for work."

Mom let go of Digger and held out her right hand. "Susan Nix. You'll have to talk to my husband about work. Right now, we're just getting things ready. When the restaurant opens, we'll need waitresses. And when the grounds are ready, we'll need guides to take the tourists around."

"There's nothin' now, ma'm?"

Ma said, "Mostly, there's just heavy labor—"

"I'm strong, ma'm," Francine said. "I was born a McKay. McKays is country people, an' we work hard. I can hoe an' haul an' cut weeds an' put up fence an' most anything. You try me."

"I'm sure you can," Ma said.

"I'll work with niggers," Francine said. "I don't mind. I'll work for nigger wages, too."

Ma said, "We try to pay a fair wage to everyone. That isn't—"

"Ma'm, I don't mean to beg, but I want you to know I'm willin' to do most any kind of work, honest."

Ma nodded. "I'm sure of that. There might be some kind of part-time work you can do."

"I'm huntin' full-time work, ma'm. But I'll take part-time if that's all there is."

Ma frowned. "You'd skip school?"

"Ma'm, I done finished ninth grade. Now I need to support my family."

"I see," Ma said. "How old are you, Francine?"

"Sixteen, ma'm."

"And your father made you quit school to get a job?"

"No, ma'm. But Pa says since I got married, it's my husband's job to support me, only Cal ain't found no steady work quite yet. He ain't about to do nigger work, but I don't mind."

Ma glanced at Little Bit and Digger. Little Bit said, "Digger's hungry, Ma."

Ma looked at Francine. "You said your family. Do you have a child?"

Francine nodded. "Little Cal, yes'm. My sister don' mind lookin' after him, since she's got plenty of her own. He's a good baby. He won't cause me to miss no work or nothin'."

Ma looked up at the parking area, but the station wagon was still gone. She asked, "Have you eaten this morning?"

Francine said, "No'm. I'm not hungry, ma'm."

Ma nodded. "Come up to the restaurant. You might as well join us while we wait for Luke."

"I ain't askin' for handouts, ma'm."

"I know. I have to make breakfast, and Luke gets upset when there are leftovers. So, if there's any extra, you'd be doing me a favor."

I frowned and said, "There's *always* leftovers, Ma."

Ma laughed. "See? Come on."

"Well, all right," said Francine.

Little Bit looked up at her. "My name's Let'bet. D'you have a dog?"

Francine nodded. "We got a few. Best one's a coon dog."

"How many we got, Chris?" Little Bit asked.

I held up both hands and opened and closed my fingers, over and over again.

Francine nodded again. "That's a lot o' dogs."

"They're mostly loaned to us," Ma said. "Don't brag, you two."

Mayella, James, and Seth all said good morning as we approached. Ma smiled at them and began unlocking the kitchen door, saying, "This is Francine. She'll be working here, for a few days, anyway. Seth and James, since Luke's not back yet, you're welcome to come in for some coffee."

Seth said, "Thank you, ma'm. That'd be nice."

Mayella and James stared at him. Then James dipped his head, saying, "Thank you, Mis' Nix. I'd 'preciate that."

In the kitchen we three kids went immediately to our usual seats. Mayella followed Ma over by the sink, where she said, "What'd you like me to do, ma'm?"

Ma said, "Start lots of coffee. James?"

He, Seth, and Francine were standing by the door. "Yes'm?"

"You'll find some chairs in the front room."

"Yes'm."

"I'll help," said Seth, following him.

"How many you want?" said Francine, starting after Seth and James.

Ma caught her arm. "Let the men do it. You sit."

Little Bit nodded and hit the chair beside her with the flat of her hand. "Sit here!"

Francine nodded and took the chair. "All right."

Ma said, "Who's eaten?"

I said, "Not me!"

Little Bit said, "Not me! Not Digger!" Digger nodded several times.

Ma said, "Besides you three?"

Francine said, "I ain't hungry, ma'm."

"I done ate," said Mayella.

"I watched James eat," said Seth. "That took care of my appetite."

"You dog!" said James. "You put away as much as I did."

"What'd you have?" asked Ma.

"Ethorne made grits an' eggs an' biscuits," said Mayella. "He's the best cook in these parts. For a colored man, that is, ma'm. He scrambled up the eggs with onion an' thyme an' rosemary. His biscuits is like clouds in a crust. Folks say Ethorne talks to the food an' it tells him how to fix it best."

"My mama makes better grits," said James.

Seth said, "It's good to see a boy stick up for his mama."

James faked a punch at Seth, and Seth blocked it. Everyone laughed, including Francine, though her face quickly slid back to its usual somber expression.

"There ain't much call for grits in No'the'n hotels," said Mayella.

"Well," said Ma, "my kids will just have to make do with French toast."

"Yum, good!" I yelled.

When Pa arrived, Francine was eating her second stack of French toast. Seth and James stood up from the table, both saying something like, "Thanks for the coffee, Mis' Nix, that was sure nice, we'll go find Ethorne and get right to work now, Mist' Nix, sir."

I thought Pa was going to be furious about how Ma had cooked way too much more food, but Ma said, "We have to talk," and he and Ma went into the front room. When they came back, Pa never said a word about the waste. He just told Francine to catch up to Ethorne, so she could start learning about the care of the dogs, and we'd see how things went.

After almost everyone had left the kitchen, Mayella, washing dishes, told Ma, "That poor girl. Some folks has it rough."

That night in my parents' bedroom, watching TV, Ma said something similar: "Poor Francine. Did you know she walked three miles to get here? And she plans to walk that every day."

Pa nodded without looking up from a cowboy book. "Walking's good for you."

Ma pressed her lips together, shook her head, then smiled. "Oh, Luke."

Pa set his book onto a table by the bed. "You know how far it is to Hawkins Corner?"

Ma said, "To where?"

"That bunch of houses where Ethorne and the others live."

Ma blinked. "No."

"Nearly five miles. Sometimes they catch rides with neighbors. Sometimes they don't."

"I didn't mean Francine had it worse than anyone else. Can't you just let yourself feel for someone?"

"Feel what?"

"Feel—I don't know. Feel sorry."

Pa nodded. "So you can feel superior?"

"No! How can you say—"

"It's a hard world, Susan. These people aren't asking for favors. They just want to be treated like everyone else."

"I'm not saying we should do anyone favors. I'm just saying—" Ma shook her head. "Oh, I don't know what I'm saying."

"Just let 'em do their work, Susan. That's doing 'em a big favor."

Ma frowned. "Are you saying I shouldn't've had them in the kitchen this morning?"

Pa nodded. "No need to make 'em watch the white folks eat."

"I invited them to eat! I practically had to force Francine to take anything!"

"I'm not talking about Francine. People have their pride."

"Luke, the Hawkinses told me what they had for breakfast. They eat a lot better than we usually do."

Pa said, "You mean they get along fine the way they are, but it's too bad about that little white girl."

Ma gnawed her lower lip.

"Well?" Pa said.

"I'm not talking about any 'they.' I'm talking about Seth and James and Mayella. They say Ethorne's a fine cook."

"I'm a pretty good cook myself," Pa said. "So?"

"So they ate well this morning, that's all. And Francine hadn't eaten anything. So I made extra French toast. Four slices of bread, two eggs, and a splash of milk. Is that too much?"

I had the bad feeling as I listened. I slid closer to the

TV set, but Little Bit looked back at Ma and Pa and said, "An' surp an' coffee an' a glass of milk. Francy was *hungry.*"

Ma looked from Little Bit to Pa. "And syrup and coffee and a glass of milk. Is that what we're arguing about? A little food?"

Pa looked at Little Bit, then at Ma. "We're not arguing." He picked up his book.

Ma said, "Luke? Did something happen?"

Pa said, "I ran into Artie Drake this morning."

"Oh?"

"He says people are wondering why we're not giving work to whites here."

Ma's eyes went wide. "No one asked! Except for Handyman. We gave him some work."

Pa nodded. "That's what I said. Artie says they're beginning to think we only call in whites when there's work niggers can't do. The hell of it is, that part's true."

"But we didn't mean—"

"*Mean* doesn't mean anything, Susan. It's what you do."

Ma squinted at him. "Is that why you hired Francine?"

Pa inhaled, drawing air between his teeth, making the sound we kids knew was the same as a rattlesnake's rattle, but that Ma often failed to recognize. Then he exhaled, saying quietly, "Is that what you think?" as he turned the page of his cowboy book.

Ma watched him read for a long moment, then kissed his cheek. He did not look up. He did not move away. Ma looked at us and said, "I think it's the kids' bedtime."

On the day before Dogland's restaurant opened to the public, I was playing behind the kitchen near the door to the utility room. I found a piece of bare wire, maybe six inches long, near the place where Handyman had extended the electrical lines. I tested the wire on different things, sticking it in dirt and through leaves and into dry pieces of bark, and I scratched patterns in the gravel, mostly for the satisfaction of seeing the dust fly up behind the wire. As I played with it, I worked my way toward the front of the restaurant.

Digger, sitting on a blanket in the sun in front of a plate-glass window, watched me, then walked over and held out his hand. I shook my head. He grabbed the wire and yanked. I pulled back, and as the wire began to slide from his hands, his face began to contort in a promise of tears and yelling. I imagined Pa asking what I'd done to my brother, and Ma asking why we couldn't play together in peace. I said, "Okay, Digger, you can have it. Don't cry, okay?" Digger smiled. I decided that I had been finished with the wire anyway, and I left to build a racetrack under the Heart Tree for my toy cars.

As I walked off, Ma came outside, calling, "Georgie? Where are—There you are! Didn't I tell you to stay by the blanket where I could see you? Now you have to come inside. I hope that teaches you something. And hurry up, because Mommy has a lot of work to do. Tomorrow's a very big day."

Ma had put childproof plugs in all the electrical outlets in our house, but none in the restaurant. Digger took the piece of wire into the front room of the restaurant, where Ma and Mayella were hanging crepe streamers from the fluorescent ceiling lights. Ma said, "Georgie, stay in the corner and don't get in the way, all right?" Digger nodded, crawled under one of the tables, squatted by an electrical socket, and poked the length of wire into it.

Ma heard a scream and a hiss. Digger fell away from the socket as if he had been thrown. When Ma picked him up, she saw that the end of the wire must have pressed against the top of his foot. His fingers were striped lightly, but the wire had burned through his sock and into his skin.

Digger opened his eyes and began to cry. Ma yelled, "Get Luke!" at Mayella and carried Digger to the deep metal sink behind the counter. Little Bit and I came inside the front door as Ma said, "Here, Georgie, this'll make it feel better." She put his foot under a stream of cold water. Digger continued to cry while Ma pulled off his sock and shoe.

Pa ran in, saw Ma, and said, "What now?"

Ma pointed at the outlet. The wire still dangled from it. "George did that."

"He's all right?"

"He didn't go unconscious."

Pa gave a tight smile as Digger continued to scream. "Well, he's sure breathing fine."

Ma said, "He's got a bad burn on his foot."

"Kids get burned all the time." Pa looked at us. "Stay away from that wire. I'll shut off the electricity."

Little Bit and I said, "Yes, sir." We had heard Digger; we weren't about to touch that wire. We followed Pa around back to the utility room, where he removed a fuse, and all the lights went out inside the restaurant.

When we went back in, Pa said, "Any idea where he got that wire?"

Ma said, "I've never seen it before."

Pa said, "He had to've found it somewhere. What about you two?"

Little Bit shook her head. I said, "Maybe Handyman dropped it, sir."

Pa said, "You need to look out for your little brother."

As Little Bit and I nodded, Ma said, "The burn's deep, Luke."

Pa said, "Chris, get the first-aid kit."

Ma said, "I want to know he's all right."

Pa said, "You can hear he's all right."

Ma lifted Digger up and stood him on the counter. Pa saw his foot and winced. "All right. We'll help that bastard buy his boat."

After bandaging Digger, Dr. Lamont said, "That's a tough little kid you've got there."

Pa said, "I know that. Not too lucky, though."

Dr. Lamont said, "I don't know about that. He's still alive. If he hadn't fallen away from that socket—" He looked at Ma. "You don't need to bring him back unless it starts to smell or just, well, looks unhealthy. Change the bandage every other day, or when it gets dirty. If it sticks to the burn, soak it in cool water until you can lift it off. Don't break the blisters or put any antiseptic on it, nothing but clean water. His body'll heal itself if you let it."

Ma nodded.

Dr. Lamont looked from Digger's tennis shoes to my cowboy boots. "George might've been so lucky because his rubber soles kept him from being grounded. If your boy in the leather boots had been holding that wire—"

Little Bit said, "Digger's always groun'ed."

Pa smiled and rubbed her head with the palm of his hand. "Not like Dr. Lamont means, li'l darling."

Driving home, Ma said, "Luke?"

Pa shook his head. "We open the restaurant tomorrow. We got to keep a better eye on the kids, is all."

That night we heard an automobile park by the restaurant. Pa looked through his and Ma's screen door, said, "It's Mrs. DeLyon. I'll see what she wants."

Ma was sitting on the bed with Digger in her lap. Little Bit sat next to them, and they were playing a game that involved touching Digger's toes and his nose and his stomach, and everyone laughing. Ma said, "Invite her in, if she can stay."

Pa nodded and headed out the door. There wasn't anything good on television, just Ed Sullivan's variety show with some stupid singers and dancers and nothing really good except for Topo Gigio, a little mouse puppet. I said, "I'll come, too," and I ran to catch up with Pa.

Behind me, Ma said, "Such brave guardians I have," and I felt good.

Mrs. DeLyon was standing beside her green sports car, petting Ranger. She was the only person who didn't work at Dogland that Ranger would not bark at when the sun went down. Ranger had his head turned to one side so she could scratch behind his ear, and his tongue lolled in bliss.

Pa said, "Don't want to make him too happy. He's supposed to be our watchdog."

"He's a most excellent watchdog."

Pa looked at her car. "Alfa-Romeo? Nice little rig."

"It gets me where I wish to go. You like sports cars?"

"Had a few before I got married. Now I drive whatever gets me where I need to be."

Mrs. DeLyon nodded. "Would you like to try her sometime? There are stretches of highway where she'll really open up."

Pa said, "I can tell."

I put both hands in front of me and twisted them together. "Vroom, vroom!"

They both laughed. Mrs. DeLyon said, "How've you been, Christopher?"

"Fine, ma'm. Me an' Ethorne are gonna go to Texas an' be cowboys."

Mrs. DeLyon nodded solemnly. "Ethorne would make an excellent instructor for anyone who wished to become a vaquero."

"A what?" I asked.

"A vaquero," she said. "It's Spanish. In English, you now say buckaroo. Your American cowboys learned the art of ranching from those who were there before them."

"I'm a buckaroo an' a buccaneer," I said. "Ethorne says so."

"Does he?" said Mrs. DeLyon. Ranger turned his head so she could scratch at his other ear. "Buccaneer's French. It means one who eats barbecued meat. The buccaneers lived on islands in the Caribbean and ate a lot of barbecued meat."

"I like barbecue," I said. "We went to the Ol' South Pit Bar-B-Q for dinner the other night, an' it was *good.*"

Mrs. DeLyon said, "Then you'd be a fine buccaneer."

"Digger got burned today," I said. "He might have a scar. But it's on his foot, so you couldn't see it 'less he goes barefoot. A pirate should have a scar here." I traced a jagged line on my cheek.

Mrs. DeLyon said, "Don't worry about what shows. It's what's inside that makes you a buccaneer."

Pa said, "Like barbecue."

Mrs. DeLyon said, "To start."

Pa said, "You're welcome to come inside, if you'd like."

Mrs. DeLyon shook her head. "I heard about Digger's burn." She reached into the car and brought out a gallon jug filled with clear liquid.

Pa said, "Doc said we shouldn't put anything on it."

"Except clean water," said Mrs. DeLyon. "This is from the springs. You'll find no purer water anywhere."

Pa laughed and took the jug. "You ought to be selling the stuff."

Mrs. DeLyon shook her head. "What is truly good, you do not sell—you share."

Pa laughed. "You and old Gideon."

"His heart is good," said Mrs. DeLyon.

"Oh, sure," said Pa. "I just wonder about his mind." He shrugged. "We're all entitled to our eccentricities."

Mrs. DeLyon said, "Even you?"

Pa said, "When I've got time for 'em. Right now, I've got a family to raise and a business to run."

Mrs. DeLyon said, "Yes." The word hung in the air for a moment.

"What about Ethorne?" Pa asked.

Mrs. DeLyon frowned. "What about him?"

"You've known him for a while."

"You could say that."

"Is he dependable?" Pa shrugged. "I mean, he's bright and he works hard. I can tell that. But I'm thinking of making him our cook, and you want to know your cook'll be there on time and ready to go most days."

"He used to drink," Mrs. DeLyon said. "But that was a long time ago."

"Then I think I'll offer him the job."

Mrs. DeLyon smiled. "I'm glad. I hope you will be, too."

"Ethorne's a good cook," I said. "He cooked for a Spanish man named Cowhead once, and he says he's been cooking for people ever since."

Pa laughed and rubbed my crew cut. "Only cowhead here is you, Kit Carson."

Mrs. DeLyon smiled and got into her car. Ranger looked up at her window as if he wanted to lean on her door, but he didn't. Mrs. DeLyon said, "Don't be a stranger," and started her engine.

Pa nodded, lifting the jug of water. "Thanks, neighbor."

When we went back into the house, Ma said, "What did Mrs. DeLyon want?"

Pa set the jug of water on top of a dresser near the sink. "Brought some spring water for Digger's burn."

"Oh, that's sweet," Ma said. "She's such a nice woman."

Little Bit said, "She's smart."

Ma said, "When you grow up, you'll be smart, too."

Little Bit nodded. "I know."

5

Things Seen in Color, Part One

E veryone woke early on the day that Dogland's restaurant opened. Everything that needed to be done in advance had been done: white wire tables and chairs stood on the restaurant's green concrete patio, and a sign painter had lettered each of the restaurant's windows: DOGGY GIFTS and SNACK BAR and GUIDED TOURS and BRING YOUR CAMERA! and ENTRANCE with a stylized hand with a finger pointing toward the restaurant's front door. Ma, Mayella, and Francine had scrubbed the front room and the kitchen "from top to bottom," as Ma proudly announced several times. She wished her mother could come to visit, because she knew the place would never be so clean again.

James had mowed the open land, and Ethorne had walked the grounds with a clippers and a knife, saying he had every intention of improving on perfection. Seth had lettered several sheets of poster board with the information that the kennels would not formally open until more dogs had arrived, people were welcome to stroll along the viewing path for free, and please don't feed the dogs.

We woke at sunrise. Because this was a special day, Pa left to pick up the workers. Ma dressed us, telling us to stay clean and not to talk to customers unless they talked to us first and to stay by the house and not to get in the way and to always be polite and not to yell or make noise unless someone wanted us to get in their car or go anywhere with them without Ma or Pa saying it was okay first, and then we were to scream for all we were worth.

Little Bit didn't want to wear a dress. When Ma asked if she wanted to be a little lady, she gave a decided "No," so Ma let her wear shorts, T-shirt, and cowboy boots like Digger and me.

While Ma helped Little Bit, I moved my rattlesnake fang from my plastic coin purse to my shirt pocket. I always kept it close, so if people did something bad, I could show it to them, and they would know that they had to be good right away, because if they were bad twice, I would scratch them with the fang and they would die.

We walked to the kitchen in the cool, dark morning and were just sitting down to bowls of Sugar Frosted Flakes when Pa entered, saying, "Thought you'd've finished by now."

Ma was dropping slices of French toast onto the griddle, where they spattered and sizzled. "Your daughter didn't like her wardrobe. She wants to be a cowboy, too."

Ethorne followed Pa inside. "My, you surely do look pretty today, Mis' Susan. Now, you get away from there and le' me do what I been hired to do, hear?"

Ma let him take the spatula. "You look very handsome yourself, Ethorne." She glanced at the others. "You all do."

I squinted. Pa didn't look any different; he wore a short-sleeved white shirt, tan slacks, and brown engineer boots that he had polished the night before. Ma's hair was pulled back with a white scarf, and she wore a new green cotton dress that I had never seen. Ethorne was dressed something like Pa, only he wore a black tie. His slacks were black, too, his socks were white, and his black shoes

gleamed like his hair and his moustache. Seth wore dark
sunglasses, a red-and-white checked shirt, black slacks,
and black loafers. James wore a striped white and blue
shirt, blue slacks, and black high-top tennis shoes. Mayella
wore a pink dress with white socks and low white tennis
shoes, and her hair was pinned up in a bun. Francine
wore the faded blue and white dress that she had worn
when she came looking for work, but a white plastic clip
on either side of her head held her hair back from her face.
She and James grinned when Ma spoke; Seth merely
touched his sunglasses and nodded.

I said, "I got to get my cowboy hat."

Ethorne said, "You got to eat your breakfast. Everyone
what counts knows you's a cowboy."

Pa studied Seth, James, and Francine. "You
shouldn't've dressed up to work with the dogs. Clean and
neat is all we ask."

"It's the first day," Francine said.

Seth looked at James. "Splash me and die."

"Splash you?" James said. "Li'l water won't hurt that
trash none. But these're my church clothes. You mess with
these, I kill you first, Jesus'll boot your black behind out
o' heaven, and Satan'll have you hunker in the brimstone
so folks won't notice them rags o' yours."

As Little Bit and I laughed, Ethorne said quietly, "I
think that's enough."

Pa nodded. "Dogs're getting hungry."

Seth touched his sunglasses again. "We'll get right to
it."

He and James jostled each other in the doorway.
James, the larger, got through first, as usual. Francine
looked at Ma, whispered loudly, "Don't Seth look pretty
t'day?" and giggled as she followed him out. Ma laughed,
too, but behind her, Mayella frowned.

Ethorne touched Mayella's arm. "Right now, Seth's
smarts has gone to his head. But he's bright. He'll figure
things out."

Mayella shook her head. "That boy is such a boy."

Ethorne said, "Mist' Luke? I was thinkin' 'bout the only way you'd make this restaurant prettier'd be if you had some flowers on the tables."

"You were, eh?" Pa looked like he was hiding a smile. He pulled car keys and a roll of green bills from his pocket. "Mayella, why don't you run up to Don and Roger's and see what ten dollars'll buy." Don and Roger ran the Suwannee River Gift and Floral, a business on the other side of the river that was full of things to look at and smell that only Ma liked.

Ma said, "Oh, Luke!"

Pa shrugged. "Isn't every day we start a business."

Mayella took the money and the keys. "I be right back."

Ethorne set breakfast before us. Ma bit into the French toast. "Mmm. You sprinkled this with cinnamon?"

"Simmon's good," Little Bit said.

"Simmanin," I corrected.

Ethorne said, "Yes'm. I was thinking on the specials today—"

Pa said, "Oh, oh. What'll this thinking cost me?"

Ethorne said, "Nothin' more'n what you spent. Tourists like Southern food. We can take that bag o' pecans that you bought fo' pecan pie an' offer pecan pancakes fo' next to nothin'—leastways, till we see if there's much call for 'em. An' the ground sausage for breakfast, well, come dinnertime, we can fry up a hamburger patty an' a sausage patty, put 'em on top of each other on a grilled bun, an' call it a rebel burger. They'd move at a fair clip, I reckon."

Pa nodded. "Maybe we ought to forget about the dogs and start a restaurant chain. Call it Ethorne's House of Good Eating. Have a big sign of you in a chef's cap, waving a spatula—"

"Mm-hmm!" I held out my empty plate. "More!"

Ma said, "More, what?"

Everyone was in a good mood; timing is everything. "More French toast!"

Ethorne grinned. Ma and Pa did not. Ma said, "More French toast, what?"

"More French toast, now!"

Ma and Pa frowned.

"Please?" I added. Ma and Pa smiled. Timing is everything.

Shortly after we finished breakfast, Mayella returned with a box of red and yellow carnations. While she and Ma cut the stems and put the flowers in water glasses, I walked around the restaurant.

A three-tiered glass display table had been placed in front of the dining counter. It held seashell ashtrays and night-lights, painted ceramic dogs including Boston terriers and dalmatians but no huskies or kuvaszes, dark glass beer bottles that had been melted into ashtrays, clear plastic hemispheres full of water that you could turn upside down to make snow swirl around palm trees or pretty women waterskiers, collapsible cups in red or green or blue plastic that you could carry in your pocket, white saucer ashtrays with DOGLAND or FLORIDA painted on their rims, saltwater taffy, porcelain mermaids on rocks looking wistfully into bowls that you could fill with water or use as ashtrays, spoons that said FLORIDA on their handles, ceramic alligators with hollowed backs where you could grow plants or flick cigarette ashes, thin beaded leather belts spelling Florida and showing the heads of American Indians in eagle bonnets, open-decked pirate ships that could be filled with sand to serve as ashtrays, table lamps made from cypress knees, Confederate war flags and caps and ashtrays, spice shakers with a West Highland white terrier for the salt and a Scottish terrier for the pepper, coiled rattlesnake ashtrays, and much more, all for tourists and not us kids. Pa had said if we touched any of it, we'd be spanked, no questions asked.

The Confederate soldier's cap tempted me, but there was only one thing I needed: a plastic sword with a golden hilt and a black sheath. Being a cavalryman was better than being a cowboy because you got to wear a six-gun and a saber both. I pointed at the sword. "Ma, can I have this, please, huh, please?"

Ma smiled. "If you're good."

I left the souvenir table and circled the restaurant. Things that dispensed things fascinated me; I wanted to pull the paper napkins out of their holders and tap repeatedly on the metal tongue that released plastic drinking straws from a burnished box. Things that turned fascinated me; I wanted to spin the round seats of the counter stools. Places I wasn't supposed to be fascinated me; I wanted to run behind the counter and play with the ice cream freezer and the milk shake mixer and the griddle and the shining steel refrigerators with their big latches. I wanted to go through the swinging doors into the kitchen and help Ethorne make pecan pies. I wanted to stay in the restaurant and play tag or hide-and-seek under the tables. I said, "I'm gonna watch TV."

Ma pointed at the highway. "Look, there goes the school bus." I watched a large yellow bus roll past as Ma said, "You'll be riding that in a year or two. Won't that be fun? Riding to school with all the boys and girls?"

"Mm-hmm," I said without certainty.

Mayella laughed. "My li'l brother loves to ride on the school bus. He ain't so big on school none, but he loves to ride that bus."

"What doesn't he like?" Ma asked.

"Oh, you know chil'en."

"Oh, of course," said Ma. "Do you help him with his homework? They say personal attention can make such a difference."

"Ain't no homework, ma'm. Hardly ever, leastways."

"There isn't? Why not?"

"Ain't no schoolbooks, ma'm."

"No books?" Ma turned and stared at Mayella.

"Yes'm. Well, there's some books, but there ain't enough. Not fo' all the chil'en at the colored school, you know. They takes turns takin' home the books they got. My brother, he's mighty careful with them books when it's his turn."

"No," said Ma, "I didn't know."

"The teacher, she learns 'em from magazines and such. I was meanin' to ask if them *Life* and *Newsweek* magazines you throw away, you know, if you'd mind if I took 'em for the colored school."

"No. No, I don't mind."

"That's good of you, ma'm."

"Oh, it's nothing. We'd just— That's all right. If there's anything we—" Ma bit her lip. "If there's anything you see us throw away, and you think someone can make use of it, you take it."

"Thank you, ma'm. I worked for one woman once, she fired me for takin' things from her trash. She said she didn't want to see none o' her things bein' used by niggers. That's why I ask."

"I see."

Mayella laughed. "I think she got mad 'cause I seen her hair-dye jars. Like ever'body think she was born with silver-blue hair."

Ma cocked her head to one side as she tied an apron around her waist. "Is that our first customer?"

I heard a car turn onto the gravel driveway. Mayella said, "No'm, that's Handyman."

"You can tell by the engine?"

Mayella shrugged. Ma hurried to the front door, opened the venetian blinds, said, "You're right," threw the bolt, then tugged the door open to let it rest against her hip. "Tom! Good morning! I thought you were bringing us some business!"

"No, ma'm." Handyman stepped out of his truck and grinned. "I brung you some he'p." A tall, somber woman with tanned, weathered skin came around the cab. She stood half a head taller than Handyman. Side by side, they reminded me of Jack Spratt and Mrs. Spratt.

Ma said, "Oh, good. You must be Mrs. Greenleaf."

The woman nodded. "You call me Lurleen, Mis' Nix."

She and Ma shook hands. Ma nodded at me. "Mr. Bigeyes there is Christopher, our oldest. That's Letitia building castles in the sandbox."

Lurleen nodded. Handyman said, "I'll be by 'round six." His wife nodded again. Handyman touched the bill of his cap as he smiled at Ma, then drove away.

Ma let the door close. "I'm Susan." She pointed toward the corner of the room. "That's Georgie." Digger was sleeping in the play area that Ma had built with the wooden slats from his crib. Pa had said we should hang a sign on it: DIGGER. BREED: UNKNOWN. DO NOT FEED. PET AT YOUR OWN RISK. Little Bit and I thought that was hilarious, but Ma had not laughed.

"And this is Mayella," Ma said.

Lurleen looked at Mayella for the first time. "I'm Mis' Greenleaf. You a Hawkins, ain't you?"

Mayella nodded. "Yes'm."

"Vernice's girl?"

Mayella nodded again, with a touch of a smile.

"Your mama washed for my mama. Now that I'm workin', I'll need a cleanin' girl."

Mayella's smile closed on itself. "I'm workin' here full-time, ma'm."

Lurleen looked at Ma. "She waitin' tables?"

Ma blinked. "Why, no. Mayella will be clearing tables and helping in the kitchen. Why?"

"Oh. I was wonderin', that's all."

Ma called, "Ethorne?"

He came through the swinging doors with an apron over his shirt and trousers. His arms and hands were white with flour. "Yes'm?"

"This is, ah, Mrs. Greenleaf. Lurleen, this—"

"Shoot, ever'body knows Ethorne," said Lurleen. "You fixin' sweet potato pie?"

"Pecan," said Ethorne.

"When you fix sweet potato, you make me one, hear?"

Ethorne nodded. "I best get back to it." He returned to the kitchen.

"Well." Ma looked at the clock, then smoothed her apron. "Let's open the blinds. We're ready for business."

I called, "I'll help!"

"Okay. Go outside and pick up all the litter you see, and I'll give you a nickel."

I grinned as she gave me a paper sack to put trash in, and I ran into the sunlight, leaping as far as I could from the sidewalk onto the gravel. Little Bit was squatting by the Heart Tree.

I said, "Whatchadoin'?"

"Talkin'."

"To the *tree?*"

She shook her head.

"To who?"

She pointed at a squirrel peeking around the side of the ancient live oak. When she pointed, the squirrel scurried out of sight.

"That squirrel?"

"His name's Ratatosk."

"Watta-tot?"

"Ratatosk."

"Ratty socks?"

"Ratatosk!"

"Ratta-tox. Pretty funny name."

Little Bit pointed overhead at the treetop. "There's a eagle."

"Where?"

She shrugged. "Ratatosk said."

"Oh." I kept looking, but I saw no eagles.

She pointed at an exposed root, next to one of Digger's toy trucks. "An' a big lizard lives there. Like a alligator."

"I don't see it."

"Way down. Underground."

I whispered, "In hell?"

She shrugged.

I sneered. "You're telling a story."

"Ratatosk said."

"Maybe Rattytocks is a big liar."

"He's nice. He wou'n't lie."

I considered that. "Is he friends with the eagle an' the gator?"

"Uh-huh. But the eagle an' the gator hate each other. Ratatosk runs up an' down, tellin' 'em what each one said."

"You shouldn't tell stories."

"He isn't tellin' stories. He's like a mailman."

"That's silly."

Little Bit shrugged. "Ratatosk said it's a job."

I shrugged, too. "I'm gonna pick up paper. If you help, I'll give you a penny."

A couple of cars of tourists arrived while we scoured the grounds. When we returned to the restaurant, Pa had come up from the kennels for a cup of coffee. I gave Ma my bag. There was almost nothing in it; Ethorne's crew had done a cleanup the day before that would've pleased Marine inspectors. Ma smiled. "That's very good. Here's a nickel."

"Thank you."

"And since you were helping," Ma told Little Bit, "here's a nickel for you, too."

"Thank you." Little Bit and I walked over by the front door to sit beneath the counter on the long footrest.

I said, "I'm gonna buy a Baby Ruth."

"I'm saving mine." She put her nickel in her red plastic coin purse, then held out her hand.

"What?"

She looked at her palm and shoved it closer to me.

"You got a nickel."

"You said you'd give me a penny."

"You got a nickel."

"You owe me a penny."

"Ma gave you a whole nickel."

"You said."

"Okay." I smiled. "Give me the nickel, an' I'll give you a penny."

"I'll tell Pa."

"You're not s'posed to tell stories."

"It's not a story. You said you'd give me a penny."

"You got a nickel. It's not fair."

"What's not fair?" Pa asked.

We both looked up.

"Well?"

"Chris said he'd give me a penny if I helped pick up paper."

Pa looked at me. "Did you?"

I nodded. "Ma gave her a nickel."

He kept looking at me. "Did Ma say she'd give you a nickel for picking up trash?"

"Yes, sir."

"And you told Little Bit you'd give her a penny for helping?"

I nodded again.

"Then you owe her a penny, don't you?"

"It's not fair."

"It's not fair to do what you said you would?"

"But she got a nickel from Ma."

Pa shook his head as he smiled. "You made your own bed, Chris. A man's got to stand by his word."

"When it's not fair?"

"Especially then."

I dug in my pocket for my leather coin purse with cowboys on one side and Indians on the other, took out one of three pennies, and handed it to Little Bit.

She grinned and dropped it into her coin purse. "Ha, ha."

I left without saying good-bye to anyone, crossed the gravel lot to the Heart Tree, and began kicking the bark with the toe of my cowboy boot. After a while, I saw the squirrel watching me. "Ratty socks," I whispered. As it ran away, I chanted, "Ratty socks, Ratty socks!"

"Master Christopher Nix. Wha'd that tree do to you?"

I turned. Ethorne was sitting on the back step, rolling a cigarette in one hand. "Nothin'."

"Then why you treatin' it that way?"

I shrugged.

"You like it if it treated you that way?"

I gawked at him.

He struck a match on the walk and put it to his cigarette, then said, "It's a livin' thing, ain't it? You think folks should hurt livin' things just 'cause they feel like it?"

"Stupid ol' tree." I kicked it as hard as I could, then walked toward the dog runs.

"Can't all live in Diddy Wa Diddy," said Ethorne.

I stopped, then turned back. "Where?"

"Diddy Wa Diddy." Ethorne blew a smoke ring. "You don' know 'bout Diddy Wa Diddy?"

I shook my head.

He smiled. "It's right close by, just a bit too far to get to. It's not a town, an' it's not a city. It's where the river runs with lemonade, an' hamburgers grow on bushes. If you hungry an' you sit down, fancy meals on plates come runnin' by, yellin' 'Eat me! Eat me!' till you got to pick one, knowin' the rest'll have their feelin's hurt."

I knew Ethorne was fooling, but Pa had said we should never say adults were lying.

"You don't b'lieve me?"

Pa had also said we should never lie. I shook my head.

Ethorne laughed. "What you don't believe, you can't find."

Little Bit had followed me out. She said, "Ethorne? Are you from Diddy Wa Diddy?"

He laughed, smiling at her. "Yes'm, Miss Li'l Bit. I was the Moon Regulator for a spell. But hangin' out the moon every night, that's some job. Ain't but once a month you got the strength to put up the full moon. An' then you so tired from the effort that you put up less an' less moon ever' night till they ain't hardly no moon in the sky at all. An' then you so 'shamed of yo'self that you put up a li'l moon, and then a li'l more moon, and finally you get so prideful, you put up the whole moon again. An' soon as you do that, *whoosh!*" Ethorne exhaled and slumped his shoulders. "You too pooped to pop. The whole thing jus' starts all over again. I up and left that job."

I said, "Who puts up the moon now?"

He shrugged. "Danged if I know. But I'm proud to've

turned it over to whoever's got it now. Don' you think they
doin' a fine job?"

I nodded. Little Bit said, "C'n we go to Diddy Wa
Diddy?"

" 'Fraid not, Mis' Li'l Bit."

"Don't you want to take us?"

He drew on his cigarette, then stubbed it out and
shredded the remains, letting the wind scatter the tobacco
and paper bits. "Oh, I'd take every living body in this wide
world there, if I could. But it's easier to find West Hell than
Diddy Wa Diddy." He looked up. Pa walked around the
corner from the front of the restaurant. Ethorne nodded.
"Mist' Luke."

Pa grinned. "We did all right this morning."

Ethorne smiled. "I do think so. Dinner an' supper yet
to go. I got biscuits in the oven 'bout ready to come out."

Pa's grin increased. "I might try one. Just to be sure it's
good enough for our customers, you know."

"Sure thing."

Pa looked at Little Bit and me. "Didn't I tell you not to
pester Ethorne when he's working?"

Ethorne said, "They ain't no bother."

"They know the rules."

"Well, I called to Chris, so I 'spect it's my fault."

"It's not a matter of fault. If you want to entertain them
when you're on break, that's your choice. Just so long as
it stays your choice. I don't want them taking advantage
of you."

"Us?" Little Bit blinked twice.

Pa smiled. "Poor Ethorne isn't as hard-hearted as your
old man. He's got enough to do without a pack of kids
hanging on his heels."

"But—" I began.

"Is that understood?" He used the voice that meant it
had better be. Little Bit and I nodded. "Good." Pa pushed
open the kitchen door and headed inside.

Ethorne stood. "Time for me to get back to work."

"Me, too," I said. Ethorne laughed and went inside.

Little Bit said, "Chris?"

I shook my head and ran up the tourist path.

Little Bit stamped her foot. "You're not s'posed to go back by the dogs alone!"

"Don't be a tattletale!" I yelled in a hoarse whisper, and ran on. I passed the WELCOME TO DOGLAND sign and raced through the Doggy Salon, my cowboy boots clattering on the concrete floor. Seth and Francine talked while James brushed an Afghan hound's long, fine hair. They looked up, but I didn't slow.

I ran to the northern working dogs, the Siberian husky, the Samoyed, the Alaskan malamute, the Norwegian elkhound. They jumped against the chain-link fences when they saw me. Captain stood against his gate, trying to lick my fingers as I lifted the latch. I had to push both the gate and Captain back to let myself in. I crawled inside his doghouse, which was dark and warm and smelled like Captain. He crawled in beside me, pressing me against the boards of his house. I put my arm around his shoulders. After a while, I quit crying.

"Pa's not fair," I whispered.

"Rr-ffh?"

"Pa likes Little Bit and Digger best."

Captain licked my face.

I yanked my head away. "Pa's bad." I touched the rattlesnake fang though my shirt, pressing it between my fingers and my heart. Captain lifted his head, pushing my hand away as he nuzzled my neck. I hugged him because I was cold. After a while, I slept.

I woke in darkness with someone calling my name. I peeked out of the doghouse. Captain, on the small porch, wagged his tail and licked my face. Ma was calling from the restaurant. I patted Captain good-bye and ran up the path, passing Francine, who was guiding a group of tourists. One said as I went by, "What a lucky boy." I didn't know or care who she meant.

On the green sidewalk, Ma stood with her arms akimbo. Her apron bore several stains, and a curl of her hair was clinging to her forehead. "Where'd you go?"

I pointed back at the pens.

"Never run off without telling your father or me. I thought you knew that."

I nodded.

"I don't want to have to tell your father."

I repeated my nod.

"We all have to work together if Dogland's going to succeed. I may not have as much time to spend with you as I wish, but that doesn't mean I don't want to be with you. You've got to help me, too. Okay, Chris? You're my big boy, you know."

I nodded a third time.

"Good. We won't tell your father."

I reached into my shirt. "Where's Pa?"

"Up front with two new dogs. I thought you'd want to see them."

"All right."

"What'd you take out of your pocket?"

I shrugged. "I got an itch."

We circled the restaurant. Pa and James were watching Digger stare at a low shaggy mass of golden hair with thick puffs like pompoms at each end. James wore a loose blue cotton shirt over his clothes. Seth and Francine, in the Doggy Salon, had worn similar shirts. All the grownups at Dogland were wearing work shirts or aprons, except for Pa. Pa was not like us. I watched him grin as he told Digger, "Hold out your hand, son. Whichever end sniffs it will be its head."

James laughed. "Dog like that wouldn' las' five minutes with no real dogs. But it sure is pretty."

"That's Ro-Ba," Ma said. "He's a Lhasa apso. Georgie, can you say Ro-Ba?"

Digger held his hand toward the taller puff, where hints of eyes and a nose lay beneath the hair. When Ro-

Ba licked his fingers, Digger waddled two steps backward, then sat. Ro-Ba licked his face, making him giggle. Everyone laughed, except me.

Little Bit said, "Digger figured which end was which, huh, Pa?"

"That's not very sanitary," Ma said, but she didn't move to separate Digger and Ro-Ba.

"The dogs have all had their shots," Pa said.

"Well," Ma said, "so has George." Then she heard herself and smiled.

Little Bit was crouching beside the second dog, who was also long-haired, short-legged, and golden, though he had a white crest on his chest and a smoother coat streaked with black along his sides and back. The hair on his head was swept back from his flat, black face. Little Bit held his leash in one hand and petted him with the other, saying, "Pretty funny, huh, Jo-Jo?"

As I approached Pa, Jo-Jo turned his small dark eyes my way, then bolted at me. His leash slid from Little Bit's fingers. She yelled, "Jo-Jo! Come back, Jo-Jo!"

The dog's eyes had fixed on mine. His mouth stayed grimly closed. I stood still. Ma lunged for Jo-Jo as he approached, but he slipped through her hands and bounded into the air, striking me in the chest.

I fell onto the gravel on my butt and elbows. Jo-Jo scrambled on top of me, sniffed my mouth, then scurried along my right arm. As I gasped and drew away, he batted my hand with the flat of his skull. The rattlesnake fang slipped from my fingers. Jo-Jo leaped after it, snuffled in the dust, then snatched up something in his teeth. A small crisp sound rang through a world of pristine silence. Then bits of fang fell from Jo-Jo's teeth, and he whirled proudly in a tight circle at my feet.

Pa ran toward me. "What in hell—"

Jo-Jo jumped back onto my chest to lick my face. I sputtered, and Ma laughed, saying, "Somebody's got a new friend."

Pa stopped beside her, then shook his head. "I thought Pekingeses were good with kids."

James smiled. "Looks like that one is."

I sat up, laughed, and patted Jo-Jo's head. His tongue lolled smugly. I stood, studying the ground.

"Lose something?" Pa asked.

By my boot lay half the fang, a brittle sliver of bone and nothing more. I shook my head. Jo-Jo stood on his hind legs to rest against my hip, so I scratched behind his ears. The morning was bright, warm, and clear.

A car full of tourists pulled into the driveway. Ma said, "I'd better check on Mayella and Lurleen."

Pa nodded, telling James, "Put the new dogs next to that Japanese chin. Seth should've hung up their signs by now."

"Sure thing." James took the leashes and started toward the Doggy Salon with Jo-Jo and Ro-Ba in tow.

I said, "Can I go along?"

Pa said, "You won't bother James?"

I shook my head.

"Come right back."

I smiled and ran after James.

Pa called, "Chris?" I turned, knowing he had decided I should pick up paper or sweep the sidewalk or pick up toys around the house instead. "You've been a big help. Your brother and sister are too little to understand that we all have to do what needs doing. I know that's hard on you sometimes, but it's all part of being the oldest." He shrugged. "I just wanted you to know that I'm proud of you, son."

I blushed, nodded, and ran after James. Jo-Jo and Ro-Ba pranced ahead of us. All of the small dogs in the Doggy Salon barked as we passed through. James laughed. "These li'l runts got hearts big as a St. Bernard."

Two pens had been left empty between Tano the Japanese chin and Pierre the Brussels griffon. While James studied the signs on the gates, Seth approached. "Got a problem, nigger?"

James nodded. "Mist' Nix said to put these dogs away."

"So?"

"This one's a Pekingese and that one's a Lhasa apso."

"Yeah?" Then Seth's voice softened. "Oh." He pointed at the signs. "You were prob'ly right. That 'g' in Pekingese is silent, and so's that 'h' in Lhasa apso."

James nodded, opened the gates, and let the dogs in. "Why they do that? They want it to be hard fo' folks to read?"

"There's lots of reasons. Foreign words brought into English hardly ever follow the usual rules. Course, English words hardly ever follow the usual rules, either. Most letters that're silent now were pronounced when the printing press was invented. Then people started sayin' some words differently."

"Should've started writin' 'em differently, too."

Seth grinned. "Hell, that'd make too much sense for white folks."

He and James left to see if any dog runs needed cleaning. I patted Jo-Jo and Ro-Ba good-bye, and ran toward the restaurant with my arms outspread, being a fighter jet in search of Nazi and Commie planes to shoot down.

Someone was talking as I flew near the Doggy Salon. The voice was Francine's, which made me expect to hear about Chihuahuas or Mexican hairless dogs and whether they were native to North America. But no one was in the main room when I stepped into the shade. I quit being a jet.

Francine was saying, "No, Cal, I can't."

The grooming and nursing area was enclosed by two wooden walls that stopped a foot short of the ceiling. Ma had hung strings of wooden beads in its open doorway, and the sign beside it said, STAFF ONLY. You could only see inside if you stood at the edge of the rear door of the Doggy Salon.

A short boy with blond ducktailed hair had backed Francine against the far wall. An acne rash decorated the side of his neck. His thin arms were dark, though a pale band of flesh showed beneath the cigarettes rolled into one sleeve of his white T-shirt. "C'mon, Francy. Tell 'em the baby's sick."

"I won't lie."

"Then tell 'em we're short on cash. That's God's truth, ain't it?"

"Well. Yes."

"So tell 'em. All I need's four-five dollars. Make it ten. Tell 'em to take it out on payday."

"No, Cal. You don't need it."

"You tellin' me what I need?"

"No. I ain't, honest."

"That's what I heard."

"Weren't what I meant."

"You tellin' me I'm hearing wrong?"

I barely heard her whisper, "No, Cal."

"Then what you tellin' me?"

"Nothin'."

He nodded. "Ten dollars. I'll wait here."

"No, Cal. I'll get paid on Friday, an' I'll give the money to my sister."

"Your sister?" He laughed. "Why'n hell'd you do that?"

"To pay her back for lettin' us live with her."

"Hell, don't she love you?"

Francine whispered again. "Yes."

"You heard her say it weren't no trouble to take us in."

"Till we were set up."

"Well, we ain't set up yet. You give her the next paycheck, if that's what you want. I need t' have some fun with this one."

"No."

"Ain't you s'posed to honor and obey me?"

She looked up. "I got to think of us, too!"

He slapped her hard, knocking her head back against the wooden wall of the Doggy Salon. *"I'm* thinkin'. Hear me? I'm thinkin' for us. Understand? Or you goin' to make me hit you again?"

I would have run for the restaurant and Pa, but that

meant passing through the building and close to Cal. Perhaps I would have done that anyway, or maybe I would have circled around the building to get Pa, if I had not seen Seth and James crossing the field toward the exercise pen.

I ran into the sunlight yelling, "Seth! James! Hurry!"

Someone came after me from the Doggy Salon. I ran as fast as I could, but Cal caught me by the back of my shirt and laughed. "What's got in your shorts, li'l fellow?"

"Help!" I yelled. "Seth, James, help!"

A button popped from my shirt as I struggled. When the hand released me, I ran forward, then turned to look up at Cal. He smiled easily; I thought he looked handsome like a singer on Ed Sullivan, like Pat Boone or Fabian except for the acne. He quit laughing to look over my head. "What you want?"

I followed his gaze. Seth and James stood side by side before us, saying nothing. Seth wiped his palms on his trousers. James merely stood there, watching. I ran to stand between them.

Cal said, "I'm talkin' to you niggers."

James squinted. Seth said, "You—"

James interrupted. "Mist' Nix's boy called us." He looked at me. "You wantin' somethin', Chris?"

"He hit Francine." I turned and saw her step into the doorway of the Doggy Salon. Behind me, I heard an intake of breath from Seth or James. I said, "Didn't he, Francine?"

She shook her head as Cal laughed. "That weren't no hit. She's my wife."

"I saw," I told Seth and James.

Cal said, "Ain't none o' your business, Yankee-boy."

"Is!" I said. "I saw! An' I was born in South Carolina. So I'm not a Yankee, neither!"

Cal smiled. "Shoot, that sets me straight."

Francine told Seth and James, "You best take that Italian Greyhound out o' the exercise pen. Mist' Nix said the blue tick hound and the Airedale seem to get along together. Try 'em out, but keep an eye on 'em, hear?"

After a long moment, James nodded at Francine. "Yes'm." Seth continued to stare. James touched his arm and turned him. "You one lazy fool, sometimes. Le's get some work done."

I watched them walk away. Cal said to me, "Ain't you got somethin' else to do, boy?"

I shook my head.

He laughed. "You best find somethin' to do."

"Francine's s'posed to be workin'," I said.

"I'm just talkin' to her durin' her coffee break."

"She's s'posed to be workin'. Pa says when people are s'posed to be workin', it doesn't mean they can do any da"—I modified his original statement—"rn thing."

Cal saluted me like a soldier. "Well, yes, sir!" As his posture relaxed, he said, "You don't mind none if I say g'bye to my very own wife, now do you, boss-boy?"

I looked at Francine. She wasn't looking at me. I shrugged.

"All right, then." He stepped close to her. "Don't you worry 'bout your lovin' husband gettin' all bored an' havin' nothin' to do the whole day long. I 'preciate you workin' till my luck turns. Which it will." He held out his arms. "Forgive me, sweet thing?"

She embraced him. "Oh, Cal, I'm tryin' to think what's best for us an' the baby."

"I know you are, honey." They kissed, and I looked away. He said, "Tha's my job, too, you know."

She said gently, "Cal?"

He cut her off. "That nigger boy botherin' you?"

She frowned. "Which nigger boy?"

"That one with the glasses."

"Seth Hawkins? Botherin' me?"

"I seen how he looked at you."

She laughed. "He di'n't! Him an' James, they ain't but perfect gen'lemen 'round me."

Cal squinted. "Not like some you could name?"

"Oh, Cal, I didn't mean it like that. You treat me the best."

"An' don't you forget it." He looked at me as he stepped away from her. "See you later, boss-boy."

"Bye." I watched Cal walk away. He looked back once and waved. Only Francine waved back.

She said, "You don' have to tell your folks 'bout Cal. He's my husband. They un'erstand that."

I shrugged.

"Your pa really say that about workin'?"

"He said it about kids. I don't know about grown-ups."

She laughed. "Grown-ups. Ain't you the sweetest thing?"

I looked down. "I got to go now. Bye."

A light midday rain began as Ma put Digger, Little Bit, and me at a table in the corner. The drizzle ended by the time Ethorne had fixed rebel burgers and french fries for us. I ate wishing for a Confederate soldier's gray cap with a shiny black visor. The lunch crowd kept Ma busy, but she returned to our table often, mostly to wipe ketchup off Digger's face and, sometimes, Little Bit's. I hated ketchup and I liked pulling paper napkins from the metal dispenser (which I justified by using them to wipe my face), so Ma didn't need to treat me like a baby.

The fun of eating in the restaurant lay in choosing your own food and watching the diners. Mostly they were tourists, young families consisting of parents and several kids, like our family, except most of them drove shiny new cars. Many were older couples like my grandma and grandpa. Some were solitary businessmen in rumpled suits, and a few were truck drivers.

Shortly after noon Ma pointed out the window. "Look, kids, a rainbow."

A stocky, gray-haired man with a patch over one eye entered the restaurant, followed by a larger red-bearded man. Behind them came a slender pale-haired man who held the door for a plump blond woman. The three men wore Hawaiian shirts; the woman wore a scooped-neck green sweater with white pedal pushers. They walked directly to a table near us kids.

The red-bearded man grinned at me. "What's good?"

The slender man jerked a thumb at the one-eyed man. "Ask him. He knows."

The one-eyed man looked at them, then said dourly, "Rebel burgers."

I rubbed my stomach. "They're *good.*"

Ma brought menus. "I hope the children aren't bothering you."

"No," said the pretty woman. "Not at all."

"They asked," I explained. "Are they strangers?"

"Strange," said the slender man, smiling at Ma, "but not strangers."

She smiled back at him as she told me, "It's all right to talk with anyone if your father or I are here." Then she asked the visitors, "Are you performers? I mean—"

"No," the one-eyed man said.

The slender man laughed. "Of course we are. Who's not?"

"Who's not?" The red-bearded man elbowed him. "That's good!"

The slender man winced, then indicated the one-eyed man. "He sees all and knows all. Beware, or he'll tell all. Too much knowledge of what's to come will make you glum indeed."

The one-eyed man nodded at Ma as he continued to study his menu.

"And this is the strong man, obviously. His feats of strength are only surpassed by his feats of feasting, as you shall no doubt witness."

The red-bearded man grinned. "Break anything for you, ma'm?"

"That," said the slender man, "is his idea of flirting." He glanced at Red-beard. "You know she's married."

"He does?" Ma asked.

"Of course," said the slender man. "From your care for these three fine children, and the ring upon your fair hand."

Ma smiled. "He's not the only flirt."

"No," agreed the one-eyed man.

The slender man nodded toward the blond woman. "And this is our beauteous companion. Some say she does nothing but bring joy to the world. I say, what's more important than that?"

The blond woman laughed. "He's shameless. Why do women love the company of heartless men?"

Ma said, "Because we can leave them easily?"

The slender man frowned. Red-beard elbowed him again. "Hah! Got you there!"

The slender man shrugged. "Perhaps I deserve it, for I am the honest deceiver." He turned his hand. A yellow rose lay there, which he held out to Ma.

She said, "I can't take that."

He said, "You must. It'll wither soon. Let its last days be in your company."

"It will not wither," said the one-eyed man.

"Is it synthetic?" Ma took the rose, smelled it, then offered it to Little Bit to sniff. Little Bit wrinkled her nose.

"It's as natural as any of us," said the slender man.

Ma touched the petals. "Silk," she told Little Bit, and then she asked the man, "Right?" He smiled. Ma said, "How'd you palm it? You're very good."

"Thank you. Would you really know the secret?"

Ma smiled. "No."

He nodded. "I thought not."

"He made it appear," said Little Bit. "Out of the air."

All of the adults laughed, so I did, too.

"We'll have rebel burgers," said the one-eyed man. "And fries and chocolate milk shakes. Except—"

"A green salad, please," said the woman. "And hot tea?"

"Of course." Ma took the order into the kitchen, and the four visitors began to talk in a language I did not know.

A box had arrived in the mail that Grandpa Abner had sent from his drugstore, so we kids amused ourselves at the table with its contents. For Digger, there was a metal bulldozer to go with his crane. He examined it with his fingers and his mouth. For Little Bit, there were crayons and a coloring book. I told her several times what colors things should be, but she ignored me. For me, there were comic books whose covers had been stripped and returned to the distributor for credit. I studied the bright pictures and figured out who were the good guys and who were the bad.

When Ma brought food, the four visitors ate with a great show of pleasure. Red-beard consumed three milk shakes, four rebel burgers, and two slices of pecan pie, then laughed when the slender man asked him if something had upset his appetite. Little Bit and I laughed, too; the slender man had asked with a wink at us.

Since I was concentrating on *Richie Rich, Kid Colt, Sad Sack,* and *Jimmy Olsen, Superman's Pal,* I paid no attention to the next table when they spoke in their language, but when the slender man spoke to the blond woman and laughed, Little Bit nudged me. She whispered, "There's a snake an' a wuff here. He said."

The slender man addressed us. "This is a land of snakes and wolves. Dogs are the children of wolves. Who are the children of snakes?"

The blond woman looked at him, then smiled and shook her head. "At the risk of adding fuel to the flames, I'll remind you we're only visitors."

He grinned. "Hardly, m'dear. Who expects us to sit in the wings when the last show's almost upon us?"

The red-bearded man shuddered. "We're stopping at the next bar we come to."

The one-eyed man said, "Yes."

Pa was helping behind the counter during lunch. While the one-eyed man paid their bill, Pa spoke with them about politics or business. The blond woman came back to their table where Ma was clearing away the dishes. "When he told you my part, he didn't say that I kept them from killing each other."

Ma laughed. "Men."

The blond woman smiled. "What is not acknowledged may still be valued."

Ma nodded. "A good life is its own reward."

The blond woman laughed. "I pray you continue to think so." She smiled at Ma, and then at us kids or maybe to Little Bit, who was coloring an oak tree with golden bark and leaves.

As the four were leaving, Mrs. DeLyon entered. She answered the slender man when he said something to her, then nodded and watched them disappear among the cars in the parking area.

Pa grinned at Mrs. DeLyon. They spoke together, and Mrs. DeLyon laughed, then came to the table that Ma had cleared.

Ma said, "Hi, Maggie. D'you know those people who just left?"

"Hello, Susan. When you've been here awhile, you'll find that many return to the springs and the tree."

"The Heart Tree? We ought to have Seth letter a sign for it." She looked at Mrs. DeLyon. "Have you thought about making a bigger deal about your springs? You know, putting up some signs, advertising? Luke loves water fresh from the earth. When we travel, he's always stopping to drink from natural wells or bathe in hot springs. Lots of people are like him."

"No," said Mrs. DeLyon. "Few are like him."

Ma smiled at Pa. "Well, that's true."

Mrs. DeLyon glanced at us kids. "How goes it?"

I shrugged and blushed. Little Bit said, "We got more dogs, Jo-Jo and Ro-Ba. Only they're little. What can they do if there's wuffs an' snakes?"

Ma said, "There aren't any wolves here, Letitia. And you know your daddy and I will protect you from snakes."

"Not me," said Little Bit. "Jo-Jo an' Ro-Ba an' Tano an' Mickey an' Sun-Up an' all the little dogs having to sleep outside."

"They protect each other," Mrs. DeLyon said. "Wolves will not venture near those who're united against them."

"Good," said Little Bit.

"You know how they bark if a snake comes around?" Ma added. "Snakes don't like noise and attention. All the

dogs'll be fine." She frowned. "Chris, were you telling stories about wolves and snakes?"

I shook my head.

"You don't want to scare your little brother and sister."

"This one?" Mrs. DeLyon nodded toward Little Bit.
"Nothing frightens her. She's an amazon."

"Am'zon," said Little Bit.

Ma laughed. "I'm afraid that's so. She's not afraid of the
dark or of heights, she'll taste any new food—"

I looked away. If Pa had been near, he would have
added, "She's braver than her big brother."

"Of course, you're not prejudiced," said Mrs. DeLyon.

Ma laughed. "Not a bit!"

I said, "A little bit," and the women laughed together.

"How old is your Digger?"

"George is two in February."

"He's very quiet."

Ma frowned. "Yes. Some children are slow."

Mrs. DeLyon shrugged. "Maybe he's chosen to keep his
own counsel."

Ma looked at Digger. "Maybe." She smiled. "I'm a very
lucky woman, having three wonderful children."

Mrs. DeLyon looked at Pa making root beer floats behind the counter. "Yes."

Ma followed her gaze. Mr. Drake held the door for several tourists who were leaving. As he entered, Ma waved.
"Artie! Hi!"

Pa came around the counter to grip Mr. Drake's hand.
"Artie, good to see you!"

Mr. Drake laughed with a hint of embarrassment.
"Likewise, Luke, likewise. Susan, how're you?"

"On a day like this? Fine, of course," Ma said. "Sit and
have a slice of Ethorne's pecan pie. On the house. This day
wouldn't have come about if it hadn't been for you."

Pa grinned at Mrs. DeLyon. "That has to go for you,
too, Maggie."

"I wanted to be your first customer," Mr. Drake said.
"But I see I'm a little late." The lunchtime traffic had light-

ened, but half of the tables were still occupied, keeping Ma and Lurleen busy.

"Well," Pa said, "you can be our first freeloader."

"Deal." Mr. Drake sat at the table near us.

"If you insist." Mrs. DeLyon took a seat across from Mr. Drake.

"We certainly do," said Ma.

"Susan, check on the paying customers," Pa told her. "I'll wait on our friends."

Ma smiled. "I'll be right back."

Mr. Drake grinned at her, then at me. "If it isn't Cowboy Chris. And Miss Letitia, and He Who Loves the Earth. How y'all?"

"Fine." Little Bit tucked her chin to smile up at him.

"All right!" I said.

Pa said, "You kids can run play if you want."

"I'm reading." I flipped a comic book page.

"I'm coloring." Little Bit touched up a blue woman who embraced a green man.

"R-rrn!" Digger slipped out of his chair to push his metal bulldozer around the base of the table.

"Kids," Pa said.

"Enjoy 'em," said Mr. Drake. "They'll be adults before you notice."

Mrs. DeLyon said, "How's Gwen?"

"Boy-crazy. Wouldn't be so bad if I liked the boy."

"Johnny Tepes," Mrs. DeLyon said. Mr. Drake nodded.

"Boys that age run a little wild. I did. Look at me now." Pa held his arms out wide and looked down at the apron he had donned when he went behind the counter.

Mr. Drake said, "There's wild, and there's wild."

"And it's easy to say, 'boys that age,'" said Mrs. DeLyon. "But those who behave as men must be held to the standards of men."

Ma arrived with a coffeepot and two slices of pecan pie. "Ethorne says you're to eat this up or his feelings'll be hurt."

"Small chance of that." Mr. Drake lifted his fork.

"How's Ethorne?" asked Mrs. DeLyon, blowing on her coffee.

"Fine," Pa said. "Missed work for a day or two, but nothing serious."

"Good."

"Must be nice," said Mr. Drake, "tending dogs and showing folks around who only want some entertainment while they learn a little about pets."

"Must be nice," said Pa, "selling houses and insurance to folks who only want some reassurance while they try to do the right thing for their families."

"You want to switch places," said Mr. Drake, "call me."

Ma laughed. "Luke happy in an office? You'll have a long wait for that call."

"Mmm." Mr. Drake took another bite of pie.

Mrs. DeLyon said, "The new woman fits right in."

We all looked over. Lurleen Greenleaf carried a round tray propped on one hand and one shoulder. The tray was loaded with dishes and glasses for a family of eight.

Ma nodded. "She hardly sits down to rest. I don't think Handyman appreciates what a worker she is."

Mr. Drake waggled his fork at Pa. "This is a good time to start a business in the South."

"Is it?" said Mrs. DeLyon.

"Sure," said Mr. Drake. "It's taken a hundred years, but the South's recovered from the War Between the States. We're moving on. You can thank the automobile and the air conditioner for that."

"Or curse them," said Mrs. DeLyon.

Mr. Drake smiled. "Those inventions will end New England's control of America."

Pa said, "John Kennedy's from Massachusetts. I figure he's got a better shot at the presidency than Nixon, Stevenson, or Johnson."

"I agree," said Mr. Drake. "But Kennedy's young, and a Democrat. He's not as tied to the old ways."

"Will the South vote for a Catholic?" Pa asked.

"We'd rather vote for a Texan like Johnson, but if the Democrats endorse Kennedy, the South'll vote for him. Folks down here may be Baptist, but we think a man's religion is his own business."

"Yet you teach it in your schools."

Mr. Drake grinned. "You know what our graduation rate's like? We don't force anyone to learn a thing."

"What about integration?"

"The chief justice carries the blame, not the president. You see bumper stickers saying 'Impeach Earl Warren,' not 'Impeach Eisenhower.' Everybody knows the president can't enforce integration, anyway."

Pa smiled without showing his teeth. "Who sent the National Guard into Little Rock so some Negroes could go to a decent school?"

Ma asked Mr. Drake, "Would you like to see the dogs?" She looked at Mrs. DeLyon. "We're not charging today."

Mr. Drake said, "I would," then turned his grin to Pa. "Don't know why I'm arguing. I'm one of the few around here who thinks integration's inevitable. What Yankees don't understand is you can't force it. Folks need time to get used to an idea."

Pa nodded as he stabbed a finger at Mr. Drake. "Ah, but will folks get used to an idea if they don't have to?"

Ma said, "Did I mention that we got two new dogs today?"

"No," said Mr. Drake, without turning his eyes from Pa. "The South's lived with slavery far longer than it's lived without it. We're talking patterns of behavior that're older than this nation. Can you change—"

"It'd be nice to see your dogs," said Mrs. DeLyon. "I'm a great admirer of hounds."

"Oh, good," said Ma.

Mr. Drake laughed. "Listen to me. I didn't come here to argue politics."

"Oh, Luke loves it," Ma said.

Pa shrugged. "Handyman and I get into it sometimes.

Only thing we agree on is it's nice to do a little fishing now and then."

Mr. Drake nodded. "He's in the Klan, you know."

"He is?" said Pa.

"Handyman?" said Ma.

"Oh," said Mr. Drake.

"Ku Klux Klan?" I said, then realized I had interrupted. No one noticed.

"Doesn't necessarily mean a thing," said Mr. Drake. "Poor whites down here join the Klan or the John Birchers like Yankees join the Lion's Club. I can't say I understand why grown men like to get together an' wear silly hats."

"Doesn't do much for me, either," Pa said.

I raised my hand.

"Yes, Chris?"

"Cowboy hats aren't silly, are they?"

Pa laughed. "Nothing John Wayne wears is silly."

"God's truth," said Mr. Drake. He set his fork on his bare plate and stood. "Tell Ethorne he did it again. You say you have two new dogs?"

"Jo-Jo an' Ro-Ba," Little Bit said.

"A Pekingese and a Lhasa apso," Ma said.

"Ah," said Mr. Drake. "Two demon-fighters."

"Say what?" said Pa.

"Lhasa apsos guarded Tibetan temples," said Mr. Drake. "And Pekingese were Chinese palace dogs, known as lion dogs or sun dogs. Very small ones were called sleeve dogs, because the nobility carried them in the pockets of their loose sleeves. Pekingeses are said to be descended from the Foo Dog, a kind of a household guardian god. Your family's spate of bad luck must be at an end."

Ma and Pa laughed. Mrs. DeLyon merely said, "Let's hope so."

Ma looked at us kids. "I think someone's getting tired."

"No!" I said, and added, "Ma'm," when I saw Pa's look.

"I'm not tired," said Little Bit. "I'm never tired."

Pa laughed. "She goes like a rocket right until her gas tank's empty."

Ma looked under the table. "Yes, it's naptime."

Digger was sleeping at our feet. I said, "I'm not tired."

"You don't understand, Chris," Mr. Drake said. "You have to take a nap so your parents can get some rest."

"But—"

"Christopher," Pa said.

I nodded and stood. Digger woke when Ma picked him up, but the evidence was against us. His beginning to cry made it worse. Ma patted his back. As he fell asleep again, she said, "I'll take them."

Mr. Drake said, "Need a hand? I used to be pretty good at getting kids to nap."

"Thanks." Ma passed Digger to him. Digger opened his eyes once, then rested his head on Mr. Drake's shoulder.

As the five of us walked away, Mrs. DeLyon asked Pa whether he found any similarities between working with horses and working with dogs. Pa laughed, said dogs and horses were nothing after working with kids, and the door closed behind us.

Mr. Drake paused on the green sidewalk. Little Bit and I stared at him. He was looking at Dogland, but there was nothing to see, just fences and bushes and flowers and buildings. He said, "You've done a lot in the past few months."

Ma smiled. "Luke has."

"Who decided to plant palm trees out front?"

"Well, we needed something to catch people's eyes."

"So, you did?"

Ma looked down.

"And who decorated the restaurant? I remember what it looked like."

"Well, Luke says I'm good with colors and things women worry about."

Mr. Drake nodded. "You are."

Little Bit said, "Ma writes all about the dogs, too. She wrote the signs on their doors."

"'Cause Pa told her to," I said.

Ma said, "Someone has to. We all chip in."

"Then you can all share the credit," Mr. Drake said.

"Okay," Little Bit stated, and Ma laughed. Opening the door to our room, she said, "You'll have to excuse the chaos. The restaurant gets the attention I'd like to give the house."

"Tell me about it." They both smiled at nothing I could see. Mr. Drake nodded at the masks of painted teak that hung on the cinder-block wall. One mask scowled, and the other grinned. "I like those."

"Luke and I bought them on our honeymoon. We took a boat down the coast of South America. It was a late honeymoon, actually. Luke was drafted right after we married, so Chris came along for the honeymoon."

"I did?"

Ma nodded. "Everyone said you were the prettiest baby."

Little Bit smiled at me. I made a face of disgust to answer her.

Putting Digger into bed, Mr. Drake said, "Sleeps like a baby 'possum."

Ma said, "He's the easiest child to care for that there could be."

"'Cept for me," said Little Bit.

"'Cept for me," I said.

"Oh," Ma said. "You'd better prove that by going right to sleep."

Little Bit rolled her eyes, nodded, and jumped onto her bed. "Okay."

"No fair," I said. "You tricked us."

"Oh?" said Mr. Drake. "Looks like you tricked yourself."

Ma smiled. "That's what Luke would say."

"Ah."

Little Bit lay on the bed with her arms folded like Sleeping Beauty in a glass case. Then she opened her eyes and said to Mr. Drake, "Tell a story."

"A story?"

"Don't bother Artie," Ma said. "And take off your shoes before you nap."

"Read something!" I said, running to find *The Little Engine Who Could.*

"Christopher!" Ma said.

I pumped my arms like a train. "Woo, woo!"

Ma said, "Maybe this wasn't such a good idea."

Mr. Drake said, "Oh, I reckon I'll just have to tell a story to quiet 'em down. Something boring that'll make it easy for them to sleep."

"Okay," said Little Bit.

"Here!" I handed him the book.

"No, a story out of my head," said Mr. Drake.

Ma glanced at him.

"Not one I made up. One that I know."

I set the book aside with extreme reluctance. "Okay."

Ma said, "You take off your boots, too."

I obeyed her as Mr. Drake said, "Now, I *could* tell you the story of the little insurance agent and the head office that wanted everything in triplicate."

His grin told me how to react. "Yuck!"

"No," Little Bit said. "Thank you."

"Or I could tell a story with knights on horseback and duels and magic and quests. Then you could dream about it afterward."

"That one!" I said.

"Okay," said Little Bit.

Digger rolled over and opened his eyes.

Mr. Drake took the chair by the sink, placed it in the middle of the room between the two beds, and sat. "This's also got love in it."

"Ee-yuck," I said.

"Oh, okay," said Little Bit, accepting that as the price of the story.

Ma, in the doorway beyond Mr. Drake, shook her head and smiled.

Mr. Drake began, "Once upon a time in a country far away, there was a sword stuck in a stone. Whoever could pull it out would become the rightful ruler of the land. And there was a boy—" I don't think we interrupted very often as we listened to the tale of the boy, the wizard, and the country that needed a good ruler. The boy was not as clever as the Little Tailor, or as brave as Jack the Giant-Killer, or as lucky as Jack who climbed the Beanstalk, but he pulled out the sword, married the queen, and gathered all of the knights of the country together to do good deeds under the direction of his best friend, the best knight in the world. "And that's probably all you need to know this afternoon," said Mr. Drake. "I'll tell you more some other time. It's a big story."

"They live happ'ly ever after?" asked Little Bit.

"Of course," said Ma.

Mr. Drake nodded. "Pretty happily, anyway. When the king died, he was buried in a hill. And when the country needs him again, he'll wake up and come help."

Little Bit smiled. "Did the king an' the queen have babies?"

"Well." Mr. Drake looked at Ma. "The king had a son."

Little Bit said, "What's his name?"

Ma said, "Somebody's trying to keep from taking her nap."

Little Bit said, "Does his son have a story, too?"

Mr. Drake laughed. "Yes. It's part of the story of what happened to the king and the queen and the best friend."

"An' the lady in the lake," said Little Bit. "An' the wise old magician."

"And all the others," Mr. Drake agreed. "Now you'd better go to sleep."

"All right," Little Bit said.

I asked, "What happened to the king's son?"

"Good try," Mr. Drake said. "Sleep, now."

I think I fell asleep immediately. I did not dream of the king, his sword, his city, or his knights. I dreamed that I ran through dark woods in a chase with rivals I could not see. Though I breathed deeply, I ran easily. My sleeping mind admired the grace with which I ducked low tree limbs and leaped puddles and logs. A deeper part of my mind wondered whether my running self was the hunter or the prey.

6

Things Seen in Color, Part Two

The day that Dogland's restaurant opened and the day of Dogland's official grand opening have merged in my mind, though they were separated by six months and two seasons. Our lives must have followed an uneventful course from December to May, excepting the interruption of Christmas. I'm sure at least one box came from Minnesota with clothes from Grandma and toys from Grandpa, and Ma must have commented on the strangeness of a Christmas without snow, and Pa must have been very busy and very quiet during the holidays. From Ma's holiday newsletter to family and friends, I know that Handyman and Lurleen gave us a bag of pecans, and Ethorne gave us a jug of cane syrup that he had brewed, and Mrs. DeLyon gave us a bushel basket of bayberry to decorate the motel unit that was our home.

In the world beyond Dogland, in the world that came in discontinuous bits from the television news that Pa watched every night and the radio that was always playing in the restaurant, these things happened in 1960: The

U.S. denied that it was sending reconnaissance flights over the Soviet Union until a U-2 jet was shot down and its pilot confessed. The Belgian Congo received its independence. John F. Kennedy won the Democratic nomination, chose one of his challengers, Lyndon Baines Johnson, for his running mate, and, at the age of forty-two, defeated Republican Richard Nixon to become the U.S.'s youngest president. John Updike's *Rabbit, Run,* Errol Flynn's *My Wicked, Wicked Ways,* and Harper Lee's *To Kill a Mockingbird* appeared in print. Albert Camus, Clark Gable, Oscar Hammerstein, and Mack Sennett died. Preminger's *Exodus* and Hitchcock's *Psycho* were released. The sixteen-year-old Bobby Fischer held the U.S. chess title. Floyd Patterson took back the world heavyweight boxing title. Cowboys rode the airwaves; the three TV networks carried twenty-eight westerns during prime time. Chubby Checker gave the world a new dance, the Twist; Little Bit, Digger, and I would twist naked in our bedroom to imaginary music after our nighttime baths, which made Ma laugh. "Itsy Bitsy Teenie Weenie Yellow Polka Dot Bikini" seemed to be on the radio whenever I passed it, which made me blush because it was a song about a girl who hardly had any clothes on.

The day of the restaurant opening and the day of the official grand opening are joined in a naptime dream. A dove flew near my ear and said, "Wake up, Chris. There's a surprise for you."

I rubbed my eyes with my fists. "Grandpa's here?"

Ma shook her head. "Not that kind of surprise."

Little Bit, Digger, and I followed her out of the house and through the afternoon sun. Had I been older, May and December could never have combined in my mind. In north central Florida late fall was a time for long pants and light jackets, while late spring was made for shorts and flip-flops.

The restaurant was empty except for a boy a little taller than me who sat at the table where we kids had eaten. He

looked up from a coverless comic book. Behind the
counter, Lurleen Greenleaf nodded at Ma, saying, "Mis'
Nix," as she walked over to stand beside the boy.

Handyman was stout and dark-haired, and Lurleen
was tall with strands of gray in her brown hair, but their
boy's hair was like wheat and his skin was the color of
lightly browned bread. He wore new blue jeans rolled into
a wide cuff at his ankles, scuffed tennis shoes, and a blue
short-sleeved shirt.

Lurleen set one hand on his shoulder. "This here's my
Jordy. Jordy, that's Chris Nix, an' Li'l Letitia, an' Baby
Georgie. You say hi to 'em now."

Jordy stood, smiled, and held out his hand. "Hi, y'all."

I did not move. Little Bit said, "Hi," and waved. Digger sat on the floor, then crawled toward the kitchen. Ma
caught him, aimed him toward the middle of the restaurant, and said, "Chris, go say hello to Jordy. He's Handyman's son. He got off the school bus here, all by himself.
Imagine that!"

Jordy offered his hand again. I shook my head.
"Those're my comic books."

"Chris!" Ma said. "I said he could read them. I didn't
think you'd be selfish."

"Grandpa sent 'em to me."

"Your granddaddy sent you comic books?" In Jordy's
voice was a generous acknowledgment of my good for-
tune. "Wish my granddaddy'd send me comic books."

"He doesn't?"

"Nary a one. He give me a quarter, once."

"My grandpa gave me five dollars once."

"Chris," Ma said, "don't brag."

"But he did."

"You still shouldn't brag."

"Five dollars?" said Jordy. "I'd get me a BB gun."

"You would?" I said.

"You're too young for a BB gun," Ma said.

"And so're you," Lurleen told Jordy.

He said, "I shot my daddy's twenty-two lots o' times. I shot a shotgun once, and I 'bout fell over." He rubbed his shoulder. "That thing kicks like a mule."

"It does?"

Jordy nodded.

"I never shot a gun," I said.

"And I hope you never have to," Ma said.

Little Bit said, "E'cept for cap guns."

Jordy said, "Me an' Daddy go huntin' t'gether. I near hit a squirrel once."

"Squirrel?" said Little Bit.

Jordy nodded. "Squirrel's better eatin'n chicken. Daddy says the price is right, too. I'm goin' t' hit one, next time we go out, you wait an' see. Mama makes the best squirrel you ever ate."

Lurleen shook her head. So far as I could tell, she did not know how to smile. "Now, Jordy."

"You do, Mama! It's the best ever."

She shook her head again. "Maybe you children should go play outside."

Ma leaned down to whisper in my ear. "You could show Jordy the swing set."

I said, "Do you want to see our swings? They're pretty good."

Jordy shrugged. "All right."

Little Bit said, "You got to push me."

I turned to Ma. "Just the boys."

Jordy said, "I don't mind pushin' her."

"Oh," I said. "All right."

Ma smiled as we walked outside. Little Bit made us both push her on the swing. She said if we pushed hard, she'd go all the way around the bar, but we couldn't push hard enough to prove that. When our arms had tired, I showed Jordy where there were big ants that you could cut in half with a plastic shovel, and both halves would wriggle. Then we played army with my plastic soldiers. Jordy didn't know how to divide them up and have them talk like on *Combat*. I taught him how the soldier with the pistol

could say things like, "You go around the hill. Be careful
so the Jerries don't shoot you," and the one with the rifle
could say, "Yes, sir, I will," and then he could go around a
sand mound, twisting from side to side on his plastic stand
as if he was walking, and the German with the machine
gun could say, "*Achtung!* I hear an American!" and shoot
him, but while the German was doing that, the American
with the pistol, a sergeant, could shoot the German in the
back. Since they were my soldiers, Jordy was the Germans. We took turns killing each other's soldiers, except
when Jordy tried to kill the American with the pistol and
only wounded him. When there were more Germans than
Americans, the American with the pistol threw a grenade
and I won.

"Let's play something else," Jordy said.

"Cowboys." I ran to the toy chest on our front porch.
"You're the Indian." I pulled out a cap gun with a broken
cylinder plate and a rifle with a missing hammer.

"Let's both be cowboys."

"I'm *Have Gun, Will Travel.*"

"Paladin," said Jordy. I squinted, then nodded. I never
thought of the character by his name. I thought of him by
the name of his show, his theme music, and his black gun-
fighting clothes. "Who'm I?"

I thought a second. "Rowdy Yates."

"*Wagon Train*? All right."

"Who'm I?" said Little Bit.

I didn't hesitate. "Miss Kitty."

"Then you're Marshal Dillon."

"I'm Paladin." I slapped the pistol at my hip. "Have
gun, will travel."

"Who's Marshal Dillon?"

"Digger."

"He's little. Jordy, be Marshal Dillon."

Jordy blinked at her. "Chris said I'm Rowdy."

Little Bit nodded. "I'm not playing."

I shrugged.

Jordy said, "She can be something, can't she?"

I shrugged again. "She's got long hair. She can be a Indian."

Little Bit said, "What about Digger?"

"He can be a Indian, too."

Digger grinned. He became Sitting Bull, which wasn't much work for him, and Little Bit became Geronimo. Her job was to tell Sitting Bull where the pale faces were, and then ambush them while Jordy and I rode through the desert carrying the mail to Fort Apache. Digger died every time you shot him, which would have been fine if after every death he had not immediately sat up and giggled. Little Bit never died and would only be wounded for a minute or two, even though Paladin never missed and Rowdy Yates only missed sometimes. Finally I said Little Bit was dead and I wasn't going to play anymore, so Jordy and I won, even though Little Bit said, "Did not!" and she and Digger began a war dance around the sandbox.

Ma was sitting in a lawn chair under the Heart Tree, reading a paperback. I ran and asked if I could show Jordy the dogs. She said that was fine if we stayed on the path and didn't go inside any of the pens and didn't bother any of the visitors or any of the help. I nodded, yelled, "C'mon, Jordy!" and we ran away, shooting Indians in the bushes. "Pow! Pow! Pow!" We hit every single one.

Jordy wanted to look at each dog, so I told him about them as we walked. "That's Bambi, the basenji. They don't bark, an' they keep themselves clean like cats. They're real old. There were basenjis in ancient Egypt with the pharaohs. Bambi's one of my favorites."

"You said that English Bulldog was one of your favorites."

"Bo-Peep's one of my favorites, too. That's Percy. He bit Pa real bad. Ethorne says you don't want to scare Percy." I held out my hand and let Percy lick my palm. "Here's the dachshunds. Whizkee's a wire-hair, an' Sun-Up's a reg'lar dachshund, an' Pandora's a miniature wire-hair, and Dev is a long-hair. Dev's the best, or maybe Whizkee." Whizkee's name made us both smile.

"You can play with 'em whenever you want?"

I shrugged. "That's Driver. He's a otter hound. I don't know what he oughter do." Jordy laughed, and I started running. "C'mon! This's Ranger. He's a kuvasz. He caught somebody once when Pa wasn't here. A drunk."

"He's dang big."

"Yeah." I stuck my hand in the cage and scratched Ranger through his thick white coat.

"Can I pet him?"

"If you're careful," I said, though it was daytime. Ma said Ranger loved everybody when the sun was up and only our family when the sun had set.

"Boy." Jordy grinned as Ranger let him rub his skull. "That's sure some dog."

"He guards the kings of Hungary."

"Where's that?"

"In Central Europe," Seth said behind us. "It's ruled by the Soviet Union now and hasn't had a king for some time."

Jordy and I turned. Jordy stared. "You sound like a white man."

"That's Seth," I said. "This is Jordy. He's Handyman's boy."

Seth rolled his eyes. "Should've guessed."

"How come they haven't got a king?" I asked.

"In Hungary?" Seth picked up a hose and turned on the faucet. "They got rid of them. If your oppressors won't free you, you've to free yourself." He began rinsing the dog runs. The Great Dane's run always needed cleaning. "That's what America's about, isn't it?"

Jordy and I shrugged.

Seth said, "We don't have a king, do we?"

I shook my head. "President."

"That's right. Americans don't like kings."

Jordy said, "Martin Luther King."

Seth smiled. "Well, we like one."

"No, we don't!" Jordy said. "He's a Com'nist agitator!"

As Seth frowned, I said, "King Arthur."

Seth laughed. "Yeah, we like fairy-tale kings who're so far removed from reality that they quit looking like heartless exploiters of the poor."

Jordy and I squinted at him. He waved his free hand. "Forget it. Want a sprinkle?"

Jordy glanced at me. I grinned and nodded. Seth flicked the hose, catching us in its cool spray. Jordy ran for the restaurant and I followed, laughing.

As we approached the Doggy Salon, Pa and James pushed two wheelbarrows full of warm dog food onto the viewing path. Pa let his wheelbarrow down and squatted in front of us. Jordy came to a stop, but I kept running. Pa caught me around the waist with one arm, then stood, turning me upside down and setting me back on my feet. James, Pa, and I all laughed.

"So," he said. "Who've you outlaws been terrorizing?"

Jordy pointed toward the pens. "That nigger got us wet! He turned a hose on us like we was dogs!"

Pa's face settled like the scowling mask on our bedroom wall. James watched with no expression that I could see. Pa looked at me. "That so?"

I looked at Jordy, then back at Pa and nodded.

"Why?"

"He asked. I said okay."

Jordy glanced at me. "Di'n't ask me."

"Asked us both. I said it was okay."

"I di'n't say no nigger could squirt me."

Pa said, "Seth sprinkled you?" Jordy and I nodded, and Pa did, too. "Well, then, Jordy, show me your wounds."

Jordy blinked.

"He must've hurt you pretty bad, seeing how upset you are. Just show me what he did, and I'll call the sheriff."

Jordy looked down at himself, then held out his shirt, showing the damp speckles.

"That's it?"

Jordy nodded.

"What'd he get you with?"

"Water," Jordy said.

"What else?"

"Just water."

"You melt in water?"

Jordy shook his head. James grinned, but Jordy did not.

Pa said, "I don't think the sheriff's going to be impressed."

"A nigger hosed water on me!" Jordy seemed angry enough to cry.

"His name's Seth," said Pa.

"I introduced them," I said.

Jordy said, "My daddy'll make him sorry."

James looked at Pa. Pa rolled his eyes and said, "That's what you want? To hear Seth say he's sorry?"

Jordy shrugged.

"Come on." Pa pushed the wheelbarrow to the first set of dog pens and left it sitting in the path. We walked on while most of the dogs ran back and forth, baying their bafflement at our priorities.

Pa said, "Seth?"

Seth took his thumb off the end of the hose he was using to clean the bull terrier's pen. "Mr. Nix?"

"I understand you sprayed these boys."

Seth glanced at me. I had hurt him, though I did not know how. He nodded.

Pa said, "Why?"

"I thought Chris liked it. I didn't hurt his clothes, did I?"

"No." Pa did not look at my clothes. Even if Seth had stained my best shirt, Pa would not have noticed or cared unless Ma had insisted on buying a new one. "Jordy had his feelings hurt."

We stepped up beside Pa. Jordy nodded.

"Oh? Sorry," Seth said. "Thought you both'd like a splash of cold water."

"I did," I said, and Seth grinned.

"That good enough for you?" said Pa, looking at Jordy.

"Good enough for what?" said Seth.

"Oh, the kid thought he needed an apology."

Jordy nodded. Seth squinted, saying, "Needed?"

James had followed us. He said, "Tha's fine."

Seth said, "What'd I do that needed an apology?"

"You 'pologized," James said. "That's the Christian thing to do, right or wrong."

"Wait," said Seth. "Wrong? We're not talking about a matter of right or wrong here. There was just a misunderstanding—"

"Tha's right," said James. "A misunderstanding, that's all. Chris, I seen a heap o' Indians on the far side o' your house. I bet you an' Jordy could capture 'em all if you headed out runnin'."

"We wanted to help feed the dogs."

Jordy nodded.

Pa said, "I don't know—" as Seth said, "Even if I splashed you again?"

Jordy cocked his head, then said, "I reckon."

All three men smiled. Pa said, "You two can help feed the dogs so long as you obey Seth and James. If I hear you disobey 'em, you can't come out here anymore. Is that understood?"

"Yessir," Jordy and I said together.

"All right, then. Seth, take the other wheelbarrow. I'll be up front if you need me." Pa studied Jordy and me. "If either of these two act up, let me know."

"We won't," I said.

Pa walked off. Jordy and I followed Seth and James back toward the wheelbarrows. Seth said, "New York City. When I get enough for a bus ticket and a bit to live on, I'm going to New York City."

"Ethorne be disappointed," James said.

"He can come to New York, too."

James smiled. "They's worse things to be called than college boy, y'know."

"Education's something you do, not something that's done to you."

"There's places where it's easier to do. Ever'body 'xpects you to go back next term."

"Everybody expects a lot."

Jordy said, "You really go to college?"

Seth looked down at him. "Why, yes. I really do."

"That's why you talk like that."

"Must be."

Francine was escorting a last group of tourists around the path. Seth looked at them, then glanced away with a grimace. To my surprise, Francine's husband listened at the back of the tourist group, which consisted of an old lady in Bermuda shorts, several children much older than me, three or four adults in sports clothes, a well-dressed dark-skinned couple, Cal Carter, and a taller, stockier youth with Brylcreemed hair. Cal wore wraparound sunglasses, a pink short-sleeved shirt, and crisp new jeans.

I stopped walking. Jordy stopped beside me. We listened to Francine saying, "Dogs that hunt their prey by sight are called sight hounds or gaze hounds. They tend to be large and fast, like the Irish wolfhound or the greyhound. Dogs that hunt by smell are called scent hounds. They tend to be small and tenacious, like beagles, basset hounds, and dachshunds."

She led the group from one set of runs toward another. Cal, following behind, told his companion, "Bet you'd like to take one o' those out one night, see what she could do."

The other said, "Wouldn't a li'l dachshund be more your speed?"

Cal pointed toward Francine, or perhaps just past her, at one of the racing dogs. "Nice lines on that bitch there, Victor. Looks like she could move out right quick, don't she?" He smiled and raised his voice slightly. "You can tell she gets what she's after in the dark."

The older woman in Bermuda shorts looked back at him. Francine turned to say, "Sight hounds and scent hounds both get around better in the dark than most folks.

But these dogs aren't available to rent or borrow. If you're thinkin' on buying one—"

Victor shook his head. "My ol' man's the banker. Wouldn't I just be checkin' the collateral on your loan?" When he said that, I could see that Victor looked like a younger, softer version of Mr. Dalton, who always gave us lollipops at the Dickison State Bank.

Francine said, "I really don't think so."

Victor Dalton nodded. "What's to keep someone from wandering in here to borrow a dog he fancied?"

Francine frowned, narrowed her eyes at Cal, and told Victor, "There's always someone on the grounds. Wait'll I show you the watchdog they let out at night."

Cal said, "Victor's real concerned that dogs're treated right. Which you'd understand if you ever seen him on a date."

Victor grunted in anger or amusement and shoved Cal's shoulder, knocking him off the path. Cal splashed into a shallow puddle and stood there, water seeping into his brown loafers, as he grinned. "Yep, Victor's the original hound dog. Your boss ought to put him on display."

Francine said, "I ought to put you two out to run in the exercise pen is what I ought to do."

Victor frowned. Cal smiled, stepped out of the puddle, and neatly wiped his loafers on the grass, telling Francine, "Folks're waiting, Mis' Tourist Guide. I'd hate to think they's waitin' on us."

The rest of the tourists had stopped in front of the next set of dog runs. Francine hurried to stand before them, resuming the speech that Ma had written. Jordy listened as though she were Captain Kangaroo, Shari Lewis, and Bozo rolled into one, but I knew the script by heart.

The two dark-skinned visitors did not look like the Negroes I had seen. Their hair was straight, and their clothes were conservatively expensive, and they carried themselves with an unthinking assertiveness that marked them as foreigners before they spoke. While the rest had waited for Francine, the dark couple had watched the dogs, but as Francine's speech began again, the man smiled at Victor Dalton, who frowned, and then interrupted Francine. "What do you do with the dogs who die?"

The woman in Bermuda shorts gave him a scathing glance. Francine said, "Ain't no dogs died, mister."

He turned his hands palms up. "All creatures are mortal."

"Why, um, yes, sir, that's Bible-true," said Francine. "Now—"

"Have you considered a canine mausoleum?" said the man. "With statues or paintings of the dogs who had died? A monument would require less care than living dogs do, and offer no waste or noise."

"Dogland's about livin' dogs, sir," said Francine. "Folks on vacation don't pay to look at no dead critters."

"Oh? What are dinosaurs but dead critters? What are all museums but monuments to the dead, lacking only the presence of the dead themselves? And often there's the token representative in the form of a skeleton or two of an animal or an Indian."

"Yes, sir," said Francine. "But we have to keep going if we're going to finish the tour before dark."

I glanced at the sky. The sun was low. My stomach said it was almost time for dinner.

The dark man looked at the sun. "Ah, yes. The transition time."

The woman beside him smiled at Francine. "Then I shall not ask whether you plan a Catland next. There are almost as many distinct breeds, you know."

Francine shook her head. "Ma'm, you can't never know what Mr. Nix'll be thinkin' on next." Before either visitor could speak again, she lifted her hand toward the next dog. "This is Spots, our dalmatian. No one knows where the breed's from or how old it is. Their name comes from Dalmatia, where they were first known."

The dark couple looked down the walk. A pale man strode toward us. He wore a white cotton suit that glistened in the late afternoon light, and the set of his jaw said that his days were always wonderful. Most of the tourists, including the old woman in the Bermuda shorts, smiled at the sight of him, and so did I. Cal's and Victor's glances were almost reverential.

The dark couple nodded curtly to him and returned their attention to Francine, who was saying, "Dalmatians were known for running alongside horse-drawn vehicles. That's how they came to be associated with fire engines. The breed's got many nicknames, including the plum-pudding dog and spotted dick."

"Spotted dick," Jordy whispered, and we ran ten or twenty feet away, giggling.

Behind us, Francine told the blond man, "You're welcome to join this tour, sir."

He answered, "Thank you, but I'm used to making my own way." I looked back. His voice had no accent in this land where everyone spoke like a Northerner, a Southerner, or a foreigner. His voice might have been mine.

Seth called, "So, you two want to help or not?"

I turned. Seth approached us with a heavy-laden wheelbarrow. A small tin pot was stuck into the dog food like a giant's medicine-spoon. While Jordy and I had dallied, Seth and James had begun their way around the ring of pens. I saw James across the circle, slopping dog food onto the cement run in front of Bambi, who wagged her coiled tail as she buried her nose in the food.

I looked back. The tourists had moved on. The pale man was not with them. If he had walked quickly, he might be on the far side of the circle, hidden by trees and bushes.

"Yeah!" said Jordy.

I returned his grin. "Yeah!" We ran to join Seth, then followed him as he opened each dog's gate to slap food onto its run. Jordy and I laughed at how happy the dogs were to see us, and we laughed again when Seth had to hose down the Great Dane's dog pen before he could put food in it. After the feeding was done, I wanted to help hose down pens in the final cleaning of the day, but I heard Ma call Jordy and me.

"Bye, Seth! Bye, James!" I yelled.

"Bye, now!" called Jordy.

"Bye, y'all," James answered as Seth shook his head.

Handyman was waiting behind the kitchen with Ma when we arrived. "Hey, boy," he said.

"Hey, Daddy," Jordy said. "Guess what? A nigger squirted me."

Handyman glanced at Ma.

Jordy laughed. "It were pretty funny, Daddy. He squirted Chris, too, but Chris run faster'n me. You should'a seen him go, Daddy. Dang, it were funny!"

Handyman shook his head. "I'm glad they're amusin' you, boy. C'mon. It's time to get on home, have your momma cook up some food."

"She's a hard worker," Ma said.

Handyman made a soft grunt of acknowledgment. "We best be goin'."

Ma looked at me. "Chris, you'd better go wash. Dinner'll be ready soon."

"Dinner?" said Jordy. "You ain't had dinner, and it's nigh on suppertime already?"

"That's what we mean," Ma said. "What you call dinner, we call lunch, and what we call dinner, you call supper."

"Dang," said Jordy. "That's a funny way to do things."

"Yankees," said Handyman, and he and Ma smiled.

I waved and ran back to our house. When I'd finished in the bathroom, I charged up the path toward the kitchen. The pale man in the white suit stood by the Doggy Salon, watching me.

"Christopher," he said, and I stopped.

"We're not s'posed to talk to strangers."

He smiled. "I'm no stranger to anyone." He looked over; Little Bit was leading Digger from the house to the kitchen. "I'm at home everywhere."

"Yes, sir," I said.

Little Bit looked at us and kept walking. I wondered if she would tell, then decided that there was nothing for her to tell. I was talking to a tourist. Pa said we were to be polite to tourists.

"You don't know the meaning of your name," the man said.

I shook my head.

"Christ-bearer. One who carries Jesus Christ in his heart."

"Oh." I grinned. Ma and both Grandmas would like that.

"Names do not define you, Christ-bearer. Some people try to live up to their names, some try to live down to them, some never know that their names are anything more than a sound that draws them. Do you love Christ, Christopher?"

I recognized a trick question. Jesus was a tall man with long blond hair who wore a white bathrobe and flip-flops. He liked children and sheep. If you said you loved somebody, people would laugh at you and you'd blush. "I love Ma, Grandma and Grandpa, Grandma Tess, and God."

Christ was also God. The pale man saw how clever I had been, and he laughed. "Do you believe in Christ, Christ-lover?"

Christ-lover sounded like nigger-lover, though he said it nicely. I said carefully, "Yes, sir."

"And Santa Claus?"

I nodded again.

"And Superman?"

That was another trick question, yet he smiled. I had seen pictures of Superman in comic books. I nodded again.

"Who's stronger, Superman or Jesus?"

I shrugged.

He laughed. "I wonder that myself."

"How'd you know my name?" I asked.

"Names are easy to know. Is there anything you want?"

"A Fort Apache play set."

"You have a Fort Apache play set."

"With two, I could put 'em together an' make a great big fort, an' a whole bunch of Indians could attack."

"Ah. It's good to know what you want. What would you do if you ruled the whole world?"

"I'd give everybody everything they want," I said. "Then I'd have a big war."

"You are wise beyond your years." He looked up. I followed his gaze. Ma had stepped out from the kitchen.

"Come," said the pale man. "I'll walk with you a ways."

"All right."

"Does everyone in your family believe in Christ?"

Wondering if he was a preacher, I nodded.

"Your mother?"

"Yes, sir."

"Your sister?"

"Yes, sir."

"Your brother?"

Digger prayed whenever we prayed. "Yes, sir."

"Your father?"

"Ye—" I began.

The pale man did not notice that I stopped. He smiled at Ma as we approached the restaurant. "Mrs. Nix. You have a very wise son."

Ma looked from me to him. "Yes. Sometimes a little too wise for his own good."

"He knows a great deal about your dogs, among other things."

Ma laughed. "Were you showing off, Christopher?"

"No, ma'm."

She asked the pale man, "Are you local?"

"Everywhere I go. Call me Nick. Nick Lumiere, at your service." He held out his hand.

Ma took it. "How do you do? I'm Susan Nix."

"Yes. I know your neighbors well. Mrs. DeLyon and the Reverend Shale."

"They're good people. Everyone here is."

"The Reverend sometimes, ah, wanders from his establishment. He hasn't bothered you, I trust?"

"Oh, no," Ma said quickly. "I'm not worried about him. You can tell he means well."

Mr. Lumiere smiled. "Mrs. DeLyon does not wander. I understand she's been especially friendly to your family, to you, to your husband."

Ma frowned, then laughed. "Oh, my, yes. I don't know how we would've gotten by without her."

"Perhaps I may be able to help you, too."

"Oh?"

He nodded. "If there's anything you need, call on me."

"Ah, I'm afraid—" Ma began.

"Yes?"

"I didn't catch what you do."

"Well," said Mr. Lumiere, "I'm not the law; I'm a lawyer, which gives me advantages in any company. I assure you, there's nothing I don't know about a contract."

"Artie Drake recommended someone for the filing we've had to do," Ma said. "My husband's happy with him."

"Artie Drake wouldn't recommend me," said Mr. Lumiere. "But he can't say I've been less than honest in my dealings with him."

"Oh! I didn't mean to suggest—"

"I know you didn't," said Mr. Lumiere. "I should leave you to your dinner. Ethorne's your cook."

Ma nodded.

"Some people fear a colored cook might spit in their food or worse, to take some small revenge on the white race."

"Yuck!" I said.

"But Ethorne isn't one of those, of course," said Mr. Lumiere. "I trust you'll have a good meal."

"Thank you." Ma narrowed her eyes.

"Good day," he told her. Then he grinned at me. "Go for what you want, Christopher. Don't let anything stand in your way. That's the path to happiness."

I nodded. Ma took my hand as if I were a baby, and we watched Mr. Lumiere stroll away. His white suit caught the light of the setting sun and shimmered like molten gold. Then he stepped around the corner of the restaurant, and I shook my hand free, saying, "I'm four an' three-quarters, Ma." She laughed, and we went into the kitchen.

Mayella and Ethorne bustled within a world of heat and steam that smelled of soap and the satisfaction of hunger. They glanced at us as Ma pulled me through the swinging doors into the front room. Mr. Shale said, "Hello there, young Christopher. I closed the hamburger stand a little early to share this joyous day with your family, and to bring you a present."

He sat at a small table by a window with a Bible before him and a cardboard box beside him. I felt everyone looking at me—Pa behind the counter, Jordy, Handyman, and Lurleen in front of it, Francine and Cal at one table, Little Bit and Digger at another, and people I did not know at others—but I did not have time to be embarrassed. The promise of a present drew me toward the box as Mr. Shale reached in with hands that were brown and gnarled like the roots of the Heart Tree. Something struggled, then mewed in fear and fury as he caught it. He lifted out a small gray-and-black-striped kitten.

"Ooh," said Little Bit.

"What a darling kitty," said Ma, and then she glanced at Pa.

"Mine?" I said.

Handyman laughed. "Ought to have a mouser bigger'n a mouse."

Mr. Shale said, "The Lord brought him to my doorstep, safely past gators and boars who would've swallowed him like Jonah. Maybe one did swallow him and cast him up here, safe in the hands of those who'll preserve him."

"Maybe not," Pa said.

"Or maybe not," Mr. Shale acknowledged. His cheeks were speckled with white day-old whiskers that rippled as he laughed. He held the kitten toward me. "Take him. If it's all right with your folks."

I reached out. "Gently," Mr. Shale said.

The kitten swatted my finger, drawing blood. "Ow!" I said. As Ma hurried over to me, Mr. Shale said, "He's just reminding you he's got a mind of his own. You have to show him you'll be nice."

"All right." I took the kitten into my cupped hands. He looked up at me as I stroked his forehead. When he lapped at my cut finger with his rough tongue, I smiled.

"Ain't that sweet?" said Lurleen.

"What you goin' to name him?" asked Jordy. "Tom? We got a Elvis and a Fabian. You could name him Troy."

"Tiger," I said.

"Isn't orange," Pa said. Ma was watching him. He shrugged. "I see how much say I've got in this."

Handyman grinned. "Ain't that the way of it."

Little Bit held out her hands. I twisted away from her and said, "No. Tiger's mine."

Mr. Shale laughed. "Thought that swipe might've shown you he's not a toy. Keeping a live thing is a grave responsibility. That's what it means, for something to be yours. You have to care for it."

I nodded.

Pa said, "You'll like cleaning his box."

Ma said, "Chris is a little young—"

Pa said, "I wouldn't call scooping cat turds a great challenge for a boy."

"I'll clean his box," said Little Bit.

"No!" I said. "I will."

Pa laughed. "Wouldn't've called it a privilege, either."

Tiger twisted in my hands. I started to put him back in the cardboard box, but Digger patted Tiger's head, and he began purring a loud, deep note. I let Little Bit pet him, too, and she smiled at Tiger and me.

"Y'know," Handyman said, "maybe we ought to eat here t'night. We both had a long day."

Lurleen nodded, smiling down at Handyman's scalp, as Jordy said, "All right!"

Pa said, "Did I mention the employee discount?"

"Employee discount?" said Cal, and we all looked at the table he shared with Francine.

Francine began, "Now, Cal—"

Pa nodded. "Francine gets it, too." He sounded less happy than he had been a minute before.

"Thank you, Mist' Nix," Francine murmured.

"Nothing to thank me for," Pa said. "It comes with the job."

Handyman claimed an empty table. "Then I reckon we better take advantage of Lurleen's benefits. What've the kitchen niggers cooked up?"

"Ethorne," Pa said, "has cooked up pork chops, mashed potatoes, sausage gravy, and green beans with bacon. That to your liking?"

"And biscuits." Mr. Shale lifted one to illustrate. "The lightest I've ever seen."

"They're good," Little Bit said, and I noticed that she and Digger had dirty plates in front of them.

"Sounds fine," said Handyman.

"Me an' Jordy'll eat together," I said.

"May Jordy and I eat together?" said Ma.

"Shoot," said Handyman, "once you've seen the young'uns eat together, you won't ask to eat with 'em, Mis' Nix."

Jordy laughed hard, so I did, too. Ma said, "Christopher."

"May Jordy and I eat together?"

"Yes, you may."

"And Tiger?"

Ma smiled. "We'll fix something for him." She glanced at Lurleen. "Sit. I'll take your order."

Lurleen nodded as if she'd been hit. "Yes'm."

Everyone admired my cat, even Cal, who said as he returned to his table, "I see you popped a button, boy. You ought to take better care o' your clothes."

Ma looked at me. "Oh, Chris. How'd you do that?"

I shrugged.

"You need to be careful with what you're wearing."

I nodded. Cal said, "You listen to your mama, boy. You want to be a nice young man."

Francine said, "Cal."

"Well, don't he?"

Ma said, "Yes, he does, and he will be."

"All right then," Cal said with satisfaction.

Once Jordy and I had been convinced that Tiger should be allowed to sleep, we began to play a game that involved sliding sugar packets across a Formica tabletop. When Ma brought our dinner, she put a saucer with a scrambled egg into Tiger's box and said, "I suppose you two didn't even notice the gorgeous sunset."

"No, Ma," I said, and giggled because Jordy did. Sunsets were for girls.

A long, dark convertible turned into the drive. Its lights struck the front window, turning the world into a fireburst, then snapped off, turning it into nothing at all. Mr. Shale blinked, then smiled when Gwenny Drake came through the door. I did, too. Mr. Shale's smile disappeared when a pale, dark-haired boy in a Levi's jacket stopped at the door frame.

"Y'all still open?" the boy asked politely.

Pa looked at the clock. "Sure. Come in, have a seat."

"Thank you," said the boy, and he stepped inside.

"Your date?" Pa asked Gwenny.

"Oh." She covered her mouth and laughed. "A friend. Johnny Tepes, this is Mr. Nix, and that's Mrs. Nix"—Ma waved as she carried dishes into the kitchen—"and that's my boyfriend, Christopher, and my best girlfriend, Little Bit, and my best little buddy, Digger."

I blushed and looked down. Jordy kicked my leg with a tennis shoe. "Your girlfriend?" he whispered.

I nodded.

"Wow. She's pretty."

"How d'you do." Johnny Tepes stood by the cash register, surveying the room. Cal and Francine ignored him.

"Fine," I mumbled.

"Fine," said Little Bit, walking up to Johnny with Digger's hand in her own. "Gwen's nice."

"I know," said Johnny, smiling at Little Bit.

Ma laughed. "My daughter's just a little bit protective. There's a clean table in the corner."

"Thank you." Johnny began to cross toward it, then paused. "Ethorne's cooking for you?"

Ma nodded.

"Ah. He remembers how I like my food."

"Oh." Ma frowned, then smiled. "All right. Sure. Do you know what you'd like? Or does Ethorne know that, too?"

Johnny glanced at Gwenny. She said, "A rebel burger, fries, and a Coke."

Johnny nodded. "Likewise. Water instead of Coke, please."

"Got it." Ma headed into the kitchen.

Gwenny tucked her menu between the napkin dispenser and the ketchup, then looked around and smiled. "Francy!"

Francine had been staring into the window, perhaps at the gathering night, perhaps at Cal's reflection in the glass. "Oh, Gwenny. Hi!"

Cal pursed his lips and said in falsetto, "Oh, Gwenny, hi!"

Jordy and I laughed. Francine swatted the air before Cal's nose, saying, "Oh, you," then turning back to Gwenny, "You know Cal, don't you?"

Gwen nodded. "You caught the long bomb in the second quarter of the Trenton game last fall."

He grinned. "Why, yes'm, that was me."

"This is Johnny," Gwenny said.

"Hi," said Francine. "I keep thinking we met, but I must've just seen you around."

"No doubt," said Johnny.

"Where around?" said Cal to Francine.

"Around. You know."

"No." Cal kept smiling. "I don't know. You tell me."

Francine glanced at Johnny and back at Cal. "Maybe at the Roadhouse when you took me the other night?"

Johnny shrugged with a smile. "I'm often at the Roadhouse."

Cal asked Francine, "So, you givin' boys the eye when I step outside?"

"No, Cal—" she began.

"If she has," Johnny said calmly, "I haven't been lucky enough to get that eye."

"She's my wife, you know," Cal said. "I'd like to know what makes you think—"

"Here you go!" Ma announced, bringing a tray of food toward Francine and Johnny. Setting a plate before Johnny, she said, "Very rare, no onions or garlic, right?" Johnny nodded. Ma looked at me. "What's the show, Mr. Bigeyes?"

Everyone looked at me. I pointed at the metal canister in front of Francine. "Can I have a milk shake, too?"

"Well—" She glanced up as a set of headlights hesitated on the highway, then came slowly down the driveway toward us.

"Huh?" I said.

Behind the counter, Pa set down his cowboy book. "My. Busy day."

"Hope it keeps up." Handyman stood. "Dinner was all right, but I sure don't see why anyone thinks that nigger cooks so good."

"Maybe your stomach's upset," Lurleen said. "It was just fine. Jordy! Go wash up."

"Yes'm," he said, sliding out of his chair with a last peek into Tiger's box. The kitten had eaten most of the egg and gone to sleep.

The new arrival parked. Little Bit stared at it, so I did, too. In the dark parking lot a man got out from behind the driver's seat. I could see several other people inside the car, but its ceiling light did not come on, so the people stayed shadows. Light from the restaurant surfed over the car's new paint.

The man stopped at the front door and knocked. Pa frowned, then waved his arm. "C'mon in! We're still serving!"

The door opened, and a man stood in the entryway in a business suit as dark as his skin. He said softly, "Excuse me, sir. Do you have a colored rest room?"

Pa studied him for a long instant, then said, "Yep. Two. The men's is colored blue, and the women's is colored pink."

The visitor's gaze flickered a fraction. I had not seen that he was not meeting anyone's eyes, until he looked at Pa's. Pa pointed at the door on the far side of the room. "They're on the side of the building, through there."

"Thank you." The visitor stepped back into the night. In the silence, we all heard him say, "It's all right," and a woman with two small girls got out of the car.

Ma was looking at Pa. He said, "What, is the women's green? I can't remember these things."

The black family hesitated at the front door. The woman wore a nice dress, as did the girls, who wore clothes cleaner and newer than mine or Jordy's, as though they had dressed for church or a family reunion. The man said, "Hurry up, now," and walked his family through the room.

Johnny Tepes looked away and said, "Good burger," to Gwenny, at the same time that Francine said, "We best be goin'," to Cal, who answered, "What's the hurry? Ain't but one openin' day. Don't you want to stay till closin'?"

A family of tourists went to the cash register and paid their bill. Pa said, "Hope you'll stop in the next time you're by." The parents nodded curtly and left without speaking.

The black man was the first to return from the rest rooms. He said, "Thank you," again to Pa.

Pa said, "That's what they're there for."

The man smiled a bit. "Do you fix take-out food?"

Pa nodded. "We fix take-out food and take-in food. I figure once you buy it, you can take it where you please." He gestured toward a table. "We're staying open a little late tonight, if you folks would like to sit down. It's our first official day of business."

The man looked at the woman and girls as they came into the room. "I—Thank you. Yes. We would. We had car trouble this afternoon, and we'd hoped to be home by now—"

"You haven't eaten?" Ma said. "These children must be starving."

"I think they are," said the woman.

"Yes, ma'am, we surely are," said the younger girl with a solemn nod.

"Well," said Ma. "We'll have to do something about that, won't we?"

Handyman shook his head once, then said, "Bye," and walked out. Lurleen and Jordy followed him. I waved at Jordy. Lurleen tugged his arm before he could wave back.

Cal said, "I seen enough," and he and Francine left after she told me to take good care of my Tiger. Johnny and Gwenny stayed in the corner, whispering as they ate. The black family ate their dinner and left. Pa said something about the man ordering the most expensive meal on the menu. Ma did not respond to that. After Johnny and Gwenny had gone and Pa had turned the OPEN sign around, he went to the cash register to count the day's receipts, and Ma took Digger and Little Bit back to the house since it was past their bedtimes.

I stood by the window, holding Tiger and looking out into the night. Ethorne, mopping the floor, came up to me and said, "What you see out there, Christopher?"

"Nothin'."

Ethorne nodded.

I added, " 'Cept that man on the road."

"Oh? What's he look like to you?"

"Like you, Ethorne. Only tall. An' he's got a black coat an' a high black hat."

"He's a Negro?"

I nodded.

"What's he doin'?"

"Just dancing."

Ethorne nodded. We stood there, looking out into the moonlight. The dancing man waved and went into the trees. I waved back. Ethorne said, "You seen him go?"

"Yes, sir."

"Well. It's been a long, long day, Mast' Chris. You best do like your kitty cat and get you some sleep."

7

Learning to Swim

We gave Tiger swimming lessons in our plastic wading pool. I taught the kitten the way Pa taught me: I threw him into water where he could not stand, and I watched, ready to grab him if he went under. Tiger did not thrash desperately like me. He merely paddled urgently for the edge of the plastic pool with his head high and his thin legs churning. Little Bit said, "Dog paddle," and we all laughed. "Tiger paddle," I said, and we all laughed some more, even Jordy. That was probably when Ma noticed the kitten swimming lessons and stopped them.

Our swimming lessons happened in two places. When Pa took us, we went to Hawkins Springs behind Mrs. De-Lyons' Fountain of Youth Motor Inn. When Ma took us, we drove to Mermaid Springs State Park, where we would sometimes meet Mr. Drake.

I liked Mermaid Springs better because I felt safe there. Ma could not swim, so she never made me jump off a dock into deep water, and she always insisted that I wear an orange Styrofoam cylinder on my back like a skindiver or

spaceman. Ma usually sat on a towel on the grass near the
beach, reading a magazine or a book while tanning her
legs. Every now and then she would call to us not to go
too far or not to splash each other. When she wore her one-
piece red swimming suit, she would come in up to her
waist, then lower herself to her shoulders, being careful
not to get her hair wet. On the rarest occasions, she would
wear a swimming cap and float on her back in the shallow water. Often she stayed in her shorts and shirt, adding
sunglasses and removing shoes as her concession to summer and the beach.

Mermaid Springs had several floating docks that enclosed a shallow area for little kids, and concrete and tile
changing rooms with wooden benches and flush toilets,
and a concession stand that sold hot dogs and soda pop
and Popsicles, and a walking bridge that arched over a
narrow neck of land where the springs flowed into a broad
area of weeds and saw grass on its way to the river. There
were always a lot of people at the state park, little kids like
us, big kids like Gwenny Drake, and adults like Ma and Mr.
Drake.

Besides the orange Styrofoam cylinder on my back, I
often swam with a giant red plastic baseball bat that I
clutched like a shipwrecked sailor clinging to a spar. Once,
when neither Pa nor Mr. Drake were along, I was hanging
on to the bat and swimming in the shallows by the walking bridge. Little kids played on both sides of the neck of
land, and bigger kids swam back and forth. I decided to
swim to the far side, but the current caught the plastic bat
and began pulling me toward the bridge.

I screamed. I can't remember now whether I was afraid
that I would drown, or that I would lose the red bat, or
that something among the weeds and lily pads would get
me. Maybe I only knew that something stronger than me
was taking me someplace I did not want to go.

Kids and adults stared at me. I don't know if the lifeguard was far away, or if there was no lifeguard on duty
that day. All I know is that Ma, fully dressed, ran into the

water and grabbed me before the current drew me under the bridge.

I had an early lesson about appearances at Mermaid Springs. The first time I went into the enclosed swimming area, I saw a man several yards from shore in water up to his neck. I looked at him, wondering if there was a drop-off and trying to remember if undertows were only something to worry about in the ocean. The man saw me and smiled and rose, higher and higher as water cascaded from his skin until he stood knee-deep in what had clearly been shallow water all along, yet had been mysterious depths until he stood.

Mermaid Springs was named for manatees. Ma read about them from plastic-covered papers tacked to a rough, outdoor signboard that stood under its own small roof. "See?" Ma said, pointing at a drawing of something that looked like a cross between a pig and a catfish. "That's a manatee. Sometimes they come into the springs, but I don't see any now."

"Will they get us?" I asked.

Ma pointed at a wire fence in the water around the swimming area. "They can't get through that. Even if they could, they wouldn't hurt anyone. It says they don't have any natural enemies. They're mammals. Do you remember what mammals are?"

"Like us," Little Bit said.

"Air breathers," I said.

Digger nodded.

"The Latin name's *Trichechus manatus*. That's pretty hard to say, huh? There are three kinds of tricky-chee-dee." She laughed as she stumbled over the name, so we laughed, too. "*Trichechus manatus* is found from central Florida to northern South America. That's the manatee that lives in the river here. There's also Trickycus *inunguis* in the Amazon River and Trickycus *senegalensis* in West Africa. Manatees can get to be as big as fifteen hundred pounds. That's thirty times what you weigh, Chris."

"A lot," I said.

"And the adults range in length from eight to fifteen feet. They mate, um, we'll skip that. The mothers have one baby at a time, like humans do."

"Can we see a baby?" asked Little Bit.

"We can look for one," said Ma. "Manatees eat plants in slow rivers and along the coasts. They help keep the waterways clear of vegetation. They're part of a group called sea cows, who're over fifty million years old. That's a lot of zeroes. That's before there were people."

"Dinosaurs?" I asked.

Ma shrugged. "Maybe. People used to hunt sea cows for meat, for their hides, and for oil. The biggest was Steller's sea cow, which grew as long as twenty-four feet. It was hunted to extinction thirty years after being discovered in the Bering Sea in 1741."

"Stinkshun means there's no more," I said.

"Not of that kind of sea cow, anyway." Ma kept reading. "Manatees are in danger because they float near the top of the water, and people in motorboats hit them with their propellers. Some of them are scarred on their backs from being hit many times. Poor things."

"That's not fair," said Little Bit.

"Well, people have to use the river, too," Ma said. "You like riding in boats, don't you?"

Little Bit nodded.

"Manatees don't see well. They communicate by touching their muzzles together."

"Like a kiss!" Little Bit said, laughing.

Ma smiled. "And when they're alarmed, they make a chirping sound. Like squirrels, maybe. They live alone or in families of up to fifteen or twenty. You know why this place is called Mermaid Springs?"

"Uh-uh," Little Bit and I said.

"When sailors on the ocean saw sea cows swimming far away, they thought they were mermaids."

I pointed at the drawing of a manatee. "Don't have any hair. Or arms."

Ma ruffled my crew cut. "If you'd been the lookout,

you'd've told them these were sea cows, not mermaids, right?"

"Right," I said.

"Mercows," said Mr. Drake behind us. "Moo. Glub glub glub. Moo."

We all laughed, even Ma, who said, "Fancy meeting you here. Is Gwenny along?"

"Oh, she's getting too old to be escorted by a senile, decrepit male like her dad." He grinned. "How're things?"

"Fine." Ma shrugged. "But I don't know if I'll ever get used to the climate. I expected the heat and the bugs. I never thought I'd be fighting mold and mustiness, trying to keep our shoes and luggage and belts wiped clean—" She brushed her hair back from her forehead and laughed. "Well. I came here to leave that behind, and here I drag it along with me."

Mr. Drake nodded. "How about a cold Co'Cola to help you forget?"

"Okay!" said Little Bit.

"Well," said Ma. "That'd be nice."

So we all had Cokes. I drank mine to the last drop, though it did not taste like grape or orange or anything good. Digger and I made sand castles while Ma and Mr. Drake sat on the beach, talking about concrete block houses and girls to help with housework and what the local schools were like and the funny things that children did. Ma wore her swimsuit and sunglasses that day, and Mr. Drake, in green swimming trunks and a red Hawaiian shirt, had white gunk on his nose like lifeguards wore (which he told me was war paint). In the sunlight, his hair and hers were the same color as Digger's and Little Bit's, which meant they were the same color as mine. As Ma spread tanning oil on her legs, Mr. Drake smiled and said it was a glorious day.

There were no Cokes to be had at Hawkins Springs, or flush toilets and tiled changing rooms, or young lifeguards with white grease stripes down their noses, or laughing crowds, or signboards about the history of the land or the native wildlife. There was an abandoned wooden dance hall, and the overgrown foundations of Fort Hawkins, and the springs itself, an eternal frigid bubbling of water from a bowl in the earth that might have been thirty feet deep and thirty feet across. A simple wooden platform had been built at the edge of the shore for divers, and a thick knotted rope hung from an oak for those who wished to swing out over the cool boil and drop into its heart.

The ground around the springs was steep and grassy, roughly terraced by roots and a few boulders. A wide swatch of saw grass under glass-clear waters bounded the side of the boil that gushed toward the Suwannee. Perhaps twenty yards from the boil was a steep sandy beach and a gently sloping sand-bottomed swimming area. Beyond that lay a region of weeds, lily pads, dark mud, and cypress knees.

Sometimes we rode in the station wagon to Hawkins Springs, but when the weather was warm and Pa was not in a hurry, we walked along the side of the road and past the Fountain of Youth to a dirt road that wound back beside the motel units to the dance hall, an old rectangular structure of weathered wood that had windows without glass or screens and entrances without doors. For decades, people had come to dance, drink, and make love there, moving desperately together beneath the rafters to the beat of a visiting band. Ma and Pa probably looked at the building and saw the ghosts of couples who passed warm evenings beside the springs. To me, it was only the old dance hall. It needed a saloon's swinging doors and the scars of gun duels to acquire romance in my eyes.

The dance hall overlooked Hawkins Springs and a sliver of the darker waters of the Suwannee that flowed past the springs' mouth. A narrow dirt path, rutted from rains, ran in front of the dance hall and down to the sandy beach. We would change into our swimsuits in the shadows of the echoing dance hall, leaving our clothes on the floor, and run down to the water with our towels and toys. Pa usually dropped his shirt and towel in the sand as he ran, kicked off his flip-flops, and plunged in, splashing all about him while we kids giggled, and diving underwater when he was in up to his thighs.

A raft made of wooden planks and metal barrels had been anchored between the beach and the mouth to the river. Sometimes Pa's dive would carry him under the raft, and he would rise on the far side out of our sight. Before we could worry, he would return, climbing onto the raft, then diving toward us, or merely swimming with strong overhead strokes back to where he could stand and ask why we hadn't gotten in the water yet.

Little Bit would laugh, and sometimes they'd start to splash each other while Digger, giggling, rocked up and down, slapping the water and splashing himself more than anyone else. Sometimes Pa would pick us up and toss us out into the water. Little Bit would shriek in delight, but I would try to hide my dread. I hated the shock of being swallowed by cold water, the pain of having water run up my nose, the sight of a rippling roof of water above me that might recede infinitely as I sank farther and farther until I was a corpse at the bottom of the sea, drifting for-ever among rippling grasses, sunken galleons, and curious mermaids.

We rarely saw other people at Hawkins Springs. When we did, they were usually guests of the motel who we'd never see again. If Mrs. DeLyon was working outside or by the office window when we passed, she and Pa would nod or wave. We almost never saw her at the springs, but once, when Pa was diving down into the boil to touch the opening where water gushed from the earth, the opening where two scuba divers had entered and never returned, I saw Little Bit looking up at the dance hall. Mrs. DeLyon stood there, watching from the shadows.

Little Bit waved to her, and so did Digger, and so did I. She laughed, said, "I have better things to do," then

walked down to join us. Digger, Little Bit, and I sat by the
shore where Pa had told us to stay while he swam. As Mrs.
DeLyon removed her sunglasses, Pa shot to the surface,
shaking his head like a seal. He looked toward us, and I
cannot guess what he saw; his glasses were tucked into a
grassy ledge along with a translucent plastic box that held
a white bar of soap. He said, "Hi, Maggie. It's invigorat-
ing."

"Yes," she agreed, "it is."

Pa swam to the shore and climbed up to join us. His
tanned biceps worked smoothly in both enterprises. I
thought of my thin pale arms and wished I could be an
adult instantly by one supreme effort of will. Pa said, "Taking a break?"

Mrs. DeLyon nodded. "I shouldn't be."

Pa said, "Sometimes you have to." He began soaping
himself, passing the bar over the hair on his chest and
stomach.

"Shampoo monster," Little Bit said, and Mrs. DeLyon
covered her mouth to hide a smile.

Pa said, "Seems to me I'm not the only one who needs
to wash. What would your ma say?"

Little Bit said, "I don't need a bath."

Pa said, "Queen Elizabeth the First took a bath every
year, whether she needed one or not."

Little Bit laughed. "I took one this year! I took one this
year!"

Pa shook his head, and, sudsing his legs and feet, told
Mrs. DeLyon, "I think our first mistake is teaching our
children to reason."

"It would be nice if we could," Mrs. DeLyon replied.

"Yeah. That's why we make the mistake of trying." Pa
handed the soap to Digger. "Soap all over."

Digger nodded and followed Pa's example. Pa said,
"There's nothing like this after a hot day's work." He
stepped to the bank and dove. When he came up again in
the center of the springs, he treaded water lazily and said,
"Care to join us?"

"Some other time." Mrs. DeLyon replaced her sunglasses.

"I like washing in the springs water," Little Bit said. "It's fun."

Mrs. DeLyon nodded at her. Pa called, "Meet you at the shallow area!" and began swimming across the stretch of saw grass as though there was no chance at all that the Creature from the Black Lagoon lurked there. The rest of us followed along the shore, stepping carefully across a creek that trickled from beneath the dance hall into the springs. Then Digger dropped the soap into Little Bit's hands and ran into the water. Pa caught him, swinging him high, then setting him back in shallow water because Digger swam fine underwater but did not seem to understand about swimming on the surface.

Little Bit threw the soap to me. I dropped it on the sand. "Stupid!" I said.

"You're stupid," Little Bit said.

"I'm rubber," I said, "and you're glue, and what you say bounces off me and sticks to you."

Ma had taught me that. I grinned until Little Bit spoiled my triumph. "Am not. You are."

"I think," Mrs. DeLyon said, "you're both too intelligent for this conversation."

"The soap's all dirty," I said.

"Is there a remedy?" asked Mrs. DeLyon.

I stuck out my lower lip, immediately retracted it, nodded, and carried the soap to the water to rinse it.

"That," said Mrs. DeLyon, "is all there is to being a hero."

"It's still got some dirt in it," I said pointedly, but Little Bit had already waded out to jump around until she had rinsed herself.

"That's the harder half of being a hero," said Mrs. De-Lyon. "You can never make things the same as they were."

I rubbed my chest with the soap with its embedded bits of sand. "Scratches."

"Makes you tough," Mrs. DeLyon said.

"Makes you more careful about catching what you're thrown," Pa said behind me. I had not realized he was listening. He patted the bristles of my crew cut, and I relaxed. He asked Mrs. DeLyon, "You do all right with kids. Any of your own?"

"Sometimes I serve as a teacher."

Pa nodded. "I don't know why our society doesn't value teachers more."

Mrs. DeLyon smiled. "I've quit trying to understand the why of societies. It's enough to know the what and the how."

Pa sat beside her. "I'd settle for that."

She laughed. "Would you? I think you understand much of what the South is, yet you do not settle for that."

"Don't tell me you're going to get after me for serving colored people, too?"

"Who's gotten after you?"

Pa shrugged. "A few of Dogland's shareholders. And I've seen that we don't get much business from local whites."

"Tourist attractions don't get a lot of local business."

"Restaurant should get some. And we do. From local colored people."

"That bothers you?"

"Hell, no. They're good people. Their money's green, and they generally seem glad to be spending it at our place. Which is more than I can say for some white tourists. Too many people aren't happy unless they're miserable."

"Ah."

"Watching Lurleen Greenleaf is the damnedest thing. You can tell she likes Mayella, which makes sense since Mayella's the only other Southern woman there. They'll sit in the kitchen smoking cigarettes and talking about men until I have to yell at them to pretend I'm paying them to do something. But when Lurleen's out front, she won't wait on Negroes, and Mayella might as well be a stranger. A stranger of no consequence."

"Does Mayella mind?"

Pa looked at her, then said, "You know, I can't tell."

"Do you mind?"

"Isn't my place to mind."

"Mmm."

I sat near them, digging in the sand with a sun-bleached stick. Pa called, "Don't you want to rinse that soap off?" I shrugged. The drying soap itched, but their conversation was interesting, and I was in no hurry to go in the water while Pa was watching.

He said, "Artie says once you understand the nature of defeated nations, you understand the South. And Ireland and Germany and a few other places as well. Folks look for scapegoats. Here, it's the black man. But why does one person's pride have to come at the expense of another's?"

"It's not unusual to despise those we've wronged."

Pa nodded. "I hate people."

Mrs. DeLyon laughed so hard that Digger and Little Bit quit splashing to glance at her. She said, "You're one of the most sociable men I've ever known, Luke Nix. Whenever I visit Dogland, you're talking with someone. Tourist, worker, child, old person, white, black—"

Pa looked at his toes, which he had buried in the sand. "Well, I don't mind a few people at a time. It's the herd I can't stand."

"Ah."

"Now, Susan loves people, though how you'd confuse me with her, I'd never know."

"You're much alike."

He looked at her, then at me. "What're you staring at?"

"Nothing. Sir."

"Get washed."

"Yessir."

I liked getting in cold water the way Ma did, as slowly as you could. That was the way Ma and I liked to remove Band-Aids, too. Pa was completely different. Grown-ups were usually wrong about obvious things.

Pa called, "Gonna take all day?"

I had gone to the point where the water would touch
the bottom of my swimsuit, and the suit would cling to my
legs. "No, sir."

"Then jump in."

I leaped forward, sinking to my shoulders in a crouch,
then sprang up.

"Feels great, doesn't it?"

I nodded. Becoming aware that my teeth wanted to
chatter, I let them. Digger, Little Bit, Mrs. DeLyon, and Pa
all laughed. I grinned, but it did no good. Pa called, "Now,
swim back and forth a little."

I obeyed by dog-paddling parallel to the shore.

"No," Pa called. "Overhand."

I began throwing my arms over my head, thrashing
from side to side, keeping my head high so I could see
whether alligators or water moccasins might swim from
the part of Hawkins Springs where lily pads were thick
around cypress knees and anything might wait for a small
boy who was just the right size to stick in an oven.

"Kick!" Pa yelled. "Kick harder." After I had swum back
and forth several times, he called, "There. Wasn't so bad."

I shrugged extravagantly.

Little Bit pointed across the springs, toward the opening to the Suwannee. "Lookit."

I turned. Something peered at us from close to the
bank by the river. I saw the top of a dark head with damp
hair, and then the watcher slid underwater.

"What?" Pa asked.

"Mermaid," said Little Bit.

Pa laughed. "Probably a log. In the water, things look
different."

Mrs. DeLyon said, "A manatee."

"Oh," I said.

"We saw a picture at Mermaid State Park," said Little
Bit. "They got a place to live there."

"They had the world in which to live," said Mrs. De-
Lyon. "The manatee you saw was an old one."

Little Bit nodded. "I know."

"Because of its size?" Pa asked.

Mrs. DeLyon nodded.

Pa said, "We have reservations for damn near every-thing. Manatees and American Indians. Had 'em for Japanese-Americans during the war. Sometimes I'm sur-prised we don't have one for Negroes. Hmm. Guess that's what Liberia was meant to be. Wonder why it didn't work."

"Too expensive to send people back to Africa?" said Mrs. DeLyon.

"Prob'ly," said Pa. "People are practical. By '43, Ro-mania had killed a hundred thousand Jews, which was getting expensive. So they offered to send Jews to any country that'd pay to transport 'em. A Hollywood writer named Ben Hecht took out a full-page ad in *The New York Times* with a headline, 'For Sale to Humanity, 70,000 Jews, Guaranteed Human Beings at $50 Apiece.' There were no buyers. So the Romanians kept doing what they knew how to do. Practical, yep."

An aluminum boat with a large outboard raced past on the Suwannee. I said, "I hope the man'tee dived."

"So do I," said Mrs. DeLyon. Then she spoke to Pa. "I've heard you say you admire Earl Warren."

"Among others. So?"

"He was California's attorney general during the war," said Mrs. DeLyon. "He had an important part in creating concentration camps for Japanese-Americans."

"Well, maybe he learned. Maybe it's just that when you get a job on something like the Supreme Court, you're tempted to do the right thing in spite of yourself. What's your point?"

"You have hope," said Mrs. DeLyon.

Pa shrugged. "Wouldn't have kids if I didn't have hope."

Sally and Colleen were two Yankee college girls spending their summer vacation driving around the South, taking odd jobs for a week or two, waiting tables or picking fruit, then moving on. I could not tell them apart. Many people passed through Dogland for a week or a month, and I only remember that Sally and Colleen were loud girls with nasal accents like Mr. Kennedy, the man Pa liked who was running for president against Mr. Nixon, the man Ma and Grandma Letitia and Grandpa Abner liked because they were Republicans. Sally and Colleen liked Mr. Kennedy, who was "a dreamboat" and "someone who would change things, make real changes at last, really." Maybe that was why Pa often talked with them about the coming election.

When Pa and we kids walked back from Hawkins Springs, we saw Sally and Colleen waving good-bye as Cal Carter and Victor Dalton drove away in a cloud of dust and gravel. Sally or Colleen saw us and called, "Hi, Mr. Nix! Hi, Chris and Little Bit and Digger!"

"Hi," I said.

Pa said, "So, you know someone in Latchahee County?"

"Met someone," said Colleen or Sally.

"Victor Dalton and Calvin Coolidge Carter Junior," said Sally or Colleen.

"Hmm," said Pa. "Dalton's dad is the banker. He's a good man. Cal's married to one of our girls. Susan must've mentioned her. Francine, who's gone to Georgia to care for her grandmother."

"He didn't say anything about being married," said Sally or Colleen.

"But you did tell him you had a fiancé in Rhode Island," said Colleen or Sally.

"True," said Sally or Colleen.

"Why?" said Pa, who followed this with a grin.

"We're going out Friday night," said Colleen or Sally.

"It'll be a double date," said Sally or Colleen.

"Just like in high school!" said Colleen or Sally, and they both laughed

"We're going dutch. First to the Roadhouse for dinner, then we'll catch a double feature at the"—Colleen or Sally made a face—"thee-ayter." They both laughed again.

"Sounds like fun," Pa said.

"Oh, it will be," said Colleen or Sally. "Then there's a rock and roll band from Gainesville at the Roadhouse."

"Your fiancé won't mind?" Pa asked.

"Oh, it's not that kind of date," said Sally or Colleen.

"For you," said Colleen or Sally. "*I* don't have a fiancé. And Victor's kind of cute. He isn't married, is he?"

"I don't think so," Pa said, "He's going to Tampa State, or something. Isn't it about time to feed the dogs?"

"Oh, right you are, Mr. Nix. James's probably got their food mixed and ready by now."

"Probably," Pa said.

"People are so polite down here. Have you noticed that, Mr. Nix?"

"Um-hmm. It's amazing how subtly people will suggest that the help ought to spend a little time now and then earning their pay."

The girls laughed, because Pa spoke with a grin. Laughing together, they walked toward the dog pens. Pa led us kids into the new wooden gift shop that he, Handyman, Ethorne, and a few helpers were building next to the restaurant. My part in the construction had been to crawl, hot, sticky, and itching, through the rafters in the low attic, unrolling pink fiberglass insulation.

Ethorne was building pegboard frames to hang up items for sale like Florida playing cards, smoke bombs, and plastic conquistador helmets. Digger grinned, and Little Bit and I both yelled, "Hi, Ethorne!"

He set aside his screwdriver. "How y'all? Looks like somebody fell in the water."

Digger nodded, and Little Bit said, "I did," then added, "We saw a mermaid."

"Do tell?"

"A manatee," I explained.

"Oh, a manatee. That's 'bout like a mermaid. You know, they got sea cows 'round Africa and 'round here. Both black folks and red folks tol' stories 'bout folks who turn into sea cows. Or maybe it's sea cows who turn into folks."

"That's just stories," I said.

"Those frames look good," Pa said.

Ethorne tapped one. "Comin' along."

Pa looked at us. "Why don't you kids go put away your swim stuff?"

"Okay," Little Bit answered, and I nodded. Outside the gift shop, I stooped to look at several empty paint cans while Digger and Little Bit went to the house. I touched the inside of one can, and the tip of my finger came away covered with slick white goo. I rubbed the goo off on my pants, saw what a mess that made, and rubbed dirt into it so the dirt would get the paint off. And while I was doing that, I heard Pa say, "Ethorne?"

"Yes, Mist' Luke?"

"You're proving such a help on the grounds that I think we'll let Mayella and Lurleen handle the cooking."

After a moment Ethorne said, "I don't mean nothin' again' either of 'em, but they don't exactly come up with inspirin' eatin', if you know what I mean."

Pa laughed. "I do. But, well, it seems that for all the compliments we get on your cooking, we get just as many complaints."

"Eh," said Ethorne.

"Doesn't mean anything," said Pa. "I'd eat your cooking forever."

"Eh," Ethorne repeated. "I bes' finish up this frame before quittin' time, Mist' Luke."

"I—" Pa began, but he only finished, "all right." I heard him walking away from Ethorne, so I began scrabbling more earnestly in the gravel. When Pa came out the door, he said, "What're you doing?"

"Playing," I said.

"Get changed," Pa said, walking toward the dog pens. "It's nearly dinner."

"Yessir." I ran to the house. "Playing" was the best excuse I had ever found. One day when Ma was cleaning the women's bathroom, I scuttled across the floor on my hands and knees, racing between her legs and peeking up her skirt as I went. When she asked me what I was doing,

I said, "Playing." She looked at me, then said, "Maybe you'd better play outside so I can finish in here."

When Little Bit told Mayella about the mermaid, Mayella laughed and laughed. "You don' fear no manatees, do you, girl?"

"No," Little Bit said solemnly.

"Good," said Mayella. "Manatees don' hurt nobody. They just swim along, thinkin' their deep river dreams."

"Deep river dreams?" I said. "What's that?"

Mayella smiled. "That's when everything's slow and peaceful, and there's plenty to eat, and there's company when you want it, and nothing happens in a hurry, and you can think all you want on what God is and what God wants, and you can know it don't much matter 'cause you doin' what you s'posed to, and God's doin' what God's s'posed to. That's deep river dreamin'."

Pa put a Coca-Cola machine in the Doggy Salon. Tourists commented on it because it was old, a low, squat red machine with a glass door in one side where the bottles of Coke waited to be pulled out, and because it was cheap, only a nickel a bottle though many places had begun selling Coke for a dime, and because Pa kept wooden trays of full Coke bottles stacked next to the machine. When people asked why he wasn't afraid they'd be stolen, Pa would point out that no one could smuggle trays of Coke through the gift shop and past Mrs. Stark, an older widow who worked in the gift shop as our cashier, and no one would want to drink a bottle of warm Coke on a hot day when a cold one was available for five cents.

What Pa did not know was that when one of the dispensing holes was empty because all the Cokes in the rack feeding that slot had been sold, you could shove a warm Coke bottle into the hole. And if you didn't push it in all the way, it didn't get latched inside, and if a tourist didn't

drop in a nickel and take that bottle, you could pull it out,
nice and cool, anytime you wanted and go hide in the
closet of Ma and Pa's bedroom, the absolute last place anyone would look for you, and drink the Coke, which was
probably still a little warm because who could wait?—
even though you'd have to share it with Digger and Little
Bit, not because they would tell but because they would
make too much noise laughing or begging for a drink if
you didn't let them have some.

I can't remember if I quit chilling Cokes because I realized that was stealing. I think a tourist reached for the
bottle that I had been cooling for a long half hour, and I
asked the tourist to take a different one, and the tourist
told my parents.

Most Sundays, Ma took us to Sunday school in Dickison.
On hot days we would fan ourselves with paper fans that
showed Jesus with his long blond hair and beard, dressed
in a white robe and leather sandals, holding his arms wide
for an embrace that anticipated his crucifixion. Once we
went with Mayella to her church, and though everyone
was colored, and they sang more than in the white people's church, they used the same paper fans.

We kids all showered together when we were small. Afterward, Little Bit would do the Naked Dance, whirling
from the bathroom into the kids' room wrapped in a beach
towel that she would discard while Digger and I clapped.
Ma stopped the Naked Dances and the shared showers at
about the same time. Digger and I continued to shower together, and sometimes Pa showered with us. Pa looked like
us, only bigger and hairier and more muscled. Ma wore
dresses and had long hair, but those were the only traits
she shared with Little Bit that I could tell.

* * *

Dog babies were tiny and blind, and if you scared the
mother, she might bite you. But when Ma or Pa said the
babies were old enough, you could hold one in your hands
and it would snuffle against your skin, trying to find out
if you were its mother.

Early one evening after dinner but before dark, I was circling the Heart Tree with a cap rifle when a car horn
honked. Cal and Victor got out of Victor's red Chevrolet
convertible. "Hey, boy," Victor called, "you know Colleen
and Sally?"

I looked at them and shrugged.

"Sure you do," said Cal, laughing. "You want to run tell
'em we're here, boss-boy?"

I grinned, nodded, and ran.

Colleen and Sally had a small trailer, just big enough
for two bunks and a tiny kitchen, that they had parked
next to our house. I banged on the door. Sally or Colleen
looked out and laughed even before I said, "Cal an' Victor
are here." I pointed up at the parking lot.

"Already?" said Colleen or Sally, inside the trailer.

"Already," said Sally or Colleen. Then she told me, "Tell
them to hold their horses; we'll be ready in a sec; we're
putting on our faces, okay?"

I nodded.

"You're a dear," said Sally or Colleen, and the door
closed.

I ran up to the parking lot. Victor was sitting in the passenger seat, looking in the mirror as he combed his hair
back. Cal was sitting on the front bumper, smoking a cigarette. He looked at me and said, "Well, boss-boy?"

"You're s'posed to hold the horses. They're puttin' on
their faces."

"I was figurin' on holdin' something else," said Victor.

"I'm goin' to have a white horse an' a black horse when
I grow up," I said. "I'll ride the white one in the daytime
an' the black one in the night."

Victor frowned at me.

Cal pointed away. "Umm-hmmm, lookathere."

"Where?" said Victor.

"G'night, Mayella!" I called, waving as hard as I could. She stopped in the middle of the semicircular driveway and looked at us without any expression. Ethorne had not come to work that day, or the day before, and Seth and James had left earlier, before supper, so she was walking home. "Good night, Chris," she said quietly, and she walked on.

"Brown sugar," Cal told Victor.

Victor laughed and nudged him. "You a dog. You such a dog."

"I like cimanin sugar," I said. "On toast."

"That's 'cause you're a Yankee," said Cal.

"Everyone likes cimanin sugar," I said.

"On toast," said Cal, nodding.

Victor said, "Ain't any kind of sugar that this houn' dog don't like."

Cal looked up at the sky and bayed like Colonel, our bloodhound. As I laughed, I heard Colleen or Sally say, "I do believe the gentlemen approve."

"And how," said Cal.

I turned. Colleen or Sally wore dresses, one pink and flounced at the waist, one blue and close-fitting. "You look like princesses," I said.

"Well," said Colleen or Sally. "Then I guess our work was not in vain."

"Not a'tall," said Victor.

Sally or Colleen said, "We haven't had an excuse to dress up all summer."

"Glad to provide one, ladies," said Cal. "Hop in. Dinner's calling."

"You didn't mention you were married," said Sally or Colleen as both girls got into the backseat.

"Didn't think I needed to after you mentioned your fee-oncy." Cal grinned. "Goin' dancin' don' mean goin' romancin'. Wasn't we just goin' to show you how we have fun 'round here?"

"Fine," said Sally or Colleen. "I just wanted to be sure."

I waved good-bye. Sally or Colleen waved back, one hand twisting from side to side at the wrist. When I turned, Ma had come out of the gift shop, where she counted up the money at the end of the day after Mrs. Stark had closed the building. She said, "Didn't they look nice?"

I nodded.

"I wouldn't have thought those boys owned ties, let alone sports jackets." She came and touched my shoulder. "You're getting to be a big boy, Chris."

I grinned. "Time to measure me again?" The inside bathroom door frame bore the marks and dates of the measurements of each kid's height, and I enjoyed the inexorable progress, a promise that someday I could be as tall as Pa.

Ma laughed. "I don't think you've grown that much since Sunday."

"Oh," I said.

"I was just thinking that someday I'd watch you going off on a date."

"With a girl?"

She laughed and nodded.

"Yuck!"

She said, "You'll think differently when you're older." And then she bent over and kissed my cheek.

"Yuck!" I repeated, and wiped my cheek with my hand.

"Are you getting too big to be kissed by your mother?"

I rolled my eyes and shrugged.

"You're never too big to be kissed by your mother," Ma said.

"Okay," I conceded, and Ma laughed.

"Come on. It's time to get into your peejays."

"Already?"

"Digger's sound asleep, and Little Bit's in hers."

"All right," I said sadly.

Ma laughed again. "Life sure is hard on some people."

*   *   *

I woke sometime in the middle of the night and pushed myself up onto my arms to see why. The night-light showed me that Digger, curled like a cat, was still asleep and Little Bit, on her back like a mummy, was already awake. She watched me from the corners of her eyes. Car lights shone through the window above her head. Someone was moving around in the yard. I wanted to call for Ma or Pa, then realized that I heard their voices outside.

I ran across the cold linoleum floor to stand on Little Bit's bed and peer through the louvered windows. Little Bit, without moving, said, "What you see?"

"Ma an' Pa an' C'leen an' Sally."

"Who's cryin'?"

I hadn't realized anyone was crying. I looked closer. "Ma. No. C'leen an' Sally." One was crying while Ma embraced her, and the other was furious, making fists and faces at Pa, who stood there with his hands before him in a rare gesture of helplessness.

"Who hurt 'em?"

"I dunno."

"Nobody should hurt 'em."

"They're hitchin' up the trailer! Pa's helpin'."

"They're takin' me swimmin' tomorrow. Co-leen said."

"Not no more," I said. "They're leavin'."

"Who hurt 'em?"

"I don't know!" I said, annoyed that she had asked me again.

"Somebody hurt 'em!"

"Maybe Cal an' Victor."

"Cal an' Victor."

"Maybe," I said.

I watched Colleen and Sally get into their old dark coupe and rattle toward the highway. I watched Ma and Pa looking after them as they turned north and drove out of this story of my life. I watched Pa put his arm around Ma and lead her toward the door to their room. I ducked down and off Little Bit's bed, whispering, "They left." Then I added, "Pa hugged Ma," and I returned to my bed. When

Ma looked in a moment later, Little Bit and I pretended we were sleeping as soundly as Digger. Perhaps Little Bit was.

The next afternoon Cal and Victor drove into the parking lot. Digger, Little Bit, and I were playing by the Heart Tree. I started to wave, but Little Bit made a face and turned her back, so I merely watched.

Cal called, "Hey, boss-boy! Sally or Colleen around?"

I don't know where Pa came from, perhaps from the gift shop, perhaps from the kitchen. He walked toward them with a stride that would have made me want to run in the opposite direction. He gave Cal and Victor the steady look that said you had better not run. Maybe that's why they waited. Pa asked in his calm-before-the-storm voice, "Why?"

"Oh-oh," I said.

"Good," Little Bit said.

Cal smiled. "How you, Mr. Nix? Elvis Presley's in a movie at the drive-in. We was wonderin' if the girls wanted some fun."

The door to the gift shop opened, and Ma stepped out. Mrs. Stark, who never missed anything interesting, looked through the gift-shop window. Lurleen watched from the front of the restaurant, and the kitchen door was open wide enough for Mayella to see and hear. Ethorne and the rest of the staff were back with the dogs. I was the only male observer.

"Get off my property," Pa said. The storm had yet to break.

"What's the matter?" said Victor. "We only want to talk to the girls."

"Now," Pa said.

Victor said, "Hold on," and began to open his car door. Pa stopped it with the flat of his hand, and he and Victor strained against each other. Victor was a foot taller than Pa, but I knew who was stronger. Ma called, "Luke!" as

Victor said, "This here's a public business, Mr. Nix. You can't run us off, and those girls ain't your slaves. If you—"

Pa released the door, grabbed Victor by his golf shirt, and yanked him forward, out of the car. Victor sprawled onto the gravel, and Pa put an engineer boot against the back of his head. "You hear what I said?"

"Yeah!" screamed Victor as Pa bore down on his boot. "I hear! I hear!"

Cal came running around the side of the car, but he stopped when Pa pointed at him. Cal spread his arms wide. "Mr. Nix, I—"

"Off my land," Pa said. "I don't ever want to see your face again. Either of you."

"Sure," Cal said. "Sure thing. Let him up."

Victor scrambled to his feet. The side of his face was red, and pieces of gravel clung to his skin. "My daddy was good to you."

Pa kicked the convertible's door shut as Victor reached for the handle. "Get."

"That's my car!"

"Get," Pa said, starting forward with one fist cocked at his side.

"Come on," said Cal, walking toward the highway "We'll let that damn sheriff know what happened here."

"No need," Pa said, starting after Cal and Victor. "Susan! Call the sheriff!"

Ma yelled, "Luke, don't hurt them!"

"Call the goddamn sheriff!"

Ma looked at him, then ran back inside. Cal and Victor had stopped near the top of the driveway. "Get the hell off my property!" Pa yelled, taking several quick steps after them.

Cal and Victor backed away so quickly that a passing car honked as it swerved around them. "Don't mess with my car!" Victor called.

"I won't touch your daddy's car," Pa said. "Start walking."

Victor squatted at the edge of the highway. Cal looked at him, then shrugged and stood there.

Pa said, "I won't tell you again."

Cal yelled, "We're off your land, Mr. Nix. I don't know what's got in your bonnet. We ain't done nothin' that's none of your business."

"It's—" Pa began, but he stopped and turned away.

The kitchen door closed, and Lurleen moved away from the front window. An elderly couple came out of the gift shop, looked at Pa, and hurried to their car as Mrs. Stark called, "Y'all come back soon now, hear?"

Ma came out and said, "Rooster Donati's on the way."

She stood there, looking at Pa until he said, "Good. Everyone can get back to work. What'm I paying people for, anyway?"

Mrs. Stark smiled and nodded. "Yes, sir, Luke. Everything's fine now."

Pa looked at me. "You see either of those two on the property, come get me."

"Yessir, Pa." I sat cross-legged under the Heart Tree with my cap rifle across my lap. Pa went back toward the Doggy Salon, and we kids were alone again, alone if you did not count the occasional tourist passing by or Ma looking out at us every two or three minutes with her lower lip pinched between her teeth.

Little Bit said, "Pa should've shooted them."

"He di'n't have a gun," I said.

Little Bit shrugged. "He should've shooted them anyway."

I didn't bother to answer. Victor sat on the edge of the highway, staring at his car in our lot while punching his right fist into his palm. Cal walked around behind him, talking constantly and laughing sometimes, though Victor never laughed.

After ten or fifteen minutes, Victor stood up, looked down the highway, and grinned. When the sheriff's car turned into the driveway, they followed it down. I ran back to the Doggy Salon, yelling, "Pa, Pa, they came back even though you told 'em not to! An' the police're here, too!"

Pa came out of the grooming area. James, clipping the black poodle's toenails, glanced at me and kept working, saying only, "Mist' Luke?"

Pa said, "I'll be back in a bit."

As we walked toward the back of the gift shop, Ma yelled, "Luke! Sheriff Donati's here!"

Pa nodded. We went through the gift shop and into the front. Sheriff Donati, a barrel-chested, balding man with a pistol on his hip and a hat like Smokey the Bear's, stood beside his car. Victor was telling him how they hadn't done a thing. The sheriff's eyes flicked from Victor to Pa to me with my cap rifle to Pa again.

Pa said, "I ordered them off my property."

Sheriff Donati looked at Victor. "That so?"

"Yeah," said Victor. "Then he threw me down—"

"You didn't get off his property?"

"No," said Victor. "This here's a public—"

"I reckon you better get offa here now."

"But he threw—"

"We'll straighten this out," said Sheriff Donati. "Be a little easier if you'd get, now."

Cal tugged Victor's arm, and they started toward the red convertible.

"You're not driving that off this property," Pa said.

"But—" said Victor.

"Go on up by the highway," said Sheriff Donati, waggling his fingers to shoo Victor. "Looked like you found a good place to sit." He turned his back on them immediately and held out his hand to Pa. "Luke."

"Rooster," Pa said as they shook. "Sorry to call you out." Behind them, Victor jabbed his finger at the sheriff's back, then trudged after Cal toward the highway.

"It's my business," Sheriff Donati said. "How're you, Chris?"

"Fine," I said, and stepped behind Pa.

"He's a good one," Sheriff Donati told Pa with a laugh,

and then the laugh left his face. "Susan said somethin' 'bout 'em hurting two o' your hired gals last night."

Pa nodded.

Sheriff Donati said, "I should talk to the gals."

"They headed home," said Pa. "North."

"Oh." Sheriff Donati took off his hat and fanned himself with it. "Prob'ly for the best."

Pa shrugged.

"You got no call to harass those boys, you know," Sheriff Donati said.

"They came whipping in here like they were drunk," Pa said. "How do I know they didn't steal that car? They were rude to me. You saying a free American can't kick a couple of little know-nothings off his property?"

Sheriff Donati said, "You had 'em sit in the sun for a while. You embarrassed 'em in front of each other and everyone who happened by. Story'll be all over the county by church-time tomorrow. I reckon that's pretty good."

"Oh?" said Pa.

"They ain't niggers," Sheriff Donati said.

"You didn't see the girls," said Pa.

"Yankee gals runnin' 'round with grown boys—"

"Yeah," said Pa. "They're not taking that car. Jack Dalton can come for it if he wants it."

Sheriff Donati looked at me, then nodded. "I'll have to give 'em rides home."

"You do what you have to."

"Cal don't live far," I said. "Francine used to walk all the time."

Pa and the sheriff laughed. Sheriff Donati said, "All right, one of 'em'll put a couple miles on his best shoes." Then he said, "I have three daughters of my own, you know."

Pa said, "No, I didn't."

"It ain't that I don't feel for them Yankee gals. But they made a mistake. Man can't protect ever'body from their own mistakes."

"A man protects everyone he can."

The sheriff nodded. "That's so. But in this here case, it looks like what's done is done."

Pa looked up at the boys on the highway. "They're not coming back on my property."

"I'll tell 'em," the sheriff said, putting his hat back on his head. He made a pistol with his fingers and shot me, and I laughed, then he said, "See you, Luke," got in his car, and drove away.

An hour or two later, a gleaming black car stopped by the driveway. The banker got out, and the car turned around and drove away. As the banker walked down the gravel in his suit and gleaming shoes, I called, "Hi, Mr. Dalton!" He looked at me and nodded. I called, "How're you?"

"Fine," he said quietly, and did not bring any lollipops out of his pocket. "Where's your father?"

"Here," Pa said, coming from the gift shop with a key in his hand. He smiled as though nothing had gone wrong all day. "Sorry you had to come yourself, Jack. I thought you'd send a tow truck and take it out of the boy's allowance, or something."

"Vic isn't spoiled," said Mr. Dalton, taking the key from Pa. "And he isn't wild, either."

"Umm."

"He doesn't keep the best company, but boys'll be boys, you know."

"Yeah," said Pa. "I wonder sometimes if men'll learn to be men."

I don't remember the transition from being afraid to swim to being able to swim. I remember Pa throwing me from the dock at Mermaid Springs while Ma looked nervous, and I swam straight back, but that wasn't really swimming. That was survival. Pa once said, "You just do it, and then you aren't scared." Ma once said, "I never learned, but I never had the chance to learn when I was your age. You've seen the bigger boys swimming, haven't you? You'll be just like them."

My parents volunteered those comments. I had to ask everyone else. Mr. Drake said, "You keep practicing, and you keep getting better. Everything's like that." Mrs. De-Lyon said, "Water's an environment, like the ground and the air. You learn its ways. You learn to trust it, and respect it. And then you swim."

When I asked Ethorne, he laughed and said, "Oh, that was too long ago. You 'member how you learned to walk?" I said, "I was just a baby." He said, "Well, there you is," which did not help me at all. He laughed again and said, "You want to talk to someone who knows 'bout swimmin', you talk to Mayella. She's the swimminest fool I know."

"Mayella?" I said. In my understanding of the world, all men could swim, but only some women could.

"Sure. Her momma was the queen of the sea. Ain't nobody knows more 'bout swimmin' than Mayella."

One afternoon when the restaurant was empty of customers and Lurleen was at a table smoking a cigarette while reading a copy of *Look*, a picture magazine that had letters in the middle of its name that might be two eyes if you drew in pupils or two heads if you drew in eyes and mouths, Little Bit and I sat at the counter and drank glasses of milk through plastic straws. I asked Mayella, "Could you really swim before you could walk?"

Little Bit giggled, and Mayella said, "Why, can't say I remember either. Why you ask?"

"Just askin'," I said.

"Oh, I see."

"Was it hard?"

"No, not—" She looked at me. "Well, first it was hard. But you know what?"

"What?"

"When you in the water, you just got to quit thinkin' you a land critter. Like Mr. Turtle. When he's on land, he thinks he's a land critter. But you know what he thinks soon as he's in the water?"

"He's a water critter?"

Mayella nodded.

"But how do you do that?"

"You want to think like 'em, you got to act like 'em. Do you splash around an' get all antsy when you in the water?"

I nodded.

"Do Mr. Turtle do like that?"

I shook my head. "He's a turtle."

"Well," said Mayella. "What about manatees?"

"I don't know."

"They like people," said Mayella. "They breathe the air. How you think they learn to swim?"

"They just swim?"

"Don't nothing just nothing. Everything's got to learn. Some learns easier 'n others, that's all. How you think li'l manatee babies learn to swim?"

"Their parents teach 'em?"

"Just 'cause someone teaches don' mean nobody learns. How you think they *learn?*"

I wrinkled up my forehead.

"Think on it. A li'l manatee baby in the water. What's it doin'?"

"Playing!"

Mayella laughed. "See? You got it figured out now."

Near the end of a day near the end of summer, I saw Ethorne walking down Dogland's driveway. I knew he was drunk by his walk, an awkward exaggeration of his usual saunter. I looked down at the dirt where Digger and I were playing with toy trucks, but Digger looked up and grinned at Ethorne.

"How you boys?" Ethorne called. "How you been?"

"Fine," I said.

"Tha's good. Ever'one ought to be jus' fine. Where's yo' pappy?" He laughed, though I did not know why. "Yo' pappy, he's a good man. Y'all ought to be proud of a fine man like him."

"Yes, sir," I said.

"Y'all ain' scared o' me?" Ethorne drew himself up. "Ain' nothin' to be scared of." He came close. He smelled like flowers that had festered.

"No," I said, which was a truth. I was wary, or I was prepared to be scared, but I liked Ethorne too much to be afraid just because everything he said and did was excessive.

"Is yo' pappy—"

"Hello, Ethorne," Ma said, coming up behind him.

He whirled, snatching his straw hat from his head and sweeping it low before him like a stage courtier. "Mis' Susan! How you!"

"Fine, Ethorne. We missed you the last week."

"Oh, I been—" Ethorne looked away, worked his lips so his moustache crawled like a dancing centipede, then said, " 'Round. Busy, you know. Is Mist' Luke about?"

"He went into town on errands," Ma said. "Something I can do?"

"Well, I don' know. Maybe I bes' wait fo' Mist' Luke."

"I don't know, Ethorne. You look like you've been feeling pretty good."

"Yes, ma'am." He grinned, and so did I, since Ma was not worried. "Tha's what I wanted t' talk to Mist' Luke about."

"Luke's not very understanding about drinking, Ethorne. I think it'd be best if you came back when you weren't"—she smiled—"feelin' so good." I heard something under her smile that Ethorne missed.

"Oh, no, ma'am. Tha's the problem. Tha's precisely the problem."

"What is?"

"I need me a fi'-dollar advance."

Ma's smile broadened. "You're still working here, then?"

"Oh, yes, ma'am. When I's a mind to."

"Doesn't look like your mind has much to do with whether you work today."

Ethorne grinned weakly. "Well, tha's true. I need me a li'l pick-me-up, is what I need."

"I don't know, Ethorne."

He nodded and sat in the dirt in front of Digger, who laughed. "Then I'll jus' wait on Mist' Luke."

"Oh, Ethorne, I—" Ma looked at Digger and me, then said, "I'll lend you five dollars, Ethorne. But this'll be our secret, understand?"

"Yes, ma'am, I do. Thank you, ma'am. Thank you kindly." He kissed the bill Ma gave him, then turned it, showing Lincoln's face. "Y'know, he di'n't want to free the slaves. But he freed 'em anyway when he thought it'd he'p him win the war, an' I love him fo' that."

Ma said quietly, "I thought you said you were quitting drinking."

"Tha's so. T'morrow, I quit again."

"Ethorne, why do you do that to yourself?"

"Oh, a man needs a li'l vacation now'n then. I's on the way here las' week, but Mist' Lumiere say he have a li'l job fo' me. An' when I do it, he as' me if I druther have fi' dollars or two bottles o' Jim Beam. Mist' Beam, he's good company."

As Ethorne walked away, Ma called, "We'll see you to-morrow?"

"Yes, ma'am. I'll be needin' a vacation from my vacation by then."

Ma watched with her lips pursed as Ethorne strolled off like an able seaman on a storm-tossed ship. Her hand touched my head, and she said, "Ethorne'll pay me back. Your father doesn't have to know about this."

I nodded, and her hand left my head. I looked up, followed her gaze, expecting to see Pa, and saw Mayella instead.

She said, "You di'n't give him no money, did you, ma'am?"

"I could hardly say no."

Mayella's face tightened.

Ma said, "I didn't know what to do. If Luke found him drunk—"

"Tha's all right, ma'am. Better you'n some others."

"Ethorne's good for it, I'm sure."

"Oh, yes'm. That's the problem. He always pays his debts."

"You're not"—Ma's eyes flicked toward Ethorne as he crossed to the far side of the highway—"hurting, are you? I mean, I'd hate for anyone to go hungry if we—"

"Oh, no, ma'am! It's just Ethorne I worry 'bout."

"Mmm." Ma nodded.

Seth and James walked up from the dog pens then. James called, "We all done, Mis' Nix!"

"No problems?"

"None at all, ma'am," said Seth. "Um, Mayella—"

"Them Newbury sisters? I thought you done spent all your money on 'em."

Seth smiled. "We have our ways."

Mayella said, "Um-hmm, but mos' folks forgive you for 'em."

James laughed. "We done cleared some brush fo' Mist' Lumiere over the weekend."

Ma said, "He didn't pay you in liquor?"

James frowned at her. "Why, no, ma'am."

Seth said, "Good green folding stuff, ma'am."

Ma laughed. "And it's burning a hole through your pockets."

Mayella said, "Tha's not what's burnin'."

Seth looked as if he would've blushed, if he had been paler. He looked down, adjusted his glasses, and lifted his shoulders.

James said, "Got to spend it on someone."

Mayella said, "Well, it's a pretty evenin'. I feel like a walk."

Seth and James grinned and ran for their truck. "We owe you!" called James.

" 'Bout a million an' one," said Mayella. "Ain' nobody paid me back fo' my half o' that truck yet."

Though she spoke quietly, James heard her and laughed. "We will! We will!"

Seth and James drove away, Ma and Mayella returned to the restaurant, Digger and I continued to play under the Heart Tree, and Cal and Victor drove by on the highway. Little Bit ran out of the gift shop, looking up after the red convertible. I called, "They didn't try to come in." She studied me, so I repeated, "They didn't." Seth and James were as big and as strong as Cal and Victor, and their truck may have been slower than the convertible, but it was more powerful. I wasn't afraid for them.

Mrs. Stark followed Little Bit out of the gift shop. "Who'd you see, sweetie?"

Little Bit said, "Car," and went inside. Mrs. Stark looked at her back, then smiled at me and followed Little Bit inside. Pa said Mrs. Stark wanted to be our grandma, but we already had two of them, and grandpas were better anyway.

When Mayella left half an hour later, I called, "Night, Mayella!" Digger waved to her as he usually did, but Little Bit ran to her and gave her a hug.

"Wha's got into you, gal?" Mayella asked, laughing.

"Nuffin."

"Your brothers di'n't hurt you none?"

"No'm."

" 'Cause if they do, you just got to whomp 'em good. Let 'em know they can't get away with nothin' no how."

Little Bit nodded.

Mayella pried Little Bit's arms from her legs. "I see you t'morrow."

Little Bit nodded again. As Mayella walked up to the road, Little Bit whispered, "Bye."

Early the next morning I swept the walkway around the restaurant all by myself, which was not fair. Little Bit usually did half, but she had gone to Gainesville with Ma, who had wanted company when she went to the doctor, but not as much company as all three kids would provide. I was big enough that I could stay at Dogland and help Pa. People said I was lucky being the oldest, which showed how stupid a lot of people were.

I stopped sweeping when Sheriff Donati's car turned onto the driveway. The sheriff parked near me. He got out, saying, "Hey, Deputy Chris, your pa around?" He smiled, but he did not sound like he would like to be asked if I could touch his pistol's genuine cherrywood handle.

I said, "Yes, sir. Want me to get him?" Ready to sprint, I dropped the broom onto the sidewalk.

"You can lead me."

"All right."

As we walked, the sheriff said, "Seen Mayella Hawkins today?"

"No, sir." I grinned at him. I liked helping adults.

"When's she usually come in?"

I frowned. "Is it nine yet?"

He looked at his watch. "No."

"She don't get in until nine. Doesn't, I mean."

Pa had dug a hole between two kennels to run a plumber's snake through a blocked sewage pipe. The plumber's snake did not have eyes or a mouth like I thought it should; it was only a diamond-shaped piece of steel on a long metal ribbon. Pa smiled at us, set down the plumber's snake, and said, "Rooster. You'd probably be grateful if I don't shake hands with you."

"Isn't a social call," Sheriff Donati said. "I'm looking for Mayella Hawkins."

Pa frowned. "She isn't here yet."

"Wasn't at her family's shack, either. An' I didn't see her on the road."

"She shortcuts across a field or two when she can't get a ride. Why?"

The sheriff looked at me.

Pa said, "You finish sweeping?"

"Almost."

"Almost isn't enough."

"Yes, sir." I dragged my cowboy boots in the gravel as I walked away, but the sheriff waited, then spoke too quietly for me to hear. Disgusted, I ran back to the restaurant and picked up my broom.

Then I dropped it again. "Mayella! Mayella!" I cried her name as I ran up the hill to the highway.

Her smile seemed forced. "How you, Chris?" She stood on the side of the road, waiting for me while she looked at Sheriff Donati's patrol car.

"The sheriff's here. He's looking for you."

"That Cal with him?"

I shook my head. "Are you getting up a posse?"

"I wish." She looked at me. "Chris, I bes' go. Don' tell no one you seen me, hear?"

"Yes'm. Why?"

She shook her head, turned, then turned back. "How's that swimmin' goin'?"

"Oh." I shrugged. "Pretty good."

"Good. You keep at it." She smiled, turned, and loped across the highway.

Behind me, Sheriff Donati called, "Who you wavin' at, Deputy Chris?"

He and Pa stood by the front door of the gift shop. Unable even to shrug, I stared at them.

"Cat got your—" the sheriff began.

"He was talkin' to Mayella," said Mrs. Stark, pushing past the sheriff. "Weren't you, Chris? You don't have to be shy of Sheriff Rooster, you know."

"Damn," said Sheriff Donati. "You tell her—Don't matter. That trail comes out back by the bridge, don't it?" He looked at Pa.

Pa shrugged. "Lots of side trails run off it. She could be heading anywhere."

Sheriff Donati nodded, then trotted to his car. As he backed out of his parking space, Mrs. Stark said, "Wha'd she do? I always liked Mayella, but black blood's weak, you know. Never tempt a nigger, 'cause a nigger hasn't got a white man's will. It's just how the Good Lord made 'em. Reverend Shale says—"

Pa said, "Later," and ran to our pickup truck. I followed. As I opened the passenger door, Pa said, "Stay"— my heart dipped until he finished—"out of the way."

"Yes, sir." I slammed the door, and we took off after the sheriff. This was no time to ask Pa questions. He drove as quickly as he had when Digger had been bitten. The pickup was old, used mostly for hauling dog food, and had rarely been driven quickly. Pa gripped the wheel with both fists, and we bounced high at every irregularity in the road.

The trail that Mayella had taken may have been an animal path, or maybe humans had used it since the time of the Timucua and the Apalachee. It cut through scrub and forest, passing by Hawkins Springs and leaving the woods near the bridge over the Suwannee.

The highway curved from Dogland to the bridge, meeting a county road to Trenton at the center of the curve. Whenever we walked to Hawkins Springs, we always followed the highway, even though it was at least twice as long as the trail. Ma didn't want her kids going where they might be bitten by bears, boars, or snakes. Though Pa laughed at those fears, he agreed that it was too easy for kids to get lost on the trail, and maybe end up drowned in swamplands or the river.

Pa kept his attention on the highway as he said, "She's prob'ly heading home. Nothing to be gained by crossing the county line. Not when the sheriff's in hot pursuit." We passed the Fountain of Youth Motor Inn, and Mrs. De-Lyon, in the courtyard, shaded her eyes with her hand as we roared by. Pa's next word was a low, quiet "Damn."

Mayella, on foot, was a quarter of the way across the suspension bridge with Sheriff Donati close behind her in his patrol car. He braked and jumped out, drawing his large, dark pistol with its gleaming cherrywood butt.

I heard his "Freeze!" as Pa stopped our truck behind the patrol car. Mayella kept running. Pa opened his door and stepped out, yelling, "Mayella! Surrender! We'll get you a lawyer!"

The sheriff called, "Listen to him, Mayella!" She had reached the middle of the bridge and was not slowing. The sheriff's pistol fired once. I blinked. The shot echoed over the river.

A cattle truck had stopped at the far side of the bridge. Sheriff Donati's pistol was pointed into the air. Mayella stood still with her back to us.

The sheriff called, "Don't make me shoot you, Mayella! I don't want to have to! I surely don't!"

Pa called quietly, "Rooster, you don't need to shoot anyone. You know—"

Mayella jumped up onto the railing. A breeze, or maybe her motion, pressed her dress against her body.

"Don't be—" Rooster shouted.

"No!" Pa called.

Mayella dove. Her arc carried her toward the sun. The bridge hid the end of her dive from my sight. Pa and Rooster ran to the railing to stare down at the river. A crowd of men and women, drivers who had stopped at either end of the bridge, ran to stand beside them. I pressed through the strangers and their questions: "What happened?" "That nigger crazy?" "She tryin' to kill herself?" "What's goin' on here?"

I squeezed next to Pa and looked down. The dark waters washed on to the Gulf of Mexico. A speedboat circled beneath the bridge, its driver craning like us all to see what the river might bring up.

"Pa!" I asked. "Where's Mayella?"

"I don't see her."

"But—"

"Sh." He put his hand on my shoulder, and we watched the water.

"I wouldn't'a' shot her," Rooster said.

Pa clapped Rooster's arm once. Rooster stood still like a scarecrow that had been emptied of life. Pa told me, "Come on."

"But Mayella—"

"She isn't coming up," Pa said. "Let's go."

"But she swims good."

"It's been too long."

"Wait! Pa, look!" Everyone stared at the bend of the river, where I pointed.

"Sorry, Chris," Pa said. "That's just a manatee."

"Don't see many," said someone in the crowd.

"I wouldn't 'a' shot her," Rooster repeated. "I don't think I would'a' shot her."

Pa drove back to Dogland far more slowly than he had driven to the bridge. I said, "Pa?"

"Son?"

"What'd Mayella do?"

"Nothing. She was just born the wrong—" He pressed his lips together and shook his head.

"Pa?"

"Cal Carter said she drowned Victor Dalton."

"Oh."

The pickup bumped its way down the driveway, and Pa parked on the far side of the Heart Tree so tourists could park near the gift shop. When we got out, Pa looked at me and said, "What is it?"

"Did she?"

After a moment he said, "Do you think Mayella would drown someone?"

"Not unless they were bad."

"Mmm."

"Pa?"

"Yes?"

"If there was a submarine, Mayella could'a' swum down to it, right?"

"There wasn't a sub, Chris." Pa turned to face the gift shop, where Mrs. Stark waited at the door.

"But there could'a'—"

"There wasn't a sub!" Pa shouted as he whirled toward me. I stepped back. My eyes began to water, and I tightened my eyelids to stop myself from crying. "Understand? There's no—" He lifted one fist, then opened it, looked from his palm to my face, turned, and strode away.

"Mr. Nix?" Mrs. Stark said. He brushed by her without slowing. She watched him pass, then came into the parking lot. Extending her soft arms to me, she said, "Christopher? Oh, you poor ba—"

I spun away, ran around the gift shop, and scrambled through the partially completed fence that would hide the dog kennels from the view of passersby. The Saluki and the Italian greyhound raced toward me in the exercise pen. I ignored them as they bounded onto the wire fence to thrust their long snouts through the links.

The northern working dogs noticed me next. I waited until tourists had left Captain's pen, then opened his gate. He jumped up, and I hugged him. He followed me into his house. "Frogmen could'a' took her in a sub," I said, and Captain licked my ear.

When Captain decided he would rather spend a warm summer day on his porch instead of sleeping in his tiny house with me, he crawled out, waking me. I peeked between two wall slats and saw no one, but when I poked my head out the doorway, Captain licked my nose, and on the gravel walkway, Helen, one of the guides, said, "Now, I'm sure you folks think we have a rare set of identical twin Norwegian elkhounds here, but the one in the cowboy boots is Christopher Nix, the owners' son."

People laughed, and I smiled. Someone asked if all the dogs were my family, and I said yes, and everyone laughed again. I squeezed out of Captain's pen as Helen said, "You ought to fill in for breeds that're off to the vet or that we haven't got in yet. We already have a elkhound to show folks."

"Yes'm." Helen made me more shy than any of the women at Dogland. She was older than Francine and younger than Ma or Lurleen. I saw her as tall and broad-shouldered because she worked with the dogs like the men, and she ordered Ethorne, Seth, and James around as easily as Pa did—Ma and Francine gave requests, not orders. Helen was a Seventh-Day Adventist, which meant she did not eat meat and she thought Sunday was on Saturday, which was fine by Pa because Helen never minded coming to work on Sundays.

When Helen led the tourists away, I took the path in the opposite direction. I poked my fingers in the cages of all my favorite dogs, then went into the Doggy Salon, where I ignored the little dogs and sat by Bo-Peep. The English bulldog always lay in the shade of the Doggy Salon on the hottest days of summer. He rested on his side on a rug before an electric fan and panted. Froth dripped from his lolling tongue. That was how dogs sweated, I explained to two old ladies, and they gave me a nickel. After they left, I sat with Bo-Peep, patting his ribs.

Seth and James brought the Bedlington terrier and the papillon in to be groomed. James saw me and said, "Your pa's wonderin' where you got to."

I nodded.

He said, "It's hard 'bout Mayella, ain't it?"

I nodded again.

"You seen it?"

"Uh-huh."

"She really dove? She weren't shot an' fell?"

I shook my head.

"Tha's somethin', I 'xpect."

"She dove good."

"She was always somethin' in the water. Ethorne say she got that from her mama."

I nodded.

"I 'xpect if she had to choose, she'd choose the water."

"Maybe she came up inside a beaver dam," I said. "Like Daniel Boone. An' hid there till everyone left."

"Ain't no beaver dams 'round here."

I nodded.

Seth spoke. "Fucking redneck sheriff."

James said, "Mayella ain't goin' t' be watchin' yo' mouth fo' you now."

"Things are going to change."

"Mm-hmm. Brush that poor dog a li'l more lightly. Ain't his fault."

"You ain't replacin' her," Seth said, but his touch with the brush became more gentle.

"Ain't no one replacin' her," James agreed.

They both stopped talking as they looked at the door. Pa stood there. He said, "Susan's back. Why don't you two take the weekend off?"

James said, "You sure you can get by?"

Pa nodded.

Seth said, "All right."

James said, "We just finish up with these two, then we'll go."

Pa said, "All right."

"Thanks, Mist' Nix," James said quietly.

"Hell," Pa said. "Nothing to thank me for. Chris?"

"Yessir?"

"Find Ethorne. Tell 'im Simmy and Abraham Brown can work, so he can take the weekend off. More if he wants it."

"All right, Pa."

I found Ethorne at the grooming shed on the far side of the walking circle. He was humming a church hymn as I approached. He looked up and smiled. "How you be, Mast' Christopher?"

"All right, Ethorne."

"Tha's good."

"Pa says Simmy an' Abraham can work, so you don't need to."

"Who's he got cookin'?"

I shrugged. "Pa cooks good."

"Man can't do ever'thing hisself."

"Ethorne?"

"Yes?"

"Is Mayella coming back?"

Ethorne closed his eyes. "No, Chris. She's gone to a better place."

"Miami?" Mayella had often talked about going to live in Miami.

"Better'n Miami. She goin' to loll 'round all the time, eatin' when she wants an' playin' when she wants. Her mama goin' t' be there to greet her, 'long with all kinds o' kith an' kin for company. Ain' no need to feel sad for her."

"Won't she miss you?"

"Oh, sure, she'll miss all of us. But things got so she couldn't stay here no more, so she done gone home."

"Oh." I sat beside him. "Seth's mad at Rooster."

"I 'xpect he is."

"Mis' Stark says they'll drag the river." Ethorne glanced at me. "For Mayella," I explained.

"They won't find her."

"Why?"

"River keeps secrets, same as you or me."

"Why'd Rooster chase Mayella?"

"Tha's his job."

"But he's the sheriff. He should lock up Cal."

"Oh." Ethorne nodded. When I frowned, he patted my back. "Always take it easy, Christopher Nix. Tha's the secret fo' livin' long."

"But it's not fair!"

"No, it surely ain't. That's why takin' it easy is 'bout the hardest thing there is t' do."

Ethorne asked Pa about using the kitchen before he left, then prepared a batch of sweet rolls. While the restaurant filled with the smell of baking bread, Ma said she thought he was fixing them for a church reception or a household gathering to remember Mayella, but when he took the rolls from the oven, he gave them to Ma, saying, "Eat 'em while they're warm."

Ma looked as if she wanted to say several things at once. She settled on, "Thank you."

Ethorne shrugged that off with a smile. "I be goin' now. I may be sayin' my farewell fo' a few days."

Ma said, "Oh, Ethorne."

"The Good Lord gave us ways to cope with the pains o' this earth."

"But can't you see it's hard on you?"

Pa, standing near, said, "Susan."

Ma said, "But I only—"

Ethorne said, "Oh, I don' mind, Mist' Luke. I'd rather listen to her than to some preacher who don' know me."

Pa nodded. After Ethorne left, Pa said, "It'd be harder on him not to—"

"I know!" Ma said so angrily that Pa jerked his chin back.

As Ma ran from the kitchen, Pa said, "Christ, Susan—" then looked at me. "Fetch Little Bit and Digger. It's time for another happy family meal."

Ma was in our bedroom, hugging Digger. She looked at me. I said, "It's lunchtime."

Little Bit was beside the house, pulling a piece of rope like a snake for Tiger. I said, "Pa said it's lunchtime."

"I know."

"Then how come you didn't come up to the kitchen already?"

"Because you didn't come to get me already."

"Tiger's my cat."

"I know." She kept playing with Tiger, but when I turned my back to walk up to the restaurant, Little Bit raced past. I ran, but she pushed through the kitchen door first.

Pa lifted her high into the air. "Pretty speedy, li'l darling." She laughed, and the kitchen door opened again.

Ma released Digger's hand as they stepped inside. He ran over to Pa, who set Little Bit down and swung Digger up. Pa made airplane noises as he turned Digger from side to side, then set him on his feet.

Ma said quietly, "What's for lunch?"

Pa looked at her. "Hamburgers and green beans."

"French cut?" I said. French cut string beans were my favorite vegetable. I always ran ahead in the grocery aisle to select the cans by the pictures on them.

Pa smiled. "Yep. French cut."

I nodded. "Yayy!"

Lunch went well, except for the usual moment when Pa, Little Bit, and Digger heaped ketchup on their burgers and I used none. When Ma set the plate of sweet rolls in the center of our table and handed one to each of us, a customer at the next table said, "Those look good."

Lurleen, passing by, said, "They're not for sale."

"They should be," the customer said.

I took a roll in my hands. It was as soft as flesh, as warm as a heart. I tore a strip free, popped it in my mouth, and mumbled, "Why'd Rooster think Mayella did that?"

Pa looked at me as he lifted a roll. "Ever hear anyone say that children should be seen and not heard?"

Because he smiled, I said, "But I want to know."

Ma swallowed a mouthful, then said, "Because there was a charge made. Rooster had to investigate it. That's what the police do. They find the guilty and protect the innocent."

Pa glanced away, then said, "Cal took Rooster to the body. Down one of the trails along the Suwannee." Without looking at Ma, he said, "They might as well hear it from us," and continued, "Hard to ignore a body. Cal claimed Mayella lured him and Victor down there, went crazy, and drowned Victor."

"Hmmf," said Ma. "And where was Cal supposed to be?"

"Said she knocked him down, and he bumped his head." To Ma's disbelief, he said, "Could be. There's such a thing as berserker strength."

"Rooster," said Lurleen, passing by, "has got better things to do than listen to the likes of Cal Carter."

Pa looked after Lurleen, then said, "The funny thing is, Rooster said Victor was mashed down in a mudflat near the edge of the shore. It looked like he drowned in mud.

Would've taken more'n Cal or Mayella to hold him down like that."

"What do you think happened then?" Ma asked.

"Yeah, Pa," said Little Bit. "What happened?"

"I don't know," Pa said. "Maybe Victor was drunk, and he dove off the bank not knowing there was a sandbar there. Maybe he was in a tree and fell. Or was pushed. We'll prob'ly never know."

"But why'd Cal blame Mayella?" I asked.

Pa looked from me to Ma to me. "Maybe she wouldn't do something he wanted. Maybe she saw something, like him pushing Victor off the riverbank as a joke, maybe. And Victor drowned because Cal didn't pull him out of the mud in time, so Cal had to blame someone."

"She shou'n't'a' run," Little Bit said.

"That's right," Pa agreed. "We'd'a' helped her."

I put the last of the sweet roll in my mouth. "No matter what."

Pa nodded. "No matter what."

That evening, after dinner, we kids were playing around the swing set when Ma screamed. We ran around the house to the washer-wringer where she was standing. Pa arrived a moment later. Ma pointed at Ranger and Tiger. The kuvasz sat, watching Ma with his head cocked, ready to be commanded. The kitten had his back to us all as he scrubbed his damp head with a paw. Ma pointed at them both. "I saw them just in time. Ranger was about to bite Tiger's head off."

Pa said, "Well, you wouldn't have to worry about 'em anymore, then."

Ma said, "Luke!"

Pa shrugged. "Well, you wouldn't."

Little Bit said, "Ranger likes Tiger."

Pa said, "Like Digger likes hamburgers."

"Really," I said. "See?"

Tiger stalked up to Ranger and swatted the dog's paw,

tangling his tiny claws in Ranger's thick white fur. Ranger bent down, closed his jaws around Tiger's head, and shook the kitten from side to side.

"Oh, I can't look," Ma said, turning away. Pa laughed, and so did we kids, and we all laughed harder as Tiger proceeded to the next part of the game by drying his ears with angry swipes.

After a moment Pa stepped beside Ma and said, "Damnedest thing happened today." When Ma looked at him, he said, "Second damnedest thing."

"Oh?"

"Negro family came in this evening. I headed for their table, but Lurleen said she'd get it. I told her she didn't have to, but she just said, 'I know,' so I got out of her way. She took the order, and she delivered the food to 'em. Then she said she had to have a cigarette. I told her to sit down; I'd get her an ashtray."

Ma smiled at Pa, and he smiled back. "Well," Ma said.

Pa said, "She sucked on that cigarette like a Weeki-Wachee mermaid sucking on an air tube. She didn't say a word until she'd finished. Then she went and asked 'em if they wanted dessert."

Ma put her hand on Pa's shoulder. We all watched Ranger and Tiger trying to decide who was chasing whom.

8

Seeking Plunder

The yellow school bus did not pass in front of Dogland during the summer, but I watched the highway for it most mornings. When Lurleen asked me what I wanted for my birthday, I told her, "To go to school."

She laughed, and then her face stilled. "You're a good boy, Chris."

A day or two later I was behind the restaurant, playing cars in the gravel with Digger. Pa came and sat on the green sidewalk. He prodded tobacco into his pipe, struck a wooden match against the concrete, lit his pipe, puffed twice, then said, "Chris, I hear you want to go to school."

I kept pushing a little metal sports car around the road we had made. "Yes, sir."

"Kids have to go to school when they're old enough for first grade. You've got a year to go." He watched us play, then said, "Some schools have kindergartens for kids who're five."

I looked up.

"But Dickison doesn't. Their school starts with first grade."

"Oh."

"Trenton has a kindergarten, though."

I knew Trenton. It was a small town as far from Dogland as Dickison or Chiefland.

"Problem is," Pa said, "their school bus stops a mile away. And Trenton's in another county, which means they don't have to take you. Even if they accepted you, your ma or I would have to drive you to the bus stop every morning, and one of us would have to meet you there every afternoon. It's mighty hard for either of us to get away now that we've let some workers go."

I nodded.

"They don't teach you anything useful in kindergarten. You won't learn about reading, writing, or arithmetic until first grade. That's when real school begins."

I nodded again.

"But if you want to go to kindergarten, we'll do what we have to to get you there."

I looked at him.

"Do you want us to do that?"

I worked my lip between my teeth.

"Well, Chris?"

"No, sir."

Pa studied me. "You're sure?"

I nodded.

"Well." Pa nodded, put his hands on his knees, and stood. "Your decision."

We drove to Minnesota early that August. Ma said it was for my birthday, even though we would return to Dogland before my birthday came. Pa said it was to give Ma a vacation. After a day or two, Pa left us in Rosecroix with Grandpa Abner and Grandma Letitia. He had to get back to Dogland to work.

At Rosecroix, we played with Grandma and Grandpa's

dachshund and the kids of the people who managed Grandpa's drugstore. Grandma and Grandpa had a huge white house with two stories and a basement, and you could go out onto the roof above the attached two-car garage. The backyard, bordered by Grandpa's roses and a white picket fence, extended endlessly toward the Rosecroix River. We played croquet there, as well as the usual games of hide-and-seek, chase, cowboys and Indians, and Mother, May I?

At night, Grandpa showed us movies in the basement on his 16-mm projector. Our favorite was about bear cubs that get into a campsite that has been abandoned for the day. The cubs topple things and break things and finally bring the canvas tents down on top of them before they run away. Little Bit, Digger, and I thought nothing was funnier in the world. Grandpa Abner, calling each of the cubs by our names, would cry, "Look, there's Big Boy Chris! Oh-oh, Pretty Letitia Bette's getting in the ice cream! Careful, Digger George, don't run through those hanging clothes or you'll be wearing somebody's nightie for sure!"

Grandma and Grandpa Uvdal had a color TV, which should have been wonderful, but Grandma Letitia always wanted to watch shows where people played accordions or guessed the answers to boring questions, even if the shows were in black and white and a cowboy show in color was on another channel. The only program we all liked—all except Pa, when he was there—was *Walt Disney's Wonderful World of Color.*

Several blocks away, across the Rosecroix River and two blocks into downtown, Grandpa's drugstore had two rooms, a boring one for drugs and health-care products and a better one for gifts like cameras, greeting cards, and chocolates. That room had a rack by the front window for paperback books, magazines, and comic books. The Uvdal Pharmacy's back room was dark and full of cardboard boxes and strange wonders like decorations for holidays that were months away. Next to Grandpa's drugstore was the toy store, and down the block near the movie theater was the bakery that made the best bread in the world, cylindrical loaves of cinnamon spirals cut into slices no larger than a child's hand and eaten chewy fresh or toasted crisp with a thick swash of butter.

But the best place in Minnesota was Grandma and Grandpa's cabin on Lake of the Woods. Thirty or forty small vacation homes made a multicolored ribbon between the woods of pine and birch and the wide blue-gray water. The Uvdals' had two bedrooms, one for Grandma and Grandpa and one for Ma, and a common room that faced the lake. Its walls were paneled with pale varnished boards, and the kitchen table was built like those in public parks, with two attached benches, except its coat of lacquer made it smooth to touch. Though the cabin had electricity, you had to use a hand pump to get water, and if you wanted warm water, you had to heat it on an old gas stove that had been in Grandma and Grandpa's house in Rosecroix before they had gotten an electric stove. A huge wooden box held quartered birch logs beside the cabin's stone fireplace that at night when you begged him, Grandpa would throw colored salts into, making dancing sprites of purple and blue and green and gold while a radio as big as a TV set and even older than Ma played static-filled music from the faraway land of Canada.

Catercorner to the cabin was the boathouse where Grandpa kept his fishing boat. The toilet was a room in the boathouse, which almost made it an inhouse. It was a two-holer, which Pa once said was a sign of luxury, which made Grandma Letitia say "Umf" in a way that meant Pa shouldn't joke about wealth or toilets, but Grandpa Abner laughed in a way that said it was all right. After you used the boathouse toilet, you sprinkled white powder on your number two so it didn't smell as bad and so it decomposed faster. Anything could hide down there, or in the dark rafters, so I always did my business in the boathouse toilet as fast as I could.

The rest of the boathouse was as wonderful as

Grandpa's basement. A rack by the door held two different-sized outboard motors, a smaller one for trolling and a larger one for racing. Along the wall were a set of gray oars and more bulky orange life jackets than I could count. The boathouse's shelves held toys, some of which had been Ma's and some of which had been bought for us. We kids each had tin sand buckets and sand shovels with our names painted on them in red enamel. Grandpa had a second croquet set at the cabin, as well as a badminton set, fishing poles, minnow buckets, tackle boxes, a large canvas American flag that flew on the tall white wooden flagpole between the cabin and the lake, and anything that had ever been useful to have at the lake during the last thirty years, and anything that might be useful someday.

The only permanent structure in the cabin's front yard was the wooden flagpole, encircled by a rough wooden bench. Its chalk-white surface was always stained by lake gulls. When the house was occupied, the yard also held two wooden Adirondack chairs and a picnic table, larger and darker and more crudely made than the table indoors. Many of the beach cabins had docks, but Grandma and Grandpa's did not. Large rocks had been dragged aside in the lake so Grandpa could land his fishing boat on the narrow beach of sand and gravel.

Lake of the Woods, a part of the Great Lakes, was cold in the summer, but no colder than Hawkins Springs. When you looked across the lake, you could not see land. The sea was like that, only salty. Sometimes you could see Gull Rock, a bony island on the horizon, but it had never had pirates, only gulls, so that did not excite me. During low tide, you could climb along a spine of rocks that stretched impossibly far from shore, perhaps twenty or thirty feet. You could even jump from one to the next if Ma or Grandpa was along to hold your hand and swing you while yelling, "Careful!" On sunny days, you could run around without your shirt, and the breeze from the lake kept you cool. On grim days the waves drove in to tease us with the notion of storm, and that was good, too. Then we would build the fire high and watch the wind and water play while we stayed warm and dry.

One of my favorite photos of my young self must have been taken on that trip. I stand in front of the cabin and wear black sneakers, dark trousers, and a powder-blue jacket with a black cowboy hat. A holster is on my right hip, and in my right hand I hold a cap gun. In my left I display the cover of a comic book titled *Colt 45.* At first glance my clothes might suggest the day was cool, but Digger stands nearby, hugging a birch tree and watching with something like envy. His trousers and sneakers are identical to mine, but he wears a striped short-sleeved shirt. My jacket is the color of the cowboy's on the cover of the comic, and I am holding my pistol like the cowboy holds his. Children know that style is more important than comfort.

Rosecroix's doctor and dentist had cabins next to Grandma and Grandpa's. On the first morning at Lake of the Woods, when I had been alone running around outside shooting bad guys, I stepped through the back door of what I thought was Grandpa and Grandma's cabin. A pleasant woman stared at me, and I stared at her. She seemed familiar, though the cabin did not. She smiled. "Hello. You must be Chris. You came to visit?"

I continued to stare.

"You should knock, you know."

That was the rule when you went to a strange house. But what was the rule when a strange house came to you?

"Your grandparents sure are happy to have you here." I nodded.

"Would you like something to eat?"

I shook my head. "No, thank you, ma'am."

"It's too bad your father had to hurry back to Florida."

I began examining the strange cabin, trying to find something familiar.

"Does your mother know you're here?"

I shook my head.

"Then maybe you should go tell her where you are. We'll visit some other time."

I nodded and backed out of the house. In the yard, between the gravel road and the row of cabins, all different colors but all similar in size and shape, I sought something I knew. I found nothing. I walked toward one cabin, then turned and walked toward another, then darted between two cabins to be near the lake. I saw no people. Chipmunks hid at my approach. Gulls screamed overhead, advising or mocking me.

I knew a dock stood in front of the cabin next to Grandma and Grandpa's, but docks stood near every second or third cabin. I knew I would recognize the inside of Grandma and Grandpa's cabin as soon as I saw it, but I had lost faith in my ability to know its outside. I did not dare knock on any door or peek in any cabin after walking in on the strange woman.

"Christopher!" Ma called nearby. I turned and ran toward her voice. She stood in front of a white cabin with green shutters and green shingles. When she saw me, I slowed down suddenly, and she laughed. "What've you been up to, young man?"

"Playing."

She smiled. "Just so you're having fun."

That night, I woke on the daybed in the cabin's front room. Embers remained in the fireplace. Their glow, a small night-light shielded by a seashell, and the moon were the only illumination. I could feel Digger sleeping beside me, and I could see Little Bit's still form on the couch across the way. Shadows moved in the wind outside, but if I did not look at them, they did not matter. The wind itself was a familiar and comforting sound; I doubt that woke me.

Something walked in the passageway between the two bedrooms. The refrigerator opened, spilling light into the cabin, but I could not see around the corner to see who or what was there. Then a bedroom door opened, and Grandpa whispered, "Can't sleep?"

Ma whispered back, "I hope I didn't wake you, Pop-pop."

"It isn't always easy, being an old married lady, is it?"

Ma laughed softly.

Grandpa said, "They're good kids."

"You think all kids are good kids."

Grandpa laughed, louder than Ma. "They're especially good kids."

"Sometimes it's tough to remember that. I'm really very lucky."

Grandpa said more quietly, "Luke works hard for all of you. Your mother sees that."

"Not much else."

"She wants Dogland to work out for you. We both do."

"I know, Daddy."

"We don't mind the money."

"Luke does."

"He shouldn't. We know he's good for it."

"Daddy?"

"Yes?"

"Did you and Mimmy ever—?"

The half question hung in the air for so long that I nearly fell back to sleep.

"That's why we're glad to help you. My parents helped us get started. It's natural."

"No. I mean, you two never quarrel, and Luke and I—"

Again, the question dangled. Grandpa said, "Do you miss him?" If Ma answered aloud, I did not hear her. Grandpa said, "Do you want to be a family?"

"Of course! But—"

"Then isn't that your answer?"

"Oh."

"You should sleep. You're not just sleeping for yourself, you know."

"Yes, Daddy." I heard them move apart, then Ma said, "Pop-pop?"

"Suzzy?"

"Good night."

"Sleep tight."

Their bedroom doors closed, one right after the other. I thought, *Don't let the bedbugs bite,* and fell asleep almost immediately.

I don't remember the drive back to Florida in the small Dodge that had been Ma's before her marriage, which Grandma and Grandpa had given back to her as a birthday present. Each morning, Ma had us take some medicine with our vitamins, and we were, by our standards and hers, quiet through the day.

At Dogland, the first new thing I noticed was Bridget, an Irish wolfhound who had trouble adjusting to Florida's moist heat and Dogland's concrete runs. She had been sleeping on the bed with Pa while we were gone. Now she spent her days in front of a fan in the Doggy Salon and her nights in Ma and Pa's room on a mattress from Digger's crib. I didn't like Bridget. She was big and awkward, and she slobbered on your face, and since she was a wolfhound, she might gobble you with one bite. I did not learn until a year or two later that wolfhounds hunted wolves and were not like them.

Near Dogland, just across the river from Hawkins Springs and the Fountain of Youth Motor Inn, a new tourist attraction was ready to open: Pirates' Paradise. Mr. Drake told Pa about it, saying, "I never would've thought it possible, but I think they're going to achieve a new low in historical accuracy."

"Huh," said Pa. "Business'll be booming."

"Pirates?" I whispered.

Mr. Drake nodded.

"Who's behind it?" Pa asked.

"Don't know," Mr. Drake said. "I was away on business

for a couple of weeks. Lumiere handled the paperwork."

"Seems like you've been called out of town a lot lately."

"The company's been a little busy. Reason I opened a branch in Latchahee was to have time for Gwenny and myself. Head office hasn't figured out that I've got a smooth operation 'cause nothing at all happens here, so I keep gettin' called to help when another agent's swamped. It's hard to say no."

"They have pirates?" I repeated.

Mr. Drake laughed and nodded. "And a pirate ship you can board, and a dungeon, and a Spanish village that gets raided every hour on the hour."

"Wow."

"It'll open by your birthday," Pa said. "Want to go?"

"Yeah!"

Mr. Drake said, "What else do you want for your birthday?"

"A driver's license."

Pa and Mr. Drake both laughed. Pa said, "Where're you planning to drive?"

"The bus stop."

Pa stopped smiling. Mr. Drake, watching me, grinned even more. "Why do you want to drive to a bus stop? Where'll a bus take you that you couldn't drive?"

"School," I said.

Pa looked at his wristwatch, then at Mr. Drake, then stood. "Tell Susan I had to run into town."

"Sure." Mr. Drake frowned. "Is there something—"

"Nah," said Pa. "I shouldn't be long."

We watched Pa go out to our pickup truck. As he drove off, Mr. Drake said, "So, where's this bus stop?"

"At the Stan'ard Oil. Ma and Pa have to work all day, but if I had a driver's license, I could drive there by myself. Then I could go to kin'ergarden on the school bus."

Mr. Drake said, "You have to be fourteen years old to get a learner's permit in Florida."

"Oh."

Ma hurried into the restaurant, saw us, and smiled. "Artie."

He smiled back. "Susan." After a moment he said, "Luke went into town. Said he wouldn't be long."

"That man." Ma looked at me. "It's such a nice day. You should be outside playing."

"I'm reading." Lurleen had saved several weeks of Sunday funnies for me, and I was looking at the pictures at the table next to Mr. Drake. Prince Valiant, Dick Tracy, and the Phantom were my favorites. Grandma and Grandpa's paper had Flash Gordon, which was my favorite in Minnesota, but the *Dickison Star* did not carry it.

Ma sighed. Mr. Drake said, "Take a load off your feet?"

"Don't mind if I do." She sat. The restaurant was quiet in midafternoon.

"Where're Little Bit and Digger?" said Mr. Drake.

"Napping."

"They're little kids," I explained.

"Ah." Mr. Drake glanced back at Ma. "Good trip home?"

I nodded.

Ma laughed. "A good one, but a slow one. Phenobarb's a wonderful traveling companion, but even with that we averaged about thirty miles an hour."

Mr. Drake's eyes narrowed. "Oh?"

Ma nodded. "Probably wouldn't be here yet without it. The kids weren't any real trouble, but we were still constantly stopping to find a lost toy, get a drink, go potty, fix a sandwich, you know. A flyswatter lying in view on the dash helped the phenobarb take effect."

Mr. Drake swirled his coffee. "The Victorians, the lower-class ones, at least, quieted their children, too. The drug of choice gave them a name: Gin Babies. Imagine infant alcoholics crying with the d.t.'s—"

"No!"

"Less enlightened times."

"It was just for the trip. Dr. Jim—he's our family doctor—gave me the prescription for the kids. He told me how much was safe."

"I didn't mean to pry."

Ma glanced at him.

He rolled his eyes. "Well, all right, I did. Sorry."

Ma patted his hand just as Lurleen set an iced tea in front of her. Ma drew her hand back. "Ah, thanks, Lurleen."

Lurleen looked at Mr. Drake. " 'Nother cup o' coffee, Mr. Drake?"

"Please."

Lurleen refilled his cup and returned to the counter. Ma gave a tiny laugh, then said, "Is Gwenny looking forward to her last year of school?"

"Mm-hmm."

"She still seeing that Tepes boy?"

"I guess. Seems like they break things off near every three or four weeks, he disappears for a month or so, then he's back as if he'd never left." Mr. Drake held his thumb and forefinger a quarter of an inch apart. "I'm this close to forbidding her to see him. When they're together, she loses weight and starts looking as bleached as a Klansman's sheet, but she's happy. When they're apart, she fills out and spends time in the sun till she's as brown as an Indian. I'd think she was happy if that wasn't when she runs fastest to answer the phone."

"Love is strange."

Mr. Drake smiled. "I'm tempted to demand he stay away from her. Then they'd elope and put an end to this."

"They're so young."

"Not by local standards. Look at Francine Carter."

"Francy's getting divorced and going back to school. Hadn't you heard? Talk about living life fast."

"Good for her." He sipped his coffee. "Seen much of Ethorne?"

"He hasn't been back to work all summer."

Mr. Drake shook his head. "He worked for my family

when I was a boy. Used to take me hunting and fishing. I s'pose he was more of a father to me than anyone."

"Oh?"

Mr. Drake nodded, took a pack of cigarettes from his shirt pocket, looked at them, then returned them to his shirt. "My parents died when I was younger than Chris. Father was part of the U.S. occupation of Haiti. They both took sick and died in Port-au-Prince. My uncle gave me a place in his house, but he was a traveling salesman, often away and drunk when he was home."

"I'm sorry."

"Don't be. He had a good library, and he treated me well. I can't complain."

Ma nodded.

Mr. Drake smiled. "So. What do you think of the South now that you've been here awhile?"

"I like it, but I won't ever get used to it."

"For instance?"

"Well, attitudes toward work are so different. I have a good colored woman for housework and washing now, but she's the first dependable one I've found since my girl I liked ran off with that albino evangelist. People, white or colored, down here have absolutely no sense of responsibility. They say they're coming to work and don't. We've had them leave at noon and not return, for no apparent reason as they seemed happy enough. One gal said her divorced husband was after her kids when she didn't show up. She said she'd taken her two babies and driven around the countryside all night to escape him, so she was leaving the state. She stopped here at six A.M. for her check. It's"—Ma shrugged—"not Minnesota."

Mr. Drake laughed. "No, it surely is not."

Ma's face tightened. "I shouldn't go on like this."

"You might have cause."

"Not really. People are so friendly here. I do appreciate that. The good workers, well, they're as good as any workers anywhere. And I can't say I mind the general attitude, except when it's inconvenient. I bet there are a lot fewer ulcers here than anywhere in America."

"Lot of ulcers get brought to Florida."

The bell over the front door rang as the door swung open. We all looked as Mr. Shale strode in. His face was red and damp, and his white hair stood in tufts about his head. He wore a faded black coat over his chef's apron. In one hand, he carried a green canvas bag.

"Mr. Shale!" Ma called. "You found our deposit!"

"Yes, ma'm, indeed I did."

"Come in; sit down! You didn't walk here in this heat?"

"Oh, I'm a lizard." He sat by Ma and Mr. Drake. "A lizard for the Lord. How're you, Artie?"

"Fine, Reverend, as always."

Lurleen called, "Fix you somethin', Mr. Shale?"

"The Lord provides," Mr. Shale answered.

"An iced tea? A Coke?" Ma asked, then saw him nod and called, "A Coke!"

Mr. Shale set the green canvas bag on the linoleum tabletop. "I thought you folks'd be relieved to see this."

"We are. Luke figured we'd just learned an expensive lesson."

"What happened?" Mr. Drake asked.

"Oh, Luke was talking with friends of ours from New Orleans who'd come to visit the other day, and he left the bank deposit on top of their car. We didn't figure out what had happened to it until after they'd gone."

Lurleen placed a tall glass of Coke and ice before Mr. Shale. "Men're lucky their most treasured possessions are attached to 'em, that's all I got to say. Here you go, Mr. Shale."

Ma blushed, but I didn't know why.

Mr. Shale took the Coke in both hands and lowered his head toward the straw. "You are two fine women in the eyes of the Lord."

Ma waved that away with a flicker of red-painted fingernails. "Was the deposit near your place?"

"No. I was walking and thinking upon the end. I found your money 'longside the road 'bout half a mile past Tom Hasty's Truck Stop."

Ma unzipped the bag and ran a finger through its contents. "Looks like it's all here." She plucked a bill and held it out. "You have to take a reward."

Mr. Shale shook his head. "No, ma'm, I don't, and I couldn't."

"A donation," Ma said. "You must be able to put some money to some good use."

"Oh, I don't know," Mr. Shale said. "The Lord sends enough folks needing burgers and the good word to meet all my daily needs. And I don't need much when the end is so close. The signs are all about us. The Commies will bring us to war, maybe over Cuba, maybe over Berlin. You can see it coming. Havoc has been cried, and soon the dogs of war'll be let slip."

Mr. Drake said, "Shakespeare?"

Mr. Shale nodded. "*Julius Caesar.* The signs are everywhere, if you know how to look. I find newspapers along the road, and the front pages speak of destruction. War with the godless Russians must come."

"Really?" I said, with perhaps a bit of eagerness.

"Not if we can help it," Ma said.

"There's only one who can help it," Mr. Shale lifted a finger from his Coke glass to point at the roof.

"One who expects us to do our best to keep the peace," said Mr. Drake.

"True," said Mr. Shale, and he smiled at Ma. "The Lord led me to your lost deposit for a reason. Maybe He means for your kind donation to be put to His service." He tucked the bill Ma had given him into a pocket of his apron and looked at me. "How's Tiger?"

"Okay," I said.

Ma said, "He's growing up strong and independent, just like my Christopher."

I grinned. "Yeah."

Pa returned sometime after Mr. Shale had left, but Mr. Drake had not. Ma called, "Luke, look! Gideon Shale found our deposit."

Pa grinned. "I guess I ought to pray with the old coot, next time he asks me to."

"What'd you do in town?"

"Just a little last-minute business I'd neglected."

The ship at Pirates' Paradise was far better than any real ship could have been. It was a shell built on a dock on the river, so you could look over either side and see water. It had ropes and masts and heavy iron cannon on wooden blocks that you could sit on. Above the ship, on the tallest of the three sailless masts, flew a black flag with a white skull and crossbones.

I turned in circles on the deck, trying to see it all at once. My birthday expedition included Ma, Pa, Digger, Little Bit, Mr. Drake, Gwenny Drake, and Jordy Greenleaf. Jordy and I stopped staring at the ship to stare at each other. "Whoa!" Jordy said.

"Yeah," I agreed. "Whoa!"

Mr. Drake said, "So? Where's Captain Blood?"

Someone behind us said, "Arr, matey. Cap'n Blood's a scribbler's phantasm. Why d'ye seek 'im when the boldest privateer of all walks these decks, an' that be me, Cap'n John 'Awkins."

Captain John grinned as though a spotlight should glint against his teeth. Though a small man, brown-haired and tanned as dark as some of the lighter blacks who worked at Dogland, he swaggered like a giant. His short hair was Brylcreemed back from his forehead, and a golden clip-on earring adorned one earlobe, and his white short-sleeved shirt and tan trousers would have gone unremarked anywhere in America that year, if he had not worn them with high black boots, a red sash, crossed flintlock pistols, and a cutlass.

"Now, there's a real pirate," Pa said.

I nodded, and Jordy said, "Yeah!"

"Welcome aboard me pirate ship!" Captain John cried. "What's your name, laddie? Be ye Black-hearted Bob, Bloody Bill, Dev'lish Davey, or Murd'rous Mike?"

"Chris'pher."

"Ah! Christopher, the Crimson Pirate! Aye, I've heard o' you, you scurvy dog! You parked your longboat out front and came aboard on a social call, I hope. We pirates must stick together, eh? We only raid the Spanish. And the French. And the Dutch. But not each other, eh?"

I nodded, and Ma, Pa, Mr. Drake, and Gwenny Drake laughed. Mr. Drake said, "I thought Hawkins's ship was the *Jesus of Lubeck*."

Captain John threw his head back and laughed. "Aye, *was!* Ye don't expect a rover to keep the same ship for four hundred years, do ye?" He looked at Little Bit. "And who's the pretty wench?"

"That's Cap'n Li'l Bit," I said.

"Ah, indeed. *Captain* Li'l Bit. You surely sailed with Anne Bonney and Mary Reid."

"No," said Little Bit.

"With Morgan the Pirate," I said.

"Arr! Captain Morgan. There was a man! The glorious sack of Panama! Ah, men dreamed the dreams of giants in those days."

"A little after your time, Captain Hawkins," said Mr. Drake.

Before the pirate could respond, Jordy said, "Was it a big sack?"

Captain John nodded solemnly. "Indeed, laddie. As big as all Panama."

"C'mon," said Gwenny. "I want to see the dungeon."

"Do ye?" Captain John laughed. "Careful what ye wish for, lassie."

"She's Gwenny," I said. "Lassie's a dog."

Gwenny shook her head. "Thanks, boyfriend."

Captain John slipped his fingers into his sash and withdrew several bright yellow slips of paper no bigger than calling cards. "Here, take a bit o' plunder with ye, now. You, Cap'n—"

"Jordy," Jordy said.

"Jordy," Captain John agreed. "And you—"

"He's Digger," I said.

"I dig that," said Captain John. " 'Cause I'm one hep pirate. Here's one for you, Cap'n Li'l Bit. And you, dungeon wench. And you, Cap'n Chris."

The yellow paper had a picture of a skull and crossbones, along with some words. "Thank you," I said, and folded it to put in my pocket.

Ma read over my shoulder. "It's for free french fries."

"All right!" Jordy and I said together.

Pa told Captain John, "I'm Luke Nix. This is my wife, Susan. We own Dogland, up the road."

Captain John shook Pa's hand, then kissed Ma's, which made her cover her mouth and smile. "It's good to meet you at last. Come aboard anytime."

Going down the gangplank, Ma asked, "Having fun?"

I nodded. Jordy said, "Yes'm, this is sure grand!"

The native village consisted of a couple of frond-covered huts with picnic tables beneath them. The dungeon was a small three-sided room with a skeleton manacled to one wall and a dummy dressed like a pirate stretched on a torturer's rack. A second, empty rack and an empty set of chains were by the opposite wall, where a pirate with a red scarf around his head was reading a newspaper.

As we approached, he set the paper aside, started to smile, studied us, then continued to smile. "Hi, y'all. Want to get your picture taken with a real pirate?"

Gwenny said, "Dream on, Cal Carter."

Ma looked from Cal to me to Pa. She said, "Luke."

Pa watched Cal, who said, "What about you, Chrissy-boy? I can put you in the rack and give it a crank or two, just like a pirate would."

I shook my head. Pa looked at Cal, then at me, then said, "C'mon, Chris."

Cal said, "I hear business ain't so hot at Dogland lately, Mr. Nix."

Pa looked at him. Ma glanced at Pa, but he suddenly laughed. "We'll be around awhile, Cal. Don't worry about us."

Ma and Pa walked on. Mr. Drake looked back at Cal and said, "If a pup barks at an old wolf long enough, it's going to get nipped."

"I ain't scared of no one," Cal said.

Mr. Drake nodded. "You've identified the problem. Now see what you can do about it."

As we walked away, Little Bit smiled. "We're li'l wolfs."

The restaurant, a large place paneled with dark timber planks, had long wooden tables and dim electric chandeliers. I ordered a buccaneer burger and fries. Mr. Drake told how Blackbeard would tie lit candles in his beard to make the people he attacked think he was crazy. Pa said he thought that must've worked pretty good, then said something about Cal being so concerned about Dogland when this place wasn't doing much business and didn't look like it was going to. Gwenny joked with Little Bit while Jordy and I wandered around the dining room, looking at posters for pirate movies, reproductions of paintings of sailing ships, and secondhand mannequins wearing seventeenth-century clothes and weapons. A black woman in a red circle skirt and a bare-shouldered white blouse brought our food on a tray, and my root beer came in a heavy frosted glass mug. It was my fifth birthday, and I could not imagine that it could be improved until Pa told me he'd gotten to Trenton in time to guarantee that the last available place at kindergarten would be mine, and he and Ma would be happy to get me to and from the bus stop every school day. When Ma asked if I liked that, I liked it so much that, unable to speak, I could only grin.

Early each morning Ma or Pa drove me a mile to the Standard Oil station at the end of the Trenton school bus line.

Late each afternoon one of my parents would leave the business of running a tourist attraction to meet me. Sometimes I would have to wait at the station for our car to arrive, but I became friendly with the old man who ran the station, so the delays in picking me up were merely an extension in the adventure of education.

I loved school. I have forgotten my kindergarten teacher and most of my classmates, but I have not forgotten the thrill of riding the bus, and learning to sing and color and cut out traced figures on stiff paper with dull scissors, winning praise from my teacher, my parents, and my grandparents. I crayoned suns as large as my paper and as yellow as margarine. I made stick men who were pilgrims, jet pilots, and pirates. I learned to cut on the line and color inside the line, to make the sky blue and the grass green. I sang songs whose words were meaningless expressions of joy: Frair uh jock ah, frair uh jock ah, door may voo? Door may voo? Sing cock uls an muss uls, a lie vuh lie voe. Yanky doodle went to town, London bridge is falling down, Mary had a little lamb, Baa-baa-black sheep, have you any wool? I plejaleejinced to the flag, and I prayed to Our Father Huart in Heaven. I played tag, catch, and dodgeball. I ran when girls chased me to kiss me, and when they caught me, I rubbed off their kisses to rid myself of girl cooties, screaming, "Ee-yuck!" while I laughed.

"Storm's comin'," Ethorne said, entering the kitchen.

"Yep." Pa folded the morning paper and set it aside. "Hurricane Donna. You heard it on the radio?"

"I heard."

"Gonna be a bad one. Record gales."

Ma put a bowl of Sugar Frosted Flakes in front of me. "Seems like every couple of years, there's a new record storm. How can that be?"

Little Bit smiled. "Gets bad."

Ma looked at me. "No school for you today, young man."

"Aw, Ma!"

"They'll probably close the school anyway." Ma smoothed her apron and smiled at Ethorne. "It's good to see you, Ethorne."

"It's good to see you, ma'am. How you been?"

"Fine. Went to visit my parents for a couple of weeks this summer. That was nice."

"Yes'm, I'd 'xpect so."

"How's Seth doing at college?"

"He's workin' hard, ma'm. Which is what I ought to be doin' now."

Pa laughed. "It's been months since we've seen you."

"No, Pa," I said. "We seen Ethorne—"

Pa's glance told me to be quiet. We had seen Ethorne one evening in July, staggering along the highway with a bottle in a paper bag in one fist.

"Saw," Ma corrected.

"Once or twice," Pa added. "We haven't seen Ethorne in the sense of being sociable."

"Oh."

Pa looked back at Ethorne. "We had to lay off some workers."

"Didn't come for money, Mist' Luke. That storm's movin' out. We ought to be gettin' ready for it. James is out feedin' the dogs already. You want to bring any of 'em in?"

We all looked at Pa. He said, "One advantage of building the pens yourself is you know they're built to stand."

Ma said, "What about Checky?"

Pa rolled his eyes. "All right."

"An' Bo-Peep," said Little Bit.

"And Mickey," said Ma.

"Any more requests?" Pa asked.

"Captain," I said.

"Elkhounds don't mind a little water. What, you want to bring them all in?"

Little Bit nodded. "Uh-huh."

Pa rolled his eyes. "Maybe I'll put a cot for me in the Doggy Salon till it's over."

Hurricane Donna hit America's East Coast on September 6, 1960, breaking all records for destructive storms in the U.S. One hundred forty-eight people died when Donna passed by. At Dogland, the skies grayed and lowered, and rain slapped the earth in heavy sheets, soaking within seconds anyone who stepped into it. A new-planted palm in the open field in front of Dogland blew free of the ground, and a wooden sign fell onto a customer's windshield, but, as Ma pointed out, we had insurance, and no one was hurt.

My delight in school was recognized by my teacher or my classmates. I was chosen by whim or vote to be one of the crown-bearers for the coronation of Trenton High School's homecoming king and queen. There is a black-and-white photograph of me in a white jacket and dark trousers beside the other crown-bearer, a dark-haired girl in a princess's white gown. We are both smiling. When I remember the photo, I am surprised by how healthy and clever and cheerful and willing to please we appear to be.

I practiced my duty as a crown-bearer in the school gymnasium. The girl and I had to walk side by side with the bright crowns balanced before us on crimson pillows. Later, when we walked the same route for the ceremony, the bleachers were full of students and parents, and the ceiling and walls were decked with colored crepe and cardboard. The school band must have played, though I remember no sounds. I walked, smiling and half-blind, through a wall of spotlights and flashbulbs. My only thought was balancing the crown on its pillow. After other members of the school court took the crown, I peeked at the girl beside me. She smiled back. I wondered if I would grow up to marry her.

* * *

That Christmas the Nix family drove back to Grandpa and
Grandma's. Grandpa made a skating rink in his backyard
and built a slide by shaping snow and strengthening it
with water that froze soon after it was applied. Though Ma
told Little Bit and me that we had seen snow when we
were babies, we thought we had gone to a place better
than Santa Claus's house at the north pole. That belief was
confirmed by Grandpa's Christmas decorations. At his
basement workbench he had cut elves, a Santa in a sleigh,
and a team of reindeer from plywood, then painted them
and set them up in front of the house. The elves were
putting lights and ornaments on a pine tree, and Santa
was flying above the garage with Rudolf's nose glowing red
to show him the way.

Pa did not stay with us. He visited Grandma Bette and
Uncle John and Aunt Felicity, who also lived in Minnesota,
and then, as before, he returned to Florida alone. I don't
know whether that was planned. In Minnesota we kids
raced through a cycle of childhood illnesses, chicken pox
followed immediately by mumps. Ma thought we might
have included measles in the mix, but she couldn't be sure.
We handed off the diseases so that as one kid was getting
better, another was falling ill.

We were all healthy on Christmas morning. Digger and
I ran downstairs in our pajamas and bathrobes to find Little Bit already up and sorting through the presents in the
large red felt sock embroidered with her name that hung
over the fireplace. The Christmas tree, topped with a
golden angel who brushed her halo against the ceiling,
stood in the middle of a mountain of presents. I don't remember the gifts anymore, but I remember too many
were clothes from Grandma, who always gave useless
things like fancy sweaters you couldn't play in. Grandpa,
Ma, and Santa always included toys. Grandma baked ham
and scalloped potatoes, which were wonderful, and sweet
potatoes, which I only had to take a little bite of. After we

had tested all the toys and eaten to the point of bursting (one of my favorite images at that age), we put on our snowsuits and snow boots and scarves and mittens and caps and waddled into the winter, where Ma pushed us on borrowed skates across Grandpa's ice rink, and rode with us down the riverbank and across the frozen river on the sled that had been hers when she was a girl.

Then, on New Year's Day, Grandpa rushed Ma to Doctor Jim's, where she told us everything was nice, because she got to rest in bed all day, eat soup and ice cream, and listen to the radio. After a week or two, Ma came back to Grandma and Grandpa's house, but Dr. Jim told her she couldn't travel immediately. So we learned a little of the life of a small Minnesota town. Ma took us to hockey games, which I did not enjoy because they reminded me that I could not stand on skates for long. Little Bit loved watching and yelling, "Go, Rosecroix, go!" when the high school cheerleaders prompted it. By the middle of a game, Digger would begin yelling, too, laughing as noise and steam poured from his lips in the cold arena.

I liked the museum and the library, two rooms in the same building where I could walk in quiet wonder. The museum had cases of military items, guns and buckles and medical tools, and ancient photos and antique farm implements. My favorite item was a rusted revolver, long-barreled like a cowboy's six-shooter, that had lain in the river until it changed into a pitted reddish-gray mass whose only value was its mystery. The library had more books than I had ever seen in my life, and shelf after shelf were books with pictures and words that Ma could read to me, over and over again until I gave in to her suggestion that we take these back and check out more.

Ma's favorite part of those days may have been the nights when we went to hear the high school band. She had played the snare drum when she attended Rosecroix. She pointed out each of the band instruments to us, but she dwelled on the percussion section, telling us which had been available in her day and marveling at the additions, the bongos, maracas, and a shining scratch tube.

Around us, in 1961, the United States of America (which was part of where I lived—Dogland, Latchahee County, Florida, the United States of America, the World, the Solar System, the Milky Way, the Universe) formally decided that Cuba (a tiny island near Miami), like Communist China (a faraway island so big that it was a continent), did not exist. President Eisenhower, who looked like Grandpa Abner, left office. In his farewell speech, he said, "We must guard against the acquisition of unwarranted influence, whether sought or unsought, by the military-industrial complex. The potential for the disastrous rise of misplaced power exists and will persist." John F. Kennedy, a handsome man with wavy brown hair, became the thirty-fifth U.S. President. He created the Peace Corps so Americans could help people who were not as well off as we were. U.S.-supported Cuban rebels were defeated at the Bay of Pigs by Fidel Castro's troops; Mr. Castro looked like Pa with a beard. The Berlin Wall was built, dividing a city in Germany between the Americans and the Russians. Ernest Hemingway, Dashiell Hammett, Gary Cooper, and Carl Jung died; Gary Cooper had been a movie cowboy, almost as good as John Wayne. Robert Heinlein's *Stranger in a Strange Land* and Joseph Heller's *Catch-22* appeared in print, but they were books that I would not know about for ten or more years. *West Side Story* won the Academy Award; Ma bought the LP, which meant "long player," which was not like our kids' records, which were 45s with only one song per side, like the thick 78s from Ma's childhood that were still in her bedroom in Minnesota. Yuri Gagarin of the Soviet Union was the first person to orbit the Earth, but he was a Russian, so that didn't really count. Alan Shepard of the U.S. rode in the first manned U.S. rocket into space, and he was a hero. Stretch pants and panty hose appeared in the marketplace. Far more importantly to me, so did the first issues of DC Comics' *Justice League of America* and Marvel Comics' *Fantastic Four.*

In the spring, a man and a woman arrived at Dogland in a covered wagon. Its wheels came from an automobile, but it was a wooden wagon covered with canvas like the Conestoga Grandma Bette had ridden in when she was a girl. It was drawn by two shaggy brown horses with white on their heads and hooves, followed by a black and white goat on a chain, and led by a white, three-legged dog with a black spot over one eye. Little Bit saw them first, but I ran back to tell everyone, "There's a wagon train coming!"

Pa laughed when he saw what I was pointing at. "You need more'n one wagon for a wagon train."

I didn't care. I ran out beside the restaurant to watch the covered wagon roll down our driveway. The man and the woman on the driver's bench were short, sun-browned people with thick dark hair. She wore a flowered skirt with a red gypsy blouse and tied her hair back in a ponytail. He had a beard like dour men in old pictures, and his hair, curling around the tops of his ears and touching the collar of his blue work shirt, was longer than any man's I had seen. I thought she needed a bonnet, and he, a Winchester rifle and a ten-gallon hat.

After the man said, "Whoa," and stopped the horses, Pa said, "Quite a rig."

The man smiled. "Thanks. I built it."

"Nice work."

"Do you mind us stopping here?" the woman asked.

"Not at all. You'll draw a few extra tourists."

"That's not the purpose," the man said.

"This is our home." The woman smiled at me. "Would you like to live in a wagon?"

I nodded.

Pa said, "I'm Luke Nix. That's my boy, Chris."

The man nodded. "I'm Joe. This is Mary."

"How do you do?" Mary said.

"Fine, thank you, ma'm," I said, and everyone smiled.

"Would there be a place where we could camp overnight?" Mary asked.

"We never mind a little work in exchange," Joe added. "I'm fairly handy."

Pa said, "How about under that old oak?"

Mary and Joe looked at the Heart Tree, then at each other. She told Pa, "Bless you."

He shrugged. "If you're worried about tourists"—he looked at me—"or kids pestering you, you can park by the woods."

"The oak's fine." Joe rattled the reins to prompt the horses.

As Mary and Joe got down from the wagon, Ma introduced herself and Little Bit. Lurleen and Mrs. Stark came into the parking lot to look at the newcomers. Lurleen only frowned and returned to the restaurant, but Mrs. Stark asked if Mary and Joe were real gypsies, and part of a caravan, or with the circus, or going down to the Wild West Show near Ocala, and wasn't it uncomfortable riding on that bench, and didn't passing cars make the animals nervous. Pa said we should let these people get settled, and then they could talk about doing a little work in exchange for a meal or two. Ma nodded and said, "C'mon, Chris."

"I'll help."

Mary said, "We don't mind. If he doesn't get in the way."

"He won't." Pa studied the wagon. "Must be nice, just traveling." He shook his head, told me, "Keep out of their way," and followed Dogland's staff.

On the wagon's back was a sign. I pointed at it. "Kay ee wye double-you—"

Mary began to unharness the horses. "'Key West or Bust.'"

"I know a joke."

"I like a good joke," Joe said. I followed him and Mary as they took care of the horses.

"Okay," I said. "A boy told his sister to pass the pie. An' she said if he ate another bite, he'd bust. An' he said, 'Then pass the pie an' duck!' " When I managed to stop laughing, I saw Joe and Mary were smiling.

"That's a good one," Joe said.

"Yeah." Their three-legged dog sniffed my hand. "What's his name?"

"Dog."

I frowned. Mary said, "You don't have to name everything."

I patted the dog's head and smiled as he licked my hand. "You could call him Pirate."

"Could call him lots of things," said Joe.

"Pirate's good," said Mary.

"True," said Joe. "Pirate it is." He looked up and smiled. "Ethorne!"

Ethorne and Digger came around the Heart Tree. Digger stood slightly behind Ethorne, peering around his leg. Ethorne said, "How you two been?"

"Good." Mary took his hand between both of hers, then looked at Digger. "Who's this?"

"That's Digger," I said. "He's only three."

"How do you do, Digger?" Joe squatted on his heels. "I'm Joe, and this is Mary."

As Digger looked down at his feet, I said, "Digger don't talk much."

"Not much he needs to say," Ethorne said.

"Ah." Mary smiled at Digger. "A thinker."

"No, ma'm," I said. "I'm the thinker. I'm going to be a lawyer."

"He thinks today," Ethorne said. "Thought you was thinkin' on bein' a cowboy, Kit Carson."

"A cowboy lawyer," I said.

Ethorne nodded. "Ain't many folks meetin' the demand for that line o' work just now."

Joe said, "What's Digger going to be?"

I squinted. My parents and grandparents often speculated about what Little Bit and I would do. No one had

ever suggested what Digger might be. Ethorne said,
"Whatever he sets his mind to."

Mary said, "He must be a good friend of yours."

Ethorne rubbed Digger's head. "Digger keeps me comp'ny when I got outdoor work. He likes studyin' what folks
do."

I said, "When I'm a lawyer, I'll be rich."

"That's what you want?" Mary asked.

I nodded. Pa said doctors and lawyers made the most
money, and I hated Band-Aids. "Or draw. I like drawing."

"What do you want to do, Digger?"

He looked at her and whispered, "Make things."

Behind us, someone spoke. "I understand that." I did
not recognize the tones of pleasure until I turned. Mr. Lumiere stood by the rear of the wagon.

He was dressed in a white short-sleeved shirt, white
slacks, and white tennis shoes. With the sun setting behind
him, his face glowed too brightly for me to look at him.
He spread his arms wide as if he expected an embrace
from someone.

Mary said without moving forward, "Why are you
here?"

Mr. Lumiere let his arms fall as he shrugged. "To greet
you on your return. How long has it been?"

Joe said, "You know."

"You must've expected me."

Mary said, "Never and always."

Mr. Lumiere laughed. "Thank you."

"But not so soon," Joe said.

"You hardly expected to sneak into the county in a
horse-drawn wagon?"

"No."

"You've already visited Mrs. DeLyon?" When Mary and
Joe did not answer, Mr. Lumiere squatted as Joe had to
look at Digger. "So. This is Ethorne's good friend."

Ethorne said, "World's full o' my good friends. My bad
friends, too."

Mr. Lumiere rolled his eyes as he smiled, then looked

back at Digger. "Hello, Digger. I hope you'll be my friend."

I said, "Digger don't like strangers."

Mr. Lumiere nodded. "Yes, I remember you. But we aren't strangers, are we?" When I had no answer, he smiled again at Digger. "You see? Your clever brother isn't afraid of me." Digger, staying beside Ethorne, met Mr. Lumiere's gaze, then shook his head. Mr. Lumiere laughed. "That's a brave boy!"

Digger stepped behind Ethorne's legs. Mr. Lumiere laughed again, and then Little Bit came around the front of the covered wagon. "It's not nice to scare Digger."

Ethorne said, "There's a long walk 'tween scared and careful."

Little Bit continued to glare at Mr. Lumiere. "It's not nice to make Digger be careful."

"I don't have to make anyone scared or careful, Miss Little Bit. That only happens when I fail to make them see things my way. Sooner or later, almost everyone sees things my way." Mr. Lumiere asked Digger, "Did I scare you? Sorry. I didn't mean to."

I said, "He'd cry if he was scared."

Mary squatted beside Digger and hugged him. "You're with friends."

"Yes," said Mr. Lumiere. "As am I." He inhaled. "This would be a fine evening to ride, trampling the earth beneath our hooves." He looked at me. "Would you like that, Christopher Nix?"

I smiled helplessly and shrugged.

"Well, there's nothing for me here," said Mr. Lumiere. "Now." He looked at Ethorne, then at each of us. "I'll be seeing all of you, sooner or later."

Little Bit waved. "Good-bye!"

I watched Mr. Lumiere stroll to his car, a large white tail-finned convertible with its top down. Ma stepped out of the restaurant, and he called, "Susan! You look lovely, as always."

Ma usually responded to flattery by blushing and dis-

missing it, but this time she frowned and said quietly,
"Thank you."

As Pa came out of the gift shop, Mr. Lumiere added,
"The sight of you makes all Artie's praise seem positively
laconic." He nodded at Pa. "Luke. I just stopped by to
greet two fine people I've known a long time. You must ask
them about the old days, and what they've heard from
their son. Fascinating storytellers, the pair of them."

Pa said, "Sure thing."

Mr. Lumiere drove away in a cloud of white dust. I
watched his car race toward the old county road. As he
turned onto it, he may have glanced over his shoulder and
smiled at me.

When Ma heard that Mary and Joe knew Ethorne, she invited him and James to stay for dinner. James said he had
an evening planned already, but he much appreciated the
invitation. Ethorne accepted. Ma made slum gum, one of
my favorite dishes. While she fried hamburger, onions,
and potatoes, then stirred in a can of string beans, a can
of whole kernel corn, and a can of mushroom soup,
Ethorne and Pa pushed several of the restaurant tables together, and Little Bit and I put out the silverware, then Ma
and Mary brought out plates of slum gum and toasted
bread. Pirate bounced up and down at the front door, but
Ranger came by, and after the two dogs had established
that Ranger could eat Pirate in two bites anytime he
needed a snack, they went out together to patrol Dogland.

Pa asked Joe about their travels through North America, and Ma asked Mary how she liked living in the wagon.
I listened to stories about people and places and good
times and bad, and often a name or an incident brought
a nod or a frown from Ethorne. Ma asked Mary and Joe
if they were beatniks, and before either could answer, Pa
said they called themselves beats, not beatniks, which was
a derogatory name someone gave the beats around the

time the Russians launched their Sputnik satellite. Ma said she didn't mean to make fun of anyone, and Joe laughed and said that was all right, he and Mary couldn't speak for anyone else, but they didn't call themselves anything other than travelers. Mary asked Pa about his interest in names, and Pa said it just seemed polite to call folks by what they wanted to be called; he always felt a little sorry for the female suffragists who were remembered in most history books as suffragettes, the name their opponents gave them. Joe asked if Pa was especially political, and Pa said, "What's so political about manners?" When Ma asked Joe and Mary if they ever thought about settling down, Joe simply shook his head. Mary said, "You can't go home again, but you can make a home wherever you go." After we finished Ma's slum gum, Ethorne went to the oven and brought out a pan of brown Betty that he had made with brown sugar, a few apples, and stale bread.

"Mm, good!" I said, rubbing my stomach after the first bite.

"Glad you like it, Kid Kit."

"Kit Cat!" Little Bit said.

"Kids," Ma said as Pa looked at us, and we were quiet. Pa asked Mary and Joe, "Nick Lumiere said to ask about your son. Should I?"

"I don't know why you don't like that man," Ma said.

Little Bit said, "You don' like 'im, either."

Ma laughed. "I don't know why I don't, either. Seems half the county thinks he's the finest fellow around."

"Mmm," Ethorne said.

Joe said, "Our son left us a long time ago."

Ma said, "You must've been very young when you had him."

"That's so," Mary said. "He was like your Digger. He wanted to make things."

Everyone looked at Digger, who was sleeping in Ma's arms.

"You've known Mr. Lumiere a long time?" Ma asked.

Joe smiled. "All my life. We see him every time we come to Latchahee."

Ma looked from Ethorne to them. "Is that how you met?"

"Oh, no," Mary said. "We met Ethorne through Mrs. DeLyon."

"Lots o' folks visit the Fountain of Youth," Ethorne said.

"How long—" Ma began, but then Ranger barked several times. A long black convertible turned into the driveway.

Pa said, "I put out the CLOSED sign."

A second vehicle, a new blue Buick Le Sabre, pulled in, and Ma said, "That's Artie's car."

Pa smiled tightly. "And Artie, too."

Mr. Drake got out of his car and greeted Captain John Hawkins, who got out of his. Ethorne gave a little exhalation as Pa said, "Guess we should pull up a couple more chairs. Good thing you made plenty, Ethorne."

"Oh, yes," Ethorne said softly.

Mr. Drake entered first, with Captain John just behind him. Mr. Drake glanced at Mary and Joe, then said, "If the sign in the door's meant for everyone, I'll turn right around."

"C'mon in, both of you," Pa called. "Make yourself comfortable. Mary, Joe, that's Artie."

Mr. Drake smiled at them and told Pa, "Well, I should warn you, I'm here on business." He indicated Captain John, who grinned as he watched us. "You've met John Hawkins, your neighbor across the river?"

Pa nodded. "We met. Didn't know that was your real name."

"Oh, aye," said Captain John. "Some say I take after the original John Hawkins, too."

Ethorne said, "That's so, Co'nel." He held a lit cigarette that he idly rolled end over end across the top of his fingers, a trick he had said he had learned when he spent a long time in a boring place.

Captain John laughed. "It's Captain. At least until I can open up Colonel Hawkins's Old-Time Plantation."

Ma, crossing to the counter, said, "You're going to expand? Already?"

Captain John nodded. "That's my intention. I'm rarely thwarted."

"Mmm," Pa said.

Ma said, "Can I get you some dessert?"

"No," said Mr. Drake. "I'm content."

"Ethorne's cooking," Ma said. "He made brown Betty."

"Huh. I believe I detect a hint of an appetite."

Ma smiled. "And you, Mr. Hawkins?"

"Call me John," said Captain John. "No, thanks. I'll take myself off to the Roadhouse shortly, to celebrate, I hope."

"Celebrate what?" Pa asked.

"Mind if we speak in private?" Mr. Drake said, taking a plate of brown Betty and a fork from Ma.

Pa had begun to draw a cigar from his shirt pocket. He looked from Mr. Drake to Captain John, then said as if daring them to agree, "You want to buy my land?"

Captain John said, "This was Hawkins land. What finer place for my Old-Time Plantation? Rebuild the Colonel's home on a grander scale—"

"Like your ship?" Pa grinned, and so did Ethorne. Captain John flinched slightly. Pa, scraping a wooden match across the table to light his cigar, missed his expression, but Little Bit looked at me, so I did not.

"Tourists like that stuff," Mr. Drake said.

"When they come around," Pa said.

"That'd be my worry," Captain John said.

"I can tote that bale a little farther," Pa said.

"I'd pay a fair price," Captain John said.

Pa shook his head. "I didn't build Dogland to sell it."

"I can offer top dollar now," Captain John said. "But you can't expect to hold me to that. If you're interested—"

Pa shook his head. "Nope."

"Without even hearing me out?"

Ma said, "Luke."

Pa said, "I hate to hear a man waste his breath."

"Oh, this isn't a waste of anything," Captain John said. "Learning what doesn't work is never a waste."

"An awful lot of learning there," Pa said.

Mr. Drake laughed, set aside the dessert plate, and said, "Excellent work, Ethorne, as always." He pulled out his own cigarette pack, offered one to Ma, who accepted with a smile. Mary shook her head at his offer, and Joe said, "We don't smoke . . . cigarettes."

Mr. Drake lit his and Ma's cigarettes with a silver lighter. Ma inhaled, then laughed and said, "Ethorne's last name is Hawkins, too."

Ethorne and Captain John looked steadily at each other. "Just a name," Ethorne said.

Captain John looked away first. As he rose, he told Pa, "Well. You know where to find me."

Ma said, "And you know where to find us. Don't be a stranger!" After Captain John left, she looked at us kids and added, "Somebody shouldn't be strangers to their beds, either."

Little Bit said, "We got comp'ny."

Ma said, "You've already visited with everyone."

"No," said Little Bit as Mrs. DeLyon drove her sports car into the front yard. "More comp'ny."

"Adults are going to sit and talk," Ma said. "You know how boring that is."

Little Bit shook her head. I added, "We're not sleepy."

Mr. Drake said, "Maybe you need a bedtime story."

I said, "We're not babies," as Little Bit said, "Okay."

Mr. Drake laughed. "Then you don't have to listen, Chris."

Joe reached into his jeans and drew out a plastic bag filled with shredded green leaves. "Any objection if Mary and I join you in a smoke? If it'd make anyone uncomfortable—"

Ma's face tightened. "If Mrs. DeLyon—"

Mary said, "Maggie won't object."

Pa said, "Go ahead. I tried that wacky weed in the Navy. I prefer beer myself, but your choice is your business."

Ma said, "Artie, let's get the kids to bed."

We all waved at Mrs. DeLyon as she came in the front door, and Little Bit yelled, "Hello, good night!" We hurried through the kitchen, along the dark path, and into our bedroom.

After washing our faces and donning our pajamas, we heard another piece of the story about the king and his knights. After the king united the land and made everyone equal before the law, he grew sick. The wizard told everyone that to save the king, the land, and the law, all the knights should go on a quest to find a magic cup that could only be found by the one who was pure of heart. So many knights rode forth, and they had many adventures, rescuing maidens and being rescued by maidens and fighting bad knights and sometimes becoming bad knights and sometimes becoming good knights again and maidens became wives and bad women tempted good knights to give up their quest and knights died and maidens died and mostly witches and giants and knights who were known by colors rather than names died until it seemed all of the bad people were dead and the good people were married. But nothing had changed for the king, and his wife, and the best knight in the land who wanted to find the cup to please the queen, and the young knight who wanted to find it to be as good as any other knight, and the king's son who did not go looking for the cup, but stayed home trying to find a way to become the next king. And the wizard who should have been able to fix everything was asleep in a cave.

"That's prob'ly enough for tonight," said Mr. Drake.

"More," said Little Bit.

Ma laughed and kissed her forehead. "Enough's enough, Letitia Bette."

I said, "Did anyone find the cup?"

Mr. Drake said, "You can't rush a story. But I think the point isn't finding it. I think the point's the search."

I frowned. "That's a gyp."

"What happened to the queen?" Little Bit asked.

Ma said, "That's my question, too."

Mr. Drake smiled. "That's the next part of the story."

9

One Hundred Breeds

To clean the dog runs in the morning, you had to unlatch the front of each cage and get inside without letting the dog out while you dragged a heavy green hose that snaked in your grip as cold water shot from its nozzle. Latching the door behind you, you walked up the concrete pen, stepping in dry areas while dragging the hose through the night's pee and dookey. Around you, dogs would bark for joy of seeing you, and for the promise of breakfast. Because the sun was just rising, its rays through the wire fence etched diamonds on everything they touched. Some dogs would scamper ahead of you, and some would watch calmly from their porches, and some would jump around you or on you, and some would stay down in the main part of the pen so that as you rinsed their runs clean, they could dance and spin in the spray of water.

After you had hosed the five runs of each unit, you squirted the gutter at the front of the pens to direct everything in them onto the curved metal mesh that covered the central drain. You tried to wash everything through the mesh into the drain, but hard turds did not break up easily under the spray of water, though soft turds did. Sometimes the holes in the mesh would clog with dog doo and dog hair and pine needles and oak leaves until nothing passed through. When you managed to get everything onto the mesh, you could stop, turn off the water, and move on to the next five dogs.

Pa or Ethorne or Ma or James or Helen or some other grown-up would work with you, hosing one unit while you hosed the next, and then they would bring up a green metal lawn cart, lift the metal mesh from the drain, and dump its contents into the cart by tapping the mesh against the cart's side. Sometimes a grown-up or two would start on the other end of the path with a second cart, and then you could race to the midpoint opposite the grooming shed.

When all the pens had been washed, you could follow as the adult pushed the sloshing cart down an uneven sandy path past palmetto bushes and evergreen brush to a pit banked with sand, ready to be covered when it was full. There the adult tipped the cart, and its contents slid into a murky, fetid pool. Kids weren't allowed to go back there alone, because there might be rattlesnakes or you could fall in and drown, which must be the most horrible way to die in the whole wide world, yuck! Sometimes lizards would run across the sand, and sometimes doodoo bugs would roll turds away toward their homes. You would make faces because of the smell, and you and the adult would laugh at each other's face, and then you would hurry away from the dog dookey pit, knowing it was so disgusting that it was wonderful.

After dumping the dookey cart, an adult, usually Pa, would feed the dogs. The dog food was made from meat purchased twice a week from a slaughterhouse where muscled men walked around in bloody clothes and pig carcasses hung from hooks in cool, dark rooms. The meat was hauled in clean metal garbage cans in the back of the old pickup truck to Dogland, where it was ground through

a sausage machine: an adult with a wooden plunger as big
as a Nazi's hand grenade mashed bloody organs into the
top, and cords like raw hamburger spiraled from the bottom into a clean wheelbarrow, where it was mixed by
hand with vitamins and grain. And then the dog food was
stored in laundry tubs kept in old refrigerators behind
our house, which was all hidden from the view of the
tourists by a wooden fence that Pa and Ethorne and
Handyman had built.

At feeding time, every morning and every evening, an
adult filled a wheelbarrow with dog food and pushed it
around the circle, opening each dog's door to slop chow
on the just-washed concrete and to give any medicine a
dog might need. You could follow if you wanted, but the
wheelbarrow was too heavy for a little kid who did not
have the strength to push the big dogs back into their
pens if they lunged for food or freedom. Usually I did
something else, like watching the flickering black-and-
white images of Captain Kangaroo or Shari and Lamb-
chop or Beaney and Cecil, the Seasick Sea Serpent, or
Felix the Cat, the Wonderful, Wonderful Cat.

After the dogs had been fed, both in the morning and
the evening, someone would go around again to hose the
pens. Only the morning round called for dumping the
drain mesh into the dookey cart. The rest of the time, you
could squirt out most of the pens without even going into
them, simply by standing beside the pens and aiming carefully through the fence. When the dookey was in one of
the inner runs and up against the side of a fence where
you couldn't hit it, you could stand in front of the cage and
arc the spray past the dookey to wash it down into the
drain. If it was stuck, you could blast it directly, sending
it scooting up the run. Then arcing the spray over it would
wash it down again. There are many ways to hose a dog
turd, and in my time at Dogland, I must have learned
them all.

*   *   *

A thin young black man limped up the path around the dog pens one Saturday morning. He saw me and said, " 'Member me?"

I shook my head.

"Imagine me without the chin frizz."

"Seth?"

He laughed, showing me that he had lost a tooth. "Give the man a prize."

"I'm in first grade now. I'm going to school in Dickison, not Trenton, 'cause the Dickison bus stops out front. Li'l Bit's not goin' to school. She di'n't like kin'ergarten, so Pa said she di'n't have to go. But I'm still goin'. You can't quit first grade, but I woul'n't if I could."

"How you doing?"

"Reading's hard. I got a C in reading."

"You stick with it."

"Pa says C's average, and none of his kids are average."

"Yeah, Ethorne's a hard-ass sometimes, too."

I smiled because he had said a bad word.

"Seen James?"

"Uh-huh. He's this way." I walked a pace ahead of him on the path. "He and Handyman are workin' on a drainpipe."

"Great."

"It got clogged. How come you're walking like Chester?"

Seth squinted. "On *Gunsmoke*? Marshal Dillon's gimp friend?"

I nodded.

His lips tightened, then he laughed hard. "Yeah, I 'spect I'm fit to be some white man's sidekick now."

"You'd be Chester's sidekick?"

He looked away. "Out of the mouths of babes."

"Digger di'n't say nothing. Anything."

He shook his head, then said, "I know."

"So how come?"

"I broke my leg. A couple times."

"Does it hurt?"

"Would've hurt worse not to break it."

"Why?"

"I wanted to take a bus ride."

"Ridin' the bus is fun."

"I hear you."

"So why would it hurt worse—"

"Hey, never mind, cowboy. Someday you'll get it, or maybe you won't."

"But what happened? Huh, Seth?"

"Maybe I'll tell you later. Maybe you best ask your folks about it. There's some things adults don't like to talk about sometimes."

I knew that, but before I could say so, I spotted James and Handyman kneeling by a hole they had dug. A shovel and a posthole digger stood in the dirt beside them. I yelled, "James, James! Look, it's Seth!"

James looked up, then bared bright teeth in his bony face. "Seth! They let you out!"

Seth nodded, keeping his face still. Handyman looked up, too, then said, "Hey, Seth. Hear you found yourself some hard times."

Seth nodded curtly.

"Well, life's an education for us all."

"True."

"You come back to work for Luke?"

Seth nodded again.

Handyman looked at James, who still grinned and still held the wire ribbon of the plumber's snake. "Whyn't you boys take five minutes to get reacquainted? I got this here all right for now."

James launched himself from his crouch, telling Handyman, "Thanks, boss," as he threw his arms around Seth, picking him off his feet and spinning him around. Seth said, "Hey, stop it!" then laughed as James said, "Welcome home, brother!" Handyman and I grinned at each other.

Seth twisted free, said, "Watch yourself, bro!" and

jabbed at James like his hero, Floyd Patterson. James blocked him, and they sparred for a few seconds, throwing slaps back and forth. As James skipped back, Seth stepped forward, ready to slip a hand past James's defense, but his leg gave under him, and he fell. James caught him in a hug.

For a moment they looked at each other, and I couldn't tell who was going to cry first. Then Seth straightened up and grinned. "C'mon, li'l bro, let's take the five the man offered."

"Yeah. Sure thing, Seth. Sounds good."

As they walked toward the grooming shed to share a cigarette, I asked Handyman, "What happened to Seth?"

Handyman shrugged. "The boy got a little uppity. Schoolin' does that sometimes. But Latchahee niggers ain't like big-city niggers. Seth's goin' to be all right. James an' Ethorne set a good example for him."

When I got to the grooming shed, James was saying, "I 'xpect he's off fishin'. He be glad to see you when he's back."

"Sure?"

"Course. What you thinkin' on doin' now?"

"Maybe I'll go back to school. Maybe I won't. I learned a heap in the last six months."

"Like what?"

Seth rolled his cigarette end over end between each finger of his left hand. "Want to see it with the other hand?"

James shook his head and said solemnly, "Ethorne be *real* proud o' that."

Seth laughed, and James joined him, so I did, too. Behind us, Francy said, "This somethin' only men can enjoy?" She approached the shed with one of our two full grown poodles, the black male called Prince Charming whose pen was next to a white female called Snow White.

I nudged Seth. "Do that with the cigarette again."

"Later." He stood. "How you, Mis' Carter?"

"Just fine, Mist' Hawkins."

They grinned at each other. Francy said, "I'm goin' by McKay again, though the papers ain't come through yet."

"Oh," said Seth. "Mis' McKay."

Francy laughed. "You called me Francy 'fore you left."

"Nigger needs to show respect to a white woman, don't he?"

James said, "Seth."

As the brothers looked at each other, Francy squatted to lift the poodle. Seth and James both reached for Prince, but Francy, saying, "I got him," shook her head and set the dog on the grooming table. Addressing Prince Charming, she added, "Don't I, handsome?" Picking up a curry brush, she began working on the poodle and said, "I di'n't just come over to say 'hey.' I come to say I heard what you done, and I'm proud for you." As Seth blinked at her, she said, "It's s'posed to be a free country, ain't it? I figure folks can sit where they want, if they paid for their ticket."

"Well," Seth said slowly. "Thank you."

"But I don't like that beatnik look one bit. Why you want to hide your handsome face?"

James said, "Huh. I di'n't think nobody could hush Seth's mouth."

Seth immediately asked Francine, "I thought you weren't workin' here?"

"Just weekends and when Helen or James can't. Weekdays I'm at Dickison High. Unlike some folks, I value an education."

Seth said, "The whole world's an education."

"An' schoolin's part of the whole world," Francy said. "I know you could be a lawyer if you set your mind to it. You could do a lot of good if—"

James said, "Francy, he just got back."

Seth looked away, then said, "Our five minutes must be up and then some. Course, Handyman'll understand. He knows how we are."

James and Francy looked at each other. Francy said, "Seth? I'm sorry if—"

"That's all right," Seth said in a way that meant it wasn't. "C'mon. Massa's waitin'."

As the brothers walked away, I said, "Francy? Wha'd Seth do?"

"Huh? Oh, he rode a bus."

"I ride a bus."

"Sure." She smiled at me. "But ain't nobody bombin' you or beatin' you or arrestin' you to make sure you're usin' the right waitin' room or the right washroom."

"I always use the boys. I woul'n't ever use the girls."

"That's 'cause you're a good boy."

I nodded. I liked being a good boy, but it was only satisfying so long as someone noticed. Then I frowned. "Did somebody bomb Seth?"

"No." She gave a laugh like a cough. "He was one of the lucky ones."

"Did somebody beat him?"

"You know what, Chris? Maybe you should talk to your mama or your papa about this."

"Somebody beat him for ridin' the bus?"

"It's all right now," Francy said. "You don't have to worry."

"I don't want to get beat for ridin' the bus."

Francy lost her concern and laughed hard. "You're white, Chris. You ain't got a thing to worry 'bout."

"Oh." I bit my upper lip, then smiled. "Or you, neither."

"That's right. I'm free, an' white, an' in a few years, I'll be twenty-one."

"Are you going to have more babies?"

She squinted at me, then said, "Maybe. If I find the right man. You know any two-legged Prince Charmings?"

"Cap'n John?"

She laughed. "Oh, sure. He's a bit old for me."

"Seth?"

She laughed again, even more dismissingly. "No, I don't think so."

"Santa Claus?"

"There's a notion." She set the brush aside. "I'll marry me a Santa Claus. Ain't Prince handsome?"

I shook my head. "He's *charming.*"

"I reckon you're right."

When Francy left to take Prince back to his cage, I decided to walk the long way back to the house so I could poke my fingers into most of the dogs' cages. Near the biggest dogs' pens, where the Great Dane, St. Bernard, kuvasz, and wolfhound were, I heard a harsh whisper. "Hey! Boss-boy! C'mere!"

Ranger looked at the same time I did, and he growled. Cal Carter stood behind a clump of palmettos by the path to the garbage dump. He had either driven or walked up the rough dirt road along the edge of our property to get there.

I called back, "You're not s'posed to come on the property, Cal!" But I didn't call too loudly; I did not want to be a tattletale.

"I don't want in! I want Francy!"

I moved closer. "She's workin'!"

"I know that! That's why I'm here, boss-boy. Go get her!"

"I'm not s'posed to bother her when she's workin'."

"Oh, c'mon." He grinned. "Fetch her for a minute. Fellow's got a right to talk to his own wife, don't he?"

"I dunno."

"Sure you do."

"For a minute?"

"For a minute."

"Well. All right."

Cal laughed. "Thanks, Chrissy-boy. That's right white of you."

When I returned to the grooming shed, Francy was clipping the schnauzer's toe nails. "Hey, Francy?"

"I got a lot o' work, Chris."

"Cal wants you."

She glanced around. "Where's he at?"

"Hidin'."

She shook her head. "Should'a' guessed. What's he want with me?"

I gave my shoulders-to-the-ears shrug of total igno-rance.

"You tell him—" She looked at me, then pursed her lips and shook her head.

"What?"

"I'll tell him. Where's he hidin'?"

"This way."

"All right." She unhooked the schnauzer's leash from the tie post over the dog bench and walked with the dog beside me. "You don't have to do what Cal tells you, you know."

"I know. He as'ed nice."

"Yeah, he's a good one at askin' nice."

As we approached the woods, Cal called, "Hey, Francy. You're lookin' pretty."

Francy stopped ten feet from the brush, so I stopped beside her and patted the schnauzer while they talked. I thought the schnauzer was funny-looking with her long brown beard, but she liked me, so I liked her.

Francy called, "How much money you want, Cal?"

"None, sugar. You know sometimes I just miss you."

"I ain't changin' my mind."

"C'mon back here, and let's us talk where the kid can't hear."

"I got work to do. Chris said you wanted a minute. This is it."

"A minute with just us." He looked at me. "Don't you got a place to go, Chris-boy?"

I shook my head.

Francy laughed. "You'd make a piss-poor father to any chil', Cal."

"Maybe so," he said. "But don't a fellow deserve a sec-ond chance? Specially under the circumstances?"

"Oh," Francy said quietly.

"Your mama told my mama, Francy. I want to do right by you, as best I can."

"My mama don't want us gettin' back t'gether, Cal. She said I never should'a' gone back once to a man who'd hit me."

"Christ, Francy. I ain't offerin' for your mama! She just wanted some money, tha's all. But I'm tryin' to give you what I should'a' given you in the first place." His voice grew softer. "I'm workin' hard, Francy. I saved up a li'l money. We could take proper care o' the li'l ones."

"I gave you too many chances," Francy said.

"One more."

"How many times you said that?"

"I mean it this time."

"How many times you said that?"

"Christ, Francy. You can tell this time's diff'rent. You think I'd hit a pregnant woman?"

"Men do."

"I ain't like most men."

"I 'xpect not."

His voice went even quieter. "What you mean by that?"

"Nothin'."

"What d'you mean?" He stepped closer. The tendons on the back of his hand grew taut as his fingers formed a claw.

"This is my land!" I yelled. "My land. You di'n't pay to be back here, Cal!"

He looked at me. "Don't make me hurt you, boy."

Francy stepped forward. "You ain't goin' to hurt him, Cal."

Behind us, Seth said, "You ain't goin' to hurt nobody at all, Cal Carter." I turned. Seth stood quietly behind the nearest dog pens.

Cal said, "You ain't in niggertown, boy. Watch your mouth."

Seth stepped forward, then stopped as Francy looked at him, saying, "Please."

James strolled up beside Seth and squinted at Cal.

"You ain't trespassin' now, is you? Mist' Nix say we s'pose to march any trespassers up to him, no matter if they white or Negro."

Francy said, "He ain't trespassin'. He just come to tell me somethin', and it's told. Ain't that so?"

Cal looked at all of us, then laughed. "Yeah, I reckon that's so. Be seein' y'all."

"Bye," I called, then looked at Francy when she didn't offer any farewell to Cal. She was looking at Seth and James.

"Work's a-waitin'," James said.

Francy nodded, and we all moved away from the woods. I left them to their duties and walked back toward our house. By the fence, I saw three women come through the Doggy Salon. They stood in the sun, blinking and looking at the right-and left-hand paths. Since all of the workers were busy, I approached them. "Hi, can I help you?"

"They said there would be a guide here," said the girl.

"I'll guide you, if you'd like."

"You can guide us?" asked the younger woman.

I nodded.

"Of course he can," said the older woman, which was enough for me.

"You saw the littlest dogs inside, but over this way, we got the next littlest "

Remembering details from the older guides' tours was easy. The sign on the front of each cage was enough to prompt my memory, and when it was not, simply announcing a dog's breed and name was enough to please the tourists. They did not want to hear the history of every dog. They wanted to stroll around the circle in thirty or forty minutes, learn a few snippets of lore to certify their entertainment as educational, and see happy, healthy dogs of more breeds than they had known existed.

When I grew older, I remembered my young self reading aloud the names of dogs to adults and thought the tourists were very kind to pretend I had provided any service. But now I realize that I provided several: I let them

know the Akita was pronounced A-kee-ta, and the papillon, pappy-yon. I showed them the dogs were safe by
reaching into the pens to greet whichever one I pleased. I
smiled, and I spoke politely, and I told them about feeding the dogs and playing with them. I was as much a part
of their visit as any of our dogs.

At the end of that first tour, the younger woman gave
me a dime. I had not anticipated that, but I thought it was
a good idea. I said, "Thank you," and tucked it into the
pocket of my shorts. And because another group, a family with many children, had come out of the Doggy Salon,
I walked over to them and said, "Hi, would you like a
tour?"

As I was finishing my third circuit with my third group,
I saw Pa walking toward us. I wondered if he knew about
Cal's visit, and whether I should have told him that Cal had
been here, but he looked at the tourists, a well-dressed
couple with British accents, and said, "Hi, I'm Luke Nix,
the owner. I just heard my son decided he's a tour guide."

"He's a fine one," said the woman.

"He has every making of a gentleman," said the man.

"Is that evidence of natural Southern charm?" the
woman asked him.

I wanted to say, "No, it's spankings," but things that
made people you know laugh could make other people
sad.

The man said, "The question of environment or breeding can hardly be answered when one has the advantage
of both."

"So true," said the woman.

Pa said patiently, "So, Chris hasn't been pestering
you?"

"Not at all," said the woman.

Pa studied me. "All right. You can keep guiding people, but if anyone doesn't want you along, leave 'em alone."

"Yes, sir."

"I hear you got a dime from one lady."

I nodded. "And a nickel from a man." I wondered if

that meant I would have to give up the money.

"Did you ask for tips?"

I shook my head fast.

"Don't ask anyone for a tip, got that? Not ever."

"Not ever," I repeated.

"Well," Pa told the tourists, "I'll take him away if you want to continue on in peace."

"Oh, he's been entertaining and informative," said the man.

"Well, all right, then." Pa smiled at me. "I'm glad to hear that."

He walked away, and I finished the tour. Back at the Doggy Salon, the woman gave me a dime. The man said, "You seem like a lad who's been around."

"Yes, sir?"

"Is there a place nearby that you think especially nice?"

"Like pretty?"

The woman said, "No, nice to visit. A special place that when you visit it, you simply feel well. It might also be a pretty place, of course."

The man told me, "We'd like to be able to tell people we'd been to the very best places in Latchahee County. Where do you think those places might be?"

"Besides here?"

"This is grand," said the woman. "But where else?"

"Pirates' Paradise!"

"We've been there," the woman said.

"The Fountain of Youth?"

They looked at each other. "And where's that?" the man asked.

I pointed. "Thataway. It's got a big sign."

"The motel," the man said with dismissal or disappointment.

I nodded. "It's nice. We swim there sometimes when it's warmer."

"Well." The woman looked at the man, then kissed my forehead. "Thanks just the same."

I wiped my hand across my forehead as I added, "You

can buy comic books at the Winn-Dixie in Dickison."

The man said, "I shall remember that. Thank you."

"Tut. We can't win them all." As they walked away, the woman said, "What is it about yeast in the States? You can't find good bread or beer in the entire nation."

"True." The man took her arm. "Sometimes I look at the state of this young empire and think we're well rid of ours."

At lunch, I asked Ma what Seth had done. She said, "Maybe you should ask your father about that." Since Pa had been in a good mood the last time I saw him, I went into the restaurant and found him sitting at a table, smoking his pipe while reading *Newsweek*.

"Pa?"

"Mm?"

"Wha'd Seth do?"

He turned the page. "When?"

I shrugged, then said, "On a bus, some people hurt his leg."

Pa set down the *Newsweek*. "That's about the size of it."

"Why?"

"Damned if I know." Then he shook his head. "In the South, it used to be the law that Negroes had to sit at the back of the bus when they rode one, and they had segregated waiting rooms and rest rooms at the bus stations, which weren't kept up as nice as the places for the whites."

"Like at gas stations."

"Right. Then the U.S. government said that isn't fair, that they couldn't have segregated facilities on buses or trains or anything that went from state to state, and everyone should get the same service."

I nodded. "That's fair."

"That's what I would've thought. And it's also the law. But people are funny about the laws they'll obey and the ones they won't. Some white people didn't like changing the way things had been, so they decided to ignore the government. So some other people, whites and blacks both, decided to ride buses from Washington to New Orleans to

see if the U.S. government would make the Southern
states obey. They sat together in the front of the buses, and
at the bus stations, the white ones used the colored bathrooms and the black ones used the white bathrooms.
Everything they did was perfectly legal."

"So why'd Seth's leg get broke?"

"Some white people attacked them. Some of 'em were
hurt pretty bad, worse than Seth. And then the Southern
police arrested 'em."

"But they didn't break the law, you said."

"Well, they didn't break the U.S. law. But they did break
some state laws. The U.S. says the states are s'posed to
change, but some of the states haven't yet."

"Even though they're s'posed to?"

"That's right. Things don't get better overnight, Chris,
but they do get better if you don't give up."

"Okay."

"Is that what you wanted to know?"

I nodded. "Thanks, Pa," I said, and I ran outside to play.

My first-grade teacher was a thin, leathery woman named
Mrs. Howe, whom I remember as both stern and com-
passionate, a little like Aunt Hope, Pa's oldest sister who
had cared for children since she was a child and therefore
rarely let affection interfere with efficiency. The school day
began with the Lord's Prayer, followed by the pledge of al-
legiance, followed by a Bible story, and then the four "R"s
of elementary school, reading, writing, arithmetic, and
recess. Reading was my greatest challenge. Mrs. Howe
tried to teach us to recognize the sounds that letters made,
but every letter made several, and it didn't matter what
sound they made when I could not be sure whether I was
reading an "S" or a "Z." "Saw" and "was" flip-flopped before my eyes, so Mrs. Howe put me in the slowest reading
group.

Ma met Mrs. Howe's challenge. Every weekday morning after Ma made breakfast for me, I ate at the counter

in the restaurant while she drilled me with flash cards that she had printed with a Magic Marker: Bat. Cat. Wall. Ball. 2 + 5. 7 − 3. One day, when I was looking at an issue of *The Justice League of America,* I realized that I had read every word that had been said by Superman, Batman, Wonder Woman, Aquaman, Green Lantern, Green Arrow, and J'onn J'onzz, the Martian Manhunter, as well as their opponent, Kanjar Ro, the Slaver from Space. By my second or third report card, I had moved from Mrs. Howe's slowest reading group to the fastest.

Ma's drills continued. Those mornings were our time together. Pa helped the workers prepare Dogland for the first tourists, and Little Bit and Digger usually slept late. After breakfast Ma walked me across the highway to meet the school bus to Dickison. In the afternoon the bus stopped on our side of the highway, so then I could run down the slope to Dogland alone.

On the Dickison bus, just as on the Trenton bus, little kids sat at the front and bigger kids were noisier at the back. Since Dogland was close to the end of the route, and the only kids who lived farther from school than me were much bigger than me, I had most of the bus to myself when it was near home.

The trip to and from school took us along Highway 13 to a short road that joined with the old county road. Ronnie Corbin, one of my best friends, lived there in a trailer house, perhaps two miles from Dogland. He usually sat with me on the firm bench seat for the rest of the ride. Ronnie was smaller than I, and he wore glasses. In our schoolbook pictures, he looks like a quiet, studious boy, but he liked to laugh as much as I did.

No one lived on the old county road, so the bus only followed it for half a mile to another asphalt county road that took us back to Highway 13 at the outskirts of Dickison. Along that road, too far back to be seen, was the farm where Dorrie and Wayne Lawson lived. I always looked away from them when they boarded at the dusty road back to their home. They were both loud and dirty and poorly dressed, and they didn't mind pushing or hitting anyone they wanted to. Wayne Lawson was one year ahead of me in school, but two years older because he had been held back a grade. Dorrie Lawson was in my grade but not in my class; Dickison Public School's elementary division was large enough to have two classes for each grade. We called her Dorrie Doodoo, but never when she was near. She could beat up any boy in first grade and most boys in second.

We never had a nickname for Wayne Lawson. It would have been too dangerous. Looking funny at Wayne Lawson was enough to get you hit. If you were stupid enough to call Wayne Lawson a name and he overheard you, your time on the school bus would be an unending torment of loudly whispered bad names, jabs in the arm, ostensibly accidental trippings when either of you passed, and spitballs when you and the bus driver were not looking. Bullies and politicians understand the importance of deniability.

Besides Ronnie Corbin at school and Jordy Greenleaf at Dogland, my best friends were two girls in my grade who lived close to Dickison. Pam Hutchins was blond. Her parents' farm was more prosperous than the Lawsons', and her name spelled backward was "map." Roxie Westly was brunette. Her father was a dentist or an accountant, a professional whose income let her family live in a new ranch-style house near the county road with a lawn that was always watered and mowed. Her name with its "x" was strange and exotic. I thought of Pam and Roxie like Betty and Veronica in the *Archie* comic books. Like Archie, I could never decide which one I liked best.

Pam, Roxie, Ronnie, and I were good students, the sort who usually got "A"s and "B"s on their report cards and who might get all "A"s once or twice a year. None of us were our class's best students, or perhaps we took turns being the best, or perhaps there were some brilliant or driven kids who consistently did better than anyone else and I've forgotten their names. Or perhaps one of the four of us was consistently the best, and none of us noticed because the point of doing well was to satisfy our parents and teachers, not to compete with our friends.

In kindergarten at Trenton, the girls had chased the boys and kissed them, but in first grade at Dickison, the boys chased the girls, and the girls acted like they hated it. I preferred being pursued, but I did not understand the rules well enough to try to change them. For the most part, the boys and the girls played their games apart. I would not play the girls' games, because I did not want to get cooties any more than the next boy, but I hated boys' team games like softball and touch football. I was always among the last to be picked because I threw balls and swung bats awkwardly, and I could not catch. I was always afraid someone would say I played like a girl. At Dogland when no one was around, I flung rocks into the woods to try to figure out how my arms and shoulders and hips should be moving, but thinking about it made it worse.

I liked games where you ran. I remember a large oak in the corner of the playground that had divided near to the ground so you could climb into its crotch. It was the perfect tree to tag in games that required a base, and a fine tree in which to be a sharpshooter. I liked dodgeball because I could dodge well, and because you thrust the ball from your chest with both hands, and if you missed your target, everyone thought your target had done well rather than you had done poorly.

I liked talking on the playground. Dickison Public School, like most Florida public schools, was still segregated in the early sixties, so we would talk about whether Negroes were real people, and whether they should go to school with whites. We had all heard our parents arguing with the television set, and we all knew our parents were correct. In our arguments about the nature of the world, we could summarize our disagreements without changing our opinions of each other. We did not believe the world could affect us, or we could affect it.

* * *

Mr. Drake was eating a grilled cheese sandwich at the counter of Dogland's restaurant one afternoon and I was having a glass of milk when a stout man in a gray suit walked in. He and Mr. Drake looked at each other, looked away, and then the man laughed and approached Mr. Drake with his hand extended. "Artie!"

Mr. Drake smiled, stood, and took the man's hand. "Dmitri, you old dog! How've you been?"

"Well. You get one word only for answer, or you get novel thick enough to make Tolstoy proud."

"I'm amazed. And delighted. Are you staying around here? I'll take the novel, if you've got the time."

"For tonight, I am at motel." Dmitri turned his chin in the direction of the Fountain of Youth. "Tomorrow, I travel to Miami."

"Sit down, man. You're here as—"

"Visitor." Dmitri sat between Mr. Drake and me, and laughed. "Actually, I could mail you true novel, which is story not of my life but of my mind. Except it is not translated, so it would not do you good."

"You could? That's great. You're really a writer now? You always said—"

Dmitri nodded. "That is why I am here. I am writing essays about integration."

"Oh?"

"Fiction does not pay well in my country. Is not so different here in America, I understand."

Mr. Drake shrugged. "Just traveling?"

"Yes. To compare your North with your South, your East with your West. Thirty days to comprehend America!"

They both laughed. Mr. Drake asked, "Taking lots of pictures?"

Dmitri shrugged. "Of course. I must show that as your wealthiest are much richer than we, your poorest are much poorer."

Mr. Drake waggled a finger at him. "Are we likely to convert each other now?"

"You asked."

"Guilty. What kind of fiction? World War II tales?"

"Spy stories."

"Like Ian Fleming? Kennedy told a reporter he liked the Bond books, and now Hollywood's making a movie."

Dmitri nodded. "I must send your president my next novel. This is your son?"

They looked at me. Mr. Drake said, "No, that's Chris Nix. This—"

"Call me Dmitri."

I nodded. "Hello, sir."

"Come to my place for supper," Mr. Drake told Dmitri. "You can meet my daughter."

"I'd like that very much."

My chance to enter the conversation had passed, so I returned to my copy of *Ranger Rick*. A subscription had been one of my birthday presents from Grandpa.

Mr. Drake said, "Essays and novels."

Dmitri nodded. "Someone must."

"Nothing else?"

Dmitri shrugged. "A bit of a vacation is a great deal else. It is, ah, perquisite."

"You knew I was here?"

"In Latchahee County, yes, of course. You mentioned your home so many times during war. In this restaurant, no. I hoped to surprise you, but I did not expect to surprise you so soon."

"One of our British friends was by recently. Purely on vacation. Jack's getting older, but his women aren't."

"I missed him? Perhaps it's just as well. I must stop in London when I am flying home."

After a moment of silence, Mr. Drake said, "A writer."

"A writer," Dmitri agreed. "And you, an insurance agent. Who would have believed this?"

Mr. Drake shrugged. Lurleen, who had been busy with a family in the far corner, came, and Dmitri ordered a

Coke. After Lurleen had given it to him, Mr. Drake said, "What do you make of Berlin?"

"I would not know, of course. But I believe the tanks will withdraw. We did not think you would spend so much money to hold your half of the city."

"And the wall dividing it?"

"It must stand, now that it is there. We are both fond of dignity. But Berlin—" Dmitri shook his head. "I do not think Berlin will be the battlefield. America knows to fight its wars far from the homeland. We have learned that lesson, too."

Mr. Drake said, "You must've heard we're sending troops to Vietnam."

"Of course I did. And of course you are. Diem goes from washing dishes in U.S. to presidency of South Vietnam. This is truly land of opportunity."

"He was elected, you know."

"We have elections ourselves, you know. And Diem has made sure he will not have to face another. Which must embarrass you as much as his repression of Buddhists. But he is hardly first enemy of democracy and religious freedom that U.S. has supported. I am sure you can rid yourselves of him if he becomes an embarrassment."

Mr. Drake nodded. "Vietnam."

"Perhaps."

"Nothing closer?"

"Eh. What's certain? Maybe closer, maybe farther. Maybe sooner, maybe later. The world is now so small that farther may not matter. But later matters. Later is better. Sometimes later becomes never." Dmitri patted my back. "My Ludmilla is this tall. Must our children pay for our obstinancy?"

"Khrushchev said, 'We will bury you.'"

Dmitri nodded. "He did not say we will drop missiles on your heads to save ourselves trouble of burying you. I tell you this, Artie, my old friend. Communism and capitalism, these are ideas. Neither of our nations gives flesh to vision of Karl Marx or Adam Smith. Our states could both become dust before breath of history, yet this would not mean either of our ideals had failed. Notions outlive nations."

They talked for some time after that, about a pub and two sisters. I finished my *Ranger Rick* and went outside. Dmitri took a picture of me under the Heart Tree, and when he drove away in a big blue American car, I watched Mr. Drake watch him go.

For Christmas, you're supposed to buy people stuff that you would like, so I bought Little Bit a red and yellow plastic biplane with a propeller that spun and a pilot in goggles and flight helmet who could be removed from his cockpit and balanced on a ledge or on another toy like a horse or a truck until it was time for him to take to the air to do battle with the Hun. I must have gotten something for everyone else, something along the lines of porcelain dogs from Dogland's gift shop for the Grandmas and a tie for Grandpa Abner and something red like a scarf or a glass brooch for Ma and something for a smoker like cigars or tobacco or a corncob pipe for Pa and a farm play set or a fire engine for Digger, but the biplane was the best toy of the season. I wanted to get it for myself, but Ma showed me that I did not have enough money saved from my tips and allowance to buy it and presents for everyone in the family. Ma thought I should get Little Bit a doll or a toy tea set, but I pointed out that Little Bit hated girls' toys and assured Ma that Little Bit would love the biplane.

I had a plan for the red and yellow biplane: Little Bit liked playing with boys' toys, but she tired quickly of them. I knew the biplane would soon be neglected by her, and then it would be mine to play with as I pleased.

Grandpa sent us a Christmas tree from Minnesota. Pa said there were plenty of trees in Florida if you wanted to kill one for the holiday, but Ma said Florida pines were too scrawny and ugly for a proper Christmas tree, and it was true that Grandpa's tree was a perfect green cone like you found in every illustrated Christmas tale. Ma let us pick our favorite ornaments from the cardboard box that normally stayed in the top of the closet, and we placed them where we thought best. Ma draped the colored lights and cellophane strands of fringe, but we kids tossed the clumps of silver tinsel on the branches. The tree stood in the corner of Ma and Pa's room, and I got to crawl under the branches every day or two to pour water into the red metal stand.

Grandma Letitia sent us Scandinavian holiday food baked by older Lutheran Rosecroix women who remembered Swedish and Norwegian traditions more fondly than any Swede or Norwegian. I hated the candied bits in fruit cake, and I was indifferent to the crisp flat discs that were sugar cookies, but I had a fondness for the moist small mounds that were butter cookies, and I knew the perfect Christmas treat was lefse. Grandma Letitia owned the lefse iron, a wide circular skillet, but she did not have the knack of one of Grandpa's employee's aunts, an old, plump woman, old enough to be Grandma's mother or Mrs. Santa Claus, who came over to Grandma's kitchen to turn potatoes into manna. Lefse is white like clouds, and round like the earth, and when God first tasted it, he said you should spread it with butter, sprinkle it with sugar, roll it into a tight cylinder, and eat it in your hands. And God was right.

Grandma Bette sent each of us a Christmas card that said something about Jesus. In each card, she tucked a new dollar bill, four times our weekly allowance, good for twenty different candy bars that Little Bit would hoard for weeks, and eight comic books that I would read in an hour or two, then reread for months, and one hundred pennies that Digger would put in his piggy bank and then laugh at the sound it made when he rattled it.

On the day before Christmas, Ma told each of us to pick one of our toys to give away. She bundled clothes that we had outgrown or outworn, and she gathered old issues of

Newsweek and *Life* and *Ladies' Home Journal,* and tied
them all in old sheets and towels and blankets. Pa saw us
carrying bundles to the station wagon and called, "Taking
that trash to the dump?"

Ma said, "We're going into town."

"Once a year, you give people the things you don't want.
That's not for their sake. It's for yours."

"It's Christmas, Luke."

"Yeah," Pa said, as though the point was his.

"They don't have anything."

"They have their pride. You take that away when you
give 'em hand-me-downs."

"You want me to throw this away? I'll do that, if it'll
make you happy."

"No. Go ahead, Susan. Feel better."

"As if I could, now."

"Then don't."

"What do you want, Luke? Just tell me."

"I want you to do what you want to do. You want to
give people our trash, go right ahead. Just don't think it'll
change anything. They need education and work, not
charity."

Ma looked at us kids, standing and watching with our
arms full. "Come on."

We drove in silence through the dusk. The Baptist
church for Negroes was smaller and plainer than the one
for white people, but when Ma turned off the engine, we
could hear people singing on the other side of the light-
filled windows. When the song ended, Ma said, "Everyone
needs charity."

We got out of the car with our bundles. The parking
area, like the road in the colored section of Dickison, was
packed, rutted earth, and there were no streetlights, only
a bare bulb above the church door. We were not in darkness, though. The sun had not quite set, and around us, a
few porch lights burned in low-roofed wooden houses. We
were not alone, either. Black children ran by, laughing as
they played, and a few adults in dress clothes walked to-

ward the church door. One of them, a man, removed his
hat and said, "Ma'm? Can I he'p you with them things?"

Ma said, "No, thank you. I understood they accept do-
nations here."

"For the needy," said a black woman, appearing at the
doorway. "Yes, ma'm, that's so. Clevon, grab up them bundles 'fore those chil'en give out."

"Well," said Ma. "All right." As we passed our bundles
to the adults, Ma said, "I hope there's something here
that'll help someone."

"It will," said the black woman. "There ain't no act of
kindness that don't help someone somewheres. The Lord
sees, and the Lord remembers."

We drove to Dickison's black school next. In my memory, it consisted of one large room in a wooden structure
that differed from the houses around it only in its size, but
I may remember the room and have forgotten the building. A young black woman was there, with several children, and they were decorating the walls with red and
green crepe paper. The young woman thanked Ma for the
magazines. She seemed especially pleased with the *Ranger
Rick*'s. I looked at the ground, and felt a little better about
giving them up, though I still thought Ma should not have
asked me to. The room smelled odd, a mixture of unfa-
miliar soaps and perfumes, and all the furniture was very
old, a collection of hand-me-downs from the white school
supplemented with wooden chairs and tables. The kids
watched Digger and Little Bit and me, and we watched
them.

When we left, Ma said, "There. Don't you feel better for
helping people?"

Little Bit and Digger both agreed with her. I said nothing. Their gratitude embarrassed me, and so did their
poverty, and I felt lucky to be white.

My plan for the red and yellow airplane failed miser-
ably. Little Bit loved it and rarely let me play with it.

* * *

I had always been, in Grandma Bette's words, "a little
pitcher with big ears." Until I learned to read, I made little effort to understand the world beyond Dogland, the
world Pa studied through newspapers and magazines and
radio and television and books, the world he talked about
with friends and strangers, the world that I was repeatedly
assured school was preparing me for. Reading made me
a citizen. When I looked at pictures in magazines, words
came from the captions or within the pictures themselves,
shaping a world that I knew but could not describe, a
world of people and allegiances.

In that world in January of 1962, a conference in
Geneva to end nucear tests ended a failure. Ma and Pa
both thought it would be good to ban the bomb, but Pa
doubted it would happen, saying, "Humans never give up
weapons before they've used 'em." The founder of the
John Birch Society claimed President Eisenhower was a
dedicated agent of a Communist conspiracy; the John
Birchers and the KKKers were never far apart in any
adult's conversation. "Lucky" Luciano died; he was a mob-
ster like on *The Untouchables*, except he went to Naples
instead of prison.

In February, President Kennedy stopped most U.S.
trade with Cuba, which was like laying siege to a fort.
John Glenn blasted into space on an Atlas rocket and circled the Earth three times; Mr. Shale said the U.S. was actually ahead of the Russians in space because the Russians
were faking their space program, but ours was real because God was on our side. The U.S.S.R. swapped U-2
pilot Gary Powers for a Soviet agent who had been caught
by the U.S., which was bad because we let a Commie spy
go, but good because we got back an American pilot who
had been flying high above Russia in one of our fastest
planes equipped with high-powered photographic equip-
ment. The Pentagon sent more men, money, and
weaponry to Vietnam because "this is a war we can't afford to lose," but President Kennedy said he had sent no

U.S. combat troops "in the generally understood sense of
the word" to Vietnam. The war in Vietnam was not an
American war because America had not declared war on
the North Vietnamese. America was merely helping the
South Vietnamese, because all the nations of the world
were like dominoes, and if South Vietnam fell, the Commies would win the game.

In March, President Kennedy said the U.S. would re-
sume atmospheric testing of nuclear bombs to stay ahead
of the Russians; Defense Secretary McNamara admitted
U.S. soldiers in South Vietnam as military instructors had
been in combat with Communist troops; and Fidel Castro
ordered severe food rationing in Cuba. At a New York
rally, Senator Barry Goldwater announced, "Conservatism
is young, virulent and alive!" which Pa thought funny,
though I was too young to appreciate a political slip of the
tongue. Algeria won independence from France after
seven and a half years of war; Pa said the British were better at giving up their empire than the French.

"That boy's got a touch of the tar brush," Lurleen said one
Saturday morning as a slender man in a dark suit got out
of a black sedan.

Ma laughed. "One look? You can tell with one look?"

"Most times. See how his hair's been straightened, and
his nose is a bit wide?"

"Maybe he's Greek or Italian or Cuban, and he likes
Brylcreem."

"Maybe he's the Sheikh of Araby. See how he carries
hisself? Haughty, like? He knows what he is, and he's
hopin' we don't."

Ma laughed again. "You're just looking because he's
handsome."

Lurleen's head snapped to the side as she glared at Ma.
Ma said, "Isn't he?"

Lurleen's shoulders dropped. "I don't look at no nig—

at no one that way." Only someone who knew her would know she had forgiven Ma.

"Except Handyman?"

She nodded. " 'Cept Handyman."

The bell rang as the front door opened. The man stepped inside and said with an accent I did not recognize, "Hello."

Lurleen turned away to adjust the row of empty glasses on the back counter. Ma said, "Hi. Sit anywhere."

"Thank you." There were no customers in the restaurant. He took a stool near the door, not far from where I was working on my most ambitious drawing, a smiling cowboy with pistols bigger than his head in each hand. He was encircled by as many arrow-shooting Indians on horseback as I could crayon. They all had the same face: circles for eyes, a checkmark for a nose, and an upward curve for a mouth. Even the horses smiled.

The man said, "Coffee, please."

Ma started for the pot, but Lurleen waved her back. As she set a cup and saucer in front of the man, he turned his head toward the window. "That is a very old tree, no?"

Lurleen glanced at him before she moved away. "You ain't seen a sequoia."

Ma said, "That's an old tree for Florida. No one knows how old. We think it's the biggest tree in the county. It might be the biggest in the state."

"It's very handsome."

"I think so. Do they have any like it where you're from?"

The man smiled for the first time. "No."

"Are you from France? We had a French family through just the other day."

Ethorne came through the kitchen doors with a tray of coffee cups and said, "That's no French accent."

"It's not?" said Ma.

The slender man looked at Ethorne, then at Ma, then smiled again. "No, madam. But you're close. I'm from Haiti."

"Really?" Ma grinned. "We've never had visitors from Haiti that I know of. Lots of Europeans, and some Japanese, and a nice man from India, but no one from Haiti. Oh, I'd love to go there."

"It's a beautiful land," the man said.

"*Bien sûr*," said Ethorne. "*Mais il est pauvre.*"

"*Il y a des pauvres, et il y a des riches, comme tous les pays du monde.*"

Lurleen gazed at Ethorne with one of her rare smiles. "French. If that don't beat all. You study that in prison?"

Ethorne smiled. "No'm. I just like to talk to folks wherever I go." To the visitor, he said, "*Que voulez-vous ici?*"

"*Rien. Amusement. Information. Des choses comme ça.*"

"Well," said Ethorne, "I got me a mess o' dishes to do."

"*Nous parlons en bas, Grand-père?*"

Ethorne paused between the swinging doors, then nodded.

"Oh, darn," said Ma. "Hearing you two go on is as good as a vacation."

"I'm sorry," said the man. "You must come to Haiti sometime. The people are very kind." He stood. "What do I owe?"

"Ten cents," said Lurleen.

"May I purchase a ticket for the tour here?"

Ma said, "The woman next door can help you."

He nodded and walked toward the gift shop. I slid off my stool, said, "I'm goin' outside," ran past the man, into the gift shop, said, "Hi, Mis' Stark!" as I passed the cash register, ducked under the turnstile, and did not slow down until I had circled behind the restaurant trash cans. I crouched there in the shade and watched fat ants the color of lobsters march to their sandy home at the border of the sidewalk and the gravel.

The back door opened, then footsteps approached, then Ethorne said, "Hey, cowboy. You a secret agent man now?"

I nodded. "That man's a Com'nist."

Ethorne laughed. "No, I don't think so." He looked up

as someone stepped around the corner, and, stepping forward, out of my sight, he asked, "Why you call me *Grandpère?*"

"From respect. You are Et'orne 'Awkins."

"They call me Ethorne Hawkins. An' you?"

"Ethorne Hawkins, yes. I am Antoine D'Hiver. I was told you know a great deal about these parts."

"You hang around long enough, you hear all kinds of lies."

"Eugenie said this."

Ethorne's voice softened. "She still livin'?"

"No."

"How she die?"

"In peace. In her little house. We invited her to join us in the city, but she refused. She might still be alive today, if she had not insisted that she wished to stay in the hills."

"I 'xpect she knew what was best for her spirit."

"She was my *grand-mère.*"

"She proud of you?"

"Of course!"

"Mmm-hmm. You get to my age, you hear *all* kinds of lies."

Someone lit a cigarette. Then Antoine D'Hiver spoke. "She said she loved me."

"I don' doubt that. Your daddy marry a rich woman?"

"My mother married a rich man. Does that matter?"

"Your daddy work for Papa Doc?"

"Well, yes. Why—"

"You work for Papa Doc?"

"Does that mat—"

"Papa Doc sends his Tontons Macoutes to terrorize folks and forces folks to worship the way he sees fit and keeps folks poor while he lives high. Know a man by his master."

"Your government supports ours."

"Did Eugenie?"

After a moment Antoine D'Hiver said, "I should not have come."

"You sniffin' 'round to help out Papa Doc, you right, no-body needs you. You lookin' to learn a little more about life, there's worse places'n Latchahee County."

"Does patriotism keep you here? There are countries where you do not have to be a nigger."

"Seems like someone's got to be a nigger wherever you go. Light-skinned folks got it over dark skins in Haiti."

"You'd prefer the black-skinned rule?"

Ethorne laughed. "Turnin' evil upside down don' make it good."

"Eh."

"You know, boy, if'n you read up on quests, hardly any of 'em work out like the quester figures. Findin' somethin' don' mean you can take it home. Don' even mean you can take yourself home. An' if you do get back, you find home changes while you gone. So do you."

"Would you say America is a good land?"

"I'd say most lands got some good in 'em."

"You know what I ask."

Ethorne chuckled. "America's got the finest ideals of anyplace I know. Someday, it might live up to 'em."

"A matter of time?"

"Yeah."

"Some have more time than others."

"There's a connection 'tween how much time you has an' how big a hurry you in." A cigarette butt sailed out onto the gravel.

"I confess, I hoped for more."

"You hoped for a shortcut. That's natural. But now you ain't found one, you might as well head home an' get to work."

"I see."

"You 'member Eugenie. Think on what she would'a' done."

"Yes."

Antoine D'Hiver took several steps, each a crunch of loose stone beneath new leather soles. Then Ethorne said, "You done paid your entrance fee. Might as well see the dogs 'fore you go. Got over a hun'ed breeds, you know."

"Waste not, want not?" Antoine D'Hiver laughed. "You're right. Thank you, *Grand-père.*"

"You welcome, son." I heard him walk away. Then Ethorne said, "Time for me to get back to work. I 'xpect a secret agent'd sneak away from here now."

As the kitchen door closed, I ran down the path toward our house, passing the sign warning PRIVATE. The fence on two sides of our home was seven feet tall and built of pine boards, interlaced like Popsicle sticks when you made them into a raft for toy soldiers or a fan to cool yourself. You could roll under the fence, which was designed to block visitors' sight and not the breeze, but since there might be burrs or anything in the grass, I ran through the opening, having to zigzag because a short wall beyond the passway kept tourists from seeing within. Little Bit and Digger played near the side of the Doggy Salon on the metal swing set that had come as a kit from Sears. Beside the house, Mrs. Green, one of the black women who worked for Ma, was feeding clothes through the wringer of our ancient electric washing machine. I ran without pausing through the second passway to pause at the back of the Doggy Salon and the beginning of the path around the dog pens.

"Hey, Speedy," Francy said. "What you up to?" She, James, and Seth sat on a low bench beneath the building's overhang.

"Nothin'." One of the rules was that I could not offer to guide visitors if any of the workers were available.

Antoine D'Hiver stepped out of the Doggy Salon. The three workers glanced at each other. They had established their own rules; unless she was busy, Francy guided white visitors. Seth, picking up his cane, told Francy, "He could be lynched for whistling at you," stood, and called, "Like a tour, brother?"

"I'm not—" Antoine D'Hiver nodded. "Yes. Please."

Seth smiled to the others and walked away. I was about

to follow when Francy asked me, "You miss me if I go away?"

I nodded as James told her, "You should finish school."

"I can finish somewheres else." She looked sideways at James. "Cal's goin' hear where I been. You know he will."

"I 'xpect."

"Got a better idea?"

James looked at the ground and shook his head.

"Where you goin'?" I asked.

"I'm thinkin' up north. Seth says San Francisco's s'posed to be nice."

"Rice-A-Roni," I sang. "The San Francisco treat."

Francy laughed.

James asked her, "What you got up north?"

"Maybe a chance."

They both looked up the path where Seth had gone. James said, "All right." He stood. "I best put the German pointer in the exercise pen."

"Can I help?" I asked.

"You could help me hose the pens," Francy said.

"Race to the middle?"

Francy nodded.

"I'll go this way!" I darted up the left-hand path. That side of the tour had more empty cages than the right, where most tourists began.

Only one or two runs per kennel needed hosing. I had gotten perhaps a quarter of the way around when Seth and Antoine D'Hiver approached. Seth gave the usual speech about each dog. Antoine interrupted once. Seth had said, "The basenji's an ancient breed, and very close in appearance to a true wild dog."

"How do you mean?"

"Every dog here's the product of selective breeding, some by man, some by nature. If you let 'em run wild and breed as they please, within two or three generations most of the pups would look like Bambi there. Their fur might

vary some in length and color, but the basic size and shape
of the dog would be pretty much like that. Wild dogs in
India, Africa, and Australia all are mighty similar."

"Mmm," said Antoine.

I beat Francy to the middle of the circle, but she
pointed out that I'd missed a little high up in the Great
Dane's cage, so we called it a tie. While she, Seth, and
James fed the dogs, I ran up to the gift shop. As I walked
in, I said, "Hey, Mis' Stark, guess what I know?"

"Why, I surely cannot imagine. What would that be,
Christopher?"

"Francy's goin' up north."

"No!"

"Yep!" I didn't see Ma, so I crossed into the restaurant.
Ma was standing beside Pa, reading a typewritten sheet
of paper.

Pa, grinning at her, said, "Well?"

Ma handed it back to him. "You're going to send it in?"

"I didn't write it for fun."

"Oh."

"You don't like it?"

"I didn't say that."

"I'm only responding to some damn fool."

"I know," said Ma.

"Never argue with a fool," Lurleen said. "Folks can't tell
you apart."

Pa smiled. "Isn't the editorial page where every idiot
with an opinion can express it? I might as well step up for
a turn." He glanced at Ma. "If the spelling's all right, send
that in." Ma looked at the floor tiles. Pa laughed again and
kissed her forehead. "Cheer up, Susan. They prob'ly won't
run it."

Since they seemed to have finished, I said, "Hey, Ma!
Guess what?"

Lurleen, Pa, and Ma all looked at me. I grinned.
"Francy's goin' up north!"

"She is?" Ma said.

"Damn," Pa said.

Lurleen said, "Might be best," and we all looked at her. She cocked her head to one side and said, "She can't stay here after what she's done."

"What's she done?" I asked.

"I don't fire people for what they do on their own time," Pa said.

"What'd she do, Pa?"

"That ain't what I meant," said Lurleen.

Pa looked at her. "That mean you couldn't keep working here?"

"Me?" Lurleen snorted. "You could fill this place with colored homosexual communist atheists, and I could work alongside 'em, long as they let me be."

"What'd Francy do?" I asked.

Ma looked at Pa, who said, "She spent last night at the Hawkins home."

"Captain John's?"

"No. Ethorne, Seth, and James's place."

"Oh," I said, disappointed.

Pa laughed and set his hand on my crew cut.

Ethorne, wiping his damp hands on his apron, stepped out from the kitchen. "In case you wonderin', and I know you is, I told 'em it was a fool thing to do. But Francy said she was near a divorcee now, and then she started quotin' Elvis Presley songs at me. I had to give in."

Lurleen whispered harshly, "Ethorne Hawkins, you know better'n that!"

Ethorne shrugged. "Cal Carter was comin' over to her sister's place near ever' night an' botherin' 'em. Her brother-in-law turned her out, an' her ma said Francy'd made her bed when she run off with Cal, so now it was time to lie in it. That girl walked near ten miles carryin' her baby to our place. Was I to turn 'em out, too?"

Lurleen glared at him. "You know the answer to that."

"Her an' the boy said they wanted to be together. She said she deserved a good man, an' she'd found one. Said she di'n't care who knew."

"How long you been around, Ethorne?"

He smiled sadly. "It's all right. They both leavin' after they pick up their pay."

"They decided?" Ma asked.

"They decided last night, whether they knew it or not. Only question now is where they go. Maybe Harlem. I got friends there can look after 'em."

"Or maybe San Francisco?" I said.

Ethorne smiled at me. "I got friends there, too." Then he met the gaze of the other adults in the room. "Once they gone, it'll just be somethin' for folks to gnaw over for a week or two, is all," Ethorne finished. Lurleen began to say something, but some tourists came in, and the conversation was over.

I ran back by our house to find Little Bit and Digger. They were building roads in the dirt beneath the swing set. I said, "I know something you don't."

Little Bit said, "Francy an' James are goin' north to be married."

"Not Seth?"

"Seth's immature."

"Seth's smart."

"James is smarter."

"Seth reads good."

"So?"

"So Francy should marry Seth."

"Seth," Little Bit repeated patiently as she scooped a tunnel for Digger's race car, "is immature."

"Says who?"

"Francy."

"What's 'immature' mean?"

Little Bit shrugged. "Means Francy's marryin' James."

I don't remember lunch. I probably ate a rebel burger in the kitchen with Ethorne. Digger, Little Bit, and I spent the afternoon playing in the yard within reach of the eyes and ears of Mrs. Green, who cleaned the house while clothes dried on the line. We usually turned on the TV for the Saturday afternoon movie. If it starred Tarzan or Bomba the Jungle Boy or Jungle Jim, we watched it without moving, but if it was about Dracula or Frankenstein, I said I was bored and pointed out that Digger was getting scared. Little Bit liked scary movies, so I took plastic cowboys and Indians from my toy box and played with Digger while peeking at the gray shadows on the screen and listening to every static-filled sound. The only things worse than scary movies were sad ones, because they made you cry in public. If the movie was about horses or dogs, I watched reluctantly, knowing at least I would not lie awake that night wondering what waited behind each closed door of the bedroom.

At the end of the day, Pa called, "Chris! Little Bit! Digger! Dinner!"

We all ran. I beat Little Bit, though no one noticed. Ethorne had made two batches of fried chicken, one spicy for Pa and one bland for Ma and us kids. In one pot, he had fixed rice with saffron, black pepper, pork sausage, onions, green beans, and tomatoes. In another, he had fixed something he only identified as "greens" that looked suspiciously like spinach. Ma said, "Oh, Ethorne, that's lovely, but there's too much."

Ethorne nodded. "Yes'm. There'll be travel food for the young folks."

"Oh. Of course."

I ate everything except the tomatoes, which I left on my plate, and no one said anything. I alternated bites with corn fritters and cold milk, and for desert, we ate bourbon pecan tarts that, Ethorne explained, had not been named for the kings of France.

While we were eating, the side door opened. James said, "Mist' Nix?"

"Just finishing up here, James. If you want to set out a little early, I can get your pay together in a minute."

"No, sir, that ain't it. Seth an' Francy're finishin' up out back. If'n you don't mind, I'd like to run home an' fetch the truck, so's we can light out straightaway."

"Sure. Tell Francy to knock off, and you could both go now."

James smiled and shook his head. "Might as well spare her the walk. It's a long night ahead of us."

"Well, get moving then," Pa said.

As the door closed behind him, Ma said, "Luke, you should've told them to leave earlier."

Pa closed his eyes, inhaled, then opened them. "I did tell them to leave earlier. They said they wanted to finish up here proper."

"Mmm," said Ma.

Pa said, "Pride's important."

"It's not the most important thing."

"Oh? And what is?"

"Things like this. Being together as a family."

Pa laughed. "What's that got to do with anything?"

"Which would you trade? Family or pride?"

Pa laughed again. "Why trade?" He looked at the clock, then at the parking lot that was empty of visitors' cars. "Time to check out. Want to count the ones, Chris?"

I shrugged. Ma glanced at me and flicked her eyes once toward the door. I said, "Yes, sir," and followed Pa.

As we crossed between the restaurant and the gift shop, he said, "I hear that after you give folks a tour, you've got a trick of rattling coins in your pocket till they give you a tip."

"Sir?"

"It's the same as begging. If people choose to give you money, that's their business. If not, that's life. Nixes don't beg."

"Yes, sir." I felt like I had after walking into the woman's house next to Grandpa and Grandma's cabin. I had not known I was doing anything wrong until the wrong thing was already done.

Mrs. Stark, on the telephone, said, "Oh, it's quitting time, I best be going. Bye!" She shook her head at us both. "Ain't that something 'bout Francy?"

"It sure is," I said.

"Mmm," Pa said. "How'd we do?"

"Oh, it was a good day. One woman came in, she was

all crazy about Scotties, you know, an' she spent near forty dollars on dish towels and them painted china plaques and little figurines of ever' size. I steered her to everything we had with a Scottie dog on it."

"All right," Pa said with satisfaction, and he said it again after looking at the register tape. He took the cash out of the drawer, counted out one ten, three fives, and twenty-five ones, and returned that to the drawer.

I said, "Why do you put some back?"

"So we can make change tomorrow morning."

"Oh."

He pointed at the register drawer, which he had left ajar. "You don't close that so if thieves break in, they won't break the register trying to get it open. That way, you may be out fifty dollars, but you're not also out a cash register that costs a damn sight more."

He handed me a wad of ones. While he made stacks of fives and tens and twenties, I went through the ones, making sure no larger bills had accidentally gotten in with them and orienting them so that George Washington was on top, not the eye in the pyramid. Then I counted them, told Pa the number, and watched him count them. If he started to count them a second time, I knew I had made a mistake.

As we finished, Ma came up from the house with a green deposit bag and took from it envelopes with each employee's pay. Little Bit and Digger were with her, so we ran up and down the aisles of the gift shop until Ma told us not to get too excited. Seth and Francy came in, and Francy said, "James ain't back yet?"

Pa said, "He hasn't been gone all that long."

Ma gave her and Seth their envelopes, then said, "Well, I guess you might as well take James's."

Francy smiled and mumbled, "Yes'm." A moment later she said, "Mis' Nix, there's too much—"

As Pa looked up, Ma said, "That's a little something extra to help you get settled."

Francy said, "You both been too kind."

Ethorne and Lurleen came in. Lurleen accepted her envelope with a nod. Ethorne said, "Thanks, ma'm." Then he
glanced at Seth. "Where's your brother?"

"Gone to get the truck."

Ethorne's face tightened, hard as tree bark.

Pa said, "He hasn't been gone that long."

Ethorne said, "Mist' Luke, would you mind—"

"No," Pa said. "Come on."

"Me, too!" Little Bit called.

Lurleen said, "What's goin' on?"

"Nothing," Pa said. "Susan'll take you and Mrs. Stark
home in the Dodge. Francy, you and Seth stay here in
case we miss James. You kids—"

"Ride in the back of the truck!" Little Bit called.

"There isn't room for all of them in the Dodge," Ma
said. "Little Bit—"

"Ride in the back of the truck!" she repeated. "Yayy!"

"I'm going," Pa said, which meant get in or be left behind.

Little Bit and I ran ahead of everyone and scrambled
over the tailgate into the back of our pickup. It smelled of
earth and blood and oil and rust, and you sat on rags that
did not let you forget that the bed of the truck was corru-
gated steel, and every rut in the road was announced to
you through your spinal cord, and it was better than any
carnival ride. Ethorne put Digger on the bench seat in
front, between him and Pa, and we drove away. Ma waved
without smiling, then walked toward her car with Lurleen
and Mrs. Stark, while Francy and Seth squatted on the
sidewalk, talking solemnly.

The edge of the sky began to smolder. Sunset should
be the most frightening time of the day, but familiarity
makes it safe, or perhaps we secretly yearn for endings.

Little Bit and I grinned at each other, united in the rattle and the wind as Pa drove on the highway and then the
dirt road to Ethorne's house. We had seen it often, so we
did not try to look forward through the dirty glass windows of the pickup's cab. Watching the world recede in our

dust, we knew that at the end of our trip was a wooden
house in which every door and every window was unique.
Its roof was a crazy quilt of shingles and tin and tar paper.
It stood in a clump of trees, and grass grew high around
it, so you could not be sure of its shape or its size. On one
side was a vegetable garden and a rosebush, and on the
other, slowly being reclaimed by the earth, a rusty car that
Ethorne said was so old that it had run on steam instead
of gasoline.

You could also not be sure what you'd find in Ethorne's
yard or on his porch. People and animals came and went.
We expected to see chickens, a goat, a dog named Wolf,
and a sparrow that would sit on Ethorne's shoulder. If
there were people, we expected fat women or skinny children, their skin dark and clean, their clothing worn and
simple.

The pickup slowed as we approached Ethorne's house.
I turned to look, then grabbed the side of the truck as it
bolted forward. I had seen too many automobiles in
Ethorne's yard, and five or six white men in a ring per-
forming a dance that, for several of them, consisted of
stepping forward and kicking.

Someone shouted when our truck hurtled into the
yard. As the brakes squealed, Little Bit and I slammed
against the cab, hard enough to frighten rather than hurt
us. Both doors opened, and Pa and Ethorne stepped out
on each side. Pa said, "Lie down and stay down," to us so
quietly and so calmly that Little Bit and I obeyed without
speaking.

One of the dancing men said, "God damn it, man—"

Another said, "You could'a' killed someone, drivin' like
that."

A third said, "Luke, this ain't none of your affair." By
the end of his sentence, I had recognized Handyman's
voice. "Just take them children and drive off."

"It's his brother we want," said Cal Carter, in perhaps
the most reasonable tones so far. "If'n he hadn't tried to
run off, we wouldn't'a' hurt him none at all."

I saw Ethorne's head pass the bed of the truck as he said, "Don't force yourself up."

James spoke with a thick, low voice. "I can stand."

Another white man said, "Let 'im be. You said he's not the one." I looked at Little Bit, and she nodded; that was Dr. Lamont's voice.

Cal said, "That's the nigger we got."

Pa said, "You haven't got anyone."

"Ain't your affair," Cal said.

Pa said, "These're my neighbors, my workers, and my friends. I don't see how it's not my affair."

Handyman said, "I didn't want no violence, Luke. I come to keep things from gettin' too het up."

"Mmm," Pa said. "And you, Doc? You here to fix things up if they got out of hand?"

"That's about the size of it," Dr. Lamont said.

Ethorne said, "I'm just goin' to take my boy over to the porch there."

"Hold on," Cal said. "Don't no one move."

"I'm a witness," Pa said.

"Easy, Luke," Handyman said.

"Let's all stay calm," Dr. Lamont said.

Cal screamed, "I want that lame little nigger that's fuckin' my wife!"

Handyman said, "Cal, put that down. I thought we had an agreement."

Ethorne said calmly, "Seth ain't here. I'll just—"

"I said don't!" Cal yelled, and then something exploded, louder than a cherry bomb.

Someone fell. The air stank of bitter smoke. I stared at the rusty ridged bed of the truck. Little Bit began to move beside me. I caught her hand, then touched my finger to my lips, and she stayed still.

Handyman said, "Hell," and James said, "Ethorne?" and Cal screamed, "Don't you move! Don't neither of you move!"

And then I heard someone sliding from the seat of the

truck. Little Bit peeked first, and I peeked second. Pa stood
near the rear of the truck. The group of white men stood
in a half circle around James, who stood, his face bloody,
leaning toward a rifle in Cal's hands that swiveled back
and forth between James and Pa. A few steps from the
other side of the truck, almost hidden by tall weeds, lay
Ethorne, and running toward him was Digger.

Pa shouted, "Digger! No!" and took a step forward. Cal
swung his rifle toward Digger. As he did, James lurched
forward, grabbing the rifle and wrenching it from Cal's
hands. Cal lunged toward James, but Handyman and a
man I had never seen before both grabbed Cal's shoulders.
Handyman said, "Easy, God damn it!"

Digger never turned from Ethorne. He touched
Ethorne's ankle, a ring of bare skin between pale jeans and
black work boots, and said, "Et'orne? Get up, Et'orne."

Pa held out his hand and said softly, "Digger? Come
here." Dr. Lamont stepped toward Digger and Ethorne. Pa
slapped his hand against Dr. Lamont's chest. "You're not
fit to touch him."

Digger shook Ethorne's ankle. "Et'orne? Wake up,
Et'orne, it's day."

Dr. Lamont said, "I'd help a dog live, if I could."

Pa left his hand against Dr. Lamont's chest, and Dr. Lamont did not move. Pa called, still gently but more loudly,
"Digger, come here."

James kept the rifle aimed at Cal's stomach. "How's
Ethorne?"

"I didn't mean—" Cal began.

"Shut up," Handyman said reasonably.

"Digger!" Pa repeated, loudly enough that Digger
turned and looked at him.

"Et'orne's sleepin'," Digger said. "But it's not bedtime."

Pa looked at James. "You trust the doc?"

Digger squeezed Ethorne's ankle. "Et'orne? It's time to
get up now."

James told Pa, "Someone's got to see to him."

Handyman looked at the other white men, then said, "Far as I'm concerned, this is over." Several of the others mumbled sounds of agreement.

Pa dropped his hand from Dr. Lamont's shirt. "See what you can do." He turned toward Digger, offering his open palm, and beside him, Dr. Lamont stepped forward. Then both men held still.

Ethorne's work boot twitched as Digger released his ankle. One of the white men inhaled harshly. Ethorne sat up. "Do 'bout what?"

Pa laughed as Digger walked over to take his hand. "Christ, Ethorne, I figured you for a goner for sure!"

I smiled, and Little Bit clapped her hands, saying, "Yayy, Ethorne!"

Digger looked at her, then clapped, too, his hands almost missing each other. "Yayy, Et'orne!"

Ethorne frowned, then got to his feet and grinned. Dr. Lamont said, "You're all right?" Ethorne nodded, and so did Dr. Lamont, adding, "Well. No harm done, then."

The atmosphere of relief failed at two points. James cried quietly, tears trickling over the high bones of his cheeks. The rifle did not waver. His target cringed, staring at Ethorne, whispering, almost whimpering, "I killed 'im. I killed that nigger."

Handyman clapped Cal on the back. "Ain't ever'day you got cause to be happy you're such a piss-poor shot." Cal stared at Handyman, who added, "It all got out o' hand. Now we just back off and let things be, all right? I told you before, you lucky to be rid of a woman who'd run off with a nigger."

Pa looked at Ethorne. "What now?"

Ethorne said, "James, you think that rifle'd make up for what happened here? Enough to forgive and forget?"

James shook his head.

Ethorne said, "Bruises heal."

James said nothing.

Ethorne said, "Then what else is there?"

James looked at Cal. "I'm goin' away. With Francy, who ain't your wife no more. You never wanted Seth, and you still don't."

"Hell, take the bitch for all I care," Cal said coolly, but his gaze flicked incessantly between James and Ethorne.

Dr. Lamont said, "So, Ethorne, did you faint, or were you just playin' possum?"

Ethorne shrugged.

Pa said, "You're gonna just forget what happened here?"

Ethorne said, "Di'n't say that."

Pa pointed at the group of white men. "They should be charged. We should take 'em back to Dogland and call the sheriff."

Ethorne said, "No need to embarrass Rooster like that. He'd arrest 'em if you make a fuss, but they wou'n't be convicted. If they killed a nigger and you was a witness, they might be convicted, it's hard to say. But in this case, no one local would say any real harm's been done."

Pa lifted his chin toward James. "Yeah?"

James swung the rifle butt to his shoulder. Cal and several of the men jumped back, but James swiveled toward the dirt road and made a fence post thrash until the hammer clicked on an empty chamber. "I took worse." He held the rifle toward Cal. "And I'm leavin' with Francy."

"All right," Cal said quietly, taking the rifle but still standing as though he were under its sight.

"Your brother wouldn't let 'em go," Pa said.

"No," James agreed, then looked at Ethorne. "I hear livin' is the best kind of victory."

Handyman squeezed Cal's shoulder. "Let's get." Cal shuddered, then nodded. The white men moved slowly toward their cars. Handyman paused with his hand on his door handle, looked at James, then shook his head and got into the car. None of the others looked back, not even Dr. Lamont. We watched them drive, one after another like a funeral procession, toward the highway.

Pa picked up Digger and carried him to the truck. "Let's go. If they see Seth at Dogland—"

"Fight's out of 'em," Ethorne said. "But, you right, we best get back just in case." He glanced at James. "You up to drivin'?" James nodded. Ethorne told Pa, "I'll ride with my boy."

Pa nodded. Little Bit and I did not suggest riding in the back of the truck; we got into the cab with him.

As we drove, Little Bit said, "Why'd they want to hurt James?"

Pa said, "They didn't know who they wanted to hurt."

"They wouldn't'a' hurt us?"

"No, I don't think so."

"Just James an' Seth?"

"Just James and Seth."

" 'Cause of Francy?"

"That's what they say. But Francy's a free woman."

"An' James is a free man?"

"That's right."

"What's Cal?"

"I don't know," Pa said. "But he isn't anyone who knows anything about being free."

Little Bit nodded. "You can say that again."

Pa smiled at her, and we drove on home.

At Dogland, Seth and Francy ran toward us. "Where's James? Where's Ethorne?"

"Coming," Pa said. "James got jumped by Cal Carter and some others, but he didn't get too badly hurt, 'cause they thought Francy was goin' off with Seth."

"Oh, God," Francy said.

"He's okay," Little Bit said.

"There they are," Pa said.

The truck that Seth and James owned came into the parking area and stopped beside us. James started to say something as he got out of it, but Francy threw her arms around him, and they kissed. I didn't want to stare, because kissing was embarrassing, but I had never seen a black and a white person kiss like that.

Seth said, "You better save that till you're on the other side of the Mason-Dixon line."

James said, "The one time you bein' cautious, you cuttin' in on my fun."

Francy rubbed her mouth, then rubbed lipstick from James and said, "He's right."

Ethorne said, "You two best get goin'. Once they lick their wounds, they might be back."

James said, "All right."

Ethorne said, "Let us know where you settle. You forget anything, we send it on."

Seth said, "Think on Canada or France."

Francy looked at Pa. "Say good-bye to Susan for me, please."

Pa said, "She'll be sorry she missed seeing you off."

"Oh," said Francy, then hugged Pa.

He stood there, letting her, then said, "Don't be making James jealous."

James said, "Mist' Luke—"

Pa stuck out his hand. "Don't forget to write."

Francy said, "Ethorne, when we find a good place, you got to come live with us."

Ethorne shook his head. "I done my searchin'. Now it's you folks' turn."

Seth told Francy, "I know I joshed you some 'bout bein' white—"

Francy hugged him, kissed his cheek, and said, "When your mouth is shut, you're as nice as your brother."

Little Bit laughed. "Seth is blushing!"

James said, "Take care, brother."

Seth said, "I ought to be tellin' you that."

James smiled. "You the one stayin' in the South."

"Well," said Seth.

"Hug the boy," Ethorne said. "They got to get goin'."

The brothers embraced, then Ethorne and James did. Ethorne said, "Up north ain't that much easier. An' I know you always been the sensible one, but remember, you got two to look out for now."

Francy touched her stomach. "Three."

Ethorne smiled, then put his hand where Francy's had been.

Little Bit yelled, "Hug me! Hug me!" So she got lifted up by James and Francy. She asked, "What about your little baby?"

Francy smiled. "Don't worry. My sister's taking good care of her." Then she looked at me and said, "Can you stand some girl cooties?"

I looked down and nodded, and she kissed me, too. I marched to James and stuck out my hand. He took it and said, "So long, pardner."

"So long, pardner," I said.

"Pardner," Digger said, and he received the same treatment that I had.

"Get," Pa said. "It's not like we never expect to see you again."

Francy and James scrambled into the cab, and the truck kicked up gravel as it drove up onto the highway. As they drove away, Ethorne said, "You never know."

Little Bit said, "Why're you cryin', Ethorne?"

"Danged if I know, Mis' Li'l Bit. You think it'd get easier to say g'bye as you get older, but it's the other way 'round entirely."

Pa said, "You want to come in, have something to drink?"

Ethorne shook his head. "Nah. Seth an' I best head on home."

Pa said, "Want to ride?"

Ethorne asked Seth, "What you think?"

"It's a nice night for a walk," he replied after a moment.

"Thanks, Luke," Ethorne said, and the two of them wandered away.

That night, Little Bit and I described how the rifle had gone off and Ethorne had fallen down. When we had finished, Ma said, "Someone could've been killed."

Pa said, "It was an accident. Either Cal didn't mean to fire, or he meant to shoot into the air."

"I don't like it, Luke."

"Can't say I like it either. But it's over now. Who's left to cause trouble?"

Ma only looked at him and shook her head. He laughed, and put his hand on her shoulder, and as they hugged, Little Bit nudged me and smiled.

In April, after the U.S. government helped negotiate a contract between steel companies and unions to avoid a raise in the cost of steel, six companies raised the cost anyway, then lowered it after Kennedy accused them of "a wholly unjustifiable and irresponsible defiance of the public interest." Republicans said the president shouldn't interfere with free enterprise, but Pa and I were Democrats, so we were glad the president had been tough. In New Orleans, three Catholic segregationists were excommunicated. In response, white protesters marched carrying signs such as, "Have socialist agents infiltrated the Catholic church? Integration is part of the international Communist criminal conspiracy!" and "Jesus was born of the House of David of pure white stock in Judea, a white country. It is our sacred duty to preserve the white race of Jesus!" A & P supermarkets began giving trading stamps with every sale; we kids would help Ma paste green stamps into booklets that could be mailed away for gifts, including toys. The X-15 plane set a new record by flying 46.7 miles above California. Jordy and Ronnie and I would pretend to be X-15 pilots because that was the best airplane; astronauts went into space, but all they got to do was ride in a tiny capsule, and "X-15" sounded a lot neater than "Atlas rocket."

In May, the first nuclear warhead was test fired from a Polaris submarine. President Kennedy sent troops and planes to Thailand to prevent a Communist attack from Laos, where Red Chinese were helping Laotian Communists. Red Chinese were Communists who did not have nuclear bombs or space programs. Jimmy Hoffa, presi-

dent of the AFL-CIO, was indicted for forcing a trucking
company to give him a million dollars; Mr. Shale said
mobsters and Communists were behind all unions, which
made Pa laugh and say he could see an argument for one
or the other, but that'd be quite a conspiracy, which only
made Mr. Shale nod and say "Indeed, indeed." The stock
market had its greatest fall since 1929; Republicans
claimed President Kennedy's intervention in the price of
steel was the reason. Israel hung Adolf Eichmann, the
Nazi war criminal that Israeli agents had captured in Argentina. Argentina liked Nazis, and Israel did not, but
America liked both Argentina and Israel because they
hated Communists, which should have meant that Communists were worse than Nazis, but Nazis were like the
witch who tricked people into her oven to bake them and
Communists were like Robin Hood who stole from the
rich to give to the poor, yet America loved Robin Hood and
hated Communists, which would have confused me had
I thought about it, but I didn't.

"Huh," said Pa, folding the *Dickison Star* back on itself.
"They printed my letter."

Ma did not look up from her ironing. "That's why you
sent it, wasn't it?"

"Sure. But that didn't mean they'd print it. Hey, kids!
Look here!" He pointed at the newspaper. "There's your father's name."

"Yayy!" said Little Bit, and Digger clapped his hands,
but they stayed on the foot of our parents' bed, watching
the flickering gray antics of two astronauts trapped in the
time of the cavemen.

"Luke H. Nix," I read aloud.

"You're not goin' to put that in one of your scrap-
books?" Pa asked Ma, who had picked up a scissors.

"Of course. Your letter to the editor right beside Chris's
spelling assignments."

"Whatever makes you happy." Pa picked up his pipe and tobacco and walked outside.

"Dear ed. Editor," I read. "I have been si. Silent for sev-er-al years now. But Dir. Doctor Lamont's letter has pro. Provoked me to write. What's that mean?"

"Dr. Lamont wrote a letter that made your father write his own letter to the editor."

"Oh. The Sup." I pointed. "This word."

"Supreme."

"Supreme Court ruled eight years ago that sep-er-ate but equal ed, ed-duc—"

"Education."

"Education was uncon."

"Unconstitutional."

"What's that mean?"

"Against the law."

"Oh. When South-ern states spend four times as much on Cau-casian students as on Negroes, it should be ob-vi. Obvious that the edu-cation is not equal. Anyone who has vis-i-ted Dickison Public School and the Dickison Colored School can see this. Yet Latchahee County, like most Southern counties, has not de-seg. Desegre. Desegre-gated."

"Very good."

"Doctor Lamont seems to think that deseg. Desegre-gating Southern schools will be the final vic-tory of the Un. Onion over the—"

"What?" Ma looked back over her shoulder at the news-paper page.

I pointed.

She said, "Union."

"Oh. Union over the Con-fed. Confederacy!"

"That's right."

"But it's merely doing what's right. There's no ra-ci."

"Racial."

"Racial ten-sion in Latchahee County. White people and colored people get along here. Their children would get along in school, too. I have a boy in second grade and a girl in first. Their abil. Ability to learn would not be hurt by having people with dif. Different skin colors in class with them. They might learn more about the world by having people of diff-er-ent backgrounds in class with them. I pray my children will grow up in a world where ev. Every American has the same chance to ex. Cel." I raced in triumph through the signature: "Luke H. Nix. Dogland, Hawkins Springs."

Ma was looking toward the yard rather than at me. I said, "Was that right?"

She nodded and smiled. "You read very well."

"Why's it say Hawkins Springs?"

"This whole area's called Hawkins Springs. The motel, both gas stations, Mr. Shale's, Don and Roger's Suwannee Gifts, Pirates' Paradise—it's all called Hawkins Springs. It hasn't been incorporated to become a town like Dickison."

"It's our address," said Little Bit as Speedy the Alka-Seltzer boy tap-danced on television.

"That's right," Ma said.

"So people will know where we are," Little Bit said.

"Exactly," said Ma, and she kissed Little Bit's forehead.

10

Wrestling with Angels

The next morning on the bus Wayne Lawson stopped in the aisle beside my seat. "Your daddy's that nigger-lover."

"Is not!" I said.

Wayne Lawson laughed. "My daddy read it."

"*You* coul'n't read it!"

His eyes widened just as the bus driver called, "Wayne Lawson! You forgot how to put your bottom into a seat?"

Several kids laughed. Wayne Lawson jerked his head toward the bus driver, said, "No, ma'm!" glared at me, then walked on to sit near the back of the bus.

"Oh-oh," Ronnie whispered beside me.

When Pam got on, she sat in the seat in front of us, swiveled sideways, and said, "Chris, you really want to go to school with niggers?"

"If we gotta. It's the law."

"Ain't."

"Is."

"That'd be a stupid law."

"It's still the law."

"Says who?"

"My ma."

"Oh." She turned around, and I thought the matter was resolved. But at school, after Bible reading, Pam raised her hand.

Mrs. Howe smiled at her. "Pamela."

"Mis' Howe, is it the law that niggers gotta go to school with us?"

"Negroes."

"Yes, ma'm."

Mrs. Howe picked up a piece of chalk, looked at me, then looked at Pam. "It's not the law in Latchahee County," she said kindly, and began to write the new words for the day on the chalkboard: Black. White. Red. Blue. Yellow. Green. Purple. Orange.

At recess on the playground, Pam, Roxie, Ronnie, and I were playing marbles when Wayne Lawson and several older boys approached us. One asked, "You really a nigger-lover?"

Pam said, "Y'all go 'way, Wayne Lawson. You can't play."

"Who wants to play with girls?" asked Wayne Lawson. "Don't Chris know if'n he's a nigger-lover?"

There was no point in looking for a teacher to point out that Wayne was calling names, because he would have already looked, and even if a teacher heard him, he'd squeak by on the technicality that he had asked rather than called. I said, "I don't love any Negroes."

"Oh." The boy frowned at Wayne Lawson, and Pam frowned at me.

I said, "I like some Negroes, but I don' love none."

A second boy smiled. "Oh, he's a nigger-*liker.*"

"I like niggers," Wayne Lawson said. The others stared at him, and he grinned. "Ever'one should own one." As they laughed, I walked away. Wayne Lawson called, "Bye-bye, nigger-liker!"

On the school bus home, I sat within a couple of seats of the front. I tried to look at a library picture book about

Daniel Boone, but I kept listening for Wayne Lawson. Every time I heard him laugh, my shoulders tightened. Nothing happened until we got to his stop. As he passed my seat, he flicked a spitball against my ear. "Owie!" I said, and he looked back and laughed. I watched him and his sister get off the bus.

As we drove away from the Lawson's farm, Ronnie said, "Wayne Lawson's a big bully."

"Yeah," I agreed. "Big fat bully ugly doodoobughead. And he's stupid." And we laughed together.

At Dogland, I entered the restaurant and climbed on a stool at the counter. Lurleen said, "Hey, Chris, you thirsty?"

"Yes'm."

She poured me a glass of milk and went back to reading a movie magazine about Elizabeth Taylor and Tony Curtis. I banged the bar of the drinking straw dispenser and was building a froth of bubbles on the surface of my milk when Ma came in. She said, "Hi, Chris, How was school?"

"Mmm. Okay."

"Learn anything new?"

"Noah had a ark. He put a momma and a poppa of every kind of animal on it, and when God flooded the whole earth, it rained for forty days, but it was okay because they were all in the ark."

"I don't see why that makes you sad."

"If there was a momma and a poppa of every animal, did Noah let all the animal kids get drownded?"

"Oh, Noah wouldn't do that. I'm sure Noah wouldn't do that."

"But Mrs. Howe said there was just two of everything."

"Well, there were just two of the Nixes before you were born."

"You an' Pa?"

"That's right. None of the animals had kids, I'm sure. They were all born after the ark landed."

"Oh. Okay."

"So why the sad face?"

"You're not s'pose to say nigger, right?"

"That's right. Did you?"

I shook my head. "Wayne Lawson says I'm a nigger-liker."

Ma's lips tightened, and then she said, "I'll talk to your father."

"Will he spank Wayne Lawson?"

"No. You don't spank other people's kids."

"Oh."

Ma laughed. "Would it make you happy if someone spanked Wayne Lawson?"

I nodded.

"Well, I don't think that's likely. But we'll see what we can do, all right?"

I nodded, slurped the last of my milk, and ran outside to play with my plastic army men. When I heard Pa yell, "Chris!" I abandoned my army in the dirt and ran as fast as I could toward his voice. I heard the tone that sometimes meant a spanking. The longer Pa waited, the madder he got; it was best to get up there and take whatever punishment might be coming.

He stood at the back of the restaurant. I skidded on the gravel in front of him and stood as straight as a soldier.

"Did some boy call you a name?"

"Yes, sir."

"Did you do anything to him first?"

"No, sir."

"What'd he call you?"

"A nigger-liker."

Pa blinked. "Not a nigger-lover?"

"No, sir. He as'ed if I was a nigger-lover."

"What'd you tell him?"

"I said I *liked* some Negroes."

Pa squinted at me, then smiled. "So he was tellin' the truth."

I thought, then said hesitantly, "Yes, sir."

"All right." He sat on the sidewalk and patted the concrete. "Sit a minute, Chris." I sat and looked up at him. He said, "When you get in trouble on your own, I can't say I feel good about it, but I figure a kid has to make mistakes to learn from them. But when you get in trouble 'cause of something I did, I feel bad about it.

"I don't regret writing that letter to the editor, mind you, and I'll probably be writing another one. But I regret this being hard on you and your mother."

"On Ma?"

"Somebody called up late last night, cussed her out, and hung up without leaving his name. World's full of cowards."

"Coward," I repeated.

"You know how I tell you about doing the right thing, no matter what? That's not just about admitting when you've done something wrong. It's about doing what's right when everyone else is doing something wrong."

"You're not s'posed to tell on people."

"No, this is different. First off, if someone does something really bad, you know you're s'posed to tell. Second off, when everyone around you is doin' something bad, there's no one you can tell. That's when you got to go ahead and do what's right."

"Like a cowboy."

He smiled. "Like a cowboy. Whenever something's wrong, you ask yourself what a cowboy would do."

I made a gun with my finger and shot him. "Pow-pow-pow!"

Pa did not laugh. "You don't start fights, but you finish 'em. You do what needs to be done, and you don't walk away from trouble."

"Okay."

Behind us, Artie Drake said, "You forgot to tell him to kiss his horse."

Pa laughed. "The boy already knows that."

"What's going on?"

"Eh. Chris had a little trouble in school."

"Wayne Lawson said I'm a nigger-liker."

Pa smiled. "Which Chris agrees he is, but which doesn't seem to make him happy."

"The Lawsons," Mr. Drake said. "There's a bunch that breeds true."

"Ignorance begets ignorance."

"The Lawsons beget a lot of ignorance."

"They smell," I added.

Pa frowned. "Don't make fun of folks for things they can't help."

"Yes, sir."

Mr. Drake shook his head. "Then you won't make fun of 'em for anything. You think people can overcome their past?"

"A man can," Pa said. "Or he isn't much of a man."

Mr. Drake laughed. "Why is it you champions of tolerance are so damned intolerant?"

"There comes a time to say enough's enough; what's wrong is stopping here and stopping now."

Mr. Drake sat beside us. He reached into his shirt pocket for a pack of Camels, my favorite brand of cigarette because I liked the pyramid and the palm tree and the serene camel standing at an oasis. Mr. Drake offered a cigarette to Pa, who waved it away. Mr. Drake tapped out one, lit it with an aluminum lighter, and said, "Ever read Churchill's essay about if the South had won the Civil War?"

Pa looked at him. "No."

"I can lend it to you. It got me thinking about race relations and the War Between the States."

"Yeah?"

Mr. Drake put his cigarette to his lips. "Seems to me there's two scenarios. The first is Lincoln lets the South go. No war. Constitution doesn't say states can't secede. There wasn't a lot of support up north for a war. It could've happened."

"And?"

"Well, in terms of industrialization, the South was about ten years behind the North. Without a war, we would've been well on our way from an agricultural to an industrial economy by 1870 or so. Slavery doesn't make sense in an industrial economy. You want workers you use when you're busy and lay off when you're not, instead of slaves you have to feed and house year 'round. It costs to keep slaves, even ones treated no better'n valuable animals. Second, international pressure on the U.S. to end slavery would've continued on a free Confederacy. Third, folks forget there were whites in the South who opposed slavery. Hell, most Confederates weren't slave owners, and a lot of Yankees were. Gen'l Lee freed his slaves, but your Gen'l Grant owned a couple through his wife that weren't freed till the end of the war."

Pa laughed. "*My* General Grant?"

Mr. Drake smiled. "I get a mite partisan now and then. Anyway, it seems to me that slavery would've ended by 1890 at the latest, when Cuba ended slavery."

"Twenty-five extra years of slavery doesn't sound like an improvement."

"You're not seeing the whole picture. A free Confederacy wouldn't've had to indulge itself in Jim Crow laws or lynchings or any of the horrors of segregation."

"Um," Pa said, which meant he was still listening.

"Oh, I'm not saying things'd be perfect. But Southern whites and Negroes both'd be wealthier'n they are today. You wouldn't have had the million, white and black, Northern and Southern, killed during the war. You wouldn't have the repercussions of all that dying passed from generation to generation. You'd just have folks of different colors workin' side by side to build a better world."

"Sounds nice," Pa said. "What's your second scenario?"

Mr. Drake looked at the ash on his cigarette, flicked it onto the gravel, and took another drag. "Say the war was fought, but the South won. There were times when that looked likely. Even a victorious war drains resources. The Confederacy was trying to get European recognition to get loans, but slavery was a major obstacle. Enough that Gen'l Lee and Judah P. Benjamin—Jefferson Davis's Secretary

of State and the first Jewish cabinet official in North
America—both recommended that the South free the
slaves in 1864. Davis overruled 'em. By then, the South
probably couldn't have won anyway, not with foreign help
or God's.

"But s'pose Lee won at Antietam, before Lincoln issued
the Emancipation Proclamation—which, by the way, only
freed slaves in states that'd rebelled and didn't affect Union
slave states like Maryland or Delaware. So the war ends
by early '63. The Confederacy's industrial base has been
battered, but it hasn't been destroyed. England and France
both'd see a chance to make money by lending it, but slavery's still an obstacle. Well, Gen'l Lee's a war hero, so his
feelings would mean a lot to Confederates. Judah Benjamin's a respected man, too, even if he is a Jew. Add the
fact that an awful lot of slaves helped the Southern war
effort, whether they wanted to or not. There was a battal-
ion of colored slave owners and free men in Louisiana who
volunteered to fight for the Confederacy. Southerners are
a proud and contrary bunch, as you may've noticed. It
would've been a damn sight easier for a victorious Confederacy to free the slaves than it is for a defeated one to
give the Negro any real equality."

Pa said, "That's it?"

"Yes, sir, that's it."

"It's a pretty fantasy. But none of us live in it."

Mr. Drake grinned. "Maybe not, Luke. But you got to
consider the possibility that force hurts your cause."

"How long d'you have to consider that?"

Mr. Drake looked at him. "What do you mean?"

"I've known some Negroes in my time. First ones I met
to say I knew were in the service. Hardly ever saw one
while I was growing up, but I did see a few." Pa took out
his pipe and a bag of Prince Albert, tapped tobacco into
the bowl with his index finger, and lit the pipe as he talked.
"My pa wasn't much interested in race relations, prob'ly
'cause it didn't affect his daily life, but I remember when
I was a boy, we went on a driving vacation, and we took

along my cousin, a boy about my age who spent the summer with us. One afternoon, we stopped at a lake to swim. My cousin started for the beach, then stopped cold in his tracks. Some Negro kids were playing in the water while their folks watched them. My pa asked my cousin, who was blocking the path, 'What's the matter, don't you want to go swimming after all?' And my cousin said, 'Uncle Wade, there's niggers in the lake!' My pa looked at my cousin and said, 'It's a mighty big lake.' And we all went swimming, even my cousin."

Mr. Drake said, "That's hardly an example of force."

"Eh." Pa puffed on his pipe. "It wasn't till I was in the Merchant Marine that I got to know a few Negroes. Used to swap cowboy books with one. Decent guy. After the war, in '46, I heard about Isaac Woodard. Remember him?"

"Can't say I do."

"He was a Negro vet just discharged and heading home on a bus. At one stop, he asked the bus driver if he could get out to use the rest room. The driver said no. That's one of those things that happens under segregation. Petty officials with discretionary powers use 'em in petty ways. Driver'll let whites off to use the rest room, but he'll tell Negroes he isn't stopping long enough to let everyone off. If they get off anyway, he won't let 'em back on the bus without buying a new ticket. Rinky-dink harassment."

"Which is wrong."

"Sure. But it happened, and you can't deny it still happens. Anyway, Woodard got in an argument with the bus driver. Might've been a bit of a scuffle. I don't know whether anyone hit anyone. What I do remember is that at the next stop, in a little town in South Carolina, the driver told a cop that Woodard had been making trouble. The cop took Woodard off the bus, beat him with his billy club, then hauled him off to the local jail. And in that jail, that cop took his club and mashed out Woodard's eyes."

Pa puffed twice on his pipe. Mr. Drake and I waited for him to continue. "Did I say Woodard was still wearing his army uniform? There was a big stink about the case, since the choice of victim and the choice of punishment were so extreme, even for the South. Something like twenty thousand dollars was raised in New York, which didn't do a damn thing to restore Woodard's sight. But it added to the press attention, which got the FBI to look into it. The cop was tried for violating Woodard's civil rights. Which was news right there, a cop tried for something done to a Negro.

"A jury acquitted that cop in half an hour. For all I know, he's the chief of police of that town today. When I heard about Woodard, I just thought about the fellows I knew in the service, and how it could've been any one of 'em. No point in trading cowboy books with a blind guy."

"But if things had been different—"

"They weren't. And they aren't."

Mr. Drake studied Pa, then said, "No. You've got to do what you've got to do, I guess."

"That's the size of it."

"You can still be cautious."

Pa smiled. "I thought I'd been pretty good at keeping my head down. I'm not looking for trouble."

"Well. Integration'll be fought out in the big cities. It doesn't have to touch Latchahee County."

"True."

Mr. Drake blew a smoke ring. I carefully poked my finger in its center as it expanded. Mr. Drake asked Pa, "You think the idea of race is here to stay?"

"How do you mean?"

"It's a new notion historically. The word's old, but it just meant offspring, or a group of similar things. You find old references to the Irish race, the race of women, the race of heroes—you could say Chris there's of the race of Nix. It wasn't until the 1700s that people began dividing humanity by race. An early idea was for five races, Caucasian, Mongolian, Ethiopian, American, and Malay."

I shook my head. "Caucasian, Oriental, an' Negro."

Mr. Drake said, "That's what they teach today. But there's no basis for race other than human. You can't tell

whether donated blood's from a Negro, a Jew, a China-
man, or a Caucasian. When they find bones of cavemen,
there's no way to know what color their skin was. If you
want to test for race, all you can do is look at people and
guess."

Pa said, "Maybe my best friend in the Merchant Marine was a blond Jew named Sam. We used to go on leave
together sometimes. In New York right after the war, two
geezers in beards and black suits and hats came up and
started jabbering at me. I thought they were Mennonites
or something. Sam starts grinning. The more they jabber,
the more annoyed they get, and the more Sam grins. I'm
going, 'Sorry, I don't understand, do you speak English?'
Sam isn't helping at all. Finally the old men walk off, all
disgusted. Sam's laughing like he's going to bust a gut.
When he finally calms down enough to talk, he says the
old guys figured I was Jewish. They were disgusted 'cause
they thought I was either an American Jew who'd never
learned the old language or I knew the language but wasn't
letting on in front of my blond goy friend. When they left,
they were mumbling 'bout the state of the House of David.
And Sam, who's first generation and speaks Yiddish or He-
brew or whatever the hell it was like he'd been born over
there, thought watching this was flat out hilarious."

I laughed. "It is."

"Yeah, right," Pa said, pretending he didn't agree,
which made me grin more. Then he asked Mr. Drake,
"Don't you ever want to share what you know with your
neighbors?"

"I do. Anybody in the county'll tell you I'm the biggest
bore around when it comes to history and race."

"You get calls in the middle of the night?"

Mr. Drake glanced at Pa. "Do you?"

"Prob'ly kids."

Mr. Drake said somberly, "I don't write letters to the
Star saying white people should change the way they do
things down here."

"Eh. Maybe you're right."

"But it won't stop you from writing your next letter."
Pa laughed. "It's already in the mail.

In the summer of '62, the state began turning the road in front of Dogland from two lanes into four. Ma and Pa were both pleased, thinking that would keep more tourists on the old route. I was pleased because when the construction crews were away, I had a private road to wobble along on my bicycle. I was forbidden to go farther than the Fountain of Youth to the north or Gideon's 19-cent Hamburgers to the south, but that was freedom from Dogland where Pa might notice me doing nothing and think of a chore that could use doing. I went for a ride or two on most days, and my bicycle wobbled less and less. Sometimes I would see Mrs. DeLyon, and she would nod to me, and sometimes I would see Mr. Shale, who would yell, "How you doin', Christopher Nix! You keep helpin' the Lord to help you, hear?"

That summer, the Supreme Court ruled that a New York school prayer violated the First Amendment's separation of church and state. Defense Secretary McNamara said that the struggle against the Vietnamese Communists might take a long time, and North Vietnam's Ho Chi Minh confirmed that, saying they were prepared to fight against the South and the Americans for another ten years if they must. The U.S. national debt topped $300 billion for the first time. Saskatchewan tested a universal medical insurance plan that became the model for all of Canada's provinces. The U.S. exploded a nuclear bomb at night in the atmosphere that was seen eight hundred miles away in Hawaii, where radios fell silent, burglar alarms rang, and streets lay dark as city lights failed. The U.S. launched Telstar, the world's first active communications satellite; an instrumental named for the satellite was the first British rock song to hit Number One on the American charts. The FDA concluded that birth control pills did not cause blood clotting and therefore were safe to sell to the American public. Marilyn Monroe, William Faulkner, and Hermann Hesse died. Ringo Starr joined the Beatles. On my birthday, the president said two U.S. nuclear-powered subs had traveled from the Atlantic and the Pacific to meet under the polar ice, which told Americans that our scientific power was supreme, and told the rest of the world the same thing about our military reach. Marvel Comics introduced Thor and Spider-Man. Peter Parker was a social outcast bitten by a radioactive spider; though he gained powers and a costume, he remained an outcast who fought human freaks. I preferred the lame but courageous Dr. Don Blake who found a gnarled wooden cane that, struck against the ground, transformed him into a long-haired, clean-shaven god of thunder who battled space aliens made of gray stone.

That summer, the Nix family drove through Birmingham, Alabama. I don't remember why. Maybe we were returning from seeing the grandparents, maybe Pa had decided to take a week off and we had driven to the Appalachian Mountains to sleep in tents and be in a place that was nothing like Florida or Minnesota, maybe we were making one of Pa's many sign-posting tours, when he and a few or all of us would put wooden Dogland signs in the back of the station wagon and then go driving to find places where bemused property owners would let us post a sign for a very low rent. All I remember with certainty (which is not the same as for sure) is that we were returning to Dogland, and we stopped to climb the tower of Vulcan.

Stairs are wonderful, as all kids and cats know, especially if you live in a house without stairs and your grandma and grandpa live in a house with lots of stairs. The most wonderful stairs are curved and go forever, so you can't see far ahead or behind you as you run ahead of your parents, who puff and puff and laugh about how much energy you have. I raced ahead of Digger and Little Bit to burst through the door at the top of the tower. And I could not move. A cold wind struck me, and the world fell away forever. I pressed myself against the wall. I did not think the tower would fall. I knew I would.

That summer the O'Donohues bought land next to Dogland and built a gift shop and a kennel for raising and selling Chihuahuas. The O'Donohues are not a major part of my story, though they might have been a major part of Pa's or Ma's. They were an older couple who had bought stock in Dogland, and I soon overheard enough conversations between Ma and Pa to know the O'Donohues had decided to move to Florida and be in a better position to oversee their investment.

They had an adopted son who was blind. He was several years older than I was, and taller and stronger. I remember Little Bit, Digger, and I going over to play with him once, and we all had squirt guns. He had the most powerful one, and his blindness did not seem to hinder him. I thought he was mean. Ma said we should feel sorry for him because he was blind, and now I have no idea whether he hurt us when we played because he could not see, or whether hurting us gave him a tiny bit of the power that the world had kept from him. I'm sure we had to visit him more than once to play with him. He spent most of the year boarding in a special school, so I never really had a chance to get to know him.

At Hawkins Springs, several new terrors added themselves to the mystery of the old dance hall and the eerie nature of the long saw grass that grew around the swimming area. Once, when we kids paddled out to the raft made of wood and empty metal barrels, we climbed aboard, then heard something move within it: something like a thick, dark rope was coiled between the barrels and the wood. We leaped back into the water and splashed ashore more quickly than ever before. The water moccasin raced, perhaps as quickly and with as much fear, across the clear water for safety in the swampy stretch of lilies and cypress knees.

That particular terror never returned. We learned to swim to the raft and circle it, examining the shadows to be sure nothing lay within before we climbed on top. We never met another snake there.

But that was the summer Pa decided I was old enough to jump from the tower next to the heart of the springs. We had all laughed when Pa went up there, because we knew he was bothered by heights and it was funny to see him force himself to dive as though he did not care. But soon Little Bit and Digger began to jump off the tower when Pa dived. Since they were smaller, I had no choice. When I hesitated, Pa always said he would count to three. On "one," I would stand with my toes over the rough-sawn edge of the boards, looking down at the clear water, ten or fifteen feet below, and think about belly flops and water up my nose and things that might grab me and keep me under. Then Pa would say "two." "Three" meant a spanking, so I would leap before I heard it. I was not afraid of being underwater; I liked swimming underwater, with the strange mirror of the sky above me. I hated plunging toward the bottom, and I dreaded having my foot touch something unknown, something soft and oozy. Divers had drowned down there. I could imagine skeletons in black wet suits and scuba gear, watching and smirking. When I surfaced, I always laughed, not because I had conquered my fears, but because I had survived them.

One day Pa insisted Ma come along to the springs. He drove the station wagon past the dance hall to the end of the dirt road where we rarely went, near the neck of the springs and the Suwannee, and we all got out. "This way," Pa said, and he led us down a sandy path.

A square wooden houseboat with peeling gray paint was docked beneath us. The stern was open to the rear and either side, but it was covered with a wooden deck on which were mounted spotlights, and the front was glassed. The deck over the cabin was surrounded by a steel railing that you could hold as you walked up either side to the bow. Across the stern in white letters, someone had painted DIXIE BELLE.

Pa turned to Ma and grinned as he said, "What do you think?"

"Umm?" Ma said. "The boat?"

Pa nodded, and his smile began to slide away.

"Is it ours?" Little Bit asked. "Is it, Pa? Huh, is it?"

Pa laughed. "That's right, little darling. The *Dixie Belle*. It must've been named for you. Who wants to go for a ride?"

Little Bit yelled, "I do, I do!"

Digger said, "Me, too!"

I said, "Okay."

Ma said, "Well, sure. Are there life jackets?"

"It's got everything," Pa said. "Wait'll you see." He went ahead on the dock, then stepped across and down into the boat. "Hold on." He set an unpainted wooden gangplank between the boat and the dock. "Now, isn't that civilized?"

Ma smiled. "Indeed."

Little Bit ran ahead of her, and I followed. Ma came last, holding Digger's hand.

"Wait'll you hear the diesel," Pa said. "Those engines never get old."

"Mmm," Ma said.

"And you talk about a deal. No one wanted to buy the boat 'cause they used it to trawl for corpses—"

"They what?"

"It was a long time ago, Susan. This is a boat with history. It was used by bootleggers to run alcohol during Prohibition. When the bootleggers were caught, the state got it, and I guess that's when they used it to drag the river for bodies. It's a workhorse. All it needs is a coat of paint."

"Mmm," said Ma.

"It's gr-r-r-reat!" said Little Bit like Tony the Tiger.

The open stern had several benches with thin foam mattresses, and a high captain's chair next to the wheel, which fascinated me, and a door down a couple of steps that fascinated Little Bit. Pa laughed and called, "Slow down, Little Bit!" as she pushed the door open.

Digger and I followed her in. The cabin was dark. Light came through small louvered windows at the front and each side. It had been painted an industrial color that I no longer remember, light gray or dull green. More wooden benches and foam mattresses, like the ones in the stern, lined the front and one wall. The galley was to my right, which was starboard, which I could never remember, because right is a relative concept and starboard is a fixed one, and I did not have the language to clarify the difference.

The galley had a gas range. "And, look at this," Pa said, going to the sink and pumping the handle. "Modern living!" The faucet gasped several times, then spat rusty water. "That'll clear," Pa said, and he pumped it several more times to prove he was right.

"It's got a bafroom!" Little Bit called, opening a door.

"See? Everything you could want," Pa said.

"I got to use it," Digger said.

"Not when we're at dock," Pa said. "Only when we're under way, 'cause it flushes right into the water."

"Yuck," I said.

Pa said patiently, "That's why you don't flush it when you're docked." He went to one of the benches. "These fold up into bunk beds. You just hook the chain. See? You can tell they could store a lot of corpses here—"

Ma said, "I'm leaving."

"I'm joking, Susan. They probably stacked them in the stern. I doubt they'd ever go after more than one or two at a time anyway."

"Luke—"

"Who wants to go for a ride?"

"I do, I do!" Little Bit sang.

"Me, too, me, too," Digger agreed.

"Then let's go."

Ma said, "Is it safe?"

"Christ, Susan, we've got life jackets. It's not like the Suwannee's a wide river."

"What if we sank?"

"Then we'd get wet."

Little Bit laughed, and so did I. Ma looked at us, then smiled. "All right."

"Good," Pa said, and he went up into the stern. We followed. Old musty-smelling life jackets were stored under one of the benches. They were orange, with rough cloth covering hard foam rectangles, and they tied over your head and onto your chest with white straps that you pulled tight. Everyone had to put one on, except for Pa. As he closed the bench, he said, "That's probably where they put the bodies."

"Luke!"

"It'd be convenient, you know, just to drop them in as soon as you pulled them up, and you wouldn't have to look at them this way."

"Really, Luke."

"Who'd want to look at them? They'd be all bloated—"

Little Bit laughed again, and so did I. Ma said, "Please, Luke."

"Oh, all right. Listen to this." He drew back the engine cover and adjusted something, but I think the engine started from a push of a button by the controls at the wheel. It coughed like a volley of cannon fire. Pa said, "Purrs like a kitten!"

Ma said, "What?"

Pa shouted, "Purrs like a kitten!"

Ma said, "Oh. Right."

When he closed the engine cover, it ran quieter, but it was not quiet. The sounds of the river, birds and fish and insects and wind, were gone, and the smells of mud and water grasses and pine trees were replaced by the smell of diesel. Digger looked at the engine, then clapped his hands, almost silently in the rumble, and he laughed, and so did Pa.

Ma sat on the back bench while Pa ran along the dock, thrusting the boat out into the springs. Then he leaped aboard, ran to the captain's chair and the wheel, and worked something. Ma jerked forward as the propeller at the rear coughed up a jet of water and pressed us forward, not swiftly, but powerfully and irreversibly.

The water of the springs was as clear as a new window, but the river was deep and dark, like looking through thick green glass. Maybe you could see the tops of grasses growing within it, or maybe you only saw sunlight stabbing into it and dying. We went under the bridge, turned around, went downstream to the first bend, turned again, and returned to the springs.

Ma came to like the afternoon and weekend rides on the river. Pa bought an aluminum duck boat that he tied on top of the *Dixie Belle* as a lifeboat, and like us, Ma wore an orange vest whenever she went along the gangway. She liked the sun, and she liked Pa's contentment, and she liked the time away from Dogland, I suspect.

The *Dixie Belle* added a new terror to my life. When it was on the water, Little Bit and I often stood on the bow, watching for logs. Whenever something struck the bottom of the boat, I felt I had failed Pa again.

Sometimes we went onto the boat for an hour or two and never left the dock. In some ways, those times were worse. Digger and Little Bit liked to climb onto the deck above the stern and jump into the water, so I had to, also. As I did on the diving platform near the heart of the springs, I would endure the threat of Pa's count, and the count itself to two, and leap.

By the end of summer, I must have been diving off the raft at Hawkins Springs and from the springboard at the pool at the Fountain of Youth, but I knew that people should not throw themselves off anything higher from the water than their waists when they stood beside it. After we saw a boy about Little Bit's size dive from the platform by the springs, Pa made me dive from it once or twice, and once from the top of the *Dixie Belle*.

The dives from the tower were not significantly different than jumping had been. If your choice is to be eaten by two tigers or five, most people would, I suspect, pick two, but not feel better for having had the choice.

But I remember the dive from the top of the *Dixie Belle*. Little Bit and Digger had both gone ahead of me to show how harmless it was. They paddled in place in the water, looking up at me, and Pa counted, and Ma watched with the face that said she would do something if she could, but she couldn't. As always, I launched out on "two," not caring whether I belly-flopped or died. I remember coming up in the clear water with a strange delight, that I had done this horrifying thing and had not hurt myself at all. That delight stayed with me as I swam to the side of the boat, climbed the plastic and aluminum ladder, ran along the gangway to the bow to climb onto the top of the cabin and from there onto the deck above the stern. I dived again, without anyone counting. Maybe I dove twice. I had conquered my fear, and it felt wonderful.

The next day I climbed the *Dixie Belle* to dive, and looked down, and waited, and felt everyone watching, and told myself it had been fun before, and jumped as though that was all I had ever wanted to do. Sometime later Pa told me that fear doesn't go away, that people who aren't afraid are not brave, but fools, that you conquer fear by recognizing it and not letting it stop you from doing what you wanted to do. That made sense to me, but it did not help. Fear had never stopped me from doing anything I wanted to do. Fear only stopped me from doing things Pa wanted me to do.

After a bit, no one expected me to dive from any height. I had proven to Pa I could if I had to, which seemed to be enough for everyone but me.

With all those fears, there was wonder, too. The fear of heights did not keep me from loving to swim. The responsibilities of the *Dixie Belle* never made me unable to feel the joys. When you stand at the bow of a boat, clinging to the front rail, squinting in the sunlight, cold with a breeze that would not exist without motion, whipped by your shirt and shorts and the straps of your life vest, vibrating with the hull as it drives itself against the water, you are as big and as old and as brave as you could ever want to be.

That August, I turned seven. You could argue that any age is the best age to be—I generally side with those who say that the age you are now is the best of all, for you are, at the very least, the sum of your parts. But of the ages of childhood, seven years old is among the best. I was enough of a big boy to laugh at the idea of being a big boy; that was a dream for little kids.

One day when I was reading comic books by the house, Mr. Drake stopped in to see Pa. They spoke briefly of things that were either pointless to me, like the weather, or boring, like sports or local politics. Then Pa said, "So, was it my latest letter to the paper that brought you out?"

"No." Mr. Drake dropped his cigarette and ground it beneath a polished loafer. "I quit the agency. Effective immediately."

"Going independent?"

"No. Shutting down. Gwenny's going off to school, and I just haven't got the stomach to stay a company man."

"Oh?"

"It's nothing in particular. Well, all right, maybe it was one too many trips trying to salvage a screwup on a project that should'a' never been begun. Maybe it's just that I'm tired of taking orders without questioning them."

Pa nodded. "I never did find a boss I could tolerate long. What'll you do?"

"Well, quitting means I'm bailing out of the pension plan, but I've got enough to get Gwenny through her first year of school and a little bit besides. I was thinking of investing in Dogland."

"Mmm." Pa tapped his pipe against the heel of his engineer boot, then spilled the ash onto the ground. "You've seen business isn't the greatest."

Mr. Drake nodded. "I think I know what I'm getting into."

"It's tough doing business with friends."

"I've heard that."

"Well, if you're sure, I could line you up with a share-holder or two who'd prob'ly sell out at cost."

Mr. Drake said, "I don't mean to set conditions—"

"I run Dogland as I see fit."

Mr. Drake laughed. "No, ah, fooling? I just wanted to say that after setting Gwenny's college money aside, I'll be strapped. I've been thinking I'd like a simple job, something outdoors without too much responsibility that'd pay for my groceries and leave me time to think about what I'm doing with my life."

"You're asking for a job?"

Mr. Drake nodded.

"I'll be damned."

"If it didn't work out, I'd quit in a second. A second before you fired me. Which I wouldn't want to happen."

Pa studied Mr. Drake. "We're talking minimum wage."

Mr. Drake nodded. "I know a man who's got a trailer house for sale. If I could park it around here, I'd be about set."

"Well," Pa began.

"Or I could ask Maggie, maybe park it back by the springs."

"Mmm." Pa nodded and stood. "Let's find Susan and talk this over. You planning to move down here tomorrow?"

"Hell, no. I got to put my affairs in order and put my own house on the market." Mr. Drake smiled. "Maybe the day after tomorrow?"

Pa reached out, and they shook hands. "Deal."

Mr. Drake looked at me. "You kids'll have to call me Artie now."

I said, "All right, Artie, sir."

He and Pa laughed. Mr. Drake said, "Just Artie. Got it?"

I smiled. "Got it."

Pa said, "Susan'll like having someone else on the grounds when I'm away. We quit letting Ranger out at night 'cause he kept scaring the locals when they walked by."

Mr. Drake said, "I don't mind being a human guard dog."

Pa said, "Fine. I should be getting back to work."

Mr. Drake said, "I should be going, too. I'll walk up with you."

Pa nodded. "Sure."

Mr. Drake said, "See you, Chris."

I laughed and waved. "See you, Artie."

As they walked away, Mr. Drake said, "Has Gideon Shale been acting oddly lately?"

"Not more'n usual," Pa said. "But I always thought the old coot acted pretty odd."

"Huh. I had the damnedest conversation with him before I drove over here."

That night, Ma made hamburgers for dinner. Little Bit and Digger might have been playing with the squeeze bottle of ketchup, or maybe I made a face at the amount of ketchup they used, or maybe some ketchup got onto my burger and I asked for another one. What I remember is that Pa said I should get over being finicky, and I said nothing. He said I should try a little, and I'd find it wasn't so bad. I stayed quiet. He said I should just take a taste, and he took a spoon, squirted a drop into its bowl, and said, "Here. Eat it."

Ma said, "Luke, he doesn't have to."

Pa said, "It's just a bite. It's time he learned to eat what the rest of us eat. Isn't good manners eating what's set before you?"

Ma told me, "Chris, you know a taste won't kill you. Pretend it's medicine."

"Christ!" Pa said. "You always turn everything into a big damn deal, Susan. If you wouldn't coddle him—"

"I'm not," Ma said.

"Eat the goddamn ketchup," Pa told me.

Ketchup is lumpy and slimy and the color of blood. Its smell made the back of my throat lurch, and only by swallowing could I keep from vomiting.

"Just eat the damn ketchup," Pa said.

We sat still. Digger and Little Bit waited. No one had been dismissed, and we all had hamburgers and potato chips on our plates.

"Well?" Pa said.

I shook my head. Ketchup spat from the squeeze bottle in Pa's fist, hitting me in the face. "See?" he said. "It's goddamn ketchup. It's no goddamn big deal. Why's everyone make such a goddamn big deal out of nothing?"

The next day, a Saturday, I ran out to meet the mailman (who was a woman) when I saw her station wagon pull up beside our mailbox. She squinted in the sunlight and said, "Hey, Chris, how're you?"

"Fine, ma'm. Any mail for me?"

She shook her head sadly. "No packages from Minnesota, no *Ranger Rick*s, no nothing for you."

"Oh."

"Except this." She handed me an envelope that I recognized. I had spent an entire dollar to subscribe to *Aquaman* for ten issues, which would save me two cents for each copy, but more importantly, would mean that I would not have to worry that the grocery store would miss an issue one week. I thought the person who drew *Aquaman* was the best artist in the world, and I liked the story of the blond man who lived under the sea where he rode giant sea horses and visited the sunken city of Atlantis and fell in love with Mera, the red-haired queen of an underwater civilization who had the power to shape and control water, just like the Human Torch could manipulate flame or Green Lantern could make objects out of the green ray from his ring. The only thing I did not like about Aquaman was his kid pal, Aquaboy, who wore tight little shorts and was every bit the nuisance for Aquaman that Robin was for Batman or Speedy was for Green Arrow.

"And your ma's got a letter from old man Shale. This must be the shortest delivery I ever made. He ain't moved?"

"I don't think so, ma'm."

"Maybe he's not feeling well. I don't think I ever seen him closed on a Saturday before."

I shrugged.

The mailman waved, called, "See you later, alligator." She pulled onto the highway as I called, "In a while, crocodile!"

I ran to the restaurant with letters and bills and magazines clutched to my chest and dumped them all on a table where Pa was reading a book. He began to flick through envelopes and magazines. When he came to Mr. Shale's thick letter, he frowned and studied the address, printed faintly in pencil with tiny, neat block letters. "That's for Ma," I said. "I'll take it to her."

Pa nodded. I ran out as Lurleen said, "Bye, Hurr'cane." Ma was in the front yard, near Digger and Little Bit, while that Saturday's cleaning woman shook rugs by the front porch of our house. I said, "Here comes the mailman!" Ma laughed as she set aside her *Ladies' Home Journal*, then frowned like Pa when she read the envelope.

I said, "Did Rev'rend Shale move away?"

"No," Ma said. "I don't think so, anyway." She inserted a red fingernail into the top of the envelope and sliced across it, then withdrew a tight bundle of three-hole notebook paper with the narrow blue lines like big kids used. She smiled, but then her frown returned and settled on her eyes and mouth. I started to look at the pages, but Ma said, "No, Chris," in a quiet voice, and then she flipped to the end and said, "Oh, my God," and stood.

"What is it? Huh, Ma?"

"Where's your father?"

"Up front."

"Bertha," Ma asked the cleaning woman, "watch the children, please."

"Yes'm," said the woman without looking away from the rugs.

"I'll show you where," I said quickly, and started to lead her toward the restaurant before she could tell me to stay.

In the restaurant, Ma hurried toward Pa, calling, "Luke!"

He looked up from his book. "What's wrong?"

"I don't know. Someone should check on Mr. Shale."

"Is that my job?"

"I'll go. I just—" She handed him the letter and pointed to a paragraph near the end. "I'm worried."

"You're always worried. I'd only worry if you weren't worried." Then he was quiet while he read, and then he said, "Call the sheriff."

"Someone should go. A minute could make a difference." Ma turned toward the door. "I'll wait for the sheriff there."

"No. I'll go."

"Then I'll come along."

"No need to make a big deal of it." He stood, then looked at me. "Chris can come. If everything's fine, he can have a milk shake."

I hesitated, then said, "Choc'late?"

"Sure."

Ma watched us with the expression that could mean almost anything, and then said, "Chris, stay in the car until your father makes sure Mr. Shale's all right, okay?"

I nodded and followed Pa out, then ran to circle the car and sit in the front seat. As Pa backed away, I waved at Ma, and smiled when she waved back.

Pa and I drove, as usual, in silence. Mr. Shale's letter to Ma lay on the seat between us. I wondered if he was sick, but I did not ask, since I would find out soon enough. The promise of a milk shake made me think it could be nothing serious. Some years later, I remembered this drive and wondered how Pa could take me along, and how Ma could let him. Only now have I realized that I was there to reassure everyone. Letting me go and Ma stay meant Ma and Pa both thought everything would be fine. Having me along would make it seem that Pa and I had stopped in for a milk shake, rather than to discover whether Gideon Shale had taken his shotgun and spattered his bedroom wall with his brains, which he had.

I did not see his body, either then or at the funeral. Pa went into the hamburger shack alone, then came out quickly and stood by the driver's door without opening it. After what seemed a long time, I said, "Pa?"

"We got to wait for the sheriff."

"What is it?"

"Mr. Shale's dead, Chris."

I nodded. I was sad because Pa was upset, not because I thought something bad had happened. Mr. Shale was old. Old people died. Even my grandparents would die someday in that unforeseeable time when I was an adult, and so would Ma and Pa, when I had married and had children, and so would Little Bit and Digger, in that order, after me, because I was oldest and the price of being oldest was dying first, which did not quite seem fair, but I did get to stay up half an hour longer than they did, which might be a fair trade. Pa had explained this years ago, before any of us were in school, I think; the explanation came so long ago that I cannot remember hearing it. I would say it had come before words were part of my memory, but I remember that his description of age and death had upset Ma more than it upset Digger or Little Bit or me. We found Pa's acknowledgment of death comforting. Death had always surrounded us, from swatted flies in summertime to malformed shapes on the sides of highways to nameless Nazis and Indians in movies. Death had a logic that we understood, and Pa's explanation that death embraced everyone was pleasing. It confirmed what we did not realize we already knew.

Then Pa said, "He killed himself."

Pa's tone explained suicide to me, or maybe I had encountered that idea already, and had never thought that someone I knew would choose to die. "You might kill yourself," was a phrase kids often heard. It was attached to some things you shouldn't do, like run into traffic or stand in a field during a lightning storm. Only crazy or sad people killed themselves. In stories, suicide happened in jail cells or lunatic asylums or dark houses where the spirit would seek revenge on those who had inspired the suicide. Suicide did not happen in back rooms of hamburger shacks near your home.

"Was he sad?"

"Poor crazy bastard," Pa said with a nod, not looking at me. Then he pointed at the letter. "You want to read it, go ahead." I watched Pa walk across the empty parking area, where he sat cross-legged on the grass under a tree near the edge of the gravel. I picked up the letter, got out of the car, went to sit beside Pa's knee, and began to read.

Dear Susan,

I'm writing you because my kin are gone and you've always been so kind to me. If, after you've asked the Good Lord to bless Luke, Little Bit, Digger, Chris, and all who live in your heart, you asked Him to consider forgiving me, too, I'd be grateful. His truth has always been dear to me, and a comfort since Estelle and Randy were taken. I have long been a holy fool in that comfort.

This is my Testament. I always preached that you've got to tell it straight. This is how it was, as best as I can recollect:

I was alone in my restaurant, reading Abraham's story, when I hear a car. As I look up, Artie Drake's Le Sabre turns off the highway, followed by Nick Lumiere's white convertible. Like any Christian businessman, I was pleased to have both business and company, and pleased also at the notion those two had made their peace. I see I'm wrong as soon as they get out of their cars. Nick smiles at Artie, but Artie ignores him. Once men set their minds on being asses, it's so easy for them to continue.

Nick comes in behind Artie. I say, "Welcome! You seeking food for body, mind, or soul?"

That gets a smile from Artie. He says, "All three would be grand."

Nick smiles, too, and says, "It's good to know you've come to the right place."

I say, "I'm pleased to hear that. What can I get you?"

Artie says, "The usual, Gideon."

Nick says, "I'll just sit a spell, if you don't mind."

I say, "You got it."

Artie says, "And a cup of java, black. And a chocolate milk shake. If that won't clear my head, nothing will."

In my vanity, I prepare to preach as I slap a hamburger patty on the grill. I say, "World gets in the way of a man's clearest thoughts."

Artie smiles and says, "Yeah. But should you walk away from it?"

I pour his coffee, saying, "That's not so easy to answer. Look at Jesus. Did he walk away from the world, or toward it?"

Nick says, "What do you think?"

I cannot say I thought yet. My hands shook from rheumatism as I worked the scoop through the hard vanilla, but I'll miss that hurt when I give up this body for a perfect one. Hands like doing things, even when they're hurting. Maybe especially then. Maybe my hands were saying things more true than anything coming out of my mouth.

What my mouth said was, "A little of both. Jesus was born a man, lived a man, and died a man so we'd all know we can live well. He gave up everything to walk this earth, teaching sinners and healing the sick. So he gave up the material things of the world, but he didn't give up the world itself, you see? Sometimes he went off by himself to pray and think, but he always came back to be with people. Even after death."

Artie nods as I turn on the milk-shake mixer. It makes

an ugly rackety sound, but everyone smiles when it starts up. I flip Artie's burger up high—there's a showman in every preacher, even in Jesus. As the burger lands, I turn off the mixer, pour half the shake in a tall glass, and set the glass and canister in front of Artie. I say, "If you're troubled over the present, I find it a blessing to think on the future."

Artie says, "It's thinking on the future that's got me troubled."

"Ain't but one way to know the future." I nod at the Good Book as I slip his hamburger patty on a bun and add onion the way he likes it.

"What's it tell you?"

"Everything. The beginning and the end, and what to do in between. There's peace in those pages if you're not too proud to ask for it with all your heart."

Nick says, "Tell us about the end."

I say, "You want to hear about the end?"

Artie, beginning to eat, says, "Sure. It's nice to think someone'll pull our fat out of this fire we've fixed."

I say, "That's not God's plan. Well, He'll take the truly saved up in the Rapture. But many'll suffer through the end times, through the horrors of the Great Tribulation. If you don't make good with God before the final trumpet sounds, you're damned forever."

Artie says, "God wins."

"The Book says so."

"Then the folks in Hell get out?"

"They've earned their place. God denies those who deny Him."

"So, even after the Devil's been conquered, Hell keeps a-going?"

I nod.

Artie says, "God's hard."

I say, "You're a parent. You know love's hard. God gives you a choice. You got to live with it forever."

"A choice with a deadline. That's not an ultimatum?"

"When you can't escape your own decisions, you're an

adult. God gives us each a final exam. It's our own fault if
we flunk."

"When's this supposed to happen?"

"No one knows the day or hour. That's gospel. Anyone
who tells you a date is denying the Holy Word."

"But preachers keep saying soon."

I sit back on my stool and say, "The prophets tell us of
signs so we'll know the time is near. And it's mighty near.
It's all around. That earthquake in Iran? Twelve thousand
dead. Another ten thousand hurt. Over twenty-five thousand homeless. That's a sign. Atomic bombs and hydro-
gen bombs here and in Russia. That's a sign. We have the
power to destroy the world several times over, but the end
times only call for once. There's that satellite, Telstar. Rev-
elations says the word'll be spread all around the world at
once. I don't claim to know it all. But I know enough to
see it coming."

Nick says, "Ask him how many nations are in the
Southeast Asia Treaty Organization."

I say, "How many nations in SEATO?"

Artie sets his burger down. "Mmm? Britain, Australia,
France, the Philippines, New Zealand, Thailand, Pakistan.
And us, of course. Eight."

Nick says, "How many kingdoms does that make?"

Artie says, "What is it?"

I say, "Great Britain. That's the thrones of England,
Scotland, and Wales. That's ten countries in SEATO."

Artie says, "So?"

I say, "A confederacy of ten nations. Daniel 7:7. The
beast with ten horns. Out of the confederacy comes the
Antichrist."

Artie smiles. "Wasn't that Hitler?"

"No."

"All right. Who, then?"

"I used to think the Pope. God says you'll know the
beast by his number, 666. The Pope's called the Vicar of
Christ. The numerical value of that in Latin is 666. But it's
not given to me to know who the Antichrist is, only that

he's coming. Daniel 7:25. 'He shall speak great words against the Most High, and shall wear out the saints of the Most High, and think to change times and laws.' The Good Book calls him the king of Babylon, the little horn, the man of sin, the son of perdition, the beast. There's a horde of clues, if only men were wise enough to see them. That's why we keep watching."

Artie says, "All right. Where do you watch?"

I look at Nick and say, "He'll make a pact with Israel. He'll enter the rebuilt Temple of Jerusalem. And there's his number, 666. Maybe he'll give everyone a number to keep track of them, tattoo it on their foreheads. Maybe it'll be like a social security number. He'll claim to be the Messiah, or a savior, anyway. That he won't regard the religion of his fathers might mean he'll be a Jew, or maybe a Christian, but he'll claim to bring a special teaching about Christ's teaching, like the Catholics and the Mormons. Or maybe he'll just ignore the religion he was brought up in and create one of his own. But he'll be destroyed in the great war when he fights the kings of the north and south. If he sets himself up in Jerusalem, which is most likely, the kingdom of the north would be the Russians and the kingdom of the south would be the Arabs, or maybe the Red Chinese, unless they're the kingdom of the east."

"Where's the U.S. fit in this?"

"The entire world will be Satan's battleground."

"And this comforts you?"

"Knowing I'll be saved comforts me. Knowing I'll be reunited with my loved ones comforts me."

"You said Eden was here in Florida."

I nod.

Artie says, "Then Florida's the Israel of the prophecies."

"Maybe. The Israel before the Flood, anyway. But the Temple was built in the Israel that Noah founded when the Ark came to rest."

"So Armageddon might start right here in Latchahee County?"

"You shouldn't joke about some things, Artie."

Artie shrugs and grins. "The pieces seem to fit."

"Pieces seem to fit in many ways. God has a perfect plan, but imperfect man has trouble seeing it."

"Here's a question for you, then. Who's the friend of Israel? The post-Flood Israel?"

"Why, the U.S. of A., what with the Arabs and the Russians against them."

Artie nods. "Now, if you're talking about a pre-Flood Israel right here, wouldn't Castro down in Cuba fit your Antichrist bill? Preaching communism and talking to the United Nations where the representatives of the world can hear him all at once?"

"Sure. Could be."

"Or you could argue the U.S. is the New Babylon. That'd fit with the Antichrist befriending Israel, which Castro hasn't done. If Eden's here in Florida, our military buildup along the coast would be a buildup in God's land, wouldn't it? Would that make J.F.K. the Antichrist? He's a Catholic, and he doesn't pay his church much mind."

"This is a great Christian nation, Artie. We came here to escape the tyranny of Catholics and Anglicans."

Nick says, "Really?"

Artie says, "A religious background doesn't make us a religious nation. No disrespect, but Washington said, ah, 'The government of the United States is not, in any sense, founded on the Christian religion,' and Jefferson said, 'Christianity neither is, nor ever was, a part of the common law.' You'd think they'd know."

I say, "This is a Christian nation, Artie. Look at the Declaration of Independence and the Constitution."

"They never mention Jesus."

"Right on our money, it says, 'In God We Trust.' "

"Which god? Take a gander at the dollar bill. You see the eye in the pyramid? That's no Christian symbol I ever saw. Looks more like the symbol of Mammon, whose temples are on Wall Street. Are you all right?"

I steadied myself against the counter. "Sure."

Artie says, "I don't mean this country's un-Christian. It's non-Christian. We give lip service to Christianity, but that doesn't mean a thing. On our biggest holidays, who gets more attention, the baby and the dying Jesus, or Santa Claus and the Easter Bunny? If we were a Christian nation, wouldn't we follow Jesus' advice? I don't see us selling all our goods and giving the money to the poor. I don't see us turning the other cheek when another country threatens our interests. Jesus said, 'Woe to the rich.' Aren't we the richest nation in the world? Isn't Jesus crying woe to America?"

"This is God's land, Artie. The nations of the world must choose between Him and Satan. We're the example to help them choose. He's made us the richest people in the world because we're doing His work. Just look. From Germany to—"

Nick says, "Guatemala. The U.S. intervened there in 1954."

I say, "Guatemala. We keep the world safe."

Artie says, "Sure. Take Guatemala. Would a Christian nation do that? Arbenz was democratically elected. Aren't we supposed to support democracies, not overthrow them? And Eisenhower authorized it. Can you imagine George Washington approving dirty tricks in foreign lands? Doesn't anyone remember the Monroe Doctrine? Don't other countries have a right to self-determination, same as us?"

I say, "You got to fight Satan wherever he shows himself."

Nick says, "Like America in Iran in 1953."

I say, "Like in Iran."

Artie says, "Exactly. Who knows what Iran would've done, if we hadn't put the shah back in power. Maybe they would've had elections. They were talking like they would. God knows the shah never will. If America's a Christian democracy, why're we supporting an Islamic monarch?"

I say, "That's other countries. But here in America—"

Nick says, "In the fifties, the U.S. dusted several of its cities with radioactive powder to study the threat of atomic war, and never told the inhabitants. Americans were injected with plutonium and uranium without being told what they were receiving."

Artie says, "What?"

I shake my head. "Americans weren't ever sprayed with radiation in secret tests? Or given shots of God knows what, and never told the truth?"

Nick says, "At Tuskegee, American doctors withheld treatment from syphilitic Negroes to study the effect of the unchecked disease."

I say, "Coloreds with the clap weren't treated by doctors they trusted? That can't be. The government wouldn't be so low as to lie to someone with as little as a Negro."

Artie frowns. "Where'd you hear that?"

"Do you know?" I insist, wanting Nick to be answered.

"If I did?" Artie finally says.

"Then you got to speak it. The truth is a shield."

"I've got pieces of rumors, Gideon. I don't have the big picture. I'm not supposed—" Artie pushed his plate away from him. "All right. Those rumors, I've heard them, too. I don't know how far it goes."

Nick says, "Political assassination."

I say, "Assassination?"

Artie says, "Did Dmitri stop by?"

"Who?"

"Forget it. I can't confirm anything that someone else can't deny. Suppose I thought I knew some secrets. Would they be real secrets? Real is what you verify, and you can verify anything you want when you can fake the files and the photos. What's the use of knowing secrets anyway? Wouldn't it be best just to watch TV and believe everything you're told? Wouldn't knowing secrets and not being able to do anything about them be one way of living in Hell?"

"This is America, Artie. If there are secrets, they're for our own good. It's not like living under communism. The

Russians lie to their people because they're godless. Their space program's a hoax. The Chinese lie. Satan is in their hearts, and they reject God's word."

"What's it mean if our government lies to us?"

"Pray with me, Artie. God has the answers."

"I can't anymore, Gideon. Sorry."

"You got to trust God."

"Like it says on the dollar? I feel like I'm walled up inside that stone pyramid, Gideon. Along with 99.99 percent of the country. Or the world. I don't know who's up there at the eye able to see what's really going on, but it sure isn't me."

I grip his shoulder. "Stay with God, Artie. With the end near—"

Nick says, "11:59 A.M., October 29, 1962."

Artie says, "Gideon?"

Nick says, "That's local time."

I say, "What?"

Artie says, "Look, don't give any thought to what I've been saying, hear? I jump to conclusions as fast as anyone. Maybe faster."

I say, "Sure."

My hand falls from Artie's shoulder, but he puts his on mine. "You've got an answer that works for you, Gideon. Hang on to it. And I'll think on what you've said, too. I expect you're right. God's got a plan. It's nice to know it's all going to work out."

I look at Nick. He whispers, "Boom."

Artie says, "People like hearing you preach, you know."

I say, "That's good."

"You ought to get out more. Go visit some family or friends."

"They're here."

"Well." Artie nods. "I should be going. But I'll be back next week for another talk and a meal."

"It's coming, Artie. Sooner than I ever thought. Call on Jesus. Call on Him tonight, if you won't do it now. Don't wait another day, hear?"

"Sure, Gideon."

When he reaches for his wallet, I tell him not to pay me. He leaves a dollar anyway and says to put the change to some good work. It's still lying on the counter.

As Artie drives off, Nick says, "He's right, you know. New York is New Babylon. All the leaders of all the nations of the world send their servants to Babylon to worship, and pledge their service, and pay tribute, and receive gifts. You know why that is."

I say, "Who's the beast?"

"You think the beast is in the newspapers and on TV? All you know are the names of the puppets."

"You're lying."

"What're lies from a liar worth? It's truth that no one can stand against. It's not a shield. It's a sword."

"Get out."

"You think you had it figured wrong."

"I got it figured right."

"The outline, yes. The Rapture, the Tribulation, the End. But if everything's certain, why's Jesus desperately hustling troops?"

"To save as many of us as He can."

"To save Himself. He knows He's lost."

"If you know so much, when's the Rapture?"

"Midnight, March 12." Nick smiles. "1959."

"No."

"Why'd you ever think He'd want you? You get drunk and drive your wife and boy into a tree, then you trot around preaching like God's never spoken to anyone but you. But you know what Jesus thinks of hypocrites."

I nod.

Nick says, "There are folks who recognize weakness, and forgive it."

I say, "Get."

"Where're Estelle and Randy, Gideon?"

"Get!"

And he leaves. I watch him go, like Artie, toward Dogland.

I know him for a liar in what's important. And I know how to prove that. If I have been a fool on this earth, it won't matter. If I've done some good during my days, God will forgive me. If the Rapture truly has come and His hand passed over me, I don't mind. I can catch up to Him. Not even the truth can drive me away from God.

If the final victory is really not certain, maybe that's what's important. Maybe we're none of us perfect because He made us as best He could, which wasn't good enough. Maybe He'd like us to show up and tell Him it's all right. We're grateful for what He did. And we forgive Him.

Yours with God,
Gideon Shale

Pa said, "You may not want to tell your ma I let you read that. It was addressed to her, and, well, she believes you protect kids by keeping some things from them for as long as you can."

"Things about Mr. Shale?"

Pa nodded. "Like that. You can be crazy and a good person, just like you can be sane and a son of a bitch."

"Okay."

Pa and I drove home when Rooster Donati arrived. The news about Mr. Shale reached Dogland before we did. Mr. Drake was there, standing beside Ma, who had tears in her eyes. Little Bit might have been sad, but Digger did not seem to know anything had changed. Ma said he was too young to understand, and we shouldn't tell him that Mr. Shale had died unless he asked.

The funeral was a few days later. Pa asked me if I wanted to go, and said I did not have to, then seemed disappointed when I decided to stay home. A funeral was like church, but more solemn. Wasn't it better to stay home and play?

11

Not Long Before the End

Second-graders are superior to first-graders, which sometimes meant we were kind to them, and occasionally meant we were cruel, but generally meant we ignored them because they were such small, timid, and ignorant creatures. Dorrie Doodoo had failed to pass, so she was repeating first grade, and Wayne Lawson had squeezed by with a report card full of "D"s, so he was in third grade. Though the Lawsons rode my bus, I did not have to share a class with either of them.

In second grade I took a band class twice a week, which meant three things. I was excused for an hour of the day with the other band students, I got to see Ronnie, who sat with me on the bus but was in the other second-grade class for the rest of the day, and I got to sit near Jeannie Peterson, a small, quiet girl with light brown hair just like Stephen Foster's "Jeannie With the Light Brown Hair," and for that year, she was the girl I imagined I would marry when I grew up.

Little Bit began first grade, so for a week or two, I had

to sit with her on the bus. Though it was a duty, it gave me pride to be her guardian. Once she made friends of her own, we tended to sit apart. That did not mean we thought less of each other. We had always understood that we could count on each other for anything that was important, and nothing that was not.

My second-grade teacher was Mrs. Robbins, a small, white-haired woman who smiled more often than Mrs. Howe. I remember that I liked her, but the teacher who had the greatest effect on me that year was Mrs. Pickett, who taught fifth grade. The elementary-grade teachers shared playground duty, and all the kids knew that Mrs. Pickett was the quickest to send students to the principal for a paddling. Mr. Hadley was a pleasant man who smiled and nodded at everyone, but in his office, he had two paddles, a round one that stung and a long one with holes drilled in it that whistled through the air to really hurt. Wayne Lawson was the only kid I knew who had been paddled by Mr. Hadley. He was our source of knowledge about Mr. Hadley's paddles, which would make anyone cry, except Wayne Lawson.

In the world beyond Latchahee County, September began with the earthquake in Iran that Mr. Shale had thought was a sign. On the tenth, the U.S. Supreme Court decided that the University of Mississippi should obey a federal order to enroll its first Negro student, James Meredith, a veteran of the U.S. Air Force. Three days later, President Kennedy said the national government would protect voter registration workers who had been helping to register Southern blacks in the face of legal harassment, arson, beatings, shootings, and bombings. On the seventeenth, Attorney General Robert Kennedy filed a suit to end segregation in U.S. military schools in Richmond, Virginia. He said, "It makes no sense that we should ask military personnel to make sacrifices and serve away from home and at the same time see their children treated as

inferiors by local requirements that they attend segregated schools."

Meredith tried to register at the University of Mississippi four times in September. Twice, the governor
stopped him in person. President Kennedy sent U.S.
deputy marshals to force the university to admit Meredith.
A riot began. Thirty-five marshals were shot. One of the
two men killed was a French journalist who had come to
observe the working of freedom, equality, and brother-
hood in America. After the governor of Mississippi was
threatened with fines and a jail sentence, Meredith regis-
tered on October 1 and began attending classes accom-
panied by federal guards.

At the end of September, the U.S. decided to sell missiles to Israel to help arm it against Arab neighbors who
bought their weapons from the U.S.S.R. The U.S. announced it would use "whatever means may be necessary,
including the use of arms" to stop Cuba from promoting
"subversive activities to any part of this hemisphere," and
Defense Secretary McNamara declared the U.S. would
use nuclear weapons to defend West Berlin from the
U.S.S.R.

For me, September and early October meant a new
television season. I had the week's schedule memorized for
the hours that I was home and awake, and I was always
amazed when anyone older than me didn't know the day
and time that anything aired. *The Jetsons* was silly, but it
was the future, so I watched a cartoon family in a time
where everything was pristine and gleaming, and people
had difficulties, but never had problems. *The Beverly Hill
billies* was also silly, but I liked Jed's wise patience, and I
wanted to grow big and handsome like Jethro, and Ellie
was pretty and wore tight clothes, which meant something that had a name I did not yet know. Ma liked *The
Lucy Show*, and the character that Lucille Ball played was
a caricature of Ma, pretty but not vain, often flustered yet
always tenacious. Pa liked cowboy, lawyer, and army
shows. *The Virginian* had too little shooting for my taste.

The Defenders had too much talking, but *Combat* suited both of us. We could sit together in peace while Americans and Nazis fought for the freedom of the world.

One morning before school, Pam, Roxie, and I played *Fireball XL-5.* I was the brave space pilot, Colonel Steve Zodiac; Pam was his blond girlfriend, Venus; Roxie took turns being the robot and the elderly scientist; and Ronnie was the funny furry space alien companion. Pam's Venus was more adventurous than the show's, and Roxie only played because the rest of us would not play the quieter games she preferred, and Ronnie's parents didn't have a TV, which meant I would have to make suggestions about his interpretation of his character, which he would laugh at and ignore.

We had just blasted off from Space City when I saw Wayne Lawson running at me. Colonel Steve Zodiac bolted from the pilot's seat and into the depths of space without bothering to use the air lock. I ran across the playground, darting in one direction, then another, but I knew I wasn't faster, and I was probably tiring myself more than Wayne Lawson. As his arms closed to grab me, I ducked down and tucked my head. Wayne Lawson tumbled over me. When I stood, he was still on the ground. He got up slowly, shaking himself, and I, still thinking him invincible, looked around for a playground monitor, hoping someone would see us so I would not have to commit the sin of calling for a teacher.

Wayne Lawson said, "You're pretty fast."

I nodded, seeing something had changed between us, and wondering if I could do the same thing again.

The teacher on playground duty, someone I did not know, passed by and asked, "You boys all right?"

"Just playing," Wayne Lawson said.

"Just playing," I repeated.

"Well, don't play too rough," she said, and walked away.

A crowd of kids, mostly second- and third-graders, had

formed near us. Wayne Lawson said, "I hear your pa's a ay-thee-ist."

"He's not," I said, because whatever it was, his tone told me it was bad.

"It was in the paper."

Pam and Roxie looked hard at me. If it was in the paper, how could it fail to be true? Under the pressure of the moment, I made an intellectual leap. "So what?"

"So it was in the paper," he repeated, but he knew that sounded weak. He looked as though he wished I had not managed to duck and was wondering how quickly I could duck again.

"I'll ask him," I said.

Wayne Lawson nodded. "All right."

When I got home that afternoon, I went straight to the house, dropped my books in the kids' room, and hurried out back by the dogs. Ma and Mr. Drake were by the far grooming shed, laughing at something.

Mr. Drake had parked a small aluminum house trailer inside the privacy fence surrounding our home. Though the trailer was probably ten or twenty years old, it seemed like the future to me. It had a room at one end that was large enough for a double bed, and a bathroom just big enough for a toilet and a shower, and a main room that was divided between the kitchen and living area by a dining booth with two padded vinyl benches, just like in restaurants. It had a sofa that opened into a guest bed, and a television, and everything you could want in the world. And it all could be hitched to the back of your car whenever you pleased, and you would never have to stay anywhere you did not truly want to be.

Since Mr. Drake had begun living at Dogland, he wore jeans and boots and old shirts. His hair was growing longer, curling around the tops of his ears, and he had stopped shaving. One day he'd been cleaning under dog pens, and when he came up front to eat lunch, he had a bit of dog turd in his beard, which everyone thought was funny, especially Ma, who would never have been amused if something like that had happened to us. Every time Mr. Drake tried to explain how he had found that the best way to clean under the doghouses was to take the hose, crouch in each dog's porch, and lean forward till he was hanging upside down, we would all start laughing, and so would he. Whenever I saw him during the first weeks he was at Dogland, he was smiling.

I said, "Hi, Ma, hi, Mr. Drake, what's a ay-thee-ist?"

Mr. Drake said, "I think I'll make a round of the pens."

Ma said, "You don't have to go."

He said, "Oh, yes, I do. Politics, religion, and the birds and the bees are strictly between kids and their parents." He walked away whistling.

Ma said, "Why do you ask?"

"Wayne Lawson said Pa's one."

Ma frowned. I wondered if she would tell me, and then she said simply, "An atheist is a person who doesn't believe in God."

"Then what does he believe in?"

"That's something you should ask your father."

"Isn't there a God?"

"Yes. I believe there is."

"But Pa doesn't?"

"You really should ask him yourself, Chris."

"Okay."

I found Ethorne and Helen preparing the dogs' evening meal. "Hi, Helen, hi, Ethorne."

Helen said, "Hey, Chris."

Ethorne said, "How do, Mast' Chris."

I watched them work for a long minute. "Helen? Are you a naytheist?"

Helen said solemnly, "I'm a Seventh-Day Adventist, Chris. You know that."

"Yes'm, but are you a naytheist?"

Helen looked at Ethorne. "These poor children."

Ethorne said, "He just asked, is all."

Helen smiled. I always liked people with confident smiles, the sort that said they knew all the answers, but

did not hold that against anyone who did not. She said,
"No, I ain't an atheist. Adventist means I know the Lord's
returnin' soon, and then there won't be any atheists at all."

"God?"

"That's right. You're not an atheist neither, are you?"

I shrugged and looked at Ethorne. "D'you believe in
God, Ethorne?"

He said, "What you believe don't change what is."

"But do you?"

"Well, sometimes I do, and sometimes I don't." He
grinned. "Mostly I do, I 'xpect."

Helen said, "How long's it been since you saw the inside of a church, Ethorne?"

He said, "Ain't the skies the roof of God's church?"

Helen laughed. "You should'a' been a preacher-man."

Ethorne shook his head. "No, ma'm. There's times I
think I got all the answers, but I thank the Lord of Judg-
ment those times don't last."

I said, "Is it bad to be a naytheist?"

Helen said, "It's bad for the atheist."

Ethorne said, "I wouldn't say *bad* exactly. Folks got a
right to believe what they want, long as they don't hurt no
one. But the times I'm an atheist, it's mighty lonely."

When I came through the front passway, I saw four
tourists walking toward the Doggy Salon. I ran across the
grass to jump over the little row of bushes that lined the
main path. As I approached them, I heard one say, "Listen. The ravens are gathering." The woman nodded after
the one-eyed man spoke, but none of them looked up at
the sky.

I looked up, saw no birds, and said, "Would you folks
like a guide?"

The handsome man said, "Why, it's Christopher Nix.
You must remember us?"

I shook my head.

The big man laughed at the handsome one. "Children
forget you, and women do, too. If you want to be remembered, you've got to be on television."

"Not even then," said the one-eyed man. "Who values the past in the land of tomorrow?"

The pretty woman said, "You remember us. We stopped in a couple of years ago. You've grown since then."

"Oh," I said.

"We had to return," said the handsome man. "For a last look."

The one-eyed man told him, "You needn't be so amused."

I looked around. Dogland was Dogland. Funny things had happened here, but I did not think they wanted to hear about Mr. Drake's beard.

The handsome man said, "Am I amused?"

The big man said, "You're always amused."

The woman said, "He's never amused. That's why he's never quiet."

"Me?" said the handsome man. "Never quiet?"

"Yes," the other three said together.

"Well," said the handsome man. "Observe then." He winked at me. "Not bad, eh? Care to hear it again?"

"Yes," said the one-eyed man. "And often."

The handsome man smiled. "If I agreed with you, I'd never let a secret slip. Which would you rather have, peace or wisdom?"

"Come," said the pretty woman. "Show us the dogs."

"Okay," I said, walking up the path. "We just got a rott-weiler and a Rhodesian ridgeback. The ridgeback was used for hunting lions in Africa, and the rottweiler's a working dog that goes way back to Roman times. It's got a funny name."

"Does," agreed the big man.

The woman told me, "Something's on your mind."

I nodded. "D'you believe in God?"

"Mmm," said the woman.

The big man laughed, and the handsome man said, "Do your parents?"

I said, "Ma does. I guess Pa doesn't."

"Then you should half believe."

"Oh," I said.

The one-eyed man said, "Be careful what you pay to know."

After showing the tourists around the dog pens, I found Seth in the kitchen. Pa said he wasn't as good a cook as Ethorne, but at least you never had to worry about him disappearing for days at a time. I opened the back door, and he looked back from the griddle. "Hey, Chris. Need to know something?" He had told me about the Colossus of Rhodes when I read about Colossal Boy in *The Legion of Super-Heroes*.

"No," I said. "Yes. Are you a naytheist?"

He laughed. "Sure. You have to convert when you become a Commie pinko radical to earn a 'godless' pin. Are you?"

I shrugged. "D'you know where Pa is?"

"In the gift shop. Mrs. Stark stayed home sick."

"Is she a naytheist?"

Seth laughed. "Mrs. Stark hasn't missed church in fifty years, I bet. Though lots of people go to church for reasons besides God."

"Ma likes getting dressed up."

"There you are."

"I hate getting dressed up."

"Sounds like a solid reason for atheism to me."

I nodded and ran from the restaurant to the gift shop. Pa sat behind the cash register, a place I almost never saw him, waiting on some customers.

When he looked over, he smiled and said, "Well, Mark Christopher?" The smile told me he was in a good mood, but using both of my names meant he was not annoyed with me for anything.

"A naytheist doesn't believe in God."

Pa nodded. "That's right."

"Is there a God?"

"Some say there isn't. Some say there is, but they don't agree about the details. You got Christians, Jews, Muslims, Hindus, Buddhists, and just about anything else you can think of. There's groups inside each of those groups arguing among themselves about who's worshiping right. I think when you get down to it, there's not two people in the world with the exact same idea about God."

"But is there a God?"

"Well. You can't know what you can't prove. You could ask me if there was a thousand-pound catfish in the Suwannee, and I couldn't say."

"But do you believe there is?"

Pa shrugged. "Catfish get pretty big."

"A God!"

"Mmm. Did you talk to your mother about this?"

"She said to ask you. Everybody believes in God, except Seth and sometimes Ethorne."

He laughed. "Everybody?"

"Mrs. Howe and Mrs. Robbins. Everybody at church. Ma, Helen, and Mrs. Stark, says Seth. I didn't ask Lurleen, but they take Jordy to the Baptist church. And four tourists, I think."

"You think?"

"I'm not sure if they did or didn't."

Pa nodded. "That's God-talk for you."

"Is God for women? All the women believe in God."

Pa shook his head. "No. The most famous atheist in America's probably a woman named Madelyn O'Hare."

"Oh." I stood and waited.

"Your ma and I had a deal. You kids get to decide for yourselves about God."

"But what about you, Pa? Do you believe in God?"

He studied me, then said, "No. I don't."

"Why not?"

"Well, I've seen horrible things done in the name of God, and I've seen good things done by people who aren't religious at all. So I figure religion doesn't matter. If you live a good life and there's a God worthy of the name, you're probably covered."

"Mrs. Robbins says if you don't believe in Jesus, you'll go to hell."

"If God's that petty, I'll be glad to go. I'd rather be with Einstein, Gandhi, and Thomas Jefferson than with a bunch of TV preachers. Shoot, based on what Jesus said about hypocrites, he'll be down there with us."

"You won't be in heaven with us?"

Pa laughed. "If God's got any goodness in Him at all, He'll let you come visit."

"God's bad?"

"If God was bad, He'd make things a lot worse than they are. But if God was really all wise and all powerful and all kind, He'd make 'em a sight better. So I don't think there's a God at all."

"Is everybody wrong?"

"Considering all the different things people have believed, that looks like the only way to bet. But that's one area I agree with most religious leaders. If there's a God, he wants you to believe because you believe, not because everyone you know does."

I nodded. "Okay."

On my way back to the house, I spotted Little Bit on the swing set and called, "Hey, guess what?"

"What?"

"Pa's a naytheist."

"I knew that."

"D'you know what it means?"

She shook her head.

I was torn between a smile of triumph and a scowl of despair. "Means he doesn't believe in God."

Her eyes widened, then narrowed, and then she said, "I knew that."

"If Pa doesn't believe, does that mean Digger and I can't believe?"

She turned her head and lifted her shoulder to scratch her ear. "No."

"Ma believes. Does that mean you got to believe?"

She laughed. "No."

"Why not?"

" 'Cause I b'lieve anyway."

"Why?"

" 'Cause God talks to me."

"Oh."

Digger was building a four-lane highway like the one being constructed in front of Dogland. I called, "Hey, Digger. Digger. Hey!" When he looked up, I said, "Where'd Mr. Shale go?" He looked from me to Little Bit, then back. I said, "Is he in heaven?" Little Bit nodded, then Digger nodded, too. I looked at her. "What about Kato?" Kato was a Japanese spaniel who had died. "Is Kato in heaven?"

Little Bit nodded. "Everybody's in heaven."

"What about hell?"

"Only bad people who're sorry they were bad."

"What about bad people who aren't?"

"They're in heaven. But they're not having fun."

"Why not?"

" 'Cause they're afraid God'll catch them."

"That's not what Mrs. Robbins says."

She shrugged. "That's what God says."

I went back up to the gift shop. "Pa?"

"Hmm?"

"Little Bit talks to God."

He laughed like he often did when Little Bit did something I would have been spanked for. "Some people call their conscience God. Some people call a lot of things God. If you call nature God, then I'm not an atheist."

"Was that in the newspaper?"

"That I'm an atheist? No, I just said the Supreme Court says it's against the law to teach religion in school. Some people think only an atheist's interested in obeying the law."

I spent the rest of the afternoon considering these things. I found Mr. Drake to get his answer, but all he would say was, "I want to believe there's a God. Since an atheist doesn't, I guess that makes me a believer."

At supper, Little Bit talked about everything she liked at school. When she was done, Pa said, "Let's see. You like the kids, the teachers, the recess, the games, the lunch, the bus, and the bus driver. So, you like everything about school except the school parts?"

Little Bit nodded.

Mr. Drake said, "Gwenny was just like that."

I said, "I like it all. I got to read the Bible story today."

Pa said, "You did?"

Ma looked at him just as Mr. Drake said, "Which one?"

"Samson and the foxes."

"Huh. I only remember Delilah and pulling down the pillars."

"This was before. He got three hundred foxes and tied stuff to their tails and lit it on fire. And the foxes ran through the Philistines' cornfields and burned it all down. And then Samson took the jawbone of an ass—" Realizing that they might have thought I had said a bad word, I said, "A donkey. And he slewed whole bunches of Philistines."

"Oh, yeah. I always liked it when he whales into the Philistines with that jawbone."

Ma and Little Bit laughed, and so did I. Pa said, "Huh. What'd the Philistines do to Samson?"

I said, "They had conquered the Jews."

"Okay. And what did the foxes do?"

Ma said, "Luke."

Pa said, "That's a reasonable question, isn't it?"

I said, "I dunno."

Pa said, "Were they bothering anybody? Weren't they just running around in the woods? Couldn't a good and all-powerful being find a better way to defeat Philistines than by burning up innocent foxes?"

Ma said, "Luke, that's not the point."

Pa said, "I'd imagine it was for the foxes."

Ma shook her head, and Mr. Drake laughed, and then we kids laughed, and finally Ma laughed, too.

That night I had the oldest dream that I remember. Pam was in it, and maybe Roxie, too, or maybe they turned into each other as the dream progressed. There was a white horse that might have been a unicorn. It was night, and I was in the dream, and not merely watching it. I think I was naked, but that did not embarrass me until I woke up, because I was also dead, like a zombie. Pam or Roxie was leading me somewhere that I did not want to go, but I could not stay behind. There was a knife, perhaps the knife that had killed me, and sometimes I became the unicorn and Pam or Roxie rode me, and sometimes I was just me, wanting to be alive so I could do whatever I chose, but I knew that if I had been alive, I would have chosen to be there with her.

At school the next day, the bus arrived too close to the start of the day for anyone to question me. At recess, the kids gathered around, and Wayne Lawson asked, "Your pa's an atheist, ain't he?"

I nodded. "I'm one, too."

He blinked, then said, "You're going to hell."

"Not if there isn't one."

I must have expected that there would be consequences to telling that to Wayne Lawson, but I did not think they would come from Roxie. She said, "You don't really not believe in God?" Dickison's entire second grade had added "atheist" to its vocabulary overnight.

I nodded. The world made more sense to me now, and so did Pa.

Roxie said, "You wouldn't tell a teacher that."

"I would."

Wayne Lawson said, "Bet not."

Ronnie defended me. "He said he would, didn't he?"

Roxie said, "I'll get a teacher, and you'll see."

All of the kids followed Roxie in her search for the playground monitor. I immediately went into the boys' bathroom. If they could not find me before the bell rang, I would be safe in class. I did not have a plan beyond that. Perhaps I thought everyone would forget I had said anything.

But recess had just begun, and either someone had seen me go into the boys' room or someone had realized there was no place else I could hide. A boy came in, looked

at me, and went out again. Then, just outside the door,
Roxie and Pam and several girls began chanting, "Christopher's a 'fraidy-cat, Christopher's a 'fraidy-cat."

I hurried out. "Am not. I had to go." I had used the uri-
nal, but I had done that because I knew you should never
lie, so whenever possible, you should ensure that the truth
could protect you.

Whether they accepted that because they believed it or
they did not care once they had me, I don't know. The girls
led me to where Mrs. Pickett stood smiling under one of
the covered walkways. The boys followed the girls. The
number of watchers had probably grown, but I can't remember if I noticed. In my memory, all sixty students of
both second-grade classes were there, but I doubt I had
more than eight or ten witnesses.

I had never spoken with Mrs. Pickett, but I knew the
smile she wore. It said I was a funny little boy with some
silly ideas that she could easily set straight. I was afraid
she was right. I think she was old, but not so old as Mrs.
Howe or Mrs. Robbins. Her hair was very black, and she
wore glasses that swept up into points toward either side.
She said, "You're the boy who doesn't believe in God?"

"Yes, ma'm."

"What's your name?"

Roxie said, "He's Chris."

Mrs. Pickett said, "He's capable of answering for himself. Aren't you?"

"Yes, ma'm."

"You do remember your name?"

Most of the kids laughed. Mrs. Pickett nodded slightly
to her audience.

"Yes, ma'm," I said. "Christopher Nix."

"And you don't believe in God?"

"No, ma'm."

"Why do you think you know more than what's in the
Good Book?"

"There's no dinosaurs there, ma'm."

"Just because dinosaurs aren't mentioned doesn't

mean God didn't make them. God didn't bother to list every kind of bug in the Bible, did he?"

"But dinosaurs are big. Why didn't God put them in the Bible? How'd they fit on the ark?"

"They didn't fit on the ark. Don't you think that's why there aren't any more dinosaurs?"

"But God told Noah to take two of every living creature, didn't he? He didn't say to leave out the dinosaurs, did he?"

Mrs. Pickett frowned, which should have been a warning. "The dinosaurs must've died before the flood. Maybe God didn't think they were important to people since they had all died so long ago. Not everything in the world is in the Bible, but everything that's important is there. Isn't that so?"

I shrugged to say I did not know, which, uttered aloud, would have meant she was right, which would have meant I was wrong and Pa was wrong.

"Don't you want to be a good boy?"

"Yes, ma'm."

"How can you be good if you don't believe in God?"

"The Greeks didn't b'lieve in God. They b'lieved in Zeus an' Hercules an' Mount Olympus. Didn't they?"

"That was because they lived before Jesus came."

"They were good, weren't they? And there's good Indians, aren't there?"

"Of course. But they won't go to heaven unless they accept Jesus as their savior. It says so in the Bible."

"But the Bible's a book."

"The Bible's *the* book. If you don't think it has all the important answers, where do you think the answers are?"

I shrugged.

She smiled. "Would you like to teach us what you know better than the Bible?" Most of the kids laughed again.

"No, ma'm," I said.

"If you don't believe the Bible, why should you be good?"

"Because you feel bad when you're bad."

"And why do you feel bad?"

I shrugged. "I don't know."

"Where do you go when you die?"

"I don't know."

"How was the universe created?"

"I don't know." Someone laughed, so I added, "And I don't care."

Mrs. Pickett's smile slammed shut. The quiet around me would have told all I needed to know, even if I had not been able to see her expression.

I added, "Ma'm."

"You're a rude and ignorant boy." She pointed toward a patch of sidewalk. "You can sit out the rest of the recess over there. Maybe God will show you the error of your ways."

I sat on the sidewalk, knowing everyone knew I was being punished. I never felt as though Roxie or Ronnie or Pam had betrayed me. They were my friends, and their demand that I testify to Mrs. Pickett was neither a dare nor a betrayal. It was the simplest way to see whether I believed an impossible thing.

When I remember my childhood, I know there were times when I was hot or cold, and I remember a number of sunburns because I always believed that my skin should tan like Pa's rather than blister like Ma's, but I have few specific memories of the weather making me uncomfortable. Sitting on the sidewalk in the sun during recess is one of them. The day was not cruelly hot, and I did not sit there for a particularly long time, but I remember sweating, and squinting in the late morning glare. I did not think about God. I thought about what I had said to Mrs. Pickett, and whether she was being fair. I had rarely been punished in school, and never by a teacher who wasn't my own. I liked hearing adults tell me how polite I was. My appreciation of the deadly intricacies of manners was at least as old as my love of watching urbane cowboy-

adventurers on *Bat Masterson, Have Gun, Will Travel,* and
Maverick. I sat on the concrete while kids played ball
games around me. My pride had been hurt, and my vanity had been hurt, and when Pa heard about this, my behind would hurt, too.

Riding the bus home, Pam and Roxie and Ronnie said
Mrs. Pickett should not have done what she did, but I
should not have done what I did, either. Roxie asked if I
had changed my mind about God, and I said I had not,
and then we talked about other things. My atheism did not
matter to them. I was the boy who talked like a Yankee;
not believing in God was the sort of thing they expected
from Northerners. Which I would not have minded, had
I felt like one. In Minnesota, everyone said I had a Southern accent. I was born in the South. My memories of life
before Dogland were dim memories of another Southern
state. Once when we argued on the playground about who
was the better Southerner, famous failed generals blurred
in my mind, and I claimed to be related to Robert E. Lee
rather than George Custer.

At Dogland, I told Pa what had happened at school.
When I finished, he put his hand on my shoulder and
said, "Well, Mark Christopher, you learned a valuable lesson today." He said I had given a fair answer to Mrs. Pickett's question, and there were a lot of Christians like her
in the world, though I shouldn't assume they were all like
her. He told me about the fourth Crusade, when European
knights set out to free Jerusalem from the Moors and
sacked the Christian city of Constantinople instead. He
talked about people who did the right thing regardless of
the consequences, about Gandhi and Martin Luther King
and Jesus, but the Jesus Pa talked about was not my Sunday school's handsome blond man in a pristine robe who
hugged children and sheep.

Governments adore phrases like "by whatever means may
be necessary." On October 10, the U.S. Congress employed

it in a resolution telling the world how they would defend
American interests in West Berlin.

The next Friday was the first night I ever spent away
from my family. Handyman and Jordy picked me up when
they came for Lurleen after work. Handyman had asked,
"How's your pa?" and I had said, "Fine." Then he had
asked, "How's your ma?" and I had said, "Fine" again. He
had not tried to ask anything more, because Jordy and I
were too busy telling jokes and laughing in the back of
their car.

They lived in the country in a wooden house that
seemed enormous compared with our two-room motel
unit. I figured they were rich, and the six automobiles on
blocks around their house bolstered that impression.
Jordy had a number of younger brothers, all littler than
either of us, so they could be bossed around and ignored.

I had always liked music, but the only recording that
I had loved before that visit was the theme song to the
Robin Hood TV show that Ma would sometimes play over
the loudspeakers at Dogland when I asked her. Jordy had
an enormous collection of records, twenty or thirty or
more, including one about a cowboy named Johnny Ringo
that was as good as any TV show. The prize of his collection was the funniest thing I had ever heard. One side was
"Rindercella," in which a man tried to tell the Cinderella
story and got all the words wrong. The other was the story
of a Southerner who went up north and saw a sign saying, "Hockey Here Tonight." In the course of the story, you
could tell he thought hockey meant doodoo. For the next
week or two, you could say, "Her Two Sad Blisters" or "He
dropped it, and I don't blame him," to either of us, and we
would laugh, reeling around the room, clutching the furniture and falling to the floor, unable and unwilling to
stop.

The Greenleafs prayed before supper and breakfast,
and I bowed my head to join them. Pa had said that being
an atheist didn't give me any right not to respect people's
beliefs when I was in their homes. After eating, Jordy,

Handyman, and the little brothers all thought it was funny when I took my plate and glass to the sink, but Lurleen smiled, so I didn't mind.

To thank the Greenleafs for having me over, Jordy spent Saturday at Dogland. We hosed the dog pens in the morning and followed Mr. Drake with the cart of dog dookey to the pit in back. Later, Little Bit and Digger insisted on following the two of us around, even though Jordy was my guest. Jordy had matches and a cherry bomb that he had saved since the Fourth of July. The four of us went back by the dog-turd pit. Jordy caught a lizard, or maybe he found a dead one. He put the cherry bomb in the lizard's mouth, lit it, and threw it into the dog-turd pit. Jordy, Little Bit, Digger, and I ran shrieking in horrified glee as globs of turd and lizard threatened to fall on us.

That afternoon, Ma and Lurleen stayed at Dogland while Mr. Drake, Pa, and we four kids went for a ride on the *Dixie Belle*. Mr. Drake had a six-pack of beer, I think, and I can't remember who suggested we tow the duck boat behind the houseboat with the kids in it. Pa and Mr. Drake discussed the arguments against it, and agreed that all four kids could swim, and we had life jackets, and Pa could keep the *Dixie Belle* at its slowest speed. They did not need to discuss the arguments in favor. We loudly told them how much fun it would be. They did not need to note how nice it would be to laze along the river on a day fit for summer without four kids running and shrieking around their legs.

I sat at the stern of the low, flat-bottomed duck boat, and Jordy sat at the bow. Pa hollered to ask if he should open the throttle a bit, and everyone yelled that he should. We felt we were flying over the surface of the Suwannee, though we probably traveled at four or five knots. We had promised not to stick our arms or legs outside the duck boat, so we did not, though every instinct demanded that we dip a finger or a hand into the water to create new, tiny wakes that would mingle within the large one made

by the *Dixie Belle* and the smaller one made by the duck
boat.

First we were racing along, then water was surging
over the bow of the duck boat. As soon as the hull had dug
into the Suwannee, the entire duck boat tilted forward and
to the side, or maybe the tilting began when kids began to
jump out. Since I was in the stern, I waited until the others were out of my way, and then I leaped.

The river from beneath looked oddly like it did from
above, a cool world without boundaries or gravity, de-
fined by shafts of light that seemed to fall through green
glass. My life jacket pulled me, and I thought that direction must be up, so I let it take me.

But the water grew darker as I was drawn onward.
Something hard stopped me. My head and my life jacket
were pressed against it. In the darkness, I could not see to
know where I was, but my skin recognized the smooth
sheet-metal seat of the capsized and sinking duck boat.

Something soft might have bumped my feet. I kicked,
lurching forward, and rose again, only to be stopped again
by slick metal. I gasped, and air filled my lungs. Remembering it now, I don't believe I should have had enough
light to see, but perhaps diffracted light in the water
helped me. The deck of the duck boat was a ceiling an inch
or two above my nose. I had risen into a narrow pocket of
air within it.

I pushed sideways to escape and was blocked by the
hull of the boat. The life jacket fought me as I tried to push
myself down and under. I had read about detectives with
names like the Thinking Machine who found themselves
in places with little air. I had seen people on TV locked in
vaults as others on the outside raced to free them before
the oxygen, and they, expired. I knew the duck boat was
sinking deeper with me inside it, because the light grew
darker, and I knew I had to get out quickly. I was not
frightened. I had been presented with a problem, and I
saw the solution.

As I pushed again against the boat's deck, forcing myself down, something soft may have bumped my legs again. Then I was under the hull, and then I was rising toward light, and then my head was in the air. Jordy, Little Bit, and Digger floated near me, and the *Dixie Belle* was forty or fifty yards away, drifting or backing slowly with Mr. Drake at the wheel. Pa was in the water, fully dressed, swimming directly toward me with strong, overhead strokes.

When we all had gotten into the houseboat, Pa and Mr. Drake hauled up the submerged duck boat on the line still attached to its bow. Jordy said, "Boy, that sure were fun! Can't we do that again?"

Pa said, "I don't think so."

Jordy said, "Dang."

I said, "No one was hurt."

Pa said, "Let's keep it that way," and then, "Christ, Chris, when you didn't come up, I figured you for a goner for sure."

He was looking at me, so I nodded, embarrassed about causing so much trouble over such a small thing. No one speculated whose fault it had been that the duck boat had nose-dived. Wrapped in beach towels, we sat in the back of the *Dixie Belle* and watched the water and the trees as Pa turned the boat to bring us back to Hawkins Springs and home.

Little Bit pointed. "Look. A manatee."

"I don't see it," said Mr. Drake.

Little Bit smiled. "That's all right."

As we drove from the springs to the highway, Mrs. De-Lyon walked out of the house behind her motel and waved widely to us. Pa stopped to call, "Hi, Maggie, how you been?"

She nodded to him, and gave a small smile that included us all. "I'm glad you got in a last swim before the weather turns cool."

Pa laughed. "Didn't exactly plan on it."

"We all fell in the river," said Jordy. "It were great. Chris hid under the boat. You should'a' seen it."

I shrugged. "Air got trapped there. You could breathe and everything."

"Well," said Mrs. DeLyon. "Quite the adventure."

"It was just a ducking," I said, as Pa said, "Don't rub it in."

Mr. Drake said, "All's well that ends well."

Mrs. DeLyon said, "It looks like I'm going to lose the motel."

Pa blinked, we kids stared, and Mr. Drake said, "Oh, God, Maggie, your family's had that place forever."

She smiled. "Not quite forever."

Pa said, "What happened? If there's anything we can do—"

She shook her head. "Thanks, Luke. I'd get by if it was just the construction sending tourists on the interstate, or just the Captain's Hideaway Hotel taking a big bite from my trade. But the combination—" She shook her head. "And investing in color TVs to compete was a mistake. You want a good deal on an almost new set, let me know."

Mr. Drake said, "It isn't like you to give up."

Mrs. DeLyon laughed. "Going away and starting over isn't the same as giving up. I've done it before. I can do it again."

Pa said, "You can't get a loan or a second mortgage or something?"

Mrs. DeLyon said, "I might if John Hawkins didn't want the springs, and if he wasn't teamed up with Nick Lumiere, who's got the lion's share of the Dickison State Bank stock. They're foreclosing on the first." She glanced at Pa. "I'm sure he'll let you keep your boat docked for the winter, at least."

Pa shrugged. "He's made a couple offers for Dogland. I expect he'll want to stay on my good side."

Little Bit said, "But what about the springs?"

Mrs. DeLyon laughed and touched Little Bit's forehead. "It'll be there, no matter who owns it."

Mr. Drake said, "He could close it off, turn it into a private club or something."

Mrs. DeLyon said, "If there's any way I can stop him, be sure that I will."

Pa said, "Good luck, Maggie."

She said, "Thanks, Luke. You, too."

Mr. Drake said, "If you need a hand with anything—"

She smiled at him. "I'm glad you quit the company. The beard suits you."

As we drove back to Dogland, Pa said, "Maggie's one hell of a woman."

"Yeah," said Mr. Drake. "Sometimes you fail to appreciate the ones who're closest to you."

On Saturday, October 20, 1962, the front pages of most, and perhaps all, American newspapers showed U.S. intelligence photos of Russian medium-range ballistic missile bases in Cuba, ready to deliver nuclear warheads within minutes to any American city. That same day, China's armies in Tibet seized 48,000 square miles of land along the old border between India and Tibet. On Monday the twenty-second, President Kennedy spoke on television, warning the world that the U.S. would not back down from any military threat. Barbed wire went up on the beaches of Key West. Across America, the business in bomb shelters was, well, booming.

Little if anything changed at school. Adults did not talk about atomic war when kids were present. On the bus, Wayne Lawson announced that we ought to bomb all the commies like we bombed the Japs, and a few kids cheered, but that was a sentiment of the time that may have had nothing to do with what was happening a few hundred miles from Latchahee County.

I don't remember teachers telling us what to do if bombs fell. I remember fire drills, at least one of which must have occurred during the last weeks of October. We would stand beside our desks, then march out of the building by rows to stand quietly in the dusty yard, waiting for our next instructions. Either second-graders were too

young to participate in bomb drills, or some school official decided that crouching with our heads between our
knees under wooden desks in wooden buildings would not
help anyone if bombs fell near enough for us to notice. In
those last weeks of October, my contemplation of death
centered on ghosts, witches, and vampires. Christmas
might have the best presents, but you pay for them by
dressing up and going to church and eating big meals
where you have to sit still for hours and be polite to all the
adults. Halloween is the only American holiday when fun
belongs to anyone who takes it.

On Monday night Ma worked on a pirate costume for
me. She hated sewing and seemed to stick herself whether
she wore thimbles or not. Without looking up from her
stitching, she said, "It'd be nice to go see my folks."

Pa glanced up from a magazine. "Now?"

"Well." Ma turned her hand in a way that meant she
would dismiss the thought.

Pa said, "The kids're in school."

"I didn't mean we should do it."

"Then why're we talking about it?"

"There doesn't have to be a point to everything, Luke."

"Why not?"

Ma shook her head.

Pa said, "That was a joke."

Ma said, "Oh. I think I'll call Mimmy and Pop-pop
tonight, then."

We all waited. When Pa did not say she shouldn't, I
said, "Is it a birthday?" Long-distance calls cost money,
and stamps were only three cents. I had known that as
long as I could remember.

"No," Ma said. "It'd just be nice to talk to the folks.
Wouldn't you like to talk to Grandma and Grandpa?"

"Yeah!" Little Bit said, and "Yay!" I said, and Digger
clapped his hands.

"Don't talk forever," Pa said. "Or when the phone bill
comes, we'll be wishing it was the end of the world."

I can't remember if the phone in the house was out, or

if Ma said she wanted to call from the restaurant where it'd be quieter. When all three of us kids said we wanted to talk to Grandma and Grandpa, Pa said, "Not much quieter." Ma said we could say hello, but then Little Bit and Digger had to go straight to bed. Sometimes there were advantages to being the oldest.

In the restaurant, Digger listened to the phone and laughed and said, "Yeah," a couple of times and "No" about as many. Little Bit talked about school, our cats (Tiger had been joined by an orange tabby Little Bit called Waffle), the soft yellow chicks that Pa had bought and was keeping in cages behind the house, the black-and-white goat that Mary and Joe had given us who liked to follow Digger around, and the sign Ma had made for the cage of Pirate, Mary and Joe's other gift, that said, TRIPOD HOUND— *Muttus Americanus Peglegus.* Ma finally had to tell Little Bit that was enough. While I talked, Ma gave Little Bit a flashlight, Little Bit took Digger's hand, and they went back to the house.

Grandma asked if I'd been good and how my grades were and whether I needed new clothes for school. Then Grandpa got on and asked how his big boy was, and whether I needed any more comic books, because he wouldn't want to send me any if I didn't need them, and he read off the list of titles I had mailed to him to make sure I didn't want to subtract any, which I didn't, or add any, which I did.

When Ma and I walked back to the house, I hurried ahead to show her I knew there was nothing to fear in the dark and to get back first if there was. A voice from the night startled me, but not Ma. Mr. Drake was sitting on the step of his trailer. He said, "Anything exciting?"

Ma said, "No, not really. I just called my folks."

He said, "That's nice," like the words meant what they said.

Ma said, "How's Gwenny like Jacksonville?"

"Hard to say. She doesn't have a phone in her dorm.

I'd swear she knew how to write before she went to college."

Ma laughed. "Being busy's a good sign."

"Yeah. I didn't think I'd miss her that much. You heard that Tepes boy moved up there to be with her?"

"You may just have to accept that."

"Why is it kids're so much younger than we were when we were their age?"

Ma smiled. "Does seem that way, doesn't it?"

Mr. Drake pointed at me. "Hey, Chris, I never told you the end of the story."

"What story?"

"You remember. The king and his friend, the best knight in the land. And the woman they loved."

"Oh, yeah. Is there more fighting in it?"

"You bet. I can't think of a story that doesn't have some fighting in it. Want to hear it?"

Ma said, "What about Digger and Little Bit?"

Mr. Drake said, "It's probably a little mature for them now. Digger'd fall asleep, and God only knows what Little Bit'd make of it. If I can't tell it to them later, Chris can."

"Yeah, Ma. I can do that."

"I see I'm out-voted."

"All right then." Mr. Drake tapped out a cigarette. "Want one?"

"No, thanks. I think I really have quit."

I said, "I'll get you a cigarette if you want one!" and Ma laughed. Among the novelty items sold at Dogland's gift shop were exploding slivers that you tucked into the ends of cigarettes to surprise smokers. When Ma decided she wanted to quit, she gave us permission to hide the slivers in her cigarettes. She exploded one for our benefit, and a day or two later, she decided she wanted just one cigarette. She took a pack from a drawer where she did not think Little Bit or I would have gone, and when it exploded, she decided she really wasn't starting again.

Mr. Drake lit a match, enclosing us all in a dim circle

of light, and then his glowing cigarette tip was the brightest source in the night as he talked.

The sick king stayed at his castle, and his knights returned, one by one, until only two were still hunting for the magic cup that would save them all. Then the king's best friend rode back without it. Only a crazy boy who wanted to be a knight was still out there, dead or searching, and he never returned, so no one knows his fate for sure.

The king's son gathered to his side the most bitter knights, the ones whose sense of failure drove them to do anything that would make them feel powerful again. The king's best friend stayed apart from them. The king's son saw that the friend and the queen loved each other, so he arranged for them to be arrested together on a charge of betraying the king. The king's best friend ran away with the queen, so when the king's son attacked with the bitter knights, the king was alone. The king and the king's son killed each other in battle, and the queen entered a monastery, and what happened to the best friend, I was not sure, but that did not seem to matter when everything had been lost.

"That's it?"

"That's it."

"They don't win?"

"Well, the cavalry doesn't show up, if that's what you mean. But they did a lot of good things, and today, they do even more because people try to be like them, helping people who need help and facing any opponent if the cause is just."

"Oh."

"So, d'you think the queen and the friend should'a' gone off together?"

"No!"

He was quiet, then asked more gently, "Even though they loved each other, and the king neglected the queen while he built his empire?"

"No. They got married."

Ma said, "Some people get divorced."

"Yeah. But there was the king's son."

Mr. Drake said, "He wasn't the queen's son."

"But he was her stepson, right? So he was her son. And she kept being with the king's friend instead of with the king or the son."

Ma said, "So it's all her fault?"

I was always surprised when adults did not understand stories. I shook my head. "It was the friend's fault. He was s'posed to be the best knight. If he'd'a' kept trying instead of giving up, it would'a' ended right."

"Hmm," said Mr. Drake.

Ma said, "I think it's bedtime for you, young man."

"But don't you think it's a silly ending, Ma?"

"I don't know, Chris. I suppose a lot of endings are silly."

"Not 'happily ever after.' "

"That's true." She looked at Mr. Drake, then at the bar of light that was the window of our home, then at me. " 'Happily ever after' is nice."

On Tuesday the twenty-third, the Organization of American States, whose membership included most South and North American nations except for Cuba, formally agreed to use force to keep weapons from entering Cuba. A U.S. fleet blockaded Cuba and turned away Russian ships.

Late that afternoon, I was leaning against the side of our house, rereading my comic books where Little Bit or Digger couldn't come pester me about looking at them. Pa was at the back, fixing the dogs' evening meal. I heard the meat grinder, then the mixing of dog food in a wheelbarrow with a hoe, and paid no attention to them. I stopped reading when I heard Handyman call, "Luke," as though he were identifying Pa rather than greeting him.

Pa grunted, as if lifting or setting down something, then said, "Been a while."

"I ain't changed my beliefs none."

"Then why're you here?"

"Well. That's a good question."

"Well, I'm fresh out of good answers."

"It's like this, Luke. Me'n' some of the boys were over at the Roadhouse the other night, and you kinda come up."

Pa chuckled. "It's nice to know I'm getting read instead of ignored."

"Oh, your letters're getting read, all right."

"And?"

"Well, we was talking about what's wrong with the world in general and Latchahee County in particular. Not me, mind you. I was mostly drinking and listening. Folks got a right to their opinion. Even you'd agree to that."

"Hell, that's my whole point," Pa said.

"Then why d'you want t' force folks to quit prayin' and make 'em go to school with niggers?"

"You came to get into that? I'm willing."

"No. That ain't it. Here's what it is. One o' the boys said, 'That Luke Nix is a goddamn nigger-lover.' Which I allowed was so. Then one said, 'And an atheist to boot.' And I agreed with that, too. Then another ol' boy said, 'He beats his son to make him speak out against God.' And I said, 'He don't beat that boy. He loves them kids as much as any of you love yours,' and I got up and left."

"You did?"

"I did."

"Well. Thank you."

"That ain't why I come here, Luke. What's true is true. What I said to 'em didn't make a damn bit of difference. I got a call saying the boys're resolved to get every godless nigger-loving Commie out of Latchahee County."

Pa laughed. "There's more'n one?"

"No."

Neither of them spoke for a minute or so. Then Pa said, "People say a lot of things when they're drunk."

"They do."

"Well. I appreciate this."

"It's only Christian." I listened to Handyman's steps as he turned and left. After a moment, I heard Pa's hoe sluicing through the dog food again.

I fixed a super-potion while Pa fed the dogs. The Flash could run fast because lightning struck a bank of chemicals that spilled over him; the Elongated Man drank an elixir that let him stretch his body like rubber; and Hour Man took a pill that gave him super-strength for an hour. Dr. Jekyll and the Invisible Man both drank fluids of their own invention from a flask. I hated pills, so Ma's medicine cabinet was safe. I wished I had a flask and lightning, but neither of those was crucial. Power comes from power, so I needed to find the most powerful fluids I could.

I took a chipped red plastic tumbler from our bathroom, went up to the restaurant, and asked Ma if I could have orange juice to take back in the yard where I was playing. She smiled and said I certainly could.

When Pa had trained horses, he had bought a gallon of horse tonic that he mixed in their food. Most of the gallon was full when we left Louisiana. He decided that if it was good for horses, it was good for people. He kept some in a small brown glass bottle in the kitchen. Every morning, we kids had to add as many drops as we were old to our orange juice and drink it down. Horse tonic was a dark, bitter fluid. Whether you stirred it into the orange juice, turning it all the color of rust, or let it settle on the bottom to drink in a last, bold gulp, it tasted terrible. Ma refused to drink it, but Pa did, so we had to. Now that I haven't tasted it in years, I remember a sense of amusement and shared hardship as we kids watched each other measure out the drops, counting them as they fell from a stopper, making sure no one else got by with less than we had to. Pa never told us that he had a gallon in storage, and we never thought to wonder why the little brown bottle never grew empty. The worst things in life do not require explanations when you're young.

I filled the dropper, a good thirty or forty drops, and squirted it into the orange juice. Impressed with my resolution, I filled it again and added a second blast.

As I returned to our yard, Little Bit said, "What you doing?"

"Making a potion."

"Magic?"

"No, dummy. It's science."

"Is that horse tonic? You're the dummy."

"You wait." I never went voluntarily into the pump house. It was Pa's place, where he kept tools and curious things that might someday have a purpose. He sent me there to fetch what he needed, and once I had gone in to find a hammer, and had stood there helplessly, trying to identify a hammer among all the dark shapes until Pa had walked in, asked what was taking me so long, and when I said I couldn't find it, had reached out onto the shelf in front of me, picked up the hammer, and walked out without saying another word.

The pump house held an oil gun and a grease gun and cans and bottles of fluids whose name and purpose I did not know. The place smelled of petroleum and paint and old wood. I always remembered that a snake had been found there. Though we rarely saw snakes around our house since we had moved in, things might run out or tendrils might reach up through the holes in the wooden floor.

I carried the tumbler into the shed and added liquids. Oil shot from the oil can with a particularly satisfying burst, and turpentine splashed with the scent that made paint bead up and run away, and gasoline powered every internal combustion engine I knew of. When I had finished, I stepped into the sunlight with my tumbler full to the brim.

"You're going to drink that?" Little Bit asked.

I nodded.

"No, you won't."

"Yes, I will." I lifted the tumbler to my lips. The smell stopped me. I told myself that if science was easy, someone else would have created a superpotion before me, but that did not help. I stuck my tongue into it to test it, then spat that out, ran to the side of the house, turned on a water faucet, and rinsed my mouth for a long, long time.

I expected Little Bit to laugh, but she stood beside me. When my mouth tasted clean, I said, "Promise you won't tell if I throw it away?" Throwing away something you took was wasting it. Little Bit nodded. "Okay." We went together behind the pump house and poured the potion into a clump of long weeds where no one would find the evidence. I said, "Somebody wants to hurt Pa."

She shook her head. "Nobody can hurt Pa."

At dinnertime, Rooster Donati stopped in. I did not overhear his conversation with Pa, except at the end when Rooster stood beside his car and said, "You know if I was by the phone or the radio so I got a call right away, it'd still be a good fifteen minutes 'fore you could expect me."

Pa said, "I don't expect you to do anything more'n a person can do."

Sheriff Donati drove away. He may have understood that Pa thought what people could do was a little bit more than their best.

The next day Pa and Mr. Drake left Dogland for a few hours. When they returned, Pa had an old single-barrel shotgun. He laughed as he told Ma how cheaply they'd gotten it, and how he was pretty sure it'd fire. When Ma said she didn't want it in the house, Pa said, "I'm sorry, Susan, it won't be much use anywhere else," and Ma was quiet for the rest of the day.

Pa gathered us kids together, and we walked with the shotgun back to the garbage dump. He fired the gun so we'd all hear how loud it was and see what buckshot did to glass, newspaper, and bottles. After he removed the shell, he let us each hold the gun, and showed us how to carry it with the barrel pointing down so if it went off, no one would be hurt, and he told us he doubted there would ever be any reason why we should carry it until we were all much older. Then we went back to the house, and he put it in the corner of the closet, pointing it out to us and saying he knew we were good kids so he wasn't worried, but if he ever suspected we had so much as touched the shotgun without his permission, we would get a spanking so bad we'd wish that gun had gone off and killed us.

On Thursday the twenty-fifth at the United Nations, the U.S. showed photos of the missile bases in Cuba to establish that the threat was real, and to announce to the assembled countries that the U.S. would not ignore it. Few American news commentators noted that the U.S. had missiles in Turkey long before Russia put missiles in Cuba, and those missiles presented as great a threat to the Russians as the Cuban base presented to us.

That morning, as Little Bit got off the bus at school, Dorrie Doodoo spat on her. Little Bit hit Dorrie, and Dorrie hit her back, and because they both had older brothers, they both fought with fists. I didn't see it start. I was already off the bus and halfway across the school yard talking with Ronnie when someone yelled "Fight!" I had time to see who it was, but not enough to sort through the applicable rules: Nixes should not fight at school. Nixes should not interfere in a fair fight. Nixes should protect each other.

The bus driver and a teacher separated Little Bit and Dorrie. Neither was bleeding, but their faces were flushed from blood or bruises, and their hair was tangled. As they were led away, they continued to scream at each other, Dorrie Doodoo yelling, "Your father's a nigger-lover!" and Little Bit yelling, "You're doodoo and you're stupid and everybody hates you!" I started to follow, but the teacher told us, "These girls are going to the principal. The rest of you get to class now."

I learned that Mr. Hadley spanked them both with the round paddle. If there was a paddle with holes in it, Little Bit had not seen it, but the round one had hurt enough. We both knew it wouldn't hurt as much as the spanking she would get at home for fighting.

But when the school bus let us off, Ma and Pa both came to meet us by the Heart Tree. Little Bit and I said, "Hi," very tentatively.

Ma said, "Hi, you two."

Pa hugged Little Bit and said, "You all right, little darling?"

She nodded.

Pa said, "That smug bastard Hadley gave me a call. He said you started it."

Little Bit shook her head. "She spit on me."

"I figured you didn't. You don't either of you have to worry about Hadley. I told him if he thought hitting people was a good way to solve problems, I'd be glad to meet up with him, but if he'd rather talk, he should tell me if you misbehave, and your ma and I'll figure what should be done. I don't know if I should spank my kids, but I know damn well no one else should." He smiled. "Got it?"

We laughed. "Yes, sir! We got it!"

Ma said, "You didn't have to hit that girl, Letitia."

Little Bit nodded. "She spit on me."

Ma said, "Jesus says to turn the other cheek."

"Let her spit on me twice?"

"She's not as smart as you. You don't have to lower yourself to her level."

Little Bit squinted at Ma.

Ma said, "What's the punishment for spitting on someone at school?"

"Going to the principal's office."

"So, by fighting, she got the same punishment she would've gotten, and you got punished, too."

Pa said, "I don't think that's exactly what Jesus had in mind when he said to turn the other cheek."

Ma said, "It works either way, doesn't it?"

On Friday, three or four kids were missing from my class, and the Lawsons had not gotten on the bus, but if there was anything truly unusual, I did not notice it. When I returned from school, I ran through the passway in the privacy fence, then skidded on the heels of my cowboy boots. Far to one side of the yard, close to the fence but not far from our house and Mr. Drake's trailer, Ethorne tossed dirt with a shovel from a hole several feet deep, approximately eight feed wide, and perhaps twice as long. At the other, shallower end of the hole, Digger was helping with a plastic beach shovel.

I said, "What you doing, Ethorne?"

"What's it look like?"

"Digging."

"There you are."

"But why?"

"Oh, now, that's another question entirely." He wiped his forehead with a handkerchief and continued to dig. "I'm figuring on making us all rich. First, me and Digger'll dig us this hole to China and set up a tollbooth at each end. Then anytime someone wants to get to Peking or America faster'n by jet plane, they can just pay my toll and jump on through."

I laughed. "But they'd come out upside down."

"Didn't I say there was money in this for all of us? You sit on a stool at the middle of the earth. Whenever someone comes by, you grab 'em, spin 'em right around, take your tip, and say, 'Thank you, sir,' or 'Thank you, ma'm,' just as nice as could be. You think you'd like that?"

"Yeah." I laughed again. "But why're you really digging it, huh?"

"That's a question—" Ethorne began.

Someone had stepped into the yard. As I turned and looked, Mr. Lumiere smiled and said, "Hello."

Ethorne said, "Ain't nobody here you'd be lookin' for."

"Why, Ethorne, sounds like you don't properly value yourself or either of the Masters Nix."

I said, "Hi, Mr. Lumiere. Pa's up front and Ma's out back."

He nodded. "That'd be right useful if I was lookin' for them."

"Who *is* you lookin' for?" Ethorne asked.

"You."

"Why?"

Mr. Lumiere laughed. "Same reason as usual."

"I picked who I work for."

He turned to me. "You'd miss Ethorne, wouldn't you?"

I nodded.

Mr. Lumiere said, "I got a place out the county road that just keeps on growing, and I keep on needing good supervisors. If Ethorne had a chance at a good position, wouldn't you want him working for me?"

I shrugged.

Ethorne said, "It's only me that's got a say in what I do."

"Really?" said Mr. Lumiere. "I thought you believed we all affect each other. I certainly thrive by that principle."

Ethorne said, "You got my answer."

Mr. Lumiere said, "You know I'll ask again."

"You know I'll answer the same."

Mr. Lumiere laughed. "Now, Ethorne, we both know that ain't necessarily so."

Ma and Mr. Drake, talking quietly together, came through the back gate. Ma said, "Hi, is something wrong?"

Mr. Lumiere said, "Oh, I was just trying to steal your help. How're you two?"

Ma blinked, and Mr. Drake said, "Just fine."

Mr. Lumiere nodded. "Glad to hear that. Well, things're mighty busy for me now, so I'll mosey along."

"Oh, I'm sorry," Ma said. "If we could offer you anything—"

"I'll take you up on that," Mr. Lumiere said. "As soon as I can."

Sometime after dark, after Seth and Ethorne had left and we had all gone to Ma and Pa's room to watch TV, we heard a car turn into the driveway. Ma said, "What's that?" and then, "Luke, there's a car."

Pa said, "I'll see who it is."

Ma said, "Do you think you should take, uh, a light, or something?"

Pa rolled his eyes upward. "Nah."

Ma stood by the door and watched while we kids stayed in a semicircle around the TV set. Ma put her knuckle to her mouth more than once, and then we heard Pa call toward the trailer, "Artie! Hey, Artie! You got company!"

"Oh," Ma said happily, and we had already come to the door before she said, "Look, kids."

Gwenny Drake stepped into the yellow light of the porch just as the door to Artie Drake's trailer banged open. Mr. Drake said, "Gwenny!" at the same moment she said, "Daddy!" and they hugged. Mr. Drake held her away from him and said, "I'm glad you came. Nothing's wrong at school, is it? You look great. You really do. You weren't worried about—"

She laughed and touched his lips with her finger. "I was saying it'd be nice to see you. Johnny pointed out there's no reason we couldn't."

Behind Pa, a man took shape in the darkness, then stepped into the light. Gwenny wore a loose white shirt and tight white pedal pushers, but Johnny Tepes wore a black T-shirt and jeans. He said, "Hello, Mr. Drake."

In the moment that they looked at each other, Gwenny went to Ma for an embrace and said, "Mrs. Nix, how've you been?"

"Oh, I'm always fine," Ma said. "It's wonderful you could come out this weekend."

"Well," Gwenny said with a shrug, and then she said, "Hey, Chris, hey, Little Bit, hey, Digger. How're you guys doing, huh?"

"I hit Dorrie Doo—" Little Bit looked at Ma. "Lawson."

Gwenny said, "She deserve it?"

Little Bit nodded.

"Well, good for you, then."

Beyond her, Mr. Drake said, "Hi, Johnny." He indicated the trailer. "Welcome to my home."

Johnny Tepes nodded. "Thank you."

Gwenny said, "Hey, Chris, you're getting handsomer every day. Am I still your best girl?"

I nodded. "Except for Jeannie Peterson. An' Pam and Roxie."

Ma said, "And your mother?"

I looked down. "Yeah."

They both laughed. Gwenny said, "Well, at least I'm in good company."

"Hey," Mr. Drake said, "why don't y'all come in the trailer, and we'll have a welcome home party?"

Pa said, "I don't know—"

Little Bit said, "Yayy!"

Mr. Drake said, "We'll just sit around and have a drink. Nothing special."

Pa said, "If we won't be imposing."

Mr. Drake asked Gwenny, "Gwen, how long can you stay?"

"Till Sunday, at least, if I can stay on the couch. Johnny's still got his place."

Mr. Drake said, "Oh, yeah. Where is that?"

Johnny Tepes turned his head in a way that might have meant "west" or might have meant nothing at all. He said, "Out in the woods aways."

Mr. Drake said, "Up the county road?"

Johnny Tepes nodded.

Mr. Drake said, "I hear you used to do a lot for Nick Lumiere."

"Used to," Johnny Tepes agreed.

"Well," Mr. Drake said, "Come on in, everyone."

Ma said, "Can I get anything from the kitchen?"

"Thanks," said Mr. Drake, shaking his head. "You wait till you see what's in the icebox. I was thinking to surprise you with a Halloween party."

So we all squeezed into Mr. Drake's tiny trailer. He had

soda pop for the kids, and wine for the adults, and Neapolitan ice cream for everyone, which was Ma's favorite, and he didn't mind that I cut around the strawberry to eat only chocolate and vanilla. Gwenny told us about life at the university, and Pa, Mr. Drake, and Johnny Tepes talked about history and free speech in Europe and early America, and finally Digger fell asleep on the rug, which was the signal for Ma to say all the kids had been up way past their bedtime. Little Bit said she wanted to stay, but Pa said we might as well all go. Johnny Tepes said he'd go, too, but he'd be back Saturday after supper to see Gwenny.

On Saturday the twenty-seventh, Nikita Khrushchev, Premier of the Union of Soviet Socialist Republics, wrote privately to President Kennedy, offering to remove the missiles from Cuba if Kennedy agreed to take American missiles out of Turkey and leave Cuba alone. Kennedy's advisors said the U.S. could not back down and keep the world's respect, so the American government continued preparing to invade Cuba.

That Saturday began as usual, with hosing the pens and feeding the dogs. As Ma made French toast for breakfast, which was always a treat, Ethorne returned, said hello, and said he'd get right to work.

We heard the door close behind him. Then Little Bit said, "Why's Ethorne digging that big hole?"

Ma looked at Pa, who said, "Well, you've probably heard something about trouble in Cuba. I don't think anything's going to come of it, but if something does, we'll all stay down in there till it blows over."

"In the hole?" said Little Bit.

"Sure," Pa said. "It'll have a roof and walls and a floor. It'll be like a cabin."

I had seen pictures in *Life* of people in a narrow room that looked like a ship's cabin or a prison cell with bookshelves, nice furniture, a record player, and a television set. They wore evening clothes, and the man smoked a pipe while he sat reading a book with a champagne glass near his leather chair, and the woman stood in the middle of the room with her champagne glass in one hand and a cigarette in a long holder in the other. I said, "It's a bomb shelter?"

Pa said, "That's right. I'm giving your ma an early Christmas present."

Ma said, "It's one present I don't want to use."

Little Bit said, "Will there be a war?"

Pa said, "I don't see how. It's not a war anyone can win. It's like a game of chicken where two cars are racing head-on at each other. What do you think the first one to turn aside is?"

I said, "The loser."

Pa said, "And the one who doesn't turn aside?"

"The winner."

"And if they both decide to be winners?"

Ma said, "Oh, Luke, you're so cheery some mornings," and brought another plate of French toast to the table. "Who wants seconds?"

Mrs. DeLyon visited that afternoon. Gwenny and I were helping Mr. Drake groom the dogs, which meant he gave the leash to me instead of tying it to a post, and Gwenny got her face licked by several different dogs. Mrs. DeLyon said, "Hello, Artie, Gwen, Chris."

Mr. Drake smiled over his shoulder as he brushed our borzoi. "Hey, Maggie."

I said, "Hi, Mrs. DeLyon. I hope you don't have to go."

"So do I," said Mrs. DeLyon, and Mr. Drake and Gwenny said the same thing half a second later, and then they all smiled.

Gwenny said, "It's the pits."

Mrs. DeLyon said, "I suppose so."

Mr. Drake said, "So. Playing tourist today?"

Mrs. DeLyon nodded. "Sometimes you forget why you came to a place."

Gwenny said, "Dickison's nice, I suppose, but it's mighty dead."

"Mmm," Mrs. DeLyon said. "There's a band at the Roadhouse. The something or other Cats, I forget."

Gwenny said, "Johnny and I are going."

"I was thinking I'd go, too." She looked at Mr. Drake. "Care to escort me?"

He blinked once, then smiled. "Why, of course. If we won't cramp the kids' style."

"Uh-uh," Gwenny said. "Separate cars."

Mr. Drake waggled a finger at her. "I never ask for details, young lady."

Mrs. DeLyon asked Gwenny, "So. You love Johnny?"

Gwenny nodded.

"And he loves you?"

Gwenny smiled.

Mrs. DeLyon said, "I thought so. I wanted to be sure."

"People do change. Things aren't always their fault."

"That hope's at the heart of most bad marriages."

"It's not like I've only known him for a couple of months. If I say he's changed, I don't mean he might change or he says he's going to change or I hope he's going to change. I mean he's changed. Maybe you think I'm too young to know—"

Mrs. DeLyon raised her hand. "I might think I'm too old. Maybe I shouldn't've asked. But I got the answer I hoped to hear."

Mr. Drake said, "He says it's been years since he worked for Nick."

"Mmm." Mrs. DeLyon nodded. "Who'll pick up whom?"

Mr. Drake said, "I'll be by at eight. No, make it seven, and dinner's on me."

"Done." She nodded to us, turned, and walked away.

"I'm going up front," I said, and I ran after Mrs. De-Lyon.

When I caught up with her, she said, "An escort. I'm honored."

"Mis' DeLyon?"

"Yes?"

"Do you believe in God?"

"Which one?"

"God. You know."

"Oh. Do you?"

"If God's nature."

She laughed. "I know where you got that."

"So, what do you think?"

"I think God is the moral and spiritual quality in each of us."

"So you believe in God?"

"Hmm. Listen to me. God isn't a name. It's a title. A description. An idea. You're a boy, but your name isn't Boy. John Kennedy's name isn't President. If you asked me whether I believed in the president, I would say yes, but that would not mean I believed John Kennedy existed. It would mean I believed John Kennedy was a good leader, or it would mean I believed in the office of president, that democracies are good things, and electing presidents is a good way to have a democracy. When you ask if I believe in God, you're not asking whether I believe there is a God. You're either asking whether I think God is good, or whether I think there should be a God."

"Oh. Okay."

"Oh, okay?"

"Okay, is God good, and should there be a God?"

"God is a wonderful idea. Yes, God should exist, and we should worship God with everything we do."

"So, is God good?"

She looked at me, then tapped my forehead with her finger. "You really shouldn't ask what you already know."

By that time, we were through the privacy fence and into our yard. Hammering came from beyond a long mound of dirt. Ethorne had dug it five feet deep, and now he was putting in rough wooden walls and beams to support a roof. He looked up as we came near. "Hey, Mis' De-Lyon, hey, Chris."

Mrs. DeLyon smiled. "Hi, Ethorne. Does that help?"

Ethorne said, "Well, Luke figures he's doin' something for his family, and Mis' Susan figures about the same, and the chil'en all figure they're getting somethin' to play in, and I figure I'm getting something to busy myself with. So I guess the answer is it sure does."

"You're doing nice work. As usual."

"Thank you, ma'm."

"What do you think of Johnny Tepes?"

"They say what's in the blood don't change."

"They do."

"But folks do change." Ethorne smiled. "You didn't come for answers."

She smiled, too. "I just wanted to know I wasn't alone in having none."

"What about Johnny Tepes?" I asked.

Ethorne said, "Oh, he used to be kind of wild when he was young."

"Oh. Pa was pretty wild."

Mrs. DeLyon nodded. "I expect he was."

Ethorne said, "You'll really give up the Fountain of Youth?"

Mrs. DeLyon said, "You see a way to keep it?"

"Not that wouldn't create more problems than you got."

"We may not have to worry about it anyway."

"I hear that," Ethorne said.

"Ma says you should always look on the bright side," I said. "Because tomorrow's another day."

Mrs. DeLyon smiled at me. "That's what we always hope."

The last customers of the day were a man and a woman with dark skin and expensive clothes. The woman said "Hello, again," to me in a voice like a purr, and the man said, "I'm so pleased we returned. The only sound as beautiful as silence is the salute of dogs."

I said, "It's their dinnertime. Would you like a tour?"

"Why, yes," the woman said, glancing at the man. "Who wouldn't want a chance to learn more about dogs?"

Neither of them spoke as we circled the pens. At the end of my speech, the woman thanked me. The man gave me a quarter, saying, "Always keep some money with you. You never know when you'll need a coin."

Ethorne finished the walls and cross-braces of the bomb shelter that afternoon. He asked Pa if he should work into the night, but Pa said he didn't think so. He and Ethorne covered most of it with a few sheets of plywood, then shoveled some dirt over them, and Pa said, "Good enough." Ma asked how we would get into the bomb shelter if we needed to. Pa said, "Jumping's pretty fast," and we kids all laughed. Then Pa said they'd add a ladder or steps on the next day, and Ma nodded.

For supper, Ma made squaw corn, my other favorite family meal. She boiled hot dogs, diced them, then poured them in a pan with a can of cream corn. That was its purest and best form, which sometimes she made when she was fixing food just for us kids, but that night she fried bacon, onions, and green pepper, added them to the corn, then beat in an egg to thicken it. That was the way Pa liked it, after he had darkened the top with pepper. I picked out the green pepper bits, and I didn't mind the egg as long as it was mixed in well enough that no slimy globules swam like white worms in the yellow corn.

Ma and Pa both looked up when a car entered the front drive, and they smiled when Johnny Tepes got out. He lifted a hand in greeting as he walked past the front window, and a minute or two later, he and Gwenny walked hand in hand back to his car.

Artie Drake entered the restaurant through the back door as we were finishing. He said, "I made a last walk around the pens, and everything looks fine. It'll be a few more days before Conchita has her pups, and Prince Phillip's dewclaw is healing nice and clean."

Pa nodded, and Ma said, "Thanks, Artie."

"I doubt we'll be gone long. We're sure to cramp the kids' style."

Ma said, "Or they'll cramp yours."

Mr. Drake smiled.

Pa said, "Have a good time. Get back when you get back."

Little Bit, Digger, and I each called, "Bye, Mr. Drake!" He waved and drove toward the Fountain of Youth.

The next three or four hours were like any other Saturday night. Ma counted the money while Pa did the dishes, I swept the gift shop, and Little Bit swept the restaurant. Saturday was a bath night, so we each showered during a TV show that we did not like. Digger and I were in our pajamas and bathrobes. Little Bit, as usual, had convinced Ma to put off her bath until another show had ended, so she was still in her dusty jeans, T-shirt, and tennis shoes. We three were sitting in our low chairs at the foot of Ma and Pa's bed, watching cowboys, when Ma said, "What's that?"

A car had stopped in front of Dogland. Pa said, "Artie must be back early. You don't ever want to try to keep up with teenagers." Then a second car stopped, and he said, "Guess they all wore out early. I'll go look."

Ma said, "Be careful."

"I'd say you shouldn't worry so much, Susan, if you didn't seem to thrive on it." He smiled, but then a third car stopped. Pa looked at Ma, then opened the closet, took out the shotgun, and grabbed some shells from the high shelf where none of us could reach.

Ma said, "Luke—"

"It's probably nothing."

Ma bit her lips and nodded.

Pa said, "Chris, put on your boots and grab the spotlight." Ma reached toward me, and Pa said, "I'll send him back if it looks like trouble. I just don't want my hands full."

Ma said, "I'll call Rooster."

Pa, halfway through the door, said, "Don't cry wolf," to her, and "Don't turn that on unless I say so," to me.

The night was not so dark that we could not see where we were going. As we walked, I could hear dogs barking to say they knew we had visitors. Pa opened the shotgun to drop in a shell, then snapped it shut and said, "If there's trouble, run back to the house as fast as you can."

"All right, Pa."

The shadow of the privacy fence made the world disappear, but the path's familiar ruts would have guided our feet, even if we had not walked it every day for several years. Pa headed around the side of the restaurant, and I followed with the big flashlight in both hands.

A fourth vehicle pulled in as we approached the front. Pa kept the shotgun in one hand, pointed at the ground, like at the beginning of *The Rifleman*, but I did not think that then. I was afraid, but I was used to that, and I was more afraid of having to run back to the house alone in the dark if something went wrong than I was of what might go wrong and what that might mean.

Three cars and a pickup truck had pulled in from both driveways and stopped in a half circle twenty or thirty feet away from the restaurant and the gift shop. Their headlights shone on the Heart Tree. Pa said, "Stay here," while I was still beside the restaurant, and then, "If I say to turn it on, shine it at them, not me."

"I know."

"Good." Pa stepped out from the porch of the restaurant with the shotgun close beside his leg and called, "You folks need some help?"

Two men in white sheets got out of one car, and Cal Carter yelled, "You're the one needing help, nigger-lover!"

Pa said, "Tell Ma to call Rooster. Run."

I ran with the flashlight, not daring to turn it on until I was behind the restaurant. I bumped into the fence as I rounded the privacy screen. The flashlight fell and went out. I ran on without it, shouting, "Ma! Ma! Call the sher-

iff, Ma! Call the sheriff!" I was still shouting when I rushed
through the front door and saw Ma was already on the
phone.

I turned and ran out again. Ma called my name once,
and then she called something I did not recognize, and
then I was out in the night, running as hard as I could, not
toward the front where the car lights burned, but toward
the dark circle of our dogs.

They barked louder as I came near. I thought of rattlesnakes and hairy spiders as big as your fist and nameless things I knew were in the night, but I also knew I was
running with all my might. My fear would carry me across
the backs of a thousand rattlers and none could strike fast
enough to bite me. For all I know, I did step on things in
the night that I would have avoided in daylight, but I never
slowed.

Captain, the Norwegian elkhound, barked as I passed
him by, but I did not stop until I had reached Ranger's
cage. I lifted the latch and threw the door wide. The white
kuvasz, shaggy guardian of kings, leaped out as I went to
free Percival the Doberman, the dark police dog, then Max
the lion-killing Rhodesian ridgeback, then Olaf the St.
Bernard and Spots the Great Dane, who were scary only
for their size, and then the Irish wolfhound and the mastiff and the rottweiler, then the bull terrier who killed in
pits to please gamblers and the bulldog who would grip
and never let go, not even if she was dying, and then Captain because he was smart, and the malamute and the
husky who were Captain's friends, and the ghostly gray
weimaraner who pursued big game in the dark woods of
Germany, the sleek vizsla from Hungary, and the bull-
mastiff who kept poachers away, and the chow and the
Tibetan spaniel who were lucky, and all the greyhounds,
because they were fast, and the saluki for the same reason, and Bambi the basenji because she jumped so high
on her door wanting out, and then I was simply lifting
latches as I ran, following Ranger and a third of the dogs

of Dogland to the front driveway. From the other side of
the circle, more dogs joined us that I had not freed, the
smaller dogs I had ignored like the spaniels and the terriers, the beagle, all the dachshunds, the basset hound, and
even three-legged Pirate, the dogs who would dash into
holes to fight clawed things in their lair, who would en-
circle bears, be batted away, and return to the fight though
their bones had been broken. Little Bit ran behind them.
Neither of us had breath to speak, or time, or inclination.
Ahead of us, near the highway, something was burning.

When I had run into our house shouting for Ma to call the
sheriff, she had already dialed and a deputy had just answered. When I ran out and Ma called my name, Little Bit
had said, "I'll get him!" and followed me. Ma had called
"Letitia!" and run to the door, but when she saw we were
going toward the dogs instead of the front, she had made
a decision of the kind that everyone must make sometime.
Hoping she was right, she had returned to the phone to
say where help should come, and why. Little Bit had followed me, but she never spoke, perhaps because she
wanted to see if she could catch me, perhaps because she
wanted to see where I was going. When she saw me release
Ranger, she ran to free the dogs farther along the circle.

When Ma finished talking with the deputy, I am sure
she bit her lip and looked once around the bedroom, but
I doubt she looked more than twice. Then she ran to Digger and carried him through the bathroom into the kids'
room. She certainly said something like, "Be a good boy
and stay in bed, okay?" and she probably kissed him in
the shallow indentation just above his eyes while she
wrapped one or both arms around his head, pressing his
bristly crew cut between her forearms. And then, I suspect, she said, "Mommy loves you," and ran toward the
front drive.

*   *   *

In the parking area in front of Dogland, after I had turned and run back to the house, Pa had called, "You're trespassing."

Someone laughed from behind the Heart Tree. As that sheet-clad figure stepped out from the tree's shadow, the other men had begun to laugh, too. More car doors opened, and fourteen or fifteen men, perhaps half in white sheets and half in street clothes, stepped out of the vehicles. They stood near their cars, waiting to see what Pa would do. Two of the nearest men carried gas cans, and six or seven held bats or axe handles, and the rest were half-hidden by the cars and the truck and the night.

Pa said, "The law's on my side."

Someone said, "Ol' Rooster?" and they began to laugh again.

Pa brought the butt of the shotgun to his shoulder, aimed it at the center of the nearest man's chest, and said, "I can drop as many of you as I can shoot, and the law won't hold it against me."

By the vehicles, someone cocked a rifle. One of the Lawson brothers said, "You don't want to turn this into a shooting matter."

Pa said, "I don't want to turn this into anything. But I'll protect what's mine."

"You can't shoot all of us."

"True. But I can shoot the son of a bitch in front of me. You could put a bullet in my heart right now, and it wouldn't stop my finger from squeezing. Who the hell are you in that sheet, anyway? You better hope to God you're somebody the rest of them cares about, or we're both going to hell in fifteen seconds."

Captain John Hawkins said, "Now, hold on, Luke. Boys, you hold on, too. Sure, I don't mind taking my hood off. You mind if I do?"

Pa said, "Be my guest."

Captain John dragged the hood off, then grinned at Pa. "You don't mean to shoot that."

"I'd say I do."

Captain John shook his head. "I admit, this wasn't how I thought it'd play out, but you know and I know one of us has to back down, and it has to be you."

"Who's got a gun with a real touchy trigger aimed at who?"

"You can't kill me, Luke. If you were stupid, I'd be worried."

"I get pretty goddamn stupid sometimes. The madder I get, the stupider I get, and you piss me off so bad I can't see straight. But I don't need to see straight, 'cause this is loaded with buckshot. So turn around and get the hell out of here."

"Sorry." Captain John shook his head again. "But you ain't thinking about how it is. If the Klan burns you down, you and your family can move on in peace. Hell, you can feel good about yourself, 'cause you'll know you wasn't driven out easy."

"Did I mention my finger gets a twitch sometimes?"

"You got four reasons to ease off that trigger."

"You got one to get going."

"Susan, Chris, Little Bit, and Digger. The boys can afford to have witnesses to a burning. Ain't no local jury that'd convict us on the word of Yankee troublemakers, not even if you had Polaroids of the fires being lit. But killing draws too much attention. It leaves no room for witnesses." Captain John, holding Pa's gaze, began walking toward the shotgun. "You go ahead and shoot if it'll make you feel good. But if you give a goddamn about anything besides your pride, you'll put that gun down, go back to your house, and pretend you never heard a sound up here till it was way too late." His final step brought his chest against the gun barrel. He waited, then lifted his hand and pushed the barrel aside.

Pa looked at the shotgun, then opened it and tossed it aside.

Captain John said, "I thought so."

Cal Carter exhaled loudly and said, "I didn't think he was bluffing."

Captain John said, "He wasn't bluffing. He just hadn't thought it through." He turned and waved his arm. "All right, boys. Have some fun!"

The man who had been near the Heart Tree threw a match. The tree's roots and trunk exploded in flame. The other men yelped with triumph and ran toward the gift shop and the restaurant.

Ma came from the shadows then. They all stopped when she called, "Mr. Hawkins. John. Please. Don't do this."

He looked at her, then looked at one man with a gas can. Captain John lifted his chin toward the restaurant, and the man hurled the can through the big front window that had survived Hurricane Donna.

Ma said, "Please. Our fire insurance was canceled because they heard the Klan—"

Pa said, "Don't, Susan."

Captain John looked at her, then called, "Leave their house alone!" He smiled at Pa. "See? Businessmen do have hearts."

Pa started forward, but Ma grabbed his arm. "Luke, they're buildings. They don't matter."

A second gas can went through the window in the door to the gift shop. The flames on the Heart Tree had reached its branches. Leaves and Spanish moss crackled and flared. The last two men with gas cans began splashing the walls of the gift shop.

Cal Carter said, "Ain't a bonfire pretty, Mr. Nix?" Pa said nothing. Cal whirled, driving the end of his axe handle into Pa's stomach. "Too high and mighty to answer me, nigger-lover?"

Pa staggered back. Cal brought the axe handle like a baseball bat against Pa's thigh, and Pa fell to his knees, scooping gravel in his hands. But before he could throw any, Ma stepped between them, saying, "Cal, please, if you've got any feeling—"

Captain John was on the porch of the restaurant,

pulling a cigarette lighter from his pocket. He looked over his shoulder and said, "Cal, lay off—"

Cal raised the axe handle high, to hit Ma or Pa, or simply to tell everyone he had the stage. "You don't tell me—"

Then one of the Lawson brothers said, "What the hell's that?"

Which was when everyone realized that the sounds of fire consuming the Heart Tree had been buried beneath the baying of the dogs, which not only grew louder, but nearer.

Little Bit and I rounded the restaurant in time to see the white kuvasz, the black Doberman, and the gray wolfhound leaping from the darkness into the hard, flickering firelight. We could not see that they were leaping over Pa, or that Percy struck Cal Carter's chest, knocking him back on the gravel, then baring his teeth within inches of the man's face.

Captain John and most of his men ran forward to help Cal, but several of them backed away. They all stopped when Ranger halted, facing Captain John. Bridget the wolfhound, taller, leaner, and perhaps more intimidating than Ranger, stood next to him, and Percy stayed on Cal's chest. At least one man by the pickup raised a rifle, looking for a clear shot at Percy, then glanced over his shoulder as Max the ridgeback and Bubba the mastiff circled the gift shop with more dogs behind them. The shadows around the burning tree surged with the arrival of the pack, who waited near the edge of the light.

Eight or ten dogs surrounded Ma and Pa. Pa pushed away Pirate, who nuzzled him, stood with Ma's help, and called, "If anyone shoots, I won't be able to hold 'em back."

Cal was repeating in a quiet voice that was almost sane, "This dog's crazy. Get 'im off o' me. Please, just get 'im off now, all right, please, somebody?"

Pa said, "I don't know if any of these dogs ever killed

their own food, but now's as good a time as any to find out. Unless you'd care to be going." He pointed at Captain John. "Just put that lighter back in your pocket." Captain John did not move. Pa bent over, holding his side with his left hand, and grunted as he picked up the axe handle that Cal Carter had dropped.

Ma said, "Luke—"

Pa shook his head and, using the axe handle as a cane, walked toward Captain John. He said, "Don't make it worse for yourself," then lifted the axe handle to point to the highway.

Ethorne and Seth and Simmy and Abraham Brown and five or ten other dark figures stood on the shoulder of the road with shotguns, hoes, and pitchforks in their hands. And as the first drop of rain struck my cheek, two more cars arrived. Stepping from one, Mrs. DeLyon called, "We all see you, John Hawkins. There's nothing more you can do here."

Captain John watched as the people on the rise walked down the slope where I always ran from the bus at the end of the day. Only Mr. Drake, Johnny Tepes, Mrs. DeLyon, and Gwenny Drake came with empty hands. The rain began falling in heavier drops, and then lightning tattooed the eastern horizon, and I heard thunder as loud as any cannon blast.

Captain John looked at Pa. "We'll go."

"No." Pa pointed the tip of the axe handle toward the Lawson brothers and the other men. "They'll go. You and Cal can wait here for Rooster."

"That wasn't the offer."

"I guess you should've taken it before it expired."

Captain John smiled. "That's so."

Cal, still on the ground with Percy on his chest, said, "Let me go with 'em."

Pa shook his head. "You'll be a whole lot safer inside a cell where I can't get at you."

The order of events blurs after that. The rain fell harder. Two cars and a pickup truck drove away with Cap-

tain John's followers. Most of us moved under the overhang of the restaurant. The air smelled of ozone and gasoline and burning wood. Someone brought hoses from the
dog pens and connected them to the faucets at the back
of the gift shop and the restaurant, Ethorne and Abraham
Brown helped the rain wash away the gasoline and ensure
that the walls closest to the Heart Tree were soaked. Mr.
Drake and Simmy dug shallow trenches so the gas washed
away from the fire and not toward it. Ma got us all rain-
coats and flashlights, and Seth and Little Bit and I
rounded up the dogs and returned them to their cages.
Only ten or fifteen had run away, and Seth said they'd
probably return soon. Sheriff Donati arrived to take cus-
tody of Cal Carter and John Hawkins, and Dickison's vol-
unteer fire department showed up shortly after that. Between the fire truck's hoses and the rain, the fire on the
Heart Tree was soon out, though the tree was so charred
that Pa told Ethorne it would have to come down the next
day. After the fire department left, Ma decided Pa should
have Dr. Lamont look him over, and after he protested, he
agreed. Mr. Drake said he could see that Little Bit and I
got to bed, so Pa eased himself into the passenger seat of
our station wagon, and Ma took the wheel.

Pa rested his hand on my shoulder and said, "That was
a little excessive, son, but you did good," and I smiled.

Little Bit said, "I helped."

Pa said, "You helped good."

Little Bit said, "Why'd you let them men go?"

Pa said, "The world's full of followers. It's the leaders
you got to look out for."

Ma said, "We'll be back as soon as we can. Don't wait
up!"

Pa looked at me. "Well, Mark Christopher, I guess
you're in charge till we return."

I nodded, and Mr. Drake, standing near, smiled.

After plywood had been nailed over the two broken
windows and the shattered glass had been swept into a
pile, Ethorne and Mr. Drake and Mrs. DeLyon concluded

that whatever was left should wait until morning. Simmy, Abraham Brown, and the others waved and went away. Seth said he thought he'd see if one or both of the Newbury girls was awake and interested in the story of the fire, and he left, too.

Mr. Drake, Mrs. DeLyon, Gwenny, Johnny Tepes, Ethorne, Little Bit, and I went back to the trailer for a snack. While Gwenny and Johnny Tepes made cheese sandwiches, Little Bit fell asleep on the couch, and one of two things happened. Either Mr. Drake and Mrs. DeLyon carried Little Bit into the bedroom, saying they'd look in on Digger, or I also fell asleep, and what follows is the second dream that I still remember.

12

Peace on Earth

Mr. Drake hurried into the trailer, and Ethorne Gwenny, Johnny Tepes, and I looked up as Mrs. DeLyon followed him. He looked at me. "Where would Digger go?"

I shrugged and blinked. The question made no sense; Digger would not go anywhere. When he slept, he slept for ten hours. You could toss him around like a sack of potatoes, and he would not wake up. With one exception. "Bathroom?"

Mrs. DeLyon shook her head. "No."

Mr. Drake said, "And he's not in any of the beds. We looked in all three."

Mrs. DeLyon said, "And under them. And I called for him. He wouldn't hide from me, would he?"

I shook my head. Ethorne got up, went to the door, and shouted, "Digger! Where is you, Digger-boy? You don't need to hide no more. Everything's fine now!"

The dogs barked in response, but no person answered.

Mrs. DeLyon said, "Call Dr. Lamont. Maybe Susan put him in the backseat and forgot to tell us."

Mr. Drake's voice held as little hope for that as Mrs. De-Lyon's, but he said, "All right."

Mrs. DeLyon said, "We'll get Chris to bed in the meantime."

"I'm in charge," I said.

Ethorne said, "When there's nothing you can do, you might as well sleep. Save your strength for when you need it."

Mrs. DeLyon said, "Don't worry. At least one of us will stay in the trailer until your folks get back."

Gwenny said, "C'mon, boyfriend. I'll see you to your bed."

I said, "I can go by myself."

Gwenny looked at Mrs. DeLyon, then at Johnny Tepes. "Well, that's a blow to a girl's ego."

They smiled without much humor, and Mr. Drake hung up the phone.

Ethorne said, "What is it?"

Mr. Drake said, "Let's get Chris to bed first."

I stood and went to the door. "G'night."

Gwenny started to follow, but Mrs. DeLyon caught her arm. "It's his decision."

The rain had stopped by then. I stepped into the porch light as everyone called or waved to me, and I ran to the door into our room. I turned off the porch light and stepped inside. In the glow of a night-light, Little Bit slept soundly. I went into the bathroom, through the door into Ma and Pa's room, out their front door, and back into the night. As I tiptoed through the wet grass toward the trailer, I heard a piece of their discussion:

"Why couldn't Rooster hang on to him?" asked Gwenny.

"Someone's got to stay," said Mrs. DeLyon.

"What matters now is who's got the fastest car," said Ethorne.

"How d'you know he's there?" said Gwenny.

"I don't," said Mrs. DeLyon. "I hope he's sleeping in one

of the doghouses with his favorite dog. Someone should check them all."

"Do that while we're gone," said Mr. Drake.

"You don't know what you're getting into," said Mrs. DeLyon.

"I do," said Ethorne.

"Who stays may be more important than who goes," said Mr. Drake.

"I've got the fastest car," said Johnny Tepes.

I turned, tiptoed to the path, then ran on drying mud to the parking area. As I went through the passway, I heard the trailer door open, and I hurried on, wishing for the first time in my life that I was wearing sneakers instead of cowboy boots.

Only tourists locked their cars in Latchahee County in 1962. I opened Johnny Tepes's door, scrambled into the back, and folded myself into a ball in the foot well behind the driver's seat. A leather motorcycle jacket lay on the rear cushion, so I dragged it over me.

Someone opened the driver's door and got in. As the engine started, the passenger door opened, the passenger seat folded down, and someone leaped into the back, hitting me with an elbow or a knee. The seat folded up, and the car accelerated in reverse before the third person had a chance to slam the door shut.

Ethorne said, "This thing got seat belts? I'll use mine."

The brakes caught, and I was slammed into the back of the driver's seat. Gravel spun as Johnny Tepes popped the clutch into first, and I rocked into the side of the backseat as we hurtled up the driveway and, still accelerating, onto the highway. If I had not been thinking about Digger, I would have thought it was better than any carnival ride.

Mr. Drake said, "You *have* been driving for a while?"

The engine roared as Johnny Tepes downshifted. The car slowed, fishtailed, then charged from pavement onto gravel as Johnny Tepes ratcheted back up through the gears. Though I had never traveled the route so quickly, the direction of the turn and the sound of the road told me we were on the old county road.

Shifting into the fourth and highest gear, Johnny Tepes said, "A few years."

Then we drove. I can't say how long. In my memory of the dream, we drove forever. I may have fallen asleep. I knew the road to Dickison, but it seemed we quickly passed that turnoff. The road grew rougher and bumpier, but you adjust to everything. The carpeting beneath me was new, and though the car swayed, it rarely veered abruptly. Johnny Tepes seemed to see farther than his headlights to anticipate every obstacle ahead of us. I might have fallen asleep in my dream.

Sometime in that timeless time, Mr. Drake said, "What've you got back here, anyway?"

Johnny Tepes said, "Back where?"

The jacket rose from my head. Mr. Drake and I looked at each other. Then he set the jacket aside and said, "We got a stowaway."

Ethorne said, "Chris, why'd you hide back there?"

Johnny Tepes said, "Because you wouldn't've let him come if he'd asked."

I nodded.

Ethorne said, "That ain't what I was asking."

"He's my brother," I said.

"Oh," said Ethorne. "It's a curse to have answers good enough to help you into trouble."

Mr. Drake said, "Chris, if we left you by the road with a flashlight, would you be all right till we got back?"

Before I could answer, Johnny Tepes said, "No," and Ethorne said, "We gone too far for that."

Mr. Drake nodded. "You might as well sit up on the seat. If anyone's going to punish you, it'll be your folks."

"Or life," said Johnny Tepes.

The bench seat was more comfortable than the floor, but the windows did not give me much more information than I had had with a jacket over me. I had thought the stars were coming out after the rain, but the only light I could see came from the headlights and the dashboard. The road ahead was gray, rutted, and littered with rocks. What trees we could see were stunted and misshapen in that light. Shortly after I sat up, I noticed one sign, DEAD END, and no others. The motion of the headlights suggested that things moved around us in the darkness. Once something pale passed by, and I thought of Handyman's tale of the white boar, but nothing showed itself clearly. If there were any sounds, the car engine smothered them.

When the car slowed, I sat up. A pole had been set across the road on two rests to stop travelers. Beyond it, a wooden platform jutted into a thick, swirling mist. An oil lamp burned at each end of the platform, showing what I've described, and nothing else. I said, "Are we here?"

Ethorne said, "We aren't where we're going."

"Do we walk?"

Mr. Drake said, "We'll find out."

Ethorne said, "I'll find out," got out, and called, "Hello? Is anybody here?"

From the darkness, someone called, "Go back!"

Ethorne yelled, "We got business on the other side."

An old man and a large, ugly dog that looked like a mix of mastiff, bulldog, and bloodhound stepped into the headlights. The man said, "They got business with you?"

Ethorne said, "Did a man and a boy come by in the last hour or so?"

The man stroked his beard, looked at the dog, then back at Ethorne and nodded.

Ethorne said, "Then we got business."

"This ain't no charity operation."

"We'll pay."

"Yeah. Question is, how much?"

"What'll it take?"

"All you got."

"And to get back?"

"A little bit more."

Ethorne looked at the car. Johnny Tepes said, "Sure,"
and Mr. Drake said, "If it's what we have to do."

Ethorne said, "Can the boy stay here?"

"Boy can stay anywhere."

"Will he be safe?"

"This ain't no baby-sitting service neither."

I said, "I want to go."

Ethorne said, "We'll be coming back soon."

I said, "I got to go." I leaned across Mr. Drake to thrust
my fist out the window. "Look. I can pay."

The old man took the coin that the day's last tourists
had given me. "You can go."

Ethorne said, "And come back?"

The old man nodded. "And come back. If he wants."

Ethorne pulled wadded bills and coins from his front
pockets to give them to the man. Mr. Drake took a silver
clip holding several folded bills and gave that, too. Johnny
Tepes spun something toward the old man, and when he
caught it, he grinned and said, "Billfold, too?"

Johnny Tepes shrugged. "You said everything."

"Well," said the old man, "let's get going. You could
catch your death in this damp." He lifted the pole from its
rests, then carried it onto the wooden platform. The dog
walked at his side. Ethorne got back into the car, we drove
onto the platform, the old man untied two cables at the
rear of the platform, and, using the pole, pushed us out
into the river.

I said, "Can I get out?"

Ethorne looked at me, then laughed. "We paid for the
trip. We might as well enjoy it."

So we all got out of the car. The lamp showed dark
water around us, but when I looked over the sides, I could
not see my reflection, or even the ripple of our passing.

Mr. Drake said, "What do you think?"

Johnny Tepes said, "I've seen it before."

I asked Ethorne, "Digger's all right, isn't he?"

Ethorne said, "I'm sure he is."

I walked back by the old man. His dog, sitting beside

him, looked past me. He was the biggest and ugliest dog
I had ever seen, and I saw nothing in his glassy eyes. If his
tail had wagged, I might have been able to tell if he was
feeling friendly or afraid, but it was still on the deck,
curled beside him with no more life than a rope.

I held out my hand, palm up, and waited. The old man
glanced at me, but the dog did not move, so I stepped
closer, keeping my hand before me. When I touched his
muzzle, it was cold. I said, "Good boy," and stroked his
head once, then said, "That's a good boy," again, and
scratched him behind the ears where Ranger and Captain
liked being scratched. His head swung to regard me, and
his breath was warm on my arm just before he licked my
wrist.

I said, "He's a good dog. What's his name?"

The old man pushed again with the pole. "I doubt he
remembers."

"Don't you remember?"

The old man looked down at me. "What do you think
his name should be?"

"George."

"Mmm," the old man said, and the dog licked my wrist
again.

When we reached the far shore, Johnny Tepes drove us
onto land, but he stopped almost as soon as the river was
lost in the night. Ethorne said, "What is it?"

"I don't feel so good."

Mr. Drake said, "What do you mean?"

"I feel weak."

"Weak?"

"Hungry. Someone else better drive."

"We didn't bring anything to eat."

"I can hold out."

Ethorne said, "All right. I'll drive."

The car stopped, and the two men crossed in the headlights, then got back in, and we drove on. I could no longer
see the shadows of trees to either side of us, and I wondered if we were getting close to the sea.

The road ended at a construction camp. One bright lamp on top of a tall pole showed metal trailers, trucks, bulldozers, and steam shovels arranged in a ring. The only vehicles that seemed out of place were Captain John's car and Nick Lumiere's white convertible, parked at the center of the circle.

Ethorne let off the gas and the car slowed of its own accord. When we were beside the other two vehicles, he touched the brake lightly, and we stopped.

Johnny Tepes looked at Ethorne and Mr. Drake. Mr. Drake shrugged. Ethorne said, "I think we could be hunting around here for a mighty long time."

Johnny Tepes reached over to put his hand on the horn and hold it there. At almost any other time, I would have loved the loud, long cry, but here it was only a noise that cut into the darkness, and the darkness ignored it. Ethorne shook his head. Johnny Tepes took his palm off the horn and fell back in the passenger seat.

Ethorne stepped out of the car. He looked into the shadows, and at the trailers. Electric lights burned in each of them, but nothing moved inside any. Ethorne cupped his hands around his mouth and yelled, "We're here to make a deal!"

The door of the nearest trailer opened. Nick Lumiere said, "Yes?"

"You've got Digger?"

Mr. Lumiere shook his head. The light behind him was so bright that I could not make out details inside the trailer.

Ethorne said, "Then we can't make a deal," and turned toward the car.

Mr. Lumiere said, "John Hawkins has Digger."

Captain John stepped into the doorway behind him and said, "You didn't have to tell 'em that."

"I don't have to do anything at all."

"I thought you and me had a deal."

"You and I were negotiating a deal. Now we got a few more bidders."

"But I brought the boy!"

Mr. Lumiere nodded. "Doesn't give you any more right to him than they have."

Ethorne said, "Where's Digger at?"

Mr. Lumiere turned, looked past Captain John, and held out his hand. Digger came from the bright room and took it.

Ethorne said, "Hey, Digger. You all right?"

Digger nodded and said, "Where's Ma and Pa?"

Ethorne said, "They're waiting for you."

Mr. Lumiere and Digger walked down the steps and onto the dirt. Captain John followed. Mr. Lumiere released Digger's hand, and Digger walked over to Ethorne, who squatted to hug him.

Ethorne said, "You're letting him go?"

Captain John said, "Like hell!"

Mr. Lumiere laughed. A steamroller started up behind us. As we turned to look, it rolled across the road and stopped, trapping us all in the camp. Someone was sitting at its wheel. Someone was sitting at the wheel of every machine around us. In their hard hats under the harsh overhead light, at that distance, they might as well have been faceless.

Mr. Lumiere looked into the car. "Hello, Johnny. Long time, no see."

Johnny Tepes said, "Not long enough."

"You're looking a tad peaked. Want to come back to work for me?"

Johnny Tepes shook his head.

"You don't miss that feeling of power?"

Johnny Tepes nodded. "I plan to keep on missing it."

Mr. Lumiere smiled. "How're you, Artie?"

Mr. Drake said, "I'm not here to play games."

"But that's why I'm here. So, how's your love life? I hope there's no one in your way. Maybe you need a word in the right place to get a good job in the agency? I only want to help."

"We want Digger back."

"You might not'a' had to come out for that. John Hawkins there wants the tree and the springs. If he negotiates with the Nixes, Digger'll be back with his family. Would that be acceptable to you?"

"What do you mean, if?"

"Well, I might arrange for John Hawkins to get his desire some other way. Digger's a good kid. I've always wanted a son."

Mr. Drake stared. "You couldn't."

Mr. Lumiere smiled. "I do have my means, Artie. I could, and I very well might." He looked past Mr. Drake. "Hi, Chris. Would you like it if I adopted your brother?"

I shook my head.

"You don't ever get jealous? Everyone spoils him, and that's hardly fair."

"I don't get jealous for long."

"What would you trade him for?"

I thought. Things that I wanted presented themselves to me, and finally I said, "Everything."

"Everything?"

"Everything in the whole wide world."

"We're talking, oh, ruling the world? As a king, say?"

I nodded.

"Hardly original."

I shrugged.

"But it has its appeal. And I'd get your brother?"

I shook my head. "You'd get the world. I'd get Digger."

"Well. That's touching. Don't you think, Ethorne?"

Ethorne nodded.

"And what do you want from life?"

"A trade."

"Which is?"

"Me for Digger."

Mr. Lumiere laughed. "Why would I do that? You're a little too old to shape as my son."

" 'Cause you can have me now, and it ain't likely you'll get another chance. You been asking me to join up with you for a powerful long time."

"That's so."

"And you can always get another shot at Digger."

"You must think I'm awfully patient."

"There ain't nobody more patient than you."

Mr. Drake said, "Hold on, Ethorne. That doesn't help things."

Ethorne nodded. "Sure it does. I had me plenty of time. If I can give somebody else a little, what more is there?"

Mr. Drake said, "You can't do this, Ethorne."

Johnny Tepes said, "Looks like he's doing it."

I said, "You're going to work for Mr. Lumiere, Ethorne?"

"I 'xpect he'll find something for me."

"You won't miss Dogland? Or Seth and James and Francy? Or us?"

"Oh, I'll miss all that. But I'll feel pretty good knowing it's all still going on." He looked at Mr. Lumiere. "If we got a deal."

Mr. Lumiere said, "There'll be consequences."

Ethorne said, "Always are."

Mr. Lumiere lifted a hand toward the road. The steamroller backed away, opening a space wide enough for our car. "We got a deal."

Captain John said, "Hey! What about me?"

Mr. Lumiere smiled. "Oh, I'll find something for you, too."

Digger began to cry. Ethorne squatted beside him and hugged him. When Ethorne stood, he walked Digger to the car, held their clasped hands toward Mr. Drake, then used his free hand to loosen Digger's fingers. He put Digger's hand in Mr. Drake's, and Mr. Drake picked Digger up and held him tight as if he were two years younger and still a baby.

Digger said, "I love you, Ethorne."

Ethorne nodded. "I know you do, child. I love you, too." He looked at me. "You too old to give me a hug?" I shook my head. "Then come on over here."

I got out of the car and walked to Ethorne. He said,

"You take good care of your little brother." I nodded. His eyes had watered, but he was smiling. He said, "Give me a hug, now." I nodded again, and he stooped down. His cheek was bristly against mine, and he smelled of smoke and earth and hard work. He whispered, "Nick won't figure it out for a long time, but it's all right. I won."

I pulled back to look at his face. He nodded and grinned, then rubbed the top of my head, then backed away. He called, "Hey, Johnny, take it easy now."

Johnny Tepes said, "You, too."

Ethorne said, "Remember me to everybody. Tell my boys I got faith in 'em." As he waved, standing next to Nick Lumiere and Captain John beneath that harsh light, we all got into the car and headed back into the night.

Mr. Drake drove, and Johnny Tepes sat in the passenger seat with his arms wrapped around his stomach. Digger cried for a while, and I sat beside him, not knowing what to do. Mr. Drake said, "That's all right," to him. His voice sounded as though comforting Digger kept him from crying, too. I put my arm around my brother then, and he fell asleep with his head on my shoulder.

At the ferry, the man and the dog blocked our way. The man said, "What'll you pay now?"

Mr. Drake said, "Ethorne paid."

"Mmm."

The dog did not move. I stuck my head and my arm out the window and yelled, "George, hey, George, it's me, remember?" He cocked his head, then walked to the side of the car, and I scratched behind his ear.

The old man looked across the river. "Well, people're waiting. Let's go."

When we returned to Dogland, Gwenny and Mrs. De-Lyon ran out to meet us. Gwenny said, "Hey, Digger, welcome back! Hey, Chris, you little sneak, you had us no end of worried." Then she embraced Johnny Tepes and said, "I'm glad you weren't gone long. Hey, are you all right?"

Mrs. DeLyon looked at Mr. Drake. "Where's Ethorne?"

Johnny Tepes answered. "A trade."

Gwenny said, "What?"

"He joined Nick Lumiere."

"I thought he despised the man."

Mrs. DeLyon said, "People do the—" She looked at Digger, swallowed, and said, "—most amazing things." She looked at Mr. Drake. "Luke's got a couple of broken ribs, and the doctor wants him to spend the night there, but he and Susan'll be back shortly. Digger looks exhausted."

"I'm not," I said.

"No, I can see that. Well, maybe you should go to the trailer and wait up for your folks." She glanced at Johnny Tepes, then turned to Mr. Drake and said, "I'll be back in a couple of minutes."

He said, "Drive carefully, Maggie. It's been a hell of a night."

She smiled, nodded, and left.

At Mr. Drake's trailer, Gwenny and Johnny Tepes sat on the couch with their heads close together. I sat in the dinette booth with my back against the wall and my feet up, which Ma always told me not to do and Mr. Drake never told me not to do. I watched him make tea, and I wanted to ask him about a lot of things, but I did not understand any of them well enough to form my questions.

Mrs. DeLyon returned with a big dull metal bowl that she held in both hands. I said, "What's that?"

She said, "It's the liner for the dipping basin at the fountain. When I'm in a hurry, it's the easiest way to carry water."

"Oh."

She held it out to Johnny Tepes. He looked at her. She nodded, and he put out his hands, and she set the basin into them.

Gwenny said, "Dad's got a lot of cups, you know."

Mrs. DeLyon smiled. "It's not the first time someone's drunk directly from it."

Johnny Tepes lifted the basin and held it close to his chin, as though smelling it, but I could see it was only water. Then he put it to his lips, tipped it, and drank deeply. When he was done, he handed it back to Mrs. De-Lyon. "Thank you."

She laughed. "You kids've been up so late, you might as well see the sun rise."

"Me, too?" I asked.

"No. I think you've seen plenty for one night."

On Sunday, October 28, the Nixes slept late. Helen arrived early as usual to feed the dogs, and since Gwenny and Johnny Tepes had stayed up to help her, there was no unusual barking to wake us. Five or six of the dogs who had gone missing the night before were waiting near their pens for their breakfast. The last wanderers were brought to us during the next four days by people who found them all over Latchahee County.

When we finally rose, Little Bit, Digger, and I were delighted with the bandages around Pa's chest and leg because he looked like the hero at the end of a cowboy movie. In the restaurant kitchen, Ma made waffles, the best breakfast treat of all, and Pa announced that he didn't want people babying him, and everyone laughed at that idea. Pa said he hoped he didn't have to get beaten up too often to lift everyone's spirits, and we all volunteered for the job. When Pa asked Ma why she hadn't raised a bunch of pacifists, Ma only smiled.

Sunday was Lurleen's day off, yet she came in with Handyman and Jordy. Shortly after breakfast, we all got to work sweeping and scrubbing and replacing the windows in the gift shop and the front of the restaurant.

Pa said a couple of times that he wondered where Ethorne was. Seth arrived a little later to say that Ethorne had died in his sleep during the night.

Khrushchev accepted a secret offer from Kennedy that

Sunday: the U.S. would withdraw its missiles from Turkey if Russia took its missiles from Cuba and promised to keep the terms of the agreement a secret to preserve America's pride. The Nix family and the world waited four more days for the news. On November 2, Kennedy announced that the missiles in Cuba were being dismantled.

James and Francy returned to Dickison for Ethorne's funeral. Francy, Mr. Drake, Mrs. DeLyon, Johnny Tepes, Gwenny, and my family were the only white people in the crowded church, which made me feel odd. When everyone prayed, I did, too. I figured if there was a God, he ought to know to look after Ethorne. When everyone said "Amen," Pa said it, too, as loud as anyone and maybe louder.

At school, Wayne Lawson asked if it was fun to see a drunk nigger get buried. I hit him in the nose, drawing blood, and he blacked my eye. We both went to the principal's office, but Mr. Hadley didn't paddle either of us. After that, Wayne Lawson and I were never friends, but we had a truce. I felt bad about hitting him, because it was not what Ethorne would have wanted, but I never felt too bad.

I never wondered whether Rooster Donati had let Captain John go on his word, or he had posted bond, or he had escaped Saturday night, then made a deal early in the morning with the sheriff to quiet the matter. Whatever happened, the criminal proceedings against John Hawkins did not slow the legal proceedings against Mrs. DeLyon. On November 1, she lost the Fountain of Youth to the Dickison State Bank and Captain John.

The Nix family went to the motel to see her off. All her goods fit into boxes and suitcases in the back of a pickup truck. As we arrived, she put a last box in the back of the truck, then went to the green cement fountain by the swimming pool, lifted out the metal liner of the dipping basin, and tucked it into a box of pots and pans. Then she looked around and said, "Well, I hope he thinks it was worth it," and we began the round of hugs and farewells.

The good-byes included Mr. Drake. He left the same day, driving behind Mrs. DeLyon in her sports car. They planned to leave one vehicle and most of their goods in Jacksonville with Gwenny and Johnny Tepes, then spend some time traveling around the country or the world, looking, as Mr. Drake said, for the next good place.

The last thing he said to me was, "That story about the king and the queen and the friend? Don't blame the queen. Maybe it's better to love too much than too little. And maybe the king should'a' blessed her and his friend, and stopped fretting over the past, and gotten on with the future. Who knows? Maybe his country would've never fallen, and he might've gotten together with the woman who gave him the sword, and the whole story would've ended better for everyone. Though I s'pose it might not've been told so often."

I have another memory that I cannot rationalize. Perhaps this is a bit of dream also, and not history: before Mrs. DeLyon got into her car, I asked her, "What'd Ethorne mean when he said he won?"

In surprise, she did not look like Mrs. DeLyon, but like someone very young who had been caught on stage in another actor's costume. She said, "When?"

"That last night."

"He said that?"

I nodded.

She kissed my forehead. "Thank you."

"But what's it mean?"

"He said once the only war you win is the war you never fight."

"Never?"

She shrugged. "What's never? But if you can keep putting something off, it's as good as never."

The Nix family drove back to Dogland in silence. We parked by the stump of the Heart Tree. Its burned bark had been cut away, so it looked like a place to sit, or to spread a cloth for a picnic. As we walked past, Little Bit stared at it.

Ma said, "Don't worry about the squirrels and the birds, Little Bit. They'll find a new home."

Little Bit shook her head and pointed. At the base of the tree grew a tiny green bud. Whether it came from the tree itself or a seed that had fallen, we did not know, or care.